THE MOST ASTOUNDING ADVENTURE OF ALL
SWEPT THEM TO A LAND OF PROMISE—AND THE
TERRIFYING CONSEQUENCES OF THE FRUITS
OF DESIRE

JOSHUA—Hardening his heart, the great warlord of Israel
would sound the trumpets of death for his tribe's enemies
and follow the dictates of his God from miracle to
miracle—until fate led him into a conflict that would
imperil all he loved.

IRI—His flesh disfigured but his heart pure, this Child of
the Lion would travel the seas in search of his kidnapped
wife—only to land before the walls of a legendary city
called Troy.

TIRZAH—Blond-haired and lovely, her passionate love
for an outcast armorer bound her to the Children of the
Lion—but nothing could save her from a terrible captivity
. . . and a raging desire for revenge.

HELEN—No woman would ever surpass her in beauty,
but her famous face would launch a war of horrifying
destruction . . . and make "Helen of Troy" a name
synonymous with betrayal.

PHORBUS—A loyal friend and faithful companion, he
alone would earn adoption into the Children of the Lion
clan—and learn at the side of the tormented Iri that
love alone could heal the tragedy that engulfed the
world.

Volume XII

THE PROMISED LAND

PETER DANIELSON

Created by the producers of
Wagons West, White Indian,
and **The First Americans.**

Book Creations Inc., Canaan, NY · Lyle Kenyon Engel, Founder

BANTAM BOOKS
NEW YORK · TORONTO · LONDON · SYDNEY · AUCKLAND

THE PROMISED LAND

*A Bantam Book / published by arrangement with
Book Creations, Inc.*

Bantam edition / July 1990

*Produced by Book Creations, Inc.
Lyle Kenyon Engel, Founder*

ISBN 0-553-28588-2

Published simultaneously in the United States and Canada

*Bantam Books are published by Bantam Books, a division of Bantam
Doubleday Dell Publishing Group, Inc. Its trademark, consisting of
the words "Bantam Books" and the portrayal of a rooster, is
Registered in U.S. Patent and Trademark Office and in other
countries. Marca Registrada. Bantam Books, 666 Fifth Avenue,
New York, New York 10103.*

PRINTED IN THE UNITED STATES OF AMERICA

RAD   0 9 8 7 6 5 4 3 2 1

This book is dedicated to all of the friends of the Children of the Lion, in all Lands.

THESSALY

AEGEAN

SEA

TROY

MYCENAE

SPARTA

GREAT

CRETE

TYRE

MOUNT
HERMON

MOUNT
MEROM

HAZOR

GALILEE

LAKE
CHINNERETH

BETH-SHEMESH

CANAAN

JORDAN

SHEBARIM

BETH BETHEL
HORON   AI
GEZER   GILGAL
GIBEON   JERICHO
MAKKEDAH

JERUSALEM

ASHDOD   SALT
LIBNA   SEA
ASHKELON

HEBRON

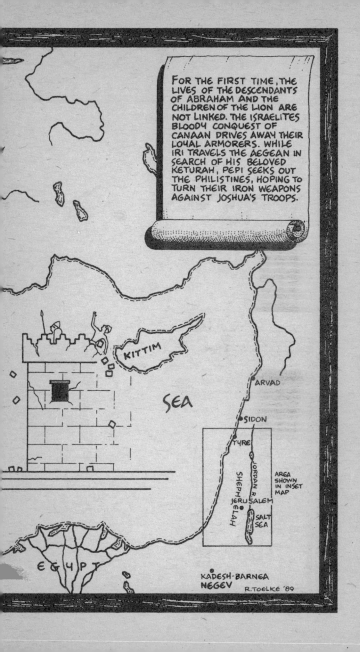

FOR THE FIRST TIME, THE LIVES OF THE DESCENDANTS OF ABRAHAM AND THE CHILDREN OF THE LION ARE NOT LINKED. THE ISRAELITES BLOODY CONQUEST OF CANAAN DRIVES AWAY THEIR LOYAL ARMORERS. WHILE IRI TRAVELS THE AEGEAN IN SEARCH OF HIS BELOVED KETURAH, PEPI SEEKS OUT THE PHILISTINES, HOPING TO TURN THEIR IRON WEAPONS AGAINST JOSHUA'S TROOPS.

KITTIM

SEA

ARVAD

SIDON

TYRE

JORDAN R.

SHEPHELAH

AREA SHOWN IN INSET MAP

JERUSALEM

SALT SEA

EGYPT

KADESH-BARNEA
NEGEV

R.TOELKE '89

stantly Pandion led him on, but he stood with a

Prologue

It was a night of shooting stars. Across the vast expanse of sky, meteors flashed like fireflies. Clustered around a dying campfire the members of the caravan watched with awe. Finally, as the showers slowed, the Teller of Tales stepped out of the shadows and stood tall and commanding before them.

"A night of auguries," the old man said, his voice ringing out into the darkness. "A night of portents. On such a night, my children, might great Joshua, warlord of the Israelite army, have stood looking across the raging Jordan upon the Land of Promise . . . the land of Israel . . . thinking of Yahweh's command to conquer it and subdue its people to the hand of the Twelve Tribes."

Somewhere in the darkness a child cried, and its mother gave it her breast. The old man looked in her direction before continuing. "So might Joshua have heard the cry of a child among his people and thought of the wild and raging child he himself had brought forth—a nation of callow warriors ordered to face older, more experienced Canaanite fighters on the battlefield.

"Picture it, my friends," he said. "He was a soldier with but four battles to his credit; on the orders of God,

1

he proposed to invade and conquer settled nations. Was Joshua afraid? Did he question his competence and courage or the mettle of his young warriors? Or did he have faith in himself and in the limitless power of Yahweh, Lord of All?"

An anticipatory murmur rose from the crowd. He smiled and raised his arms high against the dark sky, signaling that the story was to begin. "In the name of God, the Merciful, the Benevolent," he intoned, "hear now the tales of the Children of the Lion. Hear the deeds of those great men and of their endless wanderings. Hear of the great war in Canaan, as Joshua's people prepared to win a new nation—and of a great war far to the north, where, in their brief twilight, the last of the Greeks battled, brother against brother. Hear now of the men who would create a new civilization from the ruins of their nation and who sailed to every port of the Great Sea."

His voice quickened and took on a new edge. "It was a time of change," his words rang out. "And as the fortunes of men evolved, so shifted the destinies of the Children of the Lion, the caste of armorers who, from nowhere, had come to stand beside the great rulers of the world.

"Hear now," he said, "of the great war for Troy—and of the coming of those who conquered the land of milk and honey to the south—the Promised Land."

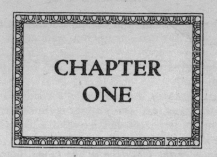

CHAPTER ONE

The Pride of Jordan

I

From the dry hills above the raging Jordan River, the forest had seemed a rich and green oasis. But now, closer, the woodland looked sinister: a dense thicket of tamarisk, willow, and poplars, their branches choked with vines. Even at low water the Jordan, raging beyond, would be a formidable barrier. Now it became an impassable barrier.

Caleb scowled. "This is the 'ford' he's chosen? It's hopeless."

Eleazar held up his hands. "Joshua has not chosen the crossing. God has chosen it."

Caleb's hawklike eyes narrowed. "Since when did Joshua start speaking with Yahweh? Since when has Joshua—and not you, the high priest—become the spiritual leader of our people? Joshua's a soldier. That was why Moses laid down the sword; he knew that God speaks to prophets, not soldiers."

"Patience," Eleazar cautioned. "God speaks to Joshua on matters of war, and the crossing of the Jordan is a military matter."

3

"That may well be," Caleb acknowledged, scratching his chin, "and it's true that God seldom gives us bad advice."

"Never gives us bad advice," the high priest corrected him gently.

"All right, never. All the more reason to distrust the choice of this crossing. The ground is quicksand, and the jungle is full of large and hostile wildlife. Bears! And my men have killed lions there."

"But," Eleazar said, "these beasts will not attack the Israelite army or the sacred Ark of the Covenant."

Caleb snorted. "Then what about the river? It's filled with treacherous mud, not to mention deep holes that can drown a man and a current strong enough to knock a man over and drag him down."

"I know," Eleazar said. "I worry about the men carrying the Ark. They bear not only a precious burden but a heavy one."

"My point exactly! Then why attempt such a foolish—"

"Because God has commanded us to do so."

Even as Eleazar said the words, the ground shook. The high priest staggered and almost fell. A crack opened in the bank, running parallel to the river and separating the two men.

Caleb, cursing loudly, stumbled back. His face turned suddenly pale as an aftershock rippled through the earth. Within seconds it was over. When all was quiet he tentatively stepped to the edge of the rift and peered down. "We could have been swallowed by the earth! It opened right beneath our feet!"

Eleazar pressed his hand to his chest. Sweat poured down his face. "All the more reason to cross the river. Once we're past the rift and onto solid ground . . ."

Caleb tested the ground with one foot. "But when? We've been waiting here for a month."

"Patience," the old man counseled, catching his breath. "You must have faith, my friend. . . ."

Caleb snorted again, then gazed across the river to

the slopes that led up to the high walls of Jericho. It was the first city they would have to conquer when they crossed into Canaan.

The Promised Land! So near yet so far.

To make sure his army did not lose its fighting edge while waiting for God's command, Joshua had ordered sword drill every morning, followed by strenuous exercise or a long, forced march. He did not want to overtrain the troops, however, and had given his men the afternoon off. Restless and worried, Joshua rode into the hills.

He had been saddling his horse when the animal had become skittish to the point of panic, and Joshua had to wrestle it into submission. Then the tremor had hit.

How strange! Joshua thought. *Does God speak to animals as He speaks to humans? Could He have alerted the horse to danger?*

Stranger things had happened. And strange indeed were the ways of the unknowable God, Who had led His people out of Egypt a generation before and brought them at last to the banks of the Jordan, where they awaited His orders to reenter the land their ancestors had abandoned.

Now, as he thought about it, Joshua felt a surge of psychic energy and suddenly knew that before the day was out, God would speak to him again.

As his horse negotiated the narrow path up the hill the army commander closed his eyes and prayed. *Please, Lord, let the move be soon. My men are losing the edge they need to conquer more experienced armies. Tell me soon, Lord, before they also lose the faith!*

The animal picked its surefooted way to the top of the hill, where Joshua could look down into the canyon. Twenty of his soldiers stood there in a rough circle around two combatants.

The commander dismounted, leaving the horse to forage, and moved closer, one cautious step at a time down the slope, until he was within range of the spectators' shouts of encouragement. Then he stopped.

He recognized the two poorly matched men in the center: The hulking braggart was a bully named Ozni, known for his physical strength and enjoyment of terrorizing recruits. The other, Shemida, whom Joshua had commended for his bravery in battle, was slightly built but quick handed. He was barely more than a boy, and handicapped by a wound that had left him lame.

Joshua's eyes narrowed. He had invalided Shemida out of the service. Yet here the young hero was, back in uniform.

As Joshua watched, Ozni feinted a clumsy blow to Shemida's face, and Shemida, limping awkwardly backward, dodged under the blow and, in a forward rush, caught Ozni on the left eye with one flashing fist.

Ozni roared with rage and charged—only to run into a flurry of lefts and rights. But none of Shemida's punches carried the force necessary to drop Ozni. Joshua shook his head. Shemida would outbox the bigger man, most likely, cut him about the face, and perhaps even close that eye; but eventually Ozni would emerge the victor. Shemida, moving on one good leg, did not have the agility that could have saved him.

Sure enough, Shemida failed to duck one of Ozni's looping punches and caught a heavy blow in the middle of his forehead. Joshua winced; he could almost feel the impact himself.

Shemida staggered and nearly fell. Ozni rushed at him, but Shemida, groggy and guided by instinct, grappled with his assailant. Finally Ozni freed his arms, grabbed Shemida around the chest, and began to squeeze.

The cheers of the crowd were for Ozni.

"Kill the little bastard!"

"Finish him off!"

Joshua was not surprised. He had trained his troops to have the killer instinct. No pity or compassion lay in these men's hearts.

Shemida struggled, and his eyes were glazed with pain. Then suddenly he pulled his head back and slammed his hard forehead into Ozni's nose. Ozni's grip loosened, and Shemida cocked his right elbow and caught the bully in the groin with his fist. As the bigger man doubled over, Shemida brought up his left fist and broke Ozni's prominent nose.

Ozni almost went down but managed to pull himself up straight, cursing and choking. He held his hand to his nose, then took it away covered with blood. Rage reddened his face and darkened his eyes. As the crowd shouted encouragement to Ozni, Shemida hopped out of range.

Joshua scanned the circle of faces. All took pleasure in seeing the bully beating a cripple.

He had taught them a violent profession, and violence was never far from their minds. Their training had been hurried and limited, with no lessons on conscience or fairness. It was the kind of schooling that could wrest a land from its standing armies.

A roar erupted from the onlookers. Ozni, seeing how clumsily Shemida moved, began to take advantage of his own greater mobility. He began to circle, throwing deadly blows at his adversary. One of his flailing swings caught Shemida in the face and brought him down to one knee. Shemida shook his head, trying to clear it.

Then Ozni moved in for the kill.

II

Avoiding Ozni's chin-down rush was impossible for Shemida. He took a solid blow to the head from Ozni's flailing fist but managed to grab at one of his assailant's ankles and trip him. Ozni fell, rolled, and righted himself before Shemida could find his feet.

Still unseen, Joshua continued to move cautiously down the slope.

"Now you've got him, Ozni! Break his neck! Don't let him get away!" shouted the men.

Get away? Joshua looked around and saw that Shemida would have no escape. The stalwart young man awkwardly rose to his feet, sidestepped paired left-and-right punches, and caught Ozni once more on his broken nose. Ozni howled with pain and counterpunched. Shemida, hurt, tried to backtrack, but his stiff leg would not hold his weight. He tottered and was about to fall.

"Stop!" Joshua ordered in the ringing voice that they had heard so many times on the parade ground or exhorting them into battle.

Ozni, fists still balled, looked up, his mouth hanging open. Shemida turned, squinting as blood dribbled from a cut on his forehead.

Joshua made no attempt to hide his anger. "Stay where you are, all of you!" he demanded, glaring at a pair of stragglers intent on sneaking away. "No one leaves until I say so!" He continued down the hill, his gaze moving from the path underfoot to the faces before him and back again. He stopped on a ledge at the men's level. "What's going on here?"

No one answered. Shemida's mouth opened for a moment, then clamped stoically shut. Ozni wiped his bleeding nose and looked rebelliously up at his leader. Finally he said, "Sir, we had a private dispute. We were settling it."

" 'Private'?" Joshua asked acidly. "With two squads looking on?" He glared at Ozni. "I remember you. You ran from the fight at Bashan and had to be whipped back into action with the flat of your officer's sword. You were a disgrace to the army then, and you're a disgrace to it now. And you—" He turned his scorn toward the spectators and saw with satisfaction how few could look him in the eyes. "Is there no one among you to stand up for a war hero who's lost the use of his leg in battle? We're supposed to be fighting the Canaanites, not each other. Your fellow soldiers are your brothers in arms."

For a moment nobody answered. Then a voice from

the second rank said: "Sir, Shemida insulted Ozni. It's a tribal dispute. We've our family pride to think of, sir."

Joshua, seething, spat on the ground. "You're all on report. Get back to camp and present yourselves to your commanders. Tell them you're to be staked out on an anthill for a day." He listened to the stunned groan that arose, but quickly continued. "That's every man of you—except Shemida and Ozni. And God protect the man who doesn't report himself."

"Y-yes, sir," a man in the first row said shamefacedly. "Will that be all, sir?"

"No!" Joshua said. "From this moment until you are released from service by death or my own personal order—and there will be no other way you'll get out, believe me—I'll hear no more talk of tribes. In this army there is only one tribe." He paused. "The tribe of Israel."

"But, sir—"

"The next man who tries to break this army into twelve warring camps won't live long enough to regret it. I have a war to win and a direct command from God to win it. Nothing—and nobody—is going to get in the way."

There was a mutter from the gathering, which Joshua took for acquiescence.

With one last scathing glance, he said, "Dismissed," and watched as the men scattered. Then he glared at Shemida. "Why are you still with the army? You are clearly disabled."

"Sir," the smaller man explained, "I haven't got a trade. I was called into service before I could be apprenticed to my uncle as a saddler. The only thing I know is the soldiering you've taught us. But you need men who can do a forced march all night and not tire, who can move from city to city in the moonlight and strike without warning. I was a fool to think I could sneak this bad leg past you."

Joshua, softening at the contrition in the young man's voice, sighed. "You, Ozni. Go back to camp. I'm letting you off this time. At least you fought fairly. But if you are brought to my attention for anything but meritorious conduct, I'll—"

"Yes, sir!" Ozni saluted, turned on his heel, then scurried away.

When he was out of sight, Joshua turned back to Shemida. "And you, my friend. What am I to do with a man who disobeys me when I discharge him?"

Shemida stood rigidly at attention. "Sir, these are days that will be remembered as long as the world lasts: the days when Joshua's army took the Promised Land. People will forever remember the conquest of Canaan. I can't bear not being a part of it because my worthless leg won't carry me to a fight." His voice lowered. "To sit by with the camp followers, like a graybeard, and watch others—the likes of Ozni—doing the work of Israel, while I have to limp around doing the work of the women . . ."

When Joshua spoke, his voice was husky. "Can you ride a horse?"

"Not well, sir. I'm slow mounting and dismounting. I'd be no good at cavalry drill."

"I'm not thinking of the cavalry," Joshua said. "I need an orderly. The only riding you'd have to do would be with me, to the scene of a battle. You'd have to help me to keep up with things: Wake me in the morning, rob the dogs for me. . . ."

"Rob the dogs, sir?"

Joshua grinned. "You know, bring my meals. Can you write?"

"Yes, sir!"

"Good! Then you can take notes for me, remind me when I've an appointment, jog my memory when someone earns promotion or deserves discipline." Joshua looked at the boy's happy smile and found his own spirits lifting.

"Sir! When do I start?"

"You just did, son. Now get back to camp and find someone to treat those cuts and bruises. Then report to Caleb and have him put you on the rolls as adjutant with an officer's uniform, pay, and benefits. Orderly isn't good enough for a war hero. How's that leg? Can you make it back to camp all right?"

"Oh, certainly, sir. I'll just—"

"Wait. I'll bring that nag of mine down here, and you'll ride back. I need the exercise anyhow. Your first assignment will be to secure us a good meal. I'm getting tired of the garbage we have to eat."

"Yes, sir. There's a fellow in the Second Troop who likes to cook. He has some ideas about how the food could be improved. He was in charge of the victory dinner we had after the triumph at Bashan."

"I remember. That was delicious."

"Another thing, sir: He told me your sutlers have been cheating the army. They're selling rotten meat and bad vegetables, and the prices—"

Joshua's eyes flashed. "Get me their names," he ordered. "The sutlers, the suppliers, everyone. And most particularly, the name of their contact in the army!"

"You'll have it all by tomorrow evening, sir."

"And sign up the fellow who cooks. An army can't do its best on bad food—"

"Yes, sir!"

But he spoke to Joshua's retreating back. The commander was stalking up the slope to bring the horse down to his newly appointed adjutant.

III

The earthquake had opened fissures in the ground in the middle of the Israelites' camp, and Caleb was inspecting them when Shemida approached. Out of the corner of one eye Caleb saw the young man limping toward him, but the second-in-command, ignoring him, continued to supervise the work detail filling in the rifts.

The tremor had left Caleb out of sorts. He, like all Israelites of his age group, had been born in Egypt, where there were no storms and the earth did not shake. The annual flood could be predicted almost to the day. There was no need for extraordinary precautions or for astrologers to tell a man when to relax and when to worry.

Caleb had been content with this aspect of Egyptian life and felt resentful when God sent down the numbing succession of plagues that compelled the Egyptians to emancipate the sons of Jacob. Caleb could still remember his terror when the sky had darkened, the rivers had run with blood, and frogs and locusts had overrun the area. He had, in fact, cowered in a corner of his family's hovel, covering his tightly shut eyes.

As he remembered his cowardice, his mood grew more testy. Thus, when he found the lame soldier looking at him, Caleb let loose his temper. "Have you nothing better to do than stand and gawk like an idiot? Speak up or return to your unit!"

"Beg your pardon, sir," Shemida said, his voice calm and his words measured. "Joshua told me to come see you."

"He did, eh! To put yourself on report, no doubt, like the other bunch of worthless no-goods."

"No, sir, as a matter of fact—"

"Spit it out!"

"Yes, sir. He said I'm to be promoted to be his adjutant. I'm to be put on the rolls to draw an officer's uniform."

"He *what?*" Caleb's tone had been known to render men of Shemida's rank paralyzed with fear. "If this is a joke, you'll quickly regret it."

"It's no joke, sir. The appointment was made not an hour ago. I would have come sooner except that he told me to stop by the physicians' tent and—"

"Am I supposed to believe this lunacy? You're a cripple. What are you doing in the army, anyhow?"

"Since the Battle of Bashan, sir, I may well have been getting in the way."

This elicited a startled stare from Caleb. "You got that

wound in Bashan?" His expression softened, and the natural respect he felt for a fellow soldier took over. "Wait, I remember. The name's Shem-something, right?"

"Yes, sir. Shemida."

"You struck a good blow or two that day."

Caleb's genuine admiration loosened Shemida's tongue. "Thank you, sir. I tried my best. Incidentally, sir, I gather that my duties for Joshua will be those of a glorified orderly. I will be out of the chain of command."

"Very well," Caleb said, his mind at ease. He was not being passed over by some jackleg from the ranks but would retain his position as Joshua's second. He smiled. "Get over to the quartermaster's. We can't have a good soldier being turned out to pasture just because he can't do forced march like a raw recruit, can we?"

"No, sir!" Shemida said, saluting smartly.

Caleb let the muscles in his shoulders relax. At first he had worried that Joshua had taken leave of his senses; if Joshua had put another man between them . . .

Enough of that. Just because he did it with Pepi of Kerma, the armorer . . .

Pepi and Joshua had been friends as children, and their camaraderie had for many years been a thorn in Caleb's side. Pepi could not have been appointed Joshua's second-in-command: Pepi was an unbeliever, one of the uncircumcised, and already an assistant and the successor to Iri, the armorer for the Israelite army during the long years of wandering.

Iri and Pepi, uncle and nephew, were Children of the Lion, members of the legendary caste of weapon makers whose destinies had been entwined with those of the Israelites ever since the dim, half-forgotten days of Abraham.

But Caleb, insecure and jealous, had felt threatened by Joshua and Pepi's closeness and had missed no opportunity to drive a wedge between them. When the break came, however, Caleb had played no part in it.

Pepi had objected to the wanton murdering of the civilian populations of conquered cities. When Joshua had explained that the massacres were ordered by Yahweh Himself, Pepi accepted neither this nor the rationalization that it was no use killing a snake unless you killed her young. The growing disagreement had driven the two friends apart until they became enemies.

Then reports had come in that Pepi had taken up with a Bashanite witch and had become a Canaanite spy. Recently an Israelite informer and a neutral trader had both reported that Pepi was inside Jericho—a guest in the home of the chief magistrate—at the very moment the Israelites were preparing to cross the Jordan and besiege the city.

The trader's report was final proof of Pepi's treason. Joshua, enraged, had put a bounty on Pepi's head.

Now the alienation was complete, and Caleb should have felt secure about his position; he had repeatedly proven his valor and fidelity to the cause, fighting with desperate bravery in battle after battle. Yet he could never believe that Joshua truly cared for him and respected him.

You've got to get a hold on yourself. You've nothing to fear from Shemida. Joshua would never appoint a common soldier as his successor.

He rubbed his shoulder, shamed by his thoughts. Joshua had known what he was doing, as usual. Adjutant—"sort of a glorified orderly," as the young fellow had put it—was a natural position for a disabled soldier. Shemida looked resourceful and intelligent and quite obviously had Joshua's confidence. It would pay to cultivate him.

IV

The new adjutant sent one of Joshua's runners to the Second Troop to fetch Nadab. The chubby, moonfaced man showed up, puffing.

"Nadab, sir, reporting for—" he began. But then his eyes widened. "Shemida, what are *you* doing here?"

"Promoting you," the young man answered. "You're chief cook for the army now."

"Is this a joke?" Nadab asked.

"No. You'll report to Caleb when I'm done with you. Draw the uniform, get put on the rolls in your new rank, and tell the chief cook he's under house arrest. Have him report to me as soon as the evening meal's been served. I'll be in the tent next to Joshua's. Tell the whole kitchen staff they're under investigation."

"But Shemida, this is so sudden."

"Not as sudden as it's going to seem to them, I'll wager. Take a squad of guards along with you. Have the crooked sutlers jailed, along with anyone else you know to be working with them. Either the sutlers will confess immediately who their contact in the army is, or they'll be tortured until they talk."

"Shemida, I'm shocked!"

"Their offense is serious. It's a crime against their fellow man and against God. They're not only cheating the army, they're selling us unclean food and claiming it's been prepared according to the Law. Caleb will back you. Joshua places the highest priority on this." He paused. "No, second highest."

Nadab blinked. "What's the first?"

A smile lit Shemida's battered face. "Tonight's dinner. Prepare a wonderful meal for Joshua and his general staff. I bragged about your talents, my friend. Make me look good."

"Tonight? But if the kitchen staff are all under suspicion . . ."

"Don't use them. Find men in the ranks who know about cooking and would like a job where they don't have to dodge arrows and spears."

"I know a dozen such, at least."

"Hire them. Pick out the best one and make him your assistant."

"I will make a splendid impression, I promise you. But Shemida, how did all this come about? Only yesterday you were talking of quitting the army altogether."

"So I was," Shemida acknowledged. "Which proves that a man doesn't always know his own mind."

Joshua had intended to go back to camp; instead, prompted by a vague urge to which he could not put a name, he continued to wander in the hills. As the afternoon wore on, he found himself atop the highest hill on the ridge, looking down at his own camp, at the enemy city of Jericho on the far slope, and at the green stripe of forest that marked the great Rift through which the Jordan ran its twisted course.

A strange mood passed over him—a feeling of great peace and calm and passivity. His head was light; his legs felt weak. He sat down on a rock, took a deep breath, and closed his eyes.

He recognized the voice echoing in his ears as his own, but it was calm and matter-of-fact. The words were simple and extraordinary:

"We will cross the Jordan tomorrow. When the sun is directly above, the army of Israel will follow the sacred Ark of the Covenant across the Jordan. The river will be bone dry, and underfoot there will be solid ground—but only for two hours. Then the Jordan will return in all its fury."

He opened his eyes and stared down at the raging, impassable Jordan. This was not like the experience his mentor, Moses, had told him about, in which he had actually spoken to Yahweh.

"This is madness," he muttered. "Was I saying that? Or was it . . .?"

He laced his fingers in an attitude of prayer and closed his eyes. "Lord," he said, "I don't understand. Even if all the water were to be taken from it, the bottom would be mud from bank to bank, with great holes full of quicksand. How can we cross it?"

A long silence enveloped his mind, and that in itself was an extraordinary occurrence: His thoughts were customarily full of turmoil. And then a single word—*trust*—came to him. He opened his eyes and stared out over the flood-swollen Jordan. The presence fled from his mind and with it, the feeling of absolute surety. Reality returned, bringing doubts.

"This is madness. I'm going to make a fool of myself."

He stood. Was he really going to muster the whole army at noon to await a miracle?

He had always anticipated that the problem of crossing the river would be solved for him, but he had imagined it would have something to do with a bridge or a rerouting of the Jordan. But this? A miracle that broke every law of nature?

"Please, Lord," he prayed. "Explain it to me. Help me to understand."

The answer came not in words but as certain knowledge. He knew how the Ark and the army and the civilian camp followers were going to cross into the Promised Land. And he knew how, when, and why he was going to take Jericho.

The moment Joshua had resigned himself to the will of Yahweh, trusting in the impossible, then and then only had come the answer, clear and credible.

A proper butcher was found and pressed into service in time for the evening meal. Fresh vegetables were brought in, and the kitchen was staffed by Nadab's men. At nightfall, when Joshua returned to camp, tempting aromas emanated from the cooking tents. As soon as dinner was ready, a detachment of three servers brought Joshua's meal to him.

"Sir," Shemida announced, "your first meal under the new regime."

The commander looked up. "Have them put it down on the table, will you? How did your first day go?"

"Taste your dinner, sir, and judge for yourself," Shemida said, nearly dancing with excitement.

Joshua made no move to eat. "We're crossing the Jordan tomorrow. At noon."

"Yes, sir. Time to get a good meal under your belt, sir, and a good night's sleep. Always best before an important day."

"Did you hear what I said?" Joshua asked, staring at him incredulously. "We're going to cross the Jordan at full flood tomorrow. Aren't you going to ask me how?"

Shemida shrugged. "No, sir. That's your job."

Joshua stared. "There's something very odd about you, Shemida. Very odd indeed."

"Yes, sir," Shemida agreed. "But I've worked very hard to prove myself worthy of my new job. Taste the lamb, sir. I guarantee you'll like it. So far Nadab is living up to my expectations."

Joshua looked at the food in front of him. "You've installed the new cook already?"

"And the new staff, sir. The old staff is in shackles, and we're smoking out the fellow who made the deals with the sutlers. Caleb has the sutlers. He's acquainting them with certain procedures he uses for obtaining information from miscreants."

Joshua gave Shemida an approving nod. "I think you're going to come in very handy, young fellow. I've needed someone efficient who does his job and minds his business."

"Thank you, sir. Was there anything else you'd like to have me attend to, sir?"

"No, unless you can find me a new armorer," he said sourly. "The trainees left behind by Pepi of Kerma are competent enough, but . . . well, never mind that. Find me a new one, will you? I'd be very grateful."

"I'll give it my best. Is that all for now, sir?"

"Yes, yes. Go along. Good work."

"Thank you, sir." He turned and was gone.

Joshua looked after him, shaking his head appreciatively. He sighed and picked up a piece of lamb. But then he sat staring morosely at the floor.

A new armorer? What wouldn't I give to have Pepi back, just as he was before.

The pain of loss was so keen that he almost cried out. But then he shook off the thought and bit into the lamb.

V

After dinner Shemida returned with Caleb. "I thought you'd want to see your lieutenant, sir. I took the liberty of asking him to come."

"Good," Joshua said. "Come in, both of you. Caleb, how did you like the evening meal?"

"Best I've had since the feast of Bashan, sir," Caleb said. He gave Shemida a tight grin. "Good man you've taken on here. Incidentally, Shemida, your suspicions were right: Just before dinner a sutler accused one of our staff, Ahikar, as the man who sold us out."

"Ahikar, eh?" Joshua mused. "Have the sutlers and cooks hanged publicly as a warning against future dishonesty. Do it tonight."

"Tonight?" Caleb asked. "Why not at dawn?"

"No time. I want you to muster the men in the morning. Shemida, send a runner to Eleazar. Tell him to come here immediately. Caleb, we're going to cross the Jordan tomorrow at noon."

"At flood tide?" Caleb asked.

"Yes," Joshua said. "It'll be dry then, believe me. Shemida, you'd better get moving."

The adjutant nodded and was gone.

At dawn the army of Israel stood at attention. Nearby, the corpses of the thieving kitchen staff swung in the breeze as Joshua spoke to his troops.

"Men, make ready for a great and historic event. God

has spoken. Today we cross over into the land promised to us!"

A great roar of excitement rose among the assemblage.

"The men you have seen hanged have sinned against God and their brethren. Let this mark the last of our trespasses. When we cross the Jordan we will be cleansed of our offenses. No man who comes with me to reclaim Canaan from the heathen will bear burdens of his past. The army that follows the Ark into the Promised Land will be free from sin."

A cheer erupted from the troops.

Joshua continued in a voice full of resolution. "After we cross to the sacred soil of the land of Israel, woe to the man who is tempted by wrongdoing. Retribution will be swift, befalling the offenders and their families."

A low, disturbed murmur rippled through the ranks.

"Are there any questions?" Joshua asked. He waited a long moment, then said, "All right. Noon. Ready to fight!"

As he spoke he heard the panicky neighing of the horses, and he realized the moment had come. The earth rolled and shook, and several men in the front rank fell to the ground. The quake continued for what seemed an eternity, causing the bravest men to cry out in terror.

When the men looked up, they could see their commander still standing, as solid as a stone statue, his massive arms crossed over his broad chest, as if nothing had happened.

Many miles upriver, where the Jordan passed through a narrow gorge, the earth shook, halving the hill above the river. Rocks broke loose, and a great avalanche hurtled down into the canyon, damming the Jordan from bank to bank. The raging river could not pass.

As the water backed up behind the great barrier, the Jordan's downstream course began to dry up. Soon the water level had fallen to the point at which a man could wade across in safety. The depth dropped, the sun beat down, and the area behind the newly created dam became first a pond, then a lake.

Caleb's mustering of the troops was a marvel of efficiency, in part because he had borrowed the services of Shemida, who had made a list and ticked off each procedure as completed. Finally Caleb left the whole task to the adjutant and joined Joshua at the river's edge.

The Jordan had fallen several feet in the last hour. In places it was little more than a trickle. Caleb removed his helmet and wiped his brow. "Who would have guessed that there was a submerged island in the center? And look—a causeway of stones leading to it."

"Just as the Voice told me," Joshua said. "Obviously there will be a short period when we can cross safely. Only one problem; we are instructed to build a cairn on the island to mark the spot. We'll have to order a detachment to build the cairn even before the Ark crosses."

"Is that proper?" Caleb asked. "As I understand it, the Ark can't be preceded by anyone."

Joshua and Caleb looked over at the slope where the priests, Eleazar at their head, were praying before the sacred Ark, the acacia-wood box that contained the holy relics of the Israelites' epic journey across the Sinai desert from Egypt.

"Not onto Canaanite soil," Joshua answered. "But the builders will be only on the island in the middle of the river. Get me a dozen big men who are good with their hands."

While Caleb set off up the slope, Joshua remained at water's edge, watching the level of the Jordan continue to fall. After a time Eleazar joined him.

"It's a great day for our people," the high priest enthused.

"It is indeed," Joshua agreed. "And I ought to feel elated. Instead I feel melancholy. Eleazar, what happens when I've conquered the Promised Land? What use will there be for me then? My wife and children hardly know me anymore. I neglect them in favor of war. I'm not a good husband, and I've been no father at all to my boys. Who am I when I'm not being a soldier?"

"I ask myself similar questions," the old priest responded sadly. "In a way, Joshua, your destiny and mine are linked, because it has fallen to us to be the two halves of Moses' successor. We will both become useless at the same time. I do not know what will become of us then. Perhaps we will both go mad."

The two men stood darkly silent for a few moments, then Joshua grasped the high priest's shoulder. "Come, my friend. Let us try to enjoy the moment. It is a great triumph!"

And so it was. The Ark, borne by four stout priests and followed by the great army of Israel, miraculously forty thousand strong, crossed the impassable river. Next came the camp followers. At last the descendants of Abraham stood on the Promised Land. Did it matter that war, destruction, and death lay ahead for them? Or that the purity Joshua sought was futile because this army, like all armies, was composed of fallible men? This day was never to be forgotten while the sun still rose over the earth.

CHAPTER TWO

Greece

I

Theon, son of Seth, leaned against the ship's railing as the vessel neared the private harbor of King Nestor of Pylos. He drew in a chestful of air and tried to concentrate on the tasks at hand. As the representative of his kinsman Demetrios the Magnificent, proprietor of the greatest merchant navy in the world, Theon had a great deal of responsibility. He was on his way now to renew a trade agreement with old Nestor and to learn what he could of political gossip that might affect shipping in the Great Sea. Nestor had proved himself to be a wellspring of information that was usually accurate.

Although Theon was a young man still in his twenties, he felt confident of his diplomatic ability and his business acumen. He had traveled widely—too widely, according to his young bride, Nuhara. Even before coming of age he had explored from Syracuse to Massilia, around the Aegean, and along the northern coast of Africa.

Yet nowhere in all his wanderings had he found a panorama to equal what lay before him now: The Great

Sea stretched out, broad, blue, and formidable; to the south were the Bay of Navarino and the Isle of Sphakteria. Ahead was the great seaport of Pylos, where King Nestor's sea-based kingdom had found its genesis decades before.

Pylos was a brawling, busy settlement, attracting ships from the four corners of the earth and teeming with lusty sailors looking for trade and trouble. And there, somewhere, was Theon's kinsman Iri—although one would never guess the two men were of the same clan. Whereas Theon was tall and elegantly formed, Iri was burly and blocky. While Theon had an easy way with people, Iri was abrasive and coarse. Theon was blessed with the face of a god, but Iri was cursed with a deep red birthmark that covered much of his face.

Iri, who was Demetrios's younger brother, was also on Theon's agenda: Theon had been charged with finding Iri and helping him to locate his wife, who had been kidnapped over a year before. Two companions, Okware and Pandion, had been brought along for that job, freeing Theon to devote his attention to Nestor and to indulge in the unparalleled hospitality that always preceded business dealings with the king.

Theon sighed, wishing Nuhara were with him. Some time together in Nestor's always-entertaining court might have gone a long way to ease their marital problems.

"Theon! Not long now, eh?" a deep voice boomed.

The young man turned to see Okware, a huge, strong, black man, stride toward him, accompanied by Pandion, whose open, round-cheeked baby face framed by dark, curly hair belied a sly and calculating mind.

Pandion placed a hand on Theon's shoulder. "Don't worry. We'll find Iri for you. Knowing our old shipmate, he's either in the taverns or in jail."

Standing atop the high walls of the palace, Theon could see King Nestor's private little bay, the caldera of a volcano framed by jutting promontories, each crowned with a fortress from which archers could defend the king's docks.

"My lord," he said to the beaming monarch beside him, "until now I thought that the loveliest sight in the world was the island my master and I call Home."

"You've a golden tongue on you," the king of Pylos said. "I see why Demetrios reposes such trust in you. What brings you to Pylos? Is the august Demetrios contemplating some revision in our treaty?"

Theon smiled and shook his head. "No, my lord. My master told me to assure you of his friendship for the great and noble lord of Pylos. He sent me here for many reasons—one of them, I suspect, was for my pleasure." Theon looked out to sea again. "He also wanted me to tell you of the capture of a famous pirate, the Minotaur, and the destruction of the brigand's fleet. The sea-lanes, Sire, are safe once again."

"I already know about the Minotaur. News travels fast in these waters. As a matter of fact," the old king said, "I heard that a very important part in this great victory was played by one Theon, son of Seth, a great hero, renowned as much for wit and cunning as for valor."

"Rumor exaggerates, my lord." Theon paused. "I fear there is also bad news. Demetrios's health is failing."

Pain seemed to cut into the old man's face.

"He is training a successor," Theon continued.

"A successor? Not *you*?"

Theon laughed. "My lord, I know my limitations. There are men who lead, and there are men who work best alone. I am one of the latter, as was my father."

"Your father was a most remarkable man. Ah, here come my servants, with olives, sweetmeats, almonds, and the golden wine of Chios."

"You will spoil me, my lord. As I was saying, Demetrios has named a successor. His name is Khalkeus of Gournia, and like Demetrios and me, Khalkeus is a Child of the Lion. He also happens to be my wife's father."

"I didn't hear you had married! Congratulations, my friend. Did you bring your wife?"

"No, my lord. She was loath to leave her father during this period of transition. The shipping empire is a most complex enterprise for one man to comprehend."

"Then you must bring your lady with you next time."

"Thank you, my lord."

"I want to hear all about Khalkeus. I had also heard rumors of there being a descendant of old Akhilleus's among you these days. Is that true?"

"Yes, my lord. His name is Okware. As a matter of fact, he is down in the port at this moment, searching for someone."

"Whom is he searching for? Could I be of service?"

Theon put down his cup of wine on the stone table before them and picked up an olive from the tray the servants had left behind. "A kinsman of mine is said to be in port. His wife, blind and pregnant, was kidnapped; he traced her as far as the Greek Isles. Our representative in Pylos sent a message saying he was here and behaving in a manner unbefitting a Child of the Lion."

"Would this be a man in his fifties, powerfully built and with a large red birthmark on his face?"

Theon nodded. "His name is Iri of Thebes. How did you hear of him?"

"Your representative Trygaeus asked my indulgence to allow Iri out of jail. Your kinsman takes to drink, falls into foul moods, and becomes the victim of his very short temper."

"My lord," Theon said sympathetically, "imagine being born with a face like that. I'm not sure whether he ever had a woman before Keturah. He'd never known love until his fifties, and then, just as he was about to experience the pleasures of fatherhood . . ."

"Poor man," Nestor said. "I ordered his release as soon as I found out who he was. He has promised to leave the wine alone while he's in Pylos."

"Thank you, Sire. Iri's not a bad sort. He's not only a

master armorer but an artist as well—a maker of fine golden jewelry."

"*That* Iri? I'd thought he'd died. There hasn't been any new work of his on the market in years."

"No, my lord. He traveled with the Israelites when they left Egypt for Canaan. He resigned as chief armorer and gave the job to his nephew, Pepi of Kerma, so Keturah could have the baby at Demetrios's 'hideaway.' Then Keturah was abducted. Iri himself was sold into slavery. I found him on a galley. He helped me to destroy the Minotaur's fleet. But now he's understandably obsessed with locating his wife."

"Shall we invite him to join us for dinner tonight?"

Theon frowned. "I'm afraid he would be uncomfortable with the courtly company and manners."

"Quite right. But I'll give the order that while he's in Pylos he's to be treated with every courtesy due a man of noble birth."

"You're very generous, my lord. Iri won't be here long, I'm certain."

"Let me take you on a tour of the new wing of the palace. I'm inordinately proud of it."

"As well you should be, my lord. Could I prevail upon you to give me some of the latest mainland gossip? Your insights are famous from one end of the Great Sea to the other."

"Gladly," Nestor agreed, with a gleam in his eyes. "We Greeks excel in intrigue and petty feuds, and there's been a surfeit of both recently. I expect war to break out any day now. Why, in Mycenae alone . . ."

II

The Pylos port was like all bustling Greek trading centers, with long piers extending into the bay. Along the docks sailors were clamoring for pay and rations, artisans were burnishing figureheads, and traders were selling corn, onions, leeks, and figs. Girls with flutes were advertising their talents, both musical and otherwise. The pipes of boatswains were shrilling, oarlocks were clanking; shipyard workers were hammering. Bellowed curses arose from every direction. The harbor was filled with ships, and the streets were teeming with hustlers and whores and vendors and practitioners of the pea-and-shells game, all eager to make money from the sailors.

Just inland from the Ropewalk lay the town square, where Pandion and Okware sought their old shipmate Iri. Trygaeus, Demetrios's agent in Pylos, had provided them with a list of Iri's favorite haunts. They had made their way into two of these already and vainly searched for Iri's distinctive face in the crowd; now they headed for the third tavern on their list, the White Dolphin.

Walking uphill from the waterfront, they passed clumsy ox-drawn wagons hauling marble down from the mountains, donkeys laden with panniers, and slaves carrying burdens on their bent backs. By their looks it was evident that the slaves came from all parts of the world: Egypt, Crete, Iberia, Nubia. The Nubians looked up, startled, as Okware passed and hailed them in their own tongue.

"I had not expected to see so many black men among the Greeks," Okware said.

"You forget, my friend," Pandion replied, "that your noble ancestor Akhilleus was a galley slave. I'm sure that even then he was not the only black man." Pandion's eyes twinkled. "Although he was the only one to become the king of Nubia."

Okware appreciated hearing the truth. Suddenly he stopped and put a hand on Pandion's wrist. "Look at all the people rushing out of that tavern."

"And the city guards are heading this way. What do you want to bet we've found Iri?"

"A fool's wager," Okware said. "What do you take me for?"

* * *

Pandion barely made it through the door before being propelled back into the street by a man trying to escape the guards. Pandion let the man pass, then he elbowed his way inside.

Roughs and cutthroats lined the walls of the dimly lit tavern. Their eyes were fixed on a burly man with great hulking shoulders who was successfully holding forth against a dozen men. It was indeed Iri. As Pandion watched, Iri picked one opponent up by the ankles and swung him around, bowling over two of his attackers with the man's body. Iri's disfigured face was set in a maniacal grin.

Pandion could hear men making wagers. Those who spoke with the local accent apparently knew Iri's reputation and were backing him; only the foreigners were betting against the red-faced man.

"Okware!" Pandion shouted over the din. "I've found him." Without waiting for his comrade, Pandion pushed his way toward his old shipmate. When he was close enough, he called out: "Iri! Iri of Thebes!" He caught Iri's eye, and one of his adversaries took advantage of the distraction to hurl a stool at his head.

A young man who had been quietly watching the fight deflected the stool with one arm, and it crashed harmlessly against the wall. The hulking man who threw the furniture cursed the boy for interfering and came at him with a punch that flattened him.

"You," Iri said in a menacing voice, thickened by alcohol, "leave the boy alone!"

Letting out a roar, he charged, head down, and caught the man in the belly. The blow drove the man against a bench, which caught him behind the knees, and he fell over backward. As he fell, two men behind Iri leaped into the melee.

"Oh, no, you don't!" Pandion warned, tackling one of them from behind. Out of the corner of his eye he saw Okware dive into the fray and take his man out with a single well-aimed punch.

Pandion had his opponent pinned to the ground and

was about to smash him in the nose when the commotion behind him grew louder. Suddenly a heavy hand fell on the back of his neck, grabbed his clothing, and hauled him to his feet.

"Break it up, you rowdies!" the burly city guardsman bellowed. "How'd the lot of you like to spend the night in jail?"

Only when all of them had been lined up against the wall did Iri look at his old shipmates. "Pandion! Okware! What are you doing here?" he asked through a mouth that was bruised and swelling.

The captain of the guards, who had worked his way down the line of prisoners, stopped before them and said, "Iri. I might have known. I thought you promised to lay off the wine and stop fighting."

"Sorry, Captain. You've been very patient. But one of these insulting idiots said that my face could only be loved by a blind woman and I . . ."

The captain looked up and down the line of prisoners. "This man is under the personal protection of King Nestor. Does everyone understand that? I'm letting you all go now, but the next person who gives him a bad time will serve six months on a galley. Now get out of here and stay out of trouble."

Pandion and Okware took Iri outside and inspected his face. He had a few cuts and bruises but no permanent damage.

"Why could you hold your temper when you were pulling an oar in the Minotaur's fleet but not ignore some idiot in a tavern?" Pandion asked.

"Look, Pandion, I—" Iri began. But then he pulled away and turned back to the tavern. "Did you see what happened to the boy who helped me in there?"

"I think he went the other way," Okware replied. "Why?"

"I wanted to thank him. Well, maybe I'll run into him later. What brings you two to Pylos?"

"Theon is busy conferring with Nestor and learning what he can of the unstable situation on the mainland. Trygaeus told Demetrios that you were here, and he sent us to find you. I take it your quest for Keturah hasn't been successful."

Iri stared out at the sea. "I've run out of leads. I thought I had located her on the mainland; but all my tips turned out to be false. All except . . ." His expression was unbearably painful. He covered his face with his big armorer's hands. "A fellow I met in port a week ago . . ."

Pandion put a comforting hand on Iri's massive shoulder.

"He may have been lying, of course," Iri continued. "He knew I'd offered a reward for information, and this would have been an easy way to collect it without having to prove anything. He said he'd seen—" Swallowing hard, he began again. "He said he'd been aboard a slaver, and he'd seen a blind slave—one with a newborn child—fall overboard during a storm and drown."

"Iri, you can't believe that," Pandion said. "Most likely he was making it up."

"That's what I'm hoping. But what if it is true? Looking for Keturah is the only thing that's keeping me alive."

"I know, Iri. Don't give up hope. The one thing that can truly seal her doom is if you quit searching for her. You know that."

Iri nodded. "Yes. But at first I had the feeling that I'd find her soon. Now the feeling's gone, and I'm getting desperate."

Pandion clapped him on the shoulder. "We're invited to Nestor's palace for dinner tonight. Come with us."

"No, no," Iri said. "I'd only disgrace myself and embarrass you. I want to find that boy who helped me. Go back and tell Theon I'm all right and he's not to worry. I'll be my old self in the morning."

*   *   *

Reluctantly Pandion let him go, but he stood with Okware, watching Iri move slowly down the hill toward the docks. "I've never seen him this bad before. Have you?"

"No," Okware answered. "On the galley he was always so tough and self-contained. I never thought he'd give up. Now I'm not so sure."

"In the morning we'll ask Theon to talk to him. He'll know how to handle Iri. At least I hope so."

The men gazed toward the end of the dock, where Iri stood disconsolately, looking down into the bay, as immobile as a statue, his massive shoulders drooping.

III

The sun was setting when at last Iri found the boy who had come to his aid in the fight. He saw him entering an inn, a dive in the worst part of town, and called out to him. "Young fellow, wait up."

The young man turned and recognized Iri. "Me?" he called.

Iri hurried forward. "Yes, you. I'd like to talk with you." As he closed the distance between them, the armorer could see how very young the fellow was; he was still smooth cheeked, Iri noted with surprise. "You helped me and took a punch for it. I wanted to thank you. It's the first time anyone has stood up for me in a long time."

The boy shrugged. "If I were a better fighter . . ."

"The least I can do is buy you dinner. You weren't thinking of going in there, were you? The food isn't fit to poison a dog."

Again the boy shrugged, and he said with a sigh, "My money's running out. I can't seem to find a job."

Iri put a friendly hand on the boy's shoulder. "What kind of a job, son? Do you have any skills?"

A cloud came over the fellow's face, and he seemed to

be debating whether to tell the truth. "I was a farmer. I wanted to go to sea. But the port's full of older men with lots of experience, so the captains always pass me by."

Iri took him by the arm. "I'm looking for work myself. Come on. We'll talk about our possibilities over a good dinner."

The boy gave Iri a startled glance when he felt his arm held in a gentle but unbreakable grip. But he let himself be led toward the more respectable inns along the Ropewalk.

Iri had more money than he knew what to do with, having cashed a draft on his funds with Trygaeus when he had first arrived, and so their dinner was the best that money could buy in Pylos.

Fearful of another uncontrollable outburst of his terrible temper, Iri watered his wine. They passed some time in small talk; then, when the first course was finished, Iri leaned across the table. "Tell me your name, where you're from, and where you're going."

Distrust flickered in the boy's eyes. Finally he said, "I'm Phorbus of Leontium. My father died a year ago, and my mother remarried a man who beat me. One day—" the boy paused, looking around cautiously "—I hit him on the back of his head with a hoe. I don't know how badly he was hurt. He may have been dead. I took off with the little money my father had left me. Now, here I am, stuck in Pylos."

"A hoe?" Iri said with a chuckle. "Better that than your fists. You're not experienced at fighting, are you, Phorbus?"

"I'm not in your league, that's for sure. But who are you? You have King Nestor's protection, but your accent's not of these parts."

"I'm Iri of Thebes, and I'm as desperate as you are. I come from an influential family. Not that I fit in with them. You can see this blotch on my face. It's made me a loner. Well, I had a wife once, but . . ." He swallowed, and when he spoke again, his voice was choked. "She's gone now. I've had a hard time of it, too. I was born to riches, but I've worked all my life—first as an armorer, then as a maker of fine jewelry." He sighed, looking at his hands. "I was a galley slave, and I helped guide a band of nomads through the desert. I was even a revolutionary once. But now . . ."

"But now what are you going to do?"

Iri shook his head. "I'm going to continue looking for my wife. She was . . . due to have our first child this month."

"Where will you look?" Phorbus asked softly.

"Everywhere. And when I find the man who enslaved her, his head will roll."

"You're good with your fists," the boy allowed. "Can you use a sword?"

Iri grinned. "I was trained in the sword by Prince Moses of Egypt, who learned the art from one of the greatest swordsmen in the world, Baliniri."

He caught the blank look on the boy's face. "All meaningless names to you, I'm sure, but they were important in their day."

Phorbus gave a sheepish smile. "I'm sorry. You must think me an innocent. I've never been anywhere or done anything. And I know nothing of fighting."

Iri looked at him. Something about the boy appealed to him, but until now he could not put his finger on it. That was it: Phorbus looked him in the eyes. Not everybody did. Most people were too embarrassed by his ugliness. This boy looked at him square in the face, as if Iri were a human being with feelings.

"Why don't you come along with me?" Iri asked. "We'll look for my wife, and I'll teach you how to fight."

"You don't know how clumsy I am. I appreciate the offer, but—"

"I've done a lot of teaching in my life, and I'm as good at that as I am at anything else I do. We'll find work along the way."

"You really mean it?" Phorbus asked cautiously. He realized his life was about to change, but he wasn't sure whether to believe his good luck or not.

Nestor's hospitality measured up to all expectations. After the last courses of the lavish meal had been taken away, Theon found himself in the mood for listening to Nestor's inimitable—and interminable—after-dinner stories. Talk soon turned to Helen of Sparta.

"Ah, there's a name I've heard of, my lord," Pandion said. "Is she as beautiful as rumor has it?"

Nestor hesitated. "Well, she's pretty enough, although she seems to me, with the blood running a bit colder in my veins than it did twenty years ago, a fairly obvious little piece. But she's got a sense of her power over men, I'll give her that, and she's more than proven her ability to twist hot-blooded males around her finger."

"As I remember, she was being courted by just about every eligible man," Theon said.

"Yes, there was going to be bad blood no matter whom she chose. Then Odysseus of Ithaca, who had the only clear head in the lot, suggested they leave the choice up to the girl and make a pact to abide by her decision and support the man she chose, even pledging to defend his household against anyone who pursued Helen after she was married. So anyone she tempts into her bed will find every young warrior in Greece pledged to hunt him down and teach him respect for chastity and fidelity. Sheer madness!" His old eyes twinkled. "We all knew that she ultimately settled upon Menelaus because he was so stupid. She'd be able to dominate him with ease and cuckold him any time she chose to."

"A potentially dangerous situation. Has anyone bedded her yet, my lord?" Theon asked, wondering what his own wife was doing at that moment.

"If they have, nobody's telling. But she flirts with everybody. She even bats her eyes at me. When her father died, he left the throne of Sparta to Menelaus, as Helen's husband."

Theon's brows lifted. "A generous inheritance . . ."

"It certainly was, especially since Helen has a sister, who is also married. I had expected their father to divide his kingdom equally between Helen's and Clytemnestra's husbands."

"To whom is Clytemnestra married?" Theon asked.

"To Menelaus's brother, Agamemnon," the old king answered.

Theon whistled low. "And is Agamemnon accepting Menelaus's good fortune with equanimity?"

Nestor snorted. "Not at all. Now that Menelaus has the power of Sparta at his command, Agamemnon wants his brother to help him get a job."

"Such as?"

"Such as recapturing Mycenae for Agamemnon to rule," the king answered. "Right now Agamemnon is a king without a throne."

Theon thought for a moment. "Mycenae was their father's kingdom!"

"That's correct. Their uncle took the throne and sent them into exile." Nestor shuddered. "It is a most repulsive family."

"This situation warrants close attention," Theon said.

"So do Helen and Clytemnestra," the old king remarked. "I know those girls, and I wouldn't leave either one alone for long. If Agamemnon and Menelaus sail from Sparta to raid Mycenae, one or the other of the husbands will be sprouting horns before long. It's going to lead to a lot of mischief, if not worse."

Aratos, mate of the slave ship *Eleia*, let his first officer off at the first whorehouse they found in Pylos and headed for the taverns. Ordinarily he would have been game to sample the brothels in port, but he had picked up some disease from the whores of the North African coast a month before, and it had cooled his ardor for the time being. Now food and drink, those were another matter. . . .

The landfall was a nonproductive one; they had stopped to reprovision only and would not be holding any sales while here. King Nestor did not like the slave trade and had imposed punitive duties that had effectively ended it in his territory, for now at least. Given the bad feeling against slavery in Pylos, it probably would not even pay to identify himself as a slave trader while he was in port. He saw no sense in doing anything that could cause controversy.

He felt lucky to have sold the one slave, the blind girl, before coming here. He had gotten a fair price for her and the infant. Aratos fingered the purse in his pocket, though, and wished it were heavier. What a pity they could not have sold one or two of the slaves in Pylos; with his percentage of the sale he could have had quite a good time. The big Lydian girl, for instance: She was a difficult one. She could fight better than any of the crew, and when the men had tried to take their pleasure on her, she had done them real damage, breaking one seaman's arm and raking another with her fingernails before they had finally subdued her.

As far as the little blind one was concerned, he was hopeful that she would be happy with her situation. He would hate to see a gentle girl like her, refined and soft-spoken, fall into the hands of a brute. Imagine having to sell her to someone like that Cretan back at the last port of call! Why, he would have raped her and brutalized her and thrown her baby overboard just for sheer, hard-hearted enjoyment.

He shuddered and offered a prayer to the gods for the blind girl's safety. The buyers seemed to have represented some fine household where she would be treated nicely. And they considered her sightlessness an advantage. Aratos wondered why. Did they have something to hide?

He sighed, needing a drink. What a trade to be in! One of these days he was going to retire, he promised himself. Just as soon as he had made a proper stake and could afford to leave the business!

IV

Iri had rented Phorbus a room next to his own at one of the better inns in the port, and when they arose in the morning for their *akratisma,* or first breakfast, they headed for the roof to take in the splendid view of the harbor and eat bread soaked in wine.

"I've been thinking over your offer of last night," Phorbus said.

"Yes?" Iri said.

"It's too good to pass up."

"So you want to travel and learn how to fight," Iri said approvingly. "You've come to the right man."

"But you said you were also a metalworker."

"Indeed, one of the best. The Children of the Lion are a metalworking family. I'm not sure you have heard of us this far away, but some of my family have ranked among the finest metalworkers in the world."

"My village of Leontium was so small you could throw a rock across it. We knew little of the outside world. Do you suppose you could show me something about working metal?"

Iri looked surprised. "You're widening your horizons fast, lad. Tell you what: Come along with me and learn how to take care of yourself in a scrap, and once you show progress in dealing with one end of a sword, maybe I'll show you a thing or two about the other end of it."

Phorbus grinned. "When do we start?"

On this they grasped hands, and Iri toasted his new apprentice. "But let me warn you about one thing: I can usually handle the mornings, particularly in a beautiful place like this, but the nights are often bad. That's a time for walking very softly around me."

"I'll remember. I suppose those are the times, like yesterday, when people go after you. They know instinctively when a fellow is feeling vulnerable."

"You're wise beyond your years, Phorbus."

"I know from experience." The boy hesitated. "I was a bastard. And people always chose my most vulnerable moments to remind me of it."

"In the world of soldiering, you can't take an insult from anyone," Iri stated. "If you swallow one insult, you'll have to swallow a hundred. Best to stop it right away."

"The way you fight, I need never fear anybody or anything again."

Iri beamed at him as proudly as a father might. But as he looked past Phorbus's shoulder, something caught his attention. "Gods! Look at that. Who do you suppose it could be?"

Phorbus turned and looked. The ship coming into the harbor was enormous, and its decks bristled with armed men. "Waiter!" he called. "Whose colors are those?"

"King Priam of Troy, sir, although I doubt Priam himself is aboard. Troy is across the Aegean. We see few of their boats here these days, sir."

"Troy, eh?" Iri said, then turned to Phorbus. "There's a thought. Maybe we could go there for a look around." Then he saw the look on the waiter's face. "I gather you don't approve?"

"Bad blood has existed between Troy and us for some years." His brow knit. "So I wonder what a ship of Troy's is doing here now. And that's no trade vessel, it's a war galley."

"Look," Phorbus said. "Way out in the bay. There are more ships bearing the same ensign. What's going on? Are the Trojans invading Greece?"

Drawn by the conversation, the innkeeper came up to the table. "I hope not, sir. The Trojans are fine fighters. Their champion, Priam's son Hector, has a reputation as being the equal of any man in the world with a sword, perhaps even the match of our Achilles. More likely, sir, it's a diplomatic mission."

"This has aroused my curiosity," Iri said. "Come on, lad, let's go down to the docks to see what we can find out."

Pylos's patrol ships, putting out to sea in the first hour after dawn, had discovered the Trojan fleet anchored off the coast and pulled alongside the flagship. As soon as the patrols returned, a messenger on horseback was sent up the hill to Nestor. He interrupted the king and his guests at a late and leisurely breakfast.

"What are the emissaries of Priam doing here?" Nestor asked.

"They say, Sire, that they're only in port to provision. They've been on a pilgrimage. Priam sent his daughter Cassandra with the fleet to Delphi to consult the oracle. I have the distinct feeling, Sire, that they're up to no good."

"Who's in command? Hector?"

"No, sir, his half brother Paris."

Nestor looked over at Theon. "I can't say I like that. Paris is high-strung and irresponsible."

The messenger spoke up. "If you'll pardon my saying so, Sire, I didn't like him at all. He was exceedingly arrogant."

Nestor leaned to speak quietly in Theon's ear. "Paris is insufferable. Thinks he's invincible with the ladies." He turned back to the messenger. "Go on. What else did they tell you?"

"Sire, I got the feeling they weren't being entirely truthful, but they did say that Paris wanted to make a temple offering. They're on their way to Cythera, to the temple of Aphrodite."

"Trips to shrines are hardly reasons to send a war fleet to Greece," Nestor muttered. "There's got to be more to it."

"Prince Paris, Sire, acted as if his being offshore was none of our business. He was very rude."

"Did they say anything about where they were going after Cythera?"

"Prince Paris is careless, Sire. He let drop one word: 'Sparta.' "

Nestor rolled his eyes heavenward. "May all the gods defend us. Mark my words, Theon, we're going to find ourselves in a war, whether we want one or not."

V

On the way to the docks Iri and Phorbus joined a crowd of curiosity-seekers, Pandion and Okware among them. As they stood watching, the Trojan flagship came in, and Pandion nodded toward the man standing in the bow. He muttered under his breath.

"What's that?" Iri asked.

"I said, 'Look at the peacock up there. It's Paris of Troy.' "

Iri looked up to where Pandion pointed. The tall, handsome man standing in the bow of the ship was the kind of fellow that all other men, particularly ugly ones like Iri, instinctively hated—and women adored. His features were as regular as a god's, and his body was smooth and graceful. His pose was the picture of elegance and confidence.

"I wonder why he is putting in here, instead of at Nestor's private harbor. Does he intend to snub the king?" Iri asked.

"I'm sure he does," Okware answered. "And he may even realize that wars have been started over less."

They watched in silence as the boat docked. Heavily armed bodyguards filed off and began clearing a path for the prince.

"Out of the way," one of the guards snarled at Iri, bumping into him on purpose. "Make way for Lord Paris!"

"There's plenty of room on the dock for both of us," Iri said, crossing his huge arms over his broad chest.

At that moment Paris came striding onto the dock. "Who is that hideous creature? Get him out of here."

Only the hard glint in Iri's eyes revealed his anger. His smile remained fixed. "There's plenty of room for you to walk on by."

Paris's eyes flashed, and his patrician upper lip curled. "Captain," he said, "deal with him."

The first guard's hand reached out toward Iri, but before anyone could see what had happened, the Trojan had been flipped over the rail to land in the water. As the bodyguards converged on their comrade's assailant, Iri immediately went on the offensive, ducking a blow and then punching another guard in the jaw.

"Guards!" Paris screamed out. "To me! Help!"

Using an obviously well-practiced maneuver, other guards separated Iri from the rest of the spectators. Iri found himself surrounded by men with drawn swords. Then a detachment of Nestor's port guards came jogging heavily up the dock from the shore. Behind them stood a squad of archers with arrows nocked, their shafts aimed at the Trojan visitors.

"Halt!" sounded the voice of the commander of the Pylos waterfront guards.

Paris's first reaction was shocked silence. Then he drew himself up and said, "You dare do this to a prince of the blood?"

"Tell your men to put down their swords and get back aboard their boat," the commander ordered. "Otherwise . . ." He sent a significant glance at his row of archers.

Iri watched Paris. The prince's eyes did not waver. Finally he motioned to his men. "Return to the ship. I'll deal with this." Reluctantly the soldiers filed back up the plank. Their faces as rigid as stone, they stood at the flagship's rail, watching. Satisfied, the commander motioned, and the archers slowly released the tension on their bows.

Paris glared at him. "I'm amazed that you would try this, knowing that a fleet of war galleys, under my command, lies out in the bay."

"Before you get any ideas," the commander said evenly, "consider that the Bay of Navarino is dotted with little coves and bights and that every damned one of them has a patrol boat in it, ready to go. And they're manned by tough Greeks who eat Trojans for breakfast."

When the guards and the crowd had dispersed, Hylas, the commander, lingered behind with Iri and his friends to watch Paris's galley head out into the bay. Iri had a wide grin across his face. "I've seen some brave actions in my day, Commander, but that tops any of them. Did you really have the authority to talk to him that way?"

The man's mouth curled into a wry smile. "Probably not. I was stretching to the limit the king's order to make sure nobody bothers you. But it gave me an excuse to do something I've longed to do for years."

Only when the ship was well out into the bay did Princess Cassandra come out on deck. Her face was pale, but not as pale as her extraordinary silvery-blue eyes. Her young body was thin and angular, and she seemed to float across the wooden planks. She watched Paris fume and curse for some minutes without saying anything. Even when he looked at her, eyes flashing, she remained silent.

This enraged him. "You keep your opinions to yourself!"

Cassandra studied him for a moment. "Do you have any idea of the damage you've done? You have snubbed a beloved king, a man the Greeks will rally around if he decides to take offense. Then, in plain sight of half the port and your own crew, you make a fool of yourself. Why my father ever decided to put you in charge of this mission, I'll never know."

"If you don't keep that mouth of yours shut, so help me I'll—"

"You'll what? I'm the daughter of the king *and* queen of Troy and a priestess of Apollo. If you lay a finger on me, the crew will cut you down. There are things that even a . . . prince of the blood . . . dare not do." Her hesitation on Paris's self-proclaimed title was deliberate. Although Priam had acknowledged his bastard son, he had never conferred a title on him.

"Your snake's tongue will betray you one day."

She let out a weary sigh. "It has already, many times. I speak the truth, to Father and everyone else, but no one believes me because I don't speak from a sulfur pit in Delphi or eat from the sacred mushroom." Turning slowly, she walked back to her cabin.

Paris stared after her, his throat full of bile. *If only she weren't princess and priestess, I'd . . .*

But he realized these thoughts were dangerous. He cast about for a suitable target for his wrath.

"That ugly red-faced bastard," he muttered. "*He* started all this. I'll remember that face. Someday I'll find him again. And when I do, he'll pay."

VI

That afternoon, Iri, Phorbus, Okware, and Pandion sat in a tavern celebrating their victory over Paris with Hylas, commander of the port guard. He regaled them with old war stories, and Iri noticed how Phorbus, wide-eyed, hung on every word.

"It may be time for you to leave Pylos," Hylas finally said to Iri. "They're hiring in Argos, no questions asked."

"Who's hiring?" Iri asked.

"Agamemnon and his brother. They're hoping to root their uncle Thyestes out of Mycenae and put Agamemnon back on their father's throne." Hylas took a long swig of wine, then looked up at Iri. "If you find work, send a message back. I may need a new job after what I did today."

Suddenly Iri jumped up. "Here's someone I want you to meet. Theon! Come over!"

Theon, who had just entered the inn, looked their way and smiled. "Iri, I was hoping you hadn't gotten away!" The group made room for him at its table, and he was introduced all around. "Ah, Commander Hylas, word has spread about your exploit."

"May the gods help me," the commander said, rolling his eyes. "Am I fired?"

"No, in fact, Nestor is bragging about you. And he sent spies after Paris to keep an eye on him. Nobody at court believes that Priam sent Paris over here to visit shrines—not with a dozen warships backing him up."

"Then why is he here?" Iri asked his kinsman.

"That's what the spies are finding out. Now, Iri, catch me up with your progress."

Iri sighed. "Phorbus, pour me my wine ration, will you, lad? Thank you. Theon, I've lost Keturah's trail, if indeed there is one. Somebody gave me a detailed description of a blind slave—a slave with a baby in her arms—he saw tossed off a slaver during a storm. I used to feel that she was alive. Now I . . . I just don't know."

"Come back to Home with me. We'll take care of you. Demetrios's men can continue the search."

"So will we," Okware offered, gesturing toward Pandion.

"I'd go crazy," Iri said. "If I'm not already. No, Theon, I need something to occupy my mind. I can't just sit around thinking of her. I've a lot of anger boiling inside me. I need to be moving around. And you don't need armorers at Home, for heaven's sake."

"You could make jewelry," Theon suggested.

Iri stared glumly at his wine. "No. Every ring I make, every bracelet, would remind me of her."

"Demetrios does so want to see you once more before he dies." Theon's voice was choked.

"Yes, I know. And I'd like to see him, too, of course. But Home . . . it's a trap. No, Theon, you go on back and live a good life. Give Demetrios my love. And take Okware and Pandion with you. Forget about me." He took a long drink and tried to get his feelings under control. "Incidentally, how's the M—" He stopped. "How's Khalkeus of Gournia doing?"

Theon raised an eyebrow. One of the best-kept secrets in the world was that Demetrios's successor had once been the notorious pirate known as the Minotaur. When Demetrios had discovered that the infamous leader of a vast association of thieves was a Child of the Lion, Demetrios had shocked everyone who knew the truth and chosen him as his successor. "Don't worry about us, Iri," Theon said. "Just take care of yourself. We have an agent in every port. Call on them for money, information, whatever you need."

Pandion leaned across the table and grasped Iri's shoulder. "We'll always be available when you need us."

Theon sighed as he went out the door into the street. Thinking about Khalkeus produced other, disquieting thoughts that he did not feel like facing tonight but could not get out of his mind.

Khalkeus, of course, was his father-in-law, father of his wife, Nuhara. And these days things were not going well between Nuhara and him.

How could anything have gone wrong? Their courtship had been wonderful, if unusual. He had infiltrated her father's pirate fleet, trying to find a way to stop the Minotaur's raids. Instead he had been captured and imprisoned. But Nuhara had taken a liking to him. One day, during the annual rendezvous of the Great Sea privateers, Nuhara and he had sneaked away to the mountains and spent the day making love and delighting in each other's company.

Not that such ecstasy could last. He knew that now. Nuhara remained her father's daughter, rather than her husband's wife and helpmate. He should have realized what would happen. Even after they were stealing moments of love aboard the pirate ship, she had betrayed him more than once to the Minotaur.

Now, in all their domestic arguments, Nuhara compared him with her father and found Theon lacking. She criticized him for not sharing her father's traits or having his wisdom.

Unfortunately, the Minotaur had not as yet proved himself equal to the task for which he had been chosen. In Theon's judgment, the man lacked vision and made one bad decision after another. And Theon was reluctant to trouble Demetrios with his opinion while the man's health was so fragile.

Theon closed his eyes and leaned for a moment against a post on the dock. *Nuhara!* If only things could go back to the way they had been before!

She was still the same dazzlingly beautiful girl she had been when they first met. Why, now, did he find himself cringing at the thought of touching her?

And why did his mind begin to wander when another attractive woman crossed his path?

He clenched his fists. No! He would not give in to temptation. He would not take the easy way out. As soon as this trip was over he would go back to Home and do what he could to make up with her. If he had to, he would take the blame upon himself.

But at the same time he would try to put some distance between Nuhara and Khalkeus. If he could wean his wife from her dependence upon her father and win some of that loyalty and devotion for himself, perhaps something could still be made of their marriage.

CHAPTER THREE

On the West Bank

I

Outside Jericho's city walls the rams' horns were blowing, as they had done for almost a week. Each day at noon the Israelites had massed in the thousands and marched around the outskirts of the city, following the priests who carried the simple acacia-wood box they called the Ark of the Covenant. Then, after one slow, portentous circuit around the city they had retired to their camp at Gilgal, where their families awaited them.

From the upper floor of Rahab's house on the city wall, Tirzah and Rahab watched the long column recede.

"Don't let your husband go to Gilgal by himself," Rahab said to the tall, blond woman beside her. "It's too dangerous."

"What can I do?" Tirzah groaned. "I might as well try to stop the wind from blowing once Pepi makes up his mind. Of course, he's not well enough to travel or, even worse, face a confrontation with Joshua."

"At least go along with him. If he has another blackout, you'll be there to take care of him."

Tirzah, wife to the armorer Pepi of Kerma, looked down at tiny, roly-poly Rahab, who until a month before had run one of the busiest brothels along the Jericho wall. "That's a good idea. I'll ask to ride along."

"If Pepi can dissuade Joshua from attacking Jericho, he'll save thousands of lives," Rahab said. "But if the attack comes, I want the two of you to stay in my house. I helped two of Joshua's spies escape from danger, and they promised to spare me and mine from the assault."

"But Rahab, we may be gone from Jericho by then. If he has no success with Joshua, we'll be leaving for Jerusalem. Pepi has relatives there."

"That won't solve anything. The Israelites will attack Jerusalem, too. My astrologer says Joshua will take Jericho with ease. And if he can take Jericho, with our thick Hai walls built by the Shepherd Kings, the walls of Jerusalem aren't going to stop him. The only thing that can save you is my dispensation."

"Rahab, surely you don't believe—"

"Those two Israelite spies promised to spare my house and everyone in it. One of them was a Levite. Levites don't lie. They'll honor their pledge. After all, I risked my life to help them escape from the city guards."

Tirzah looked her in the eyes. "But will Joshua honor it? Will Caleb? Or will the troops? You don't know what soldiers are like when they're on a killing spree. They are like wild beasts."

Rahab nervously rubbed one palm against the other. "I know, dear. I remember when the Sea Peoples attacked us."

"All right, Rahab. If we're still here, we'll take you up on your kind offer of sanctuary, I promise."

The older woman stared out the window and down the long street that ran next to the wall. "Here comes Pepi now. Your husband looks so healthy. Who would suspect there was anything wrong with him?"

Tirzah sank onto the bed, and her face became very solemn. "It's all my fault, Rahab. I thought he was one of the Israelites coming to steal my land, and I threw a rock at him. I'm big and strong, and I threw it very hard. Ever since, these blackouts come over him without warning."

"Poor Tirzah. It's so sad. I'm sure you feel terrible."

"He never had a day's illness before in his life. Look at him. He's a blacksmith, as strong as a young bullock."

"Well, what's done is done. Feeling guilty isn't going to help, so treat him well and watch over him. And make sure you go with him to Gilgal."

The two women locked eyes as Pepi's footfalls, surprisingly light for a man of his commanding size, sounded on the stairs.

Joshua was wandering along the bank of the Jordan, looking at the cairn his men had built to commemorate the crossing of the river. One moment he was aware of the world about him. The next moment everything seemed to stop. Before him stood a man arrayed in white robes, holding a gleaming sword in one hand. Joshua had not seen him approach; he just suddenly appeared.

Startled, Joshua reached for his weapon. "Are you one of us?" he demanded. "Or one of our enemies?"

The man's eyes burned. "*I am captain of the host of Yahweh.*" The voice rang in Joshua's ears.

Joshua's heart began beating wildly. He fell to his knees and refused to look at the apparition. "Command me," he implored in a quaking voice. "What would you have me do?"

"Stand," the figure ordered in his strangely soft voice. "Remove your sandals. You are on holy ground."

Hastily Joshua did so. Afraid to look on that which even Moses had not seen, he covered his eyes. "C-command me," he said again.

"You have heard His voice in your sleep; now you hear it awake. He has told you to march the army around the walls of Jericho for six days, blowing the trumpets. This you have done. And tomorrow Jericho shall be delivered into your hands."

Joshua tried to speak but found he could not.

The voice continued. "On the seventh day, the march around the city will begin at dawn. You will circle it seven times as the priests blow the rams' horns. Then they will blow a single long blast. When the people hear this, they will give a mighty shout, and the city wall will collapse."

Suddenly Joshua realized he could hear the river again, and the sounds of the horns. When he removed his hands from over his eyes, he saw that the man was gone.

Exhausted, he sank to the ground.

At last, he thought, *at last He has spoken to me. I had thought I would go to my grave without ever hearing His voice. I must fix this moment in my mind for all time. It may never happen again.*

Shemida found him lying on the ground. "There's an inspection in an hour, sir. You'll want to change your uniform. Your wife and sons have sent a message from Gilgal. They would like to see you later if it's convenient."

Still Joshua did not notice him.

Worried, Shemida knelt beside him. "Is there anything wrong, sir?"

Only then did Joshua look up. "Tomorrow," he said in a distant voice. "Tomorrow we'll take Jericho. Send Caleb to me. Tomorrow Jericho will be destroyed."

"And your family? They'd like to—"

"No time for them now. Tell them I'll see them after the battle."

II

Security was tight at the main gate of Jericho, but the tablet Pepi presented at the guardhouse, bearing the seal of the chief magistrate, allowed them to pass through. Beyond the gate they mounted up, with Tirzah unobtrusively assisting Pepi, then swinging easily into her own saddle.

From time to time Tirzah would look over at her husband. He gave no indication that there was anything wrong with him; he was in a cheerful mood, talkative and enthusiastic. He had high hopes of being able to talk Joshua out of his plan to destroy Jericho.

"You know," he said, "going out in the marketplace is a very instructive experience. I spoke with the stall owners, the fruit vendor, the butcher, and the baker. They're not a bad lot. If only Joshua could meet any of them, he'd realize that the Canaanites are not a faceless enemy to be destroyed, but real people who share the same basic concerns as the Israelites. I haven't spent so much time in a city for many years. I've been enjoying myself."

"Let's pick out a city we like and settle down," Tirzah suggested.

He smiled at her. "Or we could do a bit of traveling. That might be fun."

"Would that be safe? Your blackouts are becoming more frequent."

"I promised to show you the place my uncle Demetrios calls Home. Maybe we'll like it enough to settle there." He put his hand up to shield his eyes from the glare of the sun. The tent city spread out across the landscape was impressive. "There's the Israelite camp. It's so large. Joshua must have been doing more recruiting. I'd guess the army was up to maybe forty thousand men."

"It looks as if they're preparing to break camp," Tirzah said. "You don't suppose they're getting ready to mount the attack?"

They rode closer. "Look over there," Pepi said. "I see Caleb. I think I'll—"

Tirzah laid a cautionary hand on his arm. "Be careful. You know you've never gotten along with him."

He pulled his arm away gently. "Caleb is an honorable man. He's just ambitious and has always resented my close relationship with Joshua. But there's no reason for him to be jealous now that Joshua and I are at odds. Stay here while I go talk to him."

"Pepi. I'm going with you."

"No, don't. I'll just be a moment." Pepi urged his horse to where Caleb was supervising the dismantling of a staff tent. "Caleb!"

Joshua's second-in-command wheeled around, and his hand grasped his sword hilt.

Pepi dismounted and held up empty hands. "I'm here to speak with Joshua. There's no reason for us to quarrel."

Caleb's eyes narrowed. "Do you think I'd allow you anywhere near Joshua? He doesn't need to see a turncoat who keeps company with the enemies of Israel." In a single swift motion, he pulled his sword out of its scabbard.

Still Pepi refused to draw his. "Caleb, you've got it all wrong."

Caleb, looking beyond Pepi, saw Tirzah edging closer. "And there's the Bashanite witch. I hear you two are living in Jericho, as guests of the chief magistrate. A fit place for spies!"

"Wait a minute. Tirzah's my wife. I won't have anyone insulting her."

"Wife?" Caleb said with a snort. "That foreign slut?"

"Caleb, I'm going to forget I heard that. Tirzah isn't even Bashanite. Look at her blond hair and blue eyes. Did you ever see a Bashanite with—"

Caleb's blood was up. "What are they paying you to sell us out? What's the going rate for betraying your childhood friends, the people you shared dangers with all those years in the desert?"

Pepi's face was contorted with shock. "Calm down, Caleb! You're speaking nonsense. I have, in fact, been doing some spying—"

"Ah! Now it's out at last!"

"Let me finish! Yes, I've been spying, but for you, not against you. And I've got information if—"

"I've half a mind to cut you down, limb from traitorous limb."

"Caleb, do you honestly think I want to see any of your people die storming the walls? This is Pepi talking! We were friends once."

"Are you going to leave quietly or—"

"You just won't be satisfied until you've drawn me into a fight, is that it, Caleb?"

Caleb's face was red. His mouth was set in a hard line. "Draw that sword, damn you!"

"Pepi, no!" Tirzah cried out.

But it was too late. With a great sigh of reluctance he drew his weapon.

Caleb grinned maliciously, then moved with lightning speed, lunging and almost catching Pepi in the chest. But Pepi managed to sideslip and deflect Caleb's sword long enough to allow him to position himself properly.

"Caleb," he said wearily, "I can't believe this. We're fighting as if we were enemies. You know I'm on your side and mean you no harm." Caleb attacked. Pepi parried with ease. "But you also know that you could never equal my ability with a sword. Even if your sword were a handspan longer than mine . . ."

His words incited Caleb. Pepi met and deflected his attacks but refused to make an offensive move of his own.

A crowd of Caleb's men was beginning to gather around them. He could have stopped and called for Pepi's arrest at any time, but this match had been inevitable for years.

"Caleb, you can't win this," Pepi grunted as he turned aside a sword strike. "All you can do is make the two of us look idiotic."

Caleb flew into a black rage, attacking with an insane fury. Pepi was obliged to put up a serious defense.

"Caleb, you've improved. You're really not a bad swordsman at all now."

That Pepi could carry on a conversation while defending himself obviously infuriated Caleb. Half-exhausted, he fell back momentarily.

"Don't mock me," Caleb warned. "Let's see how good you are. Curse you, you son of a bitch! Attack!"

"But I don't want to attack you, Caleb. All I want is to see Joshua."

Tirzah stood nearby, holding the horses. "Please, Pepi," she cried. "Leave now, while you can!"

Caleb sneered. "Yes. Run along. Hide behind a woman's skirts. Return to Jericho. Tomorrow we'll destroy the city and you with it, you turncoat!"

"Tomorrow?" Pepi echoed.

Caleb, realizing he had said too much, attacked furiously and drove Pepi back.

Then, suddenly, Pepi's eyes glazed over. His jaw slackened, and the sword fell from his inert hands. As the pain hit he pressed his palms to his temples, and his massive body swayed. He fell to his knees, then pitched forward, unconscious.

Caleb, pressing forward for the kill, stopped abruptly, his sword hanging at his side. He could not strike the deathblow now. Cursing, he hurled his sword to the ground. He looked down at the tall blond woman, who kneeled over Pepi, anguish tightening her lovely face.

"Get him out of here," Caleb snarled. "If I ever see either of you again, I swear I'll kill you."

III

With help from several of the Israelite soldiers who had been friends of Pepi's, Tirzah managed to get him on his horse. Holding the reins, she led the animal slowly back to the Jericho gate. As they approached the city, he regained consciousness and tried to talk.

"The attack is coming tomorrow. We have to warn them."

"Hush, don't talk. The first thing is to get you home and to bed. Then I can try to warn them."

"N-no," he protested. His hands were pressed to his temples, and his eyes were squeezed shut. "You don't understand. Everyone will be slaughtered."

"Not the people in Rahab's house," Tirzah said. "We'll be safe there."

He clenched the mane of his horse to keep from screaming as pain shot through him. "No one will be spared. You don't know Joshua. Women, children, will be killed. I've got to see the chief magistrate. I've got to see the king. I've got to warn them."

"The army is on alert. Besides, those walls were built by the Shepherd Kings. No one has ever breached a Shepherd wall. You told me so yourself, dear."

"It doesn't matter," he said through clenched teeth. "They'll get inside. Joshua must have a plan, or he wouldn't be attacking tomorrow." He groaned.

Tirzah slowed her horse to ride beside him. "You're exhausting your strength. Let me get you into bed, then I can send someone to the magistrate."

Ahead the Jericho gate loomed. Studying the high, impenetrable walls, Tirzah couldn't imagine how anyone would ever breach them. No, Jericho would never fall except to siege. And the city had been stockpiling food and water for weeks. Besides, they would be safe at Rahab's.

"Tomorrow at dawn we will march around Jericho, as we have done before, with the Ark, and the priests before us blowing rams' horns. But on the seventh time the trumpeters will sound a long blast, and this will be your signal. When you hear it, I want you to shout as loudly as you can. And when the Lord hears your voices, He will destroy Jericho."

A mighty cheer arose at Joshua's words. He held up his hand to silence the troops. "The city is to be razed, and all in it are to be killed, except for the inhabitants of the house of Rahab the harlot—the woman who saved our spies. To her and those she chooses to shelter, we promised amnesty.

"Remember that God has said that all the gold and silver is reserved to Him," Joshua continued. "His wrath will descend on all of us if even one of you touches what belongs to the Lord. When the city is ours, it will be burned to the ground and everything in it destroyed. Jericho will be obliterated, never to be rebuilt on this accursed site. Cursed will be he who tries to rebuild its walls. The mighty hand of God will fall upon him."

Shemida had watched the fight between Caleb and Pepi from a distance and had heard how, in his anger, Caleb had grown loose-tongued. Now Pepi and his wife knew when the attack on Jericho would come. Presumably Pepi had gone to the captain of the Jericho garrison with the information.

Should he tell Joshua? Shemida knew that the wisest course was to stay out of the rivalry between Caleb and the armorer. Caleb could be a dangerous enemy. But Shemida knew that his first loyalty would always rest with the man who had given him the chance to prove himself.

So he sought out Joshua. As he neared the command tent, Shemida noticed the flap pulled back, and Joshua's wife emerged, to stalk angrily away. Shemida waited for a moment, then shrugged and went inside.

At first Joshua didn't notice him. Then he turned with a start and said, "I'm sorry, Shemida, my mind is elsewhere."

When Shemida saw the fixed expression on Joshua's face, he hesitated to trouble him. "Do you have any orders for me?"

"Yes, I'm going to need a small striking force, drawn from the best units in my command, to attack the town of Ai immediately after we've taken Jericho, while the troops' blood is still up. Tell Caleb to handpick the units for me. Our spies say that a force of three thousand will be sufficient to capture the town, but I want to take no chances. I want the best, leanest, hungriest units. I want to show that I don't need forty thousand men to take a Canaanite city."

"Certainly, sir. Who will be the commander?"

"Caleb, I think. He's in a bad temper these days. Maybe I can work some of it out of him."

"Very good, sir." Shemida remained in his place.

"Is there something you want to say?"

"Pepi the armorer showed up looking for you, sir. He ran into Caleb, and Caleb drove him away. The truth is, they had a fight. Pepi easily dealt with Caleb."

"I'm not surprised."

"Pepi wasn't looking for a fight."

"Why wasn't he allowed to see me?"

"You'll have to ask Caleb, sir. But what is important is that Caleb let it slip that we're attacking Jericho tomorrow."

To Shemida's surprise Joshua waved away his warning. "It won't help them."

Shemida stared openmouthed at Joshua. How could it not matter?

The physician had given Pepi a draught of something very like the drug they called *shepenn* in Egypt. Now he slept.

As they left the bedroom Tirzah said to the physician, "Tell me, is there anything that can be done?"

The doctor held up his hands, palms up. He said nothing, but his face was soft with pity.

"Then it's hopeless?"

"The blackouts and pain cannot be cured. But he's sound in every other way, and I think that you can keep the number of such attacks down. Strenuous physical exercise or distress probably bring them on. Give him this drug to dull the pain."

Tirzah's face fell. "I was hoping for better news."

"And I wish I could give it to you." He sighed wearily. "The medicine will allow him to sleep the night, and there's a good chance that when he awakes in the morning, he'll be in no pain."

Tirzah pressed several coins into his hand.

"Thank you," he said. "If I can be of any help in the future . . ."

What future? she asked herself.

At dawn the guards atop the city wall peered through the morning fog to see the same procession they had been ridiculing every afternoon for the past week: the entire Israelite army, preceded by priests bearing the plain wooden box. Seven priests led the procession, each bearing a ram's horn. After the first circuit of the city walls they blew their horns, as they always did. The sound was unpleasantly raw.

At their post above Rahab's building two guards shuddered at the noise. "What a sound to wake up to!" the taller man said. "It was bad enough listening to those horns in the afternoon!"

The shorter guard leaned out over the wall and shouted down. "Can't you boys learn a new tune or take up another instrument?"

The taller guard laughed. "A kithara would be an improvement. The sound wouldn't carry so far." He leaned over the wall and called out, "Don't you know any lullabies?"

There was no answer. Were there more troops than usual out there in the fog? Or was it just a trick of the light?

The rams' horns blew again, and still the army came on.

IV

From the first blast of the trumpets Tirzah had tried to rouse Pepi. What finally awakened him was the frightened whinnying of the horses in the stables on the street below. He sat up, shaking his head and rubbing his eyes. "I've slept all through the day and night, haven't I?" he asked in a hoarse and phlegmy voice.

"The doctor thought it best," Tirzah said.

"But Tirzah, I wanted to talk to the city fathers! I wanted to warn them!" His voice took on a plaintive tone. "The attack is about to start, and there's nothing I can do. Did you send a message to them?"

"Yes, but the messenger returned to say they wouldn't even let him in."

Pepi seemed to wilt. "It's too late, then. It's in the hands of the gods now."

"What do you mean?" Rahab asked from the shadows in a corner of the room. When Pepi noticed her, he grabbed for a blanket, but she laughed. "Don't mind me. You're not the first man—"

Tirzah handed him a rough robe, and he pulled it over his head. "The city can't be saved," he said.

Down in the street the whinnying of the horses was even louder, and outside the city wall dogs were howling. People were calling out, frightened and confused.

"Do you hear the animals? Do you know what that means? Earthquake!" He got up, grabbed Tirzah's hand, and dragged her to the door. "Rahab! Come on!"

Just as they reached the stairs the tremor hit. The sound was like the roar of a great subterranean beast. The entire house shook. Pepi, holding tightly to Tirzah, barely kept the two of them from being thrown over the side of the open staircase and into the street. Rahab fell to the ground and lay there, panting, as a huge crack appeared in the wall of her house. Pepi and Tirzah watched with held breath until the woman climbed to her feet and ran up the wooden stairs to join them.

"Outside!" Pepi cried. "Before something falls on us!"

Tirzah could barely hear Pepi's words above the rumble. As they scrambled up onto the rooftop, the staircase below them crumbled and fell into pieces.

*   *   *

In the main square of the city the roof of the temple of Dagon cracked and fell to the tile floor, smashing the mosaics. Four of the huge columns swayed, cracked, and toppled. The priest who had been lighting candles managed to get out the door just as an enormous chunk of the ceiling crashed to the ground, missing him by a handspan.

Everywhere there was screaming.

On the plain beyond the city, Joshua sat atop his horse, watching. The soldiers gathered around him, waiting for his signal to action. Screams of agony echoed across the plain. Another tremor hit, and the mammoth gate of the city broke in three pieces. The lintel fell, splintering the great oaken gate and crushing one of the soldiers guarding it.

A monstrous crack appeared in the unassailable Hai wall, followed by another tremor. Joshua's panic-stricken horse reared and had to be held down.

"Watch," Joshua said in a voice of wonder. "It is as though the mighty fist of God were crushing the city."

The next tremor opened a huge hole in the wall, and then another. Each was wide enough for two men bearing arms to pass through.

"Now, Joshua?" Caleb asked in a voice filled with impatience.

"Not yet," Joshua said. But he held up his hand, waiting for the sign.

At that moment the earth shifted, so quickly and powerfully that men fell to the ground. Joshua's horse reared again, tearing itself free from the soldiers' grasping hands. Before them the wall seemed to lurch violently, separating brick from brick. An entire section of the wall crumbled. Beyond it they could see buildings caving in and could hear the screams of terror.

For the last time the trumpets blew. And before their eyes the only remaining section of the wall trembled and fell.

"Now," Joshua said as his upraised hand swept down.

The army, forty thousand strong, swarmed across the rubble.

Pepi and the two women looked out over the devastated city from the rooftop. The prostitute's house had miraculously withstood the tremors.

Rahab knelt by the roof's wall, her face in her hands, sobbing. Tirzah might well have done the same, but Pepi's strong arm was wrapped around her. His voice was calm. "Maybe Joshua's right. Maybe his God *does* do this. I've never seen anything like it. Some power crushed Jericho as if it were an anthill."

"Oh, Pepi, look: They've set fire to the grain warehouse. Let's get out of here now, before the soldiers come this way," Tirzah said.

"There's nowhere we could go that would be safe. We must stay here."

Hearing Pepi's words, Rahab looked up. Her eyes were wild, and her face was white with fear.

Caleb kicked at his horse's flanks and led fifty horsemen through the crumbled remains of the great Hai wall and along what appeared to have been a main thoroughfare between the western gate and the center of Jericho. The street was lined with the crumbled ruins of small, squat dwellings, the walls and roofs having caved in upon the inhabitants, probably killing as many as would meet their fate on the swords of the Israelites. There was no sign of survivors.

Caleb steered his horse around large chunks of wall and deep gashes left by the earthquake. All the while he kept a sharp lookout for armed resistance, but apparently the forces of Jericho had scattered in terror when the earth shook and the great wall toppled.

Caleb and his men slowed their animals to a walk as they entered a broad marketplace. In the center stood a large well. It was eerily calm, almost quiet, save for the distant clatter of hoofbeats as the rest of Joshua's forces

but his attacker landed on top of him. They tumbled down the stairs and came to a halt at the landing. Caleb was on his back with the other man straddling him, choking him with one hand and bringing his sword to bear with the other. The point hovered mere inches from Caleb's heart. Caleb had lost his own weapon, but he managed to grasp the Canaanite's wrist and push away the sword. He gasped and sputtered as his adversary continued to choke him. When the man released his neck to grab the sword with both hands, Caleb drew in a great gulp of air.

Before the Canaanite could bear down harder on the weapon, Caleb gave a furious shove and threw the man sideways against the building, stunning him. Staggering to his feet, Caleb saw his own sword lying on the ground near the open doorway that led into the building. He vaulted over the stair railing and in two quick strides was at the sword and snatching it up.

Suddenly he heard an animallike shriek and looked up just as a figure hurtled through the doorway at him. He saw the glint of a knife blade, which slashed wildly then clattered to the ground as Caleb sent his sword hilt-deep into the attacker's belly. As he jerked the weapon free and the figure stumbled and fell into the sunlight, Caleb saw that it was the woman who had been huddled inside.

Caleb shuddered as he took the stairs two at a time, to where the man lay stunned on the landing. He was just opening his eyes when Caleb brought his sword down, piercing the Canaanite through the neck.

As Caleb glanced up the stairway, he heard his men making their way into the building. He called for them.

"There are two archers on the roof," he said as a pair of soldiers, followed by three others, stepped over the woman and joined him. "And an infant in the back room."

"It's been disposed of for us," one soldier said. "Looks as if the mother killed it so we wouldn't."

Caleb glanced at the two corpses, then turned and headed toward the back of the house as his men, already nocking their arrows, passed him on their way up the stairs to the roof.

A shout of victory drifted down to him, and Caleb guessed that at least one of his soldier's bolts had found its mark. Moving away from the building, he looked up and saw that three of his men were advancing across the roof at the remaining bowman. Within seconds the Canaanite tumbled over the roof's edge. When he did not stir, Caleb realized that the man had broken his neck.

The guard who had summoned the bowmen came running up to Caleb. "Joshua wants us at the south gate. He says that Jericho's main force is gathered near there to make a last stand."

Caleb was only half listening as he watched his men come down from the rooftop. None had been hurt in that mission. Seeing they were safe, he turned to the messenger. "The enemies of Israel," he said, his voice strong with conviction, "must all die, and their city must be destroyed, never to be rebuilt."

Caleb beckoned to his men to follow as he turned away from the building and strode back across the marketplace. He would lead them to where Jericho's defenders were putting up their last fight. He hoped to find one other enemy of Israel's—a traitor who was hiding somewhere within these crumbled walls. Though the man was a Child of the Lion and had once numbered Joshua among his friends, to Caleb he was merely one more enemy who must die.

Rahab looked across the leveled city in horror. "They've set fire to the inn! Tirzah, they're destroying the whole city and killing people right and left!" Rahab's words ended with a sob. "Where are our soldiers? Where is the army of Jericho? Why aren't they protecting us?"

"They can't." Pepi's face was drawn and set. "They're dead. Otherwise Caleb's men wouldn't have gotten this far." He frowned as he looked down into the street. "Here comes Caleb, with Joshua behind him!" As one of Caleb's soldiers impaled two fleeing women Pepi averted his eyes. "Why?" he murmured. "Why must they?"

Tirzah gripped his arm. "This is the reason you broke with them, isn't it?" She wanted to look away, but her eyes were drawn to the slaughter below. Whenever the swords flashed, she winced. "Oh, Pepi, couldn't they spare the children?"

"You're getting out of here," Pepi told Tirzah as he watched the troops coming closer. "If I can hold them off, you two could escape."

"Come down, you coward!"

Pepi looked down to see Caleb standing in the street below.

"Come down and fight, you traitor!"

Pepi hugged Tirzah close before reaching for his sword. "I'll delay him as long as I can. Get away." He paused and looked at her for a moment. "Tirzah—I love you."

"I'm not leaving you," she said. "Where would I go? The Israelites have promised to spare Rahab's friends. If they break their word and you die, I die with you."

"Let's go, then." Pepi bit his lip. "The stairs fell away. Is there another way down, Rahab?"

"Yes, through that door over there."

"All right. Stay behind me, both of you." He opened the door, and they moved cautiously down the staircase in the half-darkness toward the first floor.

There Rahab's family cowered in the shadows. "No! Don't open the door!" someone begged. "We'll all be killed!"

Pepi paused and took a deep breath. Then he opened the door and stepped into the bright sunshine.

Caleb stood before him, his sword at the ready. Behind him a line of archers nocked arrows in their bows.

"Is this the way you fight?" Pepi asked contemptuously. "Bowmen at your back, to do any killing you're not man enough for?"

Caleb turned and scowled. "Bows down!" he snarled. "I want this one for myself!" Then he turned back to Pepi.

"No tricks this time. No feigning a seizure to escape the way you did the other day."

As their blades clashed, a voice rang out. "Stop! This is the house of Rahab!"

Caleb turned. Joshua, accompanied by the spy Gedor, was riding toward them.

Joshua studied the two women. "You are Rahab?" he asked.

"Y-yes," she said in a small, frightened voice.

"And these two"—he gestured toward Pepi and Tirzah—"were staying with you when we entered the city?"

"Yes, they were," she answered. "My family is also in the house."

"Let them all go," Joshua said to Caleb. "Our sacred word must be honored."

"All?" Caleb was livid.

"All. Woman, take what you can carry and get out of the city. We're burning it to the ground. Caleb, get out of here. I want to talk to Pepi alone."

Caleb shot a last, hate-filled look at his enemy and stomped off, followed by the archers.

Pepi felt Tirzah's tentative touch on his arm, and he patted her hand. "It's all right," he said quietly. "Go on with Rahab. I'll join you later."

After the women had left, Joshua removed his helmet and ran a hand through his sweat-soaked hair. Next door to Rahab's house, a piece of wall was still standing. He gestured Pepi toward it, and the men sat down.

"It's been a long time, friend," Joshua said coldly. "Too long. Much has happened, I think, since last we met. I understand you wanted to see me. Caleb acted on his own when he wouldn't permit it."

Pepi looked into Joshua's war-hardened visage and tried to find some remnant of his boyhood companion. He was unsuccessful. "Caleb has always tried to put a wedge between us." He looked around at the destruction, the corpses, and felt a pain in his heart. "Unlike Caleb, I have outgrown thinking that we are still boys, harboring petty jealousies and playing harmless games."

"No, there are no games here. You may think that Caleb is immature, but I say he's loyal to a fault. I can't think of anyone I'd rather have protecting my back."

Pepi recoiled, stung. "You think you need to be watchful of me?"

"What am I supposed to think?" Joshua erupted. "You do nothing but hound me about the way I'm pursuing the conquest. Next, you disappear for weeks, and I have no idea where you are or what has happened to you. Then traders come into camp and tell me that you have taken a wife from among our enemies. If that weren't enough, I hear from my spies that you are living in the house of the chief magistrate of our first targeted city."

"Joshua! I would never betray you."

The commander appraised Pepi through narrowed eyes. "No, I suppose you wouldn't. But you would undermine me, questioning my ways, accusing me of being inhuman, of committing genocide."

"And isn't that what you're doing? Look at that dead child over there. What harm could she possibly have done to your 'noble' cause? Or that old man, over there? Are they truly your enemies? Wouldn't it have been possible for you to claim Jericho simply by besting the Canaanites who were similarly armed and could fight back?"

"And this is what you came to talk to me about yesterday, wasn't it?"

Pepi nodded.

"You and my wife. The two people who meant the most to me, and yet the ones who condemn me the most harshly." A look of inestimable sadness softened Joshua's features. Pepi suddenly could see his old friend behind the eyes. "I am on a sacred mission to reclaim this land. I was never given a choice about that. Nobody asked my wife and sons if they would mind giving up a husband and father to gain a commander. But it is a task I have to accomplish for the future of my people, and I won't let anyone—*anyone*—drive me off course or make me question the rightness of what I do." He stood and put on his helmet. Soldierly resolve straightened his spine. "I never want to see you again, Pepi. Whatever we meant to one another in the past is over. Nothing is more important to me than winning this war. Not this little girl"—he rolled her corpse facedown with his foot—"or that old man. And certainly not you!"

"Joshua!" Pepi called after him.

But the commander had mounted his horse and set off down the street, not listening, not looking back.

CHAPTER FOUR

In Greek Waters

I

The woman who came out of the sacred grove of the goddess Aphrodite wore a graceful, pleated garment that softly emphasized the womanly curves of her ripe body. Golden brooches, each beautifully fashioned, held it closed. Her bare white arms were of an almost childlike smoothness. Below the hem of her robe, her small feet were encased in golden sandals.

And her face . . . Framed by golden hair, her face was heart shaped with wide-set blue eyes, the eyes of Aphrodite herself. Out of them her soul seemed to look at Paris, prince of Troy, with amused interest. At the corners of her full and lovely lips the hint of a beguiling smile lingered. She regarded him with no false modesty, instead glorying in his homage to her beauty.

Shamelessly, her eyes looked him up and down. They paused at his face, at his broad shoulders, at his loins.

He blinked, and in the moment his eyes were closed he prayed: *Thank you, fair Aphrodite, for sending me the true love for whom I could have begged.*

71

When at last he was able to speak, he said, "I am Paris of Troy, my lady. I am the most fortunate of men, for I must have encountered Aphrodite herself coming out of her shrine. Or have I perhaps gone mad in the sun? Because I cannot imagine that I could have seen this vision and not been struck blind for my effrontery in looking upon one of the immortals of Olympus. Speak to me, if you please, and tell me the nature of my madness. Are you goddess or woman?"

Her smile was like the sun breaking through the clouds. "I am Helen of Sparta," she said in a voice low and thrilling to his ear. "Wife to Menelaus, who is away fighting wars that other men could fight for him, and not fulfilling the duty that only a husband can fulfill."

"A husband or a lover," Paris suggested, marveling at his own boldness.

"The prince of Troy has not only a tongue of gold but a keen mind as well," she said. "Perhaps he has second sight also and can read the mind of a stranger who stands before him?"

"Perhaps I can," he allowed. "But my gift works slowly. It will take more than a single meeting. Pity me, for I arrive as the queen of Sparta is leaving."

"I have a villa here on Cythera," the queen said, "but before I return to it, perhaps I should go back inside the shrine of Aphrodite to thank her again for many gifts." She paused. "Not the least of which is the chance meeting with the prince of Troy."

"By happy coincidence," Paris said, trying to sound calm despite his pounding heart, "the fair goddess is my own personal patroness, as, all too evidently, she is yours, my lady."

"Then the die is cast. We will thank the goddess both separately and together, if the prince of Troy pleases."

Paris bowed deeply. "Anything that would so please the goddess would not fail to please me."

Helen, too, was amazed at her own brazenness. How

dare she risk everything on a chance meeting? But it was obvious that Aphrodite was bringing them together. Who were they to deny the wishes of the goddess of love and beauty?

As they entered the grove together, she felt his hand reach out and touch hers. At first she thought of drawing back. The idea of committing sacrilege in a temple of Aphrodite frightened her. Then she realized that if Aphrodite had mated them, what could be wrong in obeying her commands?

She clasped his hand, thrilling at the warmth of his skin and the strength in his long, graceful fingers. How handsome he was. And how unlike the great boar Menelaus, with his smelly armpits and his ugly face and his disgusting lovemaking. She knew that Paris, adoring her beauty, would be a good lover, attentive to her needs and desires.

"The prince of Troy will honor Sparta and its queen by partaking of her hospitality," she said. Looking into his eyes, she did not need to hear his answer. He would come. He would always come when she wanted him.

II

Mycenae marked the southern tip of what should have been Agamemnon's domain. Cut off from the Aegean, it shared the seaport of Asine with the several other cities. It was at Asine that Iri and Phorbus landed.

Iri had taken the advice of the commander of Pylos and left town at the same time as Theon, Pandion, and Okware. Theon was on his way to Home, while Pandion and Okware had joined the search for Keturah. The men would communicate through the network of agents and ship's captains established by Demetrios the Magnificent's shipping enterprise.

As soon as Iri and young Phorbus had gone ashore they began to consider enlisting in Agamemnon's mercenary force. Iri enjoyed a good fight; Phorbus wanted to learn one end of a sword from the other; and joining up would put them in immediate touch with widely traveled mercenaries who might have seen a blind slave girl.

"We arrived at the right time," Iri said, grinning at Phorbus. All around them, Agamemnon's grubby, half-strength army was stumbling back into town after a failed assault on the hilltop fortress that housed Agamemnon's father's usurper. "What better day to show up looking for work than this?"

"And look over there, in the marketplace," Phorbus said. "Isn't that a recruiter?"

They approached and listened as the man addressed a gathering of boys just old enough to enlist. The officer's appeal, however, failed as badly as the day's attack. Not one boy signed up to fight.

"Better luck next time, friend," Iri called. "Come, let two foreigners buy you a drink."

"Best offer I've had all day," the tired-looking officer said. "My name's Boreas."

Several minutes later they were settled around a table outside the best inn in Asine. "That damned fortress," Boreas explained, "probably has six months' worth of food and water stored up. Old Thyestes can laugh at our attempts at a siege." A girl brought wine and bowls. Phorbus poured while Boreas questioned Iri.

"You say you're looking for work soldiering?" the recruiter asked.

"My friend and I are. I'm also an arms maker. A good one. A Child of the Lion, if that means anything to you."

Boreas's eyes lit up. "It does indeed."

"I'm a descendant of Kirta of Haran, the man who brought iron to Canaan, and Shobai."

"You're related to Hadad? And Seth of Thebes?"

"At your service. For a price."

Boreas paused and thought. "You interest me." He looked Iri directly in the eyes. "You two travel together?"

"Apprentice and master."

"He's a bit old for apprenticing. But then it's never too late to learn something about soldiering, is it? You look like a man who can use his fists."

Phorbus chuckled. "Iri's fists got us 'invited out' of Pylos. He insulted Paris of Troy, and a war nearly broke out on the docks."

"Paris of Troy? In Pylos?" a voice asked from behind them, and Boreas scrambled to his feet and bowed.

Iri looked up. The stranger was large and burly with the puffy face and dissolute look of a heavy drinker. "I can't say anything for sure," Iri said, "but the gossip was that he was headed for the island of Cythera. He had a large fleet of ships with him—warships. He passed through Pylos without calling on Nestor, as if he had plans he didn't intend to share with the rest of the world."

The newcomer looked at Boreas. "Could there be anything to this?" he asked.

Boreas shook his head. "I don't know, Sire. Someone from one of the ships said that the queen has taken most of the palace guard to Cythera on pilgrimage."

"Curse her!" the king said. "The damned shallow bitch, I told her to stay put until I returned."

Iri listened silently, trying not to show his amusement. This had to be Helen's husband, Menelaus.

"I've got to get back to Sparta immediately."

"Sire," Boreas said, "maybe you're jumping to conclusions."

Menelaus clenched his teeth. "Paris is a hard man to take seriously. He has the smell of a lapdog about him. But if you saw Priam's fleet of warships . . ."

"It could have been a friendly mission," Boreas suggested. "Why send an unreliable fumbler like Paris on anything but a friendly mission?"

The king looked at his officer. "Do you think we can trust these new men?"

"Yes, Sire. This man, Iri, is a Child of the Lion. That's an impeccable credential."

Menelaus thought for a moment, then looked at Iri.

"I have an assignment for you! Go to Sparta and see what's going on at my palace. Make sure you're discreet. Then report back to me."

Iri nodded. "There's just one thing: I told you I tangled with Paris. He'll recognize me."

"There's a road through the hills," Boreas said. "You can sneak into Sparta. Paris won't see you if you're careful."

III

When Paris returned at last, he found his half sister Cassandra waiting for him. She stood in the middle of the deck, her legs apart, fists on her narrow hips.

"You've been gone for two days. Where have you been? Does it take that long to make an offering to a goddess? Or have you been bedding some village slut?"

"Now, now," Paris said, coming aboard. "Cassandra, I'm happy. You can't rile me. I won't listen to you." He clasped his hands over his ears. Only when her harangue ran down did he uncover them. "Are you ready to listen now?" he asked. "I have wonderful news. We're going to Sparta."

"That's where we're supposed to go, you fool." She lowered her voice. "Have you forgotten that we're on a secret mission to find father's sister and to try to bring her back to Troy?"

"No, I haven't forgotten. And her kidnappers will greet us with open arms. Now get ready—we're sailing immediately. Captain!"

The captain approached and saluted Paris.

"Get the men aboard," Paris said. "We leave for the mainland in an hour." He clapped the captain on the shoulder familiarly, ignoring the flash of resentment in the fellow's eyes. "I'll be in my cabin," he said. "I'm leaving it all to you."

*   *   *

Cassandra, left standing behind like a servant, exchanged disgusted glances with the captain and went over to a bucket in the middle of the deck. She scooped up a bowl of water and splashed it on her warm face.

Suddenly she dropped the bowl. Water splashed her skirt and spilled over the deck. She covered her face with her hands.

The vision was brief: Her father's kingdom of Troy was afire. Greek soldiers ran through the streets, slaughtering women and children. She saw herself hiding with the other women of the palace, terrified, on the rooftop, awaiting the inevitable moment when the last defenders would fall and the Greeks would mount the stairs. By her side was a blind slave woman—someone she had never seen, but she knew this would be her confidante.

One of the sailors approached her. "My lady," he said softly, putting a hand on her arm. "Can I help you?"

The vision faded as quickly as it had come. She felt drained and angry. "Leave me alone!" she screamed. "Don't touch me. Don't you dare touch me!"

Paris had controlled himself all the way back to the ship, returning salutes and behaving like the dignified leader of a major expedition. But once he was behind closed doors, he let himself go. He tore off all his clothes and stood naked in the middle of his cabin.

His hands ran up and down his own body, savoring the tingling that still persisted two hours after he had left Helen. His hands roved, and he remembered blissfully that there was no place her burning—and expert—lips had not touched.

He shuddered with delight. Naked, she had been all creamy skin and velvety softness. She had ignited his passion until it had been unbearable. When at last he had mounted her like the stallion he felt himself to be by then, her slim feet, softer than other women's hands, had come up to caress his face as expertly as if they had been a second pair of hands. They had been perfumed, and the nails had been tinted a delicate pink to match the paint on her full lips.

All the while a blind slave girl quietly came and went, bringing not only drink and sweetmeats but sweet scented oil with which they had anointed each other.

He had found no flaw in Helen. In her soft and seductive voice, she had suggested new things for him to do to her, to increase her pleasure. And, to his surprise, he found that pleasing her was in many ways as enjoyable an experience as pleasing himself.

They had begun at sundown, with the soft lights of a dozen oil lamps flickering about them and turning her pink skin to gold. And they had made love all through the night and not gone to sleep, until they lay exhausted in each other's loving arms as the first rays of dawn had begun to peek through.

O, Aphrodite! Paris prayed. *My sincerest thanks, lady, for the priceless gift you have brought me!*

For a brief moment he had found himself wondering: *In what beds has she learned all this?* But then he had driven the thought from his mind. Why question his good fortune? One question still filled his mind: *Why does this have to stop? Why can't it go on forever?*

The answer was, of course, that insensitive, boorish, and fortunately absent husband of hers. It was obvious that a woman like Helen was wasted on a bungling oaf like Menelaus. Wasted, in fact, on any man but himself.

Little by little an idea began to suggest itself. It was sheer madness and very dangerous. Priam would never approve. But what if . . .

O, Aphrodite! Give me your benison upon what I'm about to do!

IV

After making her plans with Paris, Helen had hastily assembled her guards and retainers and returned to Sparta.

Now she was packing her entire wardrobe. She stood eyeing herself in the staggeringly expensive full-length bronze mirror her brother-in-law Agamemnon had given her on the occasion of marriage.

"I can't tell whether this is worth keeping or not," she said, holding up a sheer gown against her body.

Her servant Keturah stood quietly by the wall. Impulsively Helen shrugged off her *peplos* and hurled it at the blind slave. The girl was startled when it hit her, then picked it up from the floor and folded it.

"What good are you?" Helen demanded. "You can't help me decide what to wear or help me pack my things."

"I'm sorry, my lady," the girl whispered. "I believe your agents thought my sightlessness would guarantee secrecy and protect your . . . guests' identity. I have heard, my lady, that you are of peerless beauty, and I'm sure that whatever you wear will be captivating."

Helen's irritation ebbed, and she slipped into the gown she was holding. It was so sheer it exposed her entire golden body. A woman could wear this before no one but her husband or lover, but Menelaus had yet to see her in it.

"He'll love me in this, Keturah," the queen said. "He won't be able to wait to take it off me. He'll have me on top of the table by the third course."

"Then my lady should keep it," Keturah said with no emotion.

"I will," Helen said. "I'll wear it tonight."

"My lady, are you sure? This is a drastic step, and the consequences—"

"Don't talk to me of consequences. The consequences of staying here with a man I can't bear to have touch me are also great. But you probably wouldn't understand."

"A slave understands only too well. She is at the mercy of her captors, the ship's crew, agents. . . . Any man with a little power or a taste for violence or with a copper coin can find his pleasure on a slave."

"Do you know the father of your child, Keturah?"

"Oh, yes, my lady. I am married to a fine man. He's the brother of Demetrios the Magnificent, and a famous armorer in his own right."

Helen smirked. "Yes, girl, I'm sure that's true." She let the gown fall from her shoulders to reveal one pink-nippled breast; then she veiled both breasts, leaving her belly naked. This arrangement pleased her. "Bring me the sandals by your left foot," she said.

Keturah found the shoes, brought them to her mistress, then knelt to lace the sandals on Helen's white feet.

Helen arranged a gold stomacher with an emerald pendant so as to draw attention to the place between her rosy thighs. "He won't be able to ignore that, but maybe I should leave something to the imagination."

"I have no idea what his tastes might be, my lady."

Helen smiled like a pleased, purring house cat. "That's what I like about him. He enjoys all of it. He hadn't much experience, but he took to everything I showed him. He was the most apt pupil a woman could want. And before we parted . . ."

"I am very impressed, my lady."

Helen threw off the gown and stood naked. "He loves my legs," she said. "He loves my feet. Perhaps I'll wear a gown that bares one leg all the way up to the waist and cover up the rest. I'll tease him just a bit."

"I'm sure all of that would be satisfactory, my lady."

Helen wasn't listening. She picked up another dress. "Perhaps sheer black, so my body will show through. I wonder if he likes black. Some men don't." She dropped the gown on the floor. "Of course, I could receive him naked, wearing only my jewels."

She reached down and picked up a necklace.

As she did, the expression on her face changed. The erotic mood vanished. "Why should I leave my jewels here for the hog Menelaus to give to some other woman? If I run away with my darling Paris, we're going to need money to live on. His father might turn him out for all the trouble this will cause."

"My lady!"

"Don't worry, I'll take you and your baby along, wherever we go. Menelaus would probably sell you because you're blind and keep your baby for another woman to raise. Indeed, should I leave anything behind for that great blundering ox of a husband? He'll only pawn my jewels and sell my servants for money to spend on that ridiculous war for Mycenae."

She looked at her reflection. "He's just stupid enough to go to war against Troy over me and fight Paris. Why should I leave anything behind for him to pay his troops with, since he'll be fighting my lover? I must clean him out altogether."

"My lady, please! Many men will die if—"

"Don't you talk back to me, you little bitch! For the first time in my life I know exactly what I want, and I'm going to get it!"

The journey to Sparta took a day. When Iri and Phorbus arrived, they were surprised to find the city occupied by the military. The city guards were here, which meant Helen was back from her pilgrimage to the temple of Aphrodite. But Iri and Phorbus also spotted soldiers in Trojan uniforms.

Iri drew his apprentice aside. "Something is indeed going on, maybe even more than Menelaus suspects. What is a full complement of Trojans doing here, armed to the teeth?"

"We've got to get inside the palace and find out, don't we?" Phorbus said. "But how? Maybe I could slip in disguised as a servant, but you—" He stopped, embarrassed.

"I know. Nobody hires servants who look like me. Besides, Paris would remember my face. But if you could get in . . ."

"Yes?"

Iri studied the high walls around Helen's palace. "Then you could toss a rope down to me."

Phorbus's eyes were wide. "Look out!" he whispered,

yanking Iri back against the wall. From their cover they watched as a squad of Trojans came out of the palace of Sparta, bearing many heavily laden trunks.

When they were out of earshot, Iri let out his breath in a low whistle of astonishment. "Gods, Phorbus! Do you know what we're seeing?"

"I think so. But I'm not sure whether or not to believe my eyes."

"Neither am I. We have to find out if Paris is really looting Menelaus's house. But if he is, why aren't the city guards stopping him?"

"I think I may know why. One of the men told me the city guards owe their first loyalty to Helen and her sister, as daughters of the old king of Sparta."

"To Helen? But that means . . ."

Phorbus nodded grimly. "That means trouble."

"Big trouble," Iri said. "Get the rope from my horse. We've got work to do."

V

After supervising the loading of their trunks onto ox carts, Helen and Paris had enjoyed a leisurely dinner and then retreated, without their servants, to their own love bower on the palace roof, to continue their romance in the balmy night air. On the balcony below, musicians played soft melodies, while down in the courtyard Paris's men began to send the carts laden with jewels and coin, rich fabrics and plate, to the port.

Paris reclined on Helen's bed, which her slaves had dragged into the rooftop garden. The prince of Troy wore only his sandals; he was too lazy to remove them. What he longed for now was sleep.

But Helen sat naked before him, busily trying on jewelry in the flickering light.

"Oh, Paris, will you just *look* at this!" she said.

"Menelaus never showed me this one. My father must have made it part of my dowry. It has to be the biggest ruby I've ever seen! Look how it lies between my breasts. Isn't that the most gorgeous sight you've ever seen?"

Paris yawned. "Your breasts or the ruby, my darling?"

"Both!" She laughed and thrust out her chest. Her rouged nipples gleamed like the red jewel. "Oh, Paris, poor dear, you're all tired out. You don't want to make love to me anymore. I've exhausted you."

She took off the necklace and slid down the bed toward him. "Have I grown ugly in the last hour?" she cooed. "Have I lost my appeal for you?" But there was a mischievous smile on her red lips, and when she bent over to kiss him, long and lovingly, it was not on his mouth that her kiss fell.

"Are you sure you want to get all this started again?" Paris asked. "We have to get up very early tomorrow morning if we're to catch the tide."

She raised her golden head, smiled, and licked her lips. "There will be another tide." She looked down. "The dead arise! Just lie back, darling. Let me take off your sandals. Lie back and relax."

Paris stared at her, his interest returning.

In the darkness Iri and Phorbus crouched behind a cabinet and spoke in whispers. "Well, Phorbus," Iri said wryly, "I told you I'd help you complete your education. Have you learned anything tonight?"

Phorbus exhaled in amazement. "I had no idea that one man and one woman could connect in so many ways. I can't wait to try out some of this."

"Yes, you can," Iri told him. "Did you see that ruby she had on? I made that necklace myself more than thirty years ago for a princess of the royal court of Egypt."

"Can't we leave soon?" Phorbus asked nervously. "This has been very instructive, but I'm afraid someone will find us."

"Pretty soon. We've found what we came here for,"

Iri said slowly. "Would you sneak over there while they're indulging in this latest exercise and grab my necklace?"

"Iri, that's dangerous!"

"Sure it is. But unless we bring back some proof, Menelaus may not believe our story."

Phorbus nodded. "I'll try. But what are you going to be doing?"

"This part of the roof overhangs the wall, and I'm going to lower myself to that balcony and secure our rope so we can get out of here."

Phorbus nodded. "And the horses are below in the street. We might get out safely before anyone sounds the alarm."

As Phorbus disappeared into the darkness, Iri climbed over the wall. Before lowering himself to the balcony, he watched the two lovers for a moment. Because of his ugliness, he had always had to buy love until he had married Keturah. Now, to his amazement, he saw that it was not enough to be handsome to keep the interest of a beautiful woman—not if she had the sexual appetites of a Helen of Sparta. One had to work at it.

Apparently Paris did not mind the work. Although, to Iri, it looked like drudgery, despite Helen's beauty. The most fundamental issue of successful lovemaking, Iri knew, was that your partner be the one great love of your heart.

He sighed, put that thought out of his head, and, after finding secure hand- and toeholds, lightly dropped to the balcony one floor below. Then he carefully tied the rope to the balcony wall and tossed the hemp line down. It did not quite reach the ground, but it was long enough.

Suddenly, there was a shrill cry of alarm. Paris had obviously spotted Phorbus.

"Stop, thief!" the prince cried.

Iri scrambled up the wall and flung himself onto the rooftop. Phorbus sprinted for the roof's edge, running over the bodies of the entangled lovers on the bed. Naked, Paris leapt to his feet and grabbed his sword off the floor where it lay with the rest of his clothing.

"Guards! Guards," Paris cried. "To me! *Guards!*"

"Go down quickly," Iri said to Phorbus, grabbing the young man's wrists, helping him over the wall, and lowering him to the balcony. "I'll be right behind you. Make for the horses and ride. Don't wait for me."

"But what—?"

"Do as I say!"

Taking a deep breath, Iri drew his sword and stepped out into the moonlight. "Paris, do you recognize me, you perfumed pimp?"

But it was Helen who attacked. Her angry rush almost bowled Iri over. She pounced on him like a naked wildcat, screaming and clawing and biting. With a sigh Iri calmly knocked her cold.

Paris stood bare and motionless, the sword in his hand. "Let's finish this conversation some other time," Iri suggested. "I've got to get a message to the king of Sparta." He saluted and turned.

"You son of a—" Paris began, but Iri had leapt onto the wall and jumped off the roof into the darkness.

VI

Iri and Phorbus rode like the wind, never slowing until Iri was satisfied that Sparta was far enough behind to ensure their safety for the time being. When they reached the crossroads in the mountains and the path down the hill to Asine, Iri reined in his exhausted horse and dismounted. "It's all right," he said. "If they come after us now, we'll hear them on the road. And our animals will be rested by then."

Phorbus said, "My mind is still reeling. What do you think will come of all we've seen?"

"Well, my friend, you and I came here to find a way to teach you to fight and to find me a chance to travel. I think we've found ourselves a war. It ought to be worth several years of fighting."

"Years?" Phorbus asked. "But how will Agamemnon and Menelaus pay anyone to come with them to attack Troy? They're both broke."

"This war will be different. You forget that before Helen chose her husband, every king in this area had sworn an oath to support the man she wed."

"But all the way to Troy?"

"Most likely," Iri said. "People here tend to take matters of honor very seriously."

"That's pretty amazing, considering all the dishonorable things that have gone on in this region. From what I could see, this mess is as much Helen's idea as Paris's. Her husband ought to count her well lost and start over again."

Iri chuckled. "That would be logical. But besides the matter of honor, we must take into account the location of Troy—a fine reward for a king's victory at war."

"Meaning?"

"Troy controls a very profitable trade route through and across the Hellespont. Menelaus will use his wife's, uh . . . kidnapping as an excuse for war. He'll accuse Paris of rape, and soon Helen will be a blameless goddess of virtue."

Phorbus grinned. "Hard to imagine after you've seen her like *that*."

"I knew Paris had a reputation for being stupid, but I wonder if he really believes that Priam will welcome him home to Troy after what he's done?" Iri paused. "Maybe he hasn't thought far enough ahead to consider what his father's reaction might be."

"Would Troy be a rich enough prize to pay all the soldiers needed to conquer it?" Phorbus asked.

"Absolutely. If Menelaus and Agamemnon have a trace of brains between them, they'll leave the looting of the place to the other kings and their men and will content themselves with taking over the port and the fortress, which control access to Phrygia, Scythia, and Colchis. There's more money and power to be had that way than in a city ten times the size and worth of Troy."

Phorbus whistled. "Until I came to Pylos, I'd never seen a town I couldn't throw a rock across."

Iri's toothy grin was clear in the light of the moon. "You're a man of the world now, Phorbus. You'll see many wonderful sights in your lifetime."

They walked in silence until Phorbus said in a voice filled with awe, "This war's going to be a big one, isn't it?"

"Such as the world of the Aegean Sea never has seen, lad."

"You've been in a war before."

"Not one like this. Our war was strike and run, strike and run. We were desert rats fleeing the Egyptian army."

"You must have had a good leader."

"Yes. A great man named Moses ben Amram, born to wealth and power but who left it all to become a slave. He led his fellow slaves to freedom. I could have stayed in Egypt—I was much in demand there. But when the gods show you a man better than yourself, it means you've something important to learn from him. And once I'd met Moses, I knew I had to follow him. Lad, remember, when someone like that walks across your path, follow him."

Phorbus nodded. "I have met such a man," he said quietly. "And I will follow you wherever you go."

VII

Cassandra stood by the rail of the royal boat, waiting and watching with increasing impatience. One of the servants who had been brought along was the blind girl from Cassandra's prophetic vision. She did not know whom the girl belonged to, but Cassandra was eager to find out. Paris was the last to arrive, and when he finally appeared, Cassandra's heart sank: With Paris was Helen of Sparta.

Paris escorted the queen up the plank as if she were made of glass. He proudly led her to Cassandra. "Let me introduce you," he said. "My half sister, Princess Cassandra of Troy, meet Queen Helen of Sparta."

Cassandra gaped at them for a minute without saying anything. Then she exploded. "Paris, what in the name of the gods are you up to? We're not here to take the queen for a boat ride. We're here to strike a deal for Aunt Hesione and to show the Trojan might." She ignored Helen, who watched her with an emotionless smile on her lips but ice in her eyes. "Paris, answer me!"

"My dear," Helen said softly, "everyone knows that your father's sister does not reside in Sparta. She and her . . . husband live—"

Again Cassandra ignored her. "Do you think Father is going to stand for this behavior? Do you think he sent you on this expedition so you could carry off some adulteress who's grown tired of her husband and wants a little excitement?"

"Now, now, Cassandra. You're being rude to Helen. If you'll just calm down—"

"Calm down! How do you expect me to calm down when you've just sealed the fate of Troy and of every one of us? Paris, it's not too late. Send her back right now, and all that we'll have to smooth over will be a personal insult to her husband. But carrying her *away*? I promise you, it will have the gravest repercussions."

"Send her back?" Paris asked with a smile. "Not a chance. Cassandra, I've been looking for her all my life. I prayed to Aphrodite, and the goddess sent me Helen. Now, if I were to go against such an augury—"

"Don't you speak to me of auguries! My own dreams say that if you bring a Greek woman back from—"

"I know, I know. You already warned me. But when you make your predictions, nobody understands them until afterward, when someone manages to squeeze what really happened into your vague prophecies."

"But this time my dream was very clear."

"I know, you claim that Troy will perish. But how is Troy going to perish when we're not even going there?"

"We're not?" Helen asked, looking disappointed.

"No. We're going to let things cool down and drop anchor in the harbor at the island of Cranae."

"Cranae? But I thought—" Helen said with a touch of bitterness.

"Troy is too dangerous now. I must prepare Priam for the news. But we have more than enough to live on for quite a long while."

"You fool," Cassandra seethed. "We've just enough to keep the fleet fed until we get home." Suddenly she understood. "Those trunks you had loaded on board—they aren't . . . you didn't . . ."

"I'm afraid we did," Helen said brightly.

Cassandra stood frozen, staring open-eyed at Helen. Finally she turned to Paris. "It was true. It's going to come to pass, just as I dreamed it. You've killed us. You've killed us all."

Menelaus refused to say anything. Finally Iri held up the ruby necklace.

"She was going to steal that," Menelaus whispered, staring off into the distance.

"She took everything else," Iri said softly. "The servants even peeled the gold trim off your bedstead. Paris took some of your clothing. I remember a beautiful purple robe."

"My father's," Menelaus said tonelessly. "He was crowned in it."

His report completed, Iri withdrew. He found Phorbus waiting outside. "The king will be numb for a day or two, until it has sunk in," he told the young fellow. "Then the rage will come, and the gods help anyone who's near him when it does."

VIII

Theon looked at his wife across Demetrios's bed-chamber. Nuhara's eyes were swollen and red rimmed, but he didn't know if she grieved for Demetrios or for her father. Soon, too soon, Demetrios would breathe his last, and Khalkeus would be at the helm of the Great Sea's largest shipping empire.

Theon's eyes flicked to his father-by-marriage. Khalkeus sat rigidly in the corner, hands flexing in his lap. The big-boned pirate, once called the Minotaur, with his wild, black brows and beard and piercing eyes, had been tamed under Demetrios's tutelage. Tamed or broken? Theon wondered sadly. Insecurity seemed to have settled just beneath Khalkeus's skin, making it flush and prickle with every failed task, poor decision, and ungrasped concept.

Demetrios's labored breathing drew Theon's attention. Each exhalation caused a downward thrust of the man's head, as if he were already across death's threshold and was nodding to his forebears. His almost fleshless, clawlike fingers fluttered on the blanket.

Theon stood and threaded his way past the physician and Demetrios's wife to walk out onto the room's balcony. He leaned his hands against the railing and arched his back against the stiffness of the days-long vigil, which had begun as soon as he had returned to the island of Home from Pylos. The sun and breeze felt soothing. That life should be going on as usual in the port and harbor while his kinsman was so ill seemed mad.

A gentle hand touched Theon's shoulder. Nuhara? He turned. It was Rhodope, Demetrios's wife. "We were thankful you came back in time," she said.

"Why don't you try to get some rest, my dear? You look exhausted."

"I couldn't, not now."

"You have brought him much joy, you know," Theon said. "His last years have been his happiest."

She smiled sadly. "As they were mine, too. But now it is ending, and only the gods know what shall become of all this. Demetrios worked so hard and built so much." She leaned against the balcony wall and looked out at the harbor. "What think you, Theon? Will it all come crashing down around us or grind to a slow, wheezing halt?"

Theon hesitated, trapped between his desire to comfort Rhodope and his natural inclination toward honesty.

"These are difficult times," he said at last. "King Nestor apprised me of a situation that could jeopardize both overland and sea trade." He forced a smile and a hearty tone. "But we'll watch for developments and respond accordingly."

The physician poked his head out. "My lady? Sir? If you please . . ."

Theon followed Rhodope inside. She went to her husband's side and took his hand.

Demetrios's breathing sounded shallow and wet. Then, with a backward thrust of the great man's head, his lungs seized a draught of air, his eyes glazed, and he was no more.

CHAPTER FIVE

Canaan

I

"Defeated?" Joshua demanded. "What do you mean, defeated? I sent three thousand top men to conquer Ai."

"I'm reporting what the messenger told me, sir," Shemida said. "He'd ridden so hard, his horse expired as he reached camp. He wanted to come directly to you himself, but he was so near collapse that I ordered him to rest."

"But are you sure he tells the truth? Caleb predicted an easy victory; we outnumbered the people of Ai by a third."

Shemida looked down at his commander, who sat at the table with maps of Canaan before him, the scrolls unrolled and weighted with rocks. "Sir, I dragged every last piece of information out of him."

Joshua leaned forward. "But what happened?"

"The soldiers claimed they were the victims of witchcraft. They said their arrows went wide, and the enemy easily turned aside even our troops' most powerful blows. Swords broke when they touched the enemy soldiers' bucklers." He raised one brow. "It does seem, sir, as though there were some sort of . . . intervention. Caleb's a fine soldier, and the men were handpicked campaigners. The enemy drove them up a hill and down the other side before withdrawing and setting up a new picket line."

"How many are dead?"

"The messenger said that Caleb's first count was thirty-six. The men of Ai not only stopped them, they drove them back all the way to . . ." He looked down at the map before them. "Here. A place called Shebarim."

"And there they stand at Shebarim, unable to advance?" Joshua asked. He looked devastated.

"When the messenger awakens, I'll bring him here for questioning," Shemida assured him. He paused. "Sir?"

Hollow-eyed, Joshua looked up at him. "What is it, Shemida?"

"The messenger, sir. He claims to be Pepi's half brother. He was on his way here, to find Pepi, when he happened upon the battle."

The revelation did Joshua no good. Since the conquest of Jericho, Shemida thought the commander had been so close to physical collapse that Eleazar and the elders had prevailed upon him to rest and temporarily leave the fighting to the younger men. What happened in Jericho, Shemida wondered, to have laid Joshua so low? Now he seemed to take the whole weight of the defeat at Ai upon his shoulders.

"Don't tell Caleb about that. And don't worry him about the defeat. It isn't his fault; God never punishes without reason. One of us has sinned. Our ranks must be purified. Summon Eleazar and the priests. We will have a day of fasting, prayer, and self-castigation. Then if one of us has sinned and defied my orders . . ."

"Yes, sir."

"Tell Caleb to stay where he is and make no moves against the enemy until we have purged ourselves."

"Very good, sir. Do you want to send reinforcements?"

"Don't you understand? Even if we had an army the

size of the Shepherd Kings' we'd still lose. Now muster the entire army. Someone has betrayed us, and I'm going to find out who it is."

At dawn the next morning, Joshua and the priests of Israel lay on the ground, facedown, their clothes rent, their faces streaked with earth, before the Ark of the Covenant. It was the accepted ritual for the humbling of self before the Lord. All day long Joshua prayed, but it was not until evening that the Voice finally spoke to him.

"Arise! Tomorrow you shall catch the malefactor in the net, and then you must purge Israel's sin by destroying him and all that are his. While he lives the army of Israel will not be able to stand before its enemies. And until the transgression is healed, I will not be by your side."

After the day and night of contrition were ended, Joshua called together the entire nation of Israel. When the tribes were gathered, an unnaturally bright light from the heavens surrounded the tribe of Judah. The other tribes, frightened into silence, edged away. Women clutched their children, and men took hold of their trembling wives. Then the light narrowed and brightened, falling on the clan of Zerah. The rest of the tribe moved quickly aside to watch.

A ray of light, humming and vibrating, shot out at the nervous, shifty-eyed face of Achan, son of Zerah. So bright was its intensity, the man's skin looked white. He hid his eyes and, crying out, fell to his knees.

Joshua walked slowly toward him. "Pay honor to the Lord, Achan," he said in a low and terrible voice. "It is time to confess to Him. Withhold nothing."

Achan swallowed, and then in a broken voice he moaned, "I am sorry. In the streets of Jericho I saw a fine Shinarian cloak in a box with two hundred shekels of silver, and a gold bar. I took them and buried them under my tent."

Joshua nodded curtly to one of his lieutenants. "Dig

them up and bring them here." He looked down with disgust at the trembling, kneeling man. "You have heard our Lord's commandment that we not defile ourselves by stealing from our vanquished enemies. Yet you have broken that commandment. Our defeat at Ai rests upon your shoulders, and the death of our men is on your head."

Joshua turned away for a moment and stared at the Ark, which was bathed in a golden, supernatural glow. It seemed to pulsate with the light. As the commander stared into the aura that enveloped the Ark, he saw the horrible image of Achan and his family falling under the weight of a thousand stones. But then he felt an ineffable calm settle over him.

The luminescence surrounding the Ark dimmed, and Joshua knew that to carry out Yahweh's will, Achan and his family must be stoned to death and their remains buried along with the ill-gotten treasure.

Abruptly Joshua turned back to Achan and declared, "You know what must happen now, don't you?"

Nodding pitifully, Achan broke down and sobbed. "Please," the condemned man cried, his broad shoulders quaking, "have mercy on my wife and children."

"May your family find mercy with Yahweh."

Joshua turned to nod at the guards holding Achan's wife and two young sons. The woman, released, rushed to her husband's side, exclaiming, "What is going on? What do they mean to do to us?"

Her husband's only reply was to gather her and the boys to him, kissing them and proclaiming his sorrow and his love.

A dark and beautiful woman stood at the edge of the gathering. As Joshua walked away from the condemned family, she called his name. When he came toward her, she said, "Surely the death of that unfortunate man is more than enough to satisfy—"

"Silence!" Joshua demanded.

"But if you had sinned, would you allow our people to stone me and our sons?" the woman implored.

Joshua turned to his wife, his eyes ablaze. "If it was the only way to cleanse the sins of our people, then yes, Shayna, I would expect them to kill you and the boys. Indeed, I would be forced to hand them the first stone." He pushed past her and headed into the crowd.

A chill shuddered through the woman after her husband disappeared among the gathered masses. Her eyes filled with tears as she looked upon Achan and his family huddled together in the center of a wide circle of Israelites.

Just then a Levite stepped forward, a large rock in his clenched fist. Shayna thought to protest, but she remained silent because the Levite was sobbing as he let the rock fly. Achan looked up in surprise and uttered a name; this first blow was from one of his close friends. Then the stone struck its target, and Achan fell unconscious to the ground.

Men and women in the crowd were crying, as one and then another rock went hurtling through the air. The sobbing grew louder until it sounded like some strange, unearthly chorus.

When the younger boy was struck in the head and collapsed in his mother's arms, Shayna could stand the sight no longer. She turned her back and tried to walk away, but a strange force held her in place. Despite the horror she felt, Joshua's wife found herself looking upon the scene of death.

She expected to see a ghastly, terrifying sight. Instead, a vast calm had enveloped the area, and though rocks still sailed through the air, they could no longer be heard and seemed disconnected from reality. And instead of seeing four bloody, battered bodies, Shayna looked upon Achan's family shrouded in the golden light—a purifying light that seemed to heal even as it drew their spirits from their bodies.

Shayna felt the breath go out of her, and she dropped to her hands and knees and clutched the earth, afraid that her own life force would also be carried away. The supernatural glow started to withdraw into the heavens, and as it receded, Shayna was certain she could see within it the gentle, smiling faces of Achan and his family. She knew then that this stoning was an inexplicable, fantastic cleansing, not only of the people of Israel but of the four who had died.

Rising to her feet, Joshua's wife wondered if anyone else had experienced the same vision as she. The people around her were still throwing rocks at the lifeless bodies in their midst, and she was startled to feel something cold and hard clutched in her right hand. She looked down to see a stone she must have grabbed when she fell to her knees.

As she hefted the rock, her mind shouted that this was madness; but a deeper, surer Voice whispered that things were rarely what they seemed. Shayna surrendered to the Voice, allowing it to fill her body and guide her hand as she drew back her arm and sent the stone speeding through the air.

"You say you've never met Pepi, Micah?" Joshua asked the strapping, clear-eyed boy standing before him in the command tent.

"No, sir. But we're half brothers—we have the same mother, sir—and I've always wanted to get to know him."

"Why now?"

"Well, sir, I thought it was time for me to strike out on my own. My—our mother, sir, didn't spend much time with Pepi when he was growing up. She decided to set things right with me, though, and, well, I mean no disrespect, sir, but I can't take a piss without her wanting to know about it."

"How old are you, boy?"

He straightened his shoulders. "Eighteen, sir. Well, almost eighteen."

More like almost sixteen, Joshua thought, *the same age as my older boy*. "Did Shemida tell you that Pepi's not traveling with the army anymore?"

"Yes, sir, but I'd still like permission to stay. I could be useful. I'm a Child of the Lion, sir, and my father—his name is Baufra, sir—was trained by my uncle Iri back in Egypt. I know that Iri used to be your chief armorer. Father is chief armorer of Jerusalem's army now, and he's taught me to work metals, too."

Joshua almost laughed; either Micah's father had no idea of the boy's plans to walk boldly into the enemy's camp and innocently ask for a job, or Jerusalem's king did not view the Israelites as a threat. "And you think you have the stomach for war? It's not a game we're playing here."

"I could tell that from the stoning I watched today, sir. I'd still like to stay."

Joshua thought for a moment. For one so young, Micah had a hard glint in his eyes that made the commander believe that the boy wouldn't be a complainer like Pepi. Joshua was also satisfied that the lad was not a spy or sent on some fool's errand by his half brother. He called for Shemida, who came hurrying in. "Find my wife. Tell her she's got a guest."

"Yes, sir!" The adjutant disappeared.

Joshua looked at Micah, whose face was split in a grin. "All right, you're one of us now. Work hard, stay out of trouble, and when you see my second-in-command, Caleb, coming, run the other way."

The next day Joshua mustered the army and moved on Ai, forty thousand strong. When they reached Shebarim, Caleb met Joshua and was apologetic. But the commander shrugged off his words. "There was a traitor among us. He has been dealt with. Now let us get on with our objective. We must attack quickly, while the army of Ai still doubts our ability. You and your men attack again, as if you were repeating the earlier pattern. Then, when they counterattack, I want you to retreat."

"But sir! My men are already demoralized."

"I need you to draw the Ai defenders out of their present position."

Suddenly Caleb understood. "You want me to lure them to where they'll have no cover."

"Right." Joshua squatted and began to draw in the sand with his dagger. "Meanwhile I'll be leading our main force back here. We'll split up with one arm attacking their left flank—"

"—while the other arm is guarding their rear and cutting off the possibility of any reinforcements."

"Right. Any suggestions?"

Caleb shook his head. "What about the force you've sent back to cut off reinforcements?"

"They'll be taking Ai, which—if I've pegged them right—will have been left undefended. And once the city's taken, our men will attack the enemy from the rear. We'll box them in, and they won't stand a chance."

The attack worked perfectly. Caleb's men surged forward, then fell back in apparent disarray. The main force at Ai pursued them into the plain between two hills, only to find Joshua's army charging toward them from over the hill. The battle raged for three hours before the king of Ai spotted the black smoke rising from his undefended city. So demoralizing was the sight that his troops faltered, and the Israelites' pincers closed.

In the end the king of Ai, covered with blood, sat alone on his horse, surrounded by a circle of defenders. Joshua came into the circle, his bloody sword raised.

"Just the two of us now, eh?" he challenged.

"*Yes!*" the king spat out, and charged. The soldiers around them fell back as the two commanders came together. Joshua spurred his mount forward to rush the king from the side. The men engaged swords, and the king aimed a looping blow at Joshua's head. Joshua parried and stabbed his opponent in the shoulder. The force of the blow toppled the king from his horse. He rose groggily and staggered at Joshua, who jumped down from his horse and met him thrust to thrust as his men cheered.

Fighting desperately, the king drove Joshua back. And then suddenly he seemed to run out of power. Despair and weariness etched his face.

With a shrug Joshua ran him through. Then, holding the body up by the hair, he cut off the king's head. He waved it high in the air for all the Israelite army to see.

"On to Bethel!" he cried in a voice of triumph. "On to Gibeon!" As the entire army took up the cry the hills rang with the Israelite vow.

II

"Tell me again about your mother," Tirzah asked her husband. "I'm nervous about meeting her."

Pepi caught her hand and pulled her down onto the grass, where he sat in the shade of a tree. They were on the road to Jerusalem. Nearby, their horses lipped greenery at the oasis. "Don't worry. She'll love you." He kissed the top of her head.

"What's she like?"

"She's had a hard life. Back in Thebes, Mother had two brothers. They were the children of Sinuhe, son of Ketan, members of a rich family of metalworkers. But when the parents died, the eldest, Khian, tried to raise Mother and my uncle Iri by himself. Then a miraculous thing happened to Khian."

"What?"

"He was chosen to train as heir to a great shipping empire. Iri had to raise himself and Mother, because Khian, who called himself Demetrios, assumed the administration of the business empire."

"Isn't Iri younger than your mother?"

"Yes, and he took his responsibility very seriously. Iri is bright, strong, sensitive—and ugly as sin. The hereditary red birthmark we Children of the Lion all bear on our backs also turned up on Iri's face, making him the target of ridicule all his life. The only way for him to make a living was to become an armorer like the rest of us, but what he really wanted was to make fine jewelry."

"Poor man," Tirzah said.

"But Mother's problems were quite different. She was a spoiled rich girl, bored, with nothing to do, and no one to tell her problems to. She had no older brother available or father to negotiate a betrothal agreement. She was ripe for something awful to happen to her." He sighed. "And, of course, it did."

"What happened?"

The hand holding Tirzah's suddenly grew tense. "Down from Nubia came a man named Apedemek. . . ."

"Your father?"

He unconsciously squeezed Tirzah's fingers so hard, she winced. Realizing he was hurting her, Pepi relaxed. "He was a magus, capable of ruling the minds of others. He corrupted Mother and then tossed her away. By that time she realized she was pregnant." He tensed again. "With me. By the most evil man in the world."

"Oh, Pepi . . ."

"She blamed herself and must have gone a little mad, because she centered her anger at him on me, telling me I had tainted blood and could mature into being like my father. The worst part was that I started to believe it. And I became curious about Apedemek. Could he be as evil as she said? If he was so powerful, was it bad to take after him?"

"But Pepi, darling . . ."

"It's all right. I know now that I can be anything I want to be. But then I wasn't sure. I was ten years old when Mother, having let the matter fester in her heart, conceived a scheme to go downriver to Thebes, find Apedemek, and kill him. Of course, I ran away to follow her."

"Did you find him?"

"I did. Fortunately, Moses saved us—all of us. Father challenged Moses. His black magic against the powers of Moses' 'God.' Father was destroyed completely. I knew without a doubt that he was a weak and evil man; I knew right from wrong and that I wasn't the slave of my 'tainted' blood. And when Moses led his people out of Egypt, Mother, Iri, and I went with them."

Tirzah's hand stole behind his waist, and she gently hugged him to her.

Pepi smiled. "I haven't seen her in many years, and I don't know whether she's recovered or not. Although she does have a good man now. Baufra, an Egyptian, was an apprentice of my uncle Iri's, and he came with us out of Thebes. I hear that Baufra is a full-fledged armorer now. He works for King Adonizedek of Jerusalem, and he and Mother are well-off. They have two sons of their own, whom I've never met. But as to Mother's mental state . . ."

Tirzah hugged him to her bosom. "Oh, Pepi! You have brothers. Won't it be fun to meet them?"

He returned her hug, laughed, and kissed her. "I'm sure it will be. We'll know soon enough."

To Pepi's surprise, he barely recognized his mother or Baufra. Neftis was a fresh-faced, gray-haired woman who looked younger now than when he had last seen her. Her face was unlined, her figure was youthful, and most wonderful of all, she smiled and laughed with delight when she saw him.

Baufra was a vigorous, white-haired man. His handshake was powerful and his gaze clear. His smile was that of a contented man.

But Pepi's greatest surprise was that he had a strapping eighteen-year-old half brother, a bright and likable young man named Nimshi. The boy had been through his apprenticeship under Baufra and was now accepted at court as journeyman at the family trade. He was also, to Pepi's delight, a Child of the Lion, with the family birthmark halfway down his back like every male in his line. But, Baufra explained, his son needed training at the hands of a master craftsman before he could take his place as a full-fledged member of the clan.

"I was hoping, Brother, that I could finish my training under a man like you," the boy said.

"That you will," Pepi said. "If I stay here in Jerusalem."

"Surely you'll not even consider the possibility of leaving," Baufra said, "now that we've finally been reunited with you and this fair-haired goddess you've brought with you!"

Pepi smiled and gave Tirzah a hug. "It is indeed a joyous meeting, but I've promised to show Tirzah life at Home."

After he and Tirzah had entered the comfortable house, Neftis asked, "Isn't Micah with you?"

Pepi and Tirzah exchanged glances.

"Micah. Our younger boy. He left here over a week ago—without our permission; otherwise we would have notified you in advance—to find you and become an apprentice with the Israelite army."

"I'm . . . not with them anymore."

A silence settled. Finally Baufra spoke up.

"Well, I'm sure our friends the Israelites will take good care of Micah as soon as he identifies himself." He reached over and patted his wife's shoulder. "Don't worry—the boy will be fine. He's in good hands."

"Don't you know?" Pepi asked. "Joshua intends to take the whole of Canaan, including Jerusalem. Aren't you making plans to leave the city?"

"Leave?" Baufra scoffed. "Our roots are here. We're citizens, and I have a good job, as does Nimshi. It's a fine place to live, prosperous, peaceful—"

"Not for long," Pepi warned. "He'll come here. He'll attack the city, and it will fall."

"Nonsense. King Adonizedek has just signed a treaty with four of the most powerful rulers in the region. They've agreed to come to each other's rescue in case of attack.

Surely Joshua can't stand before the combined might of armies like these. This is good news, Pepi! If Joshua is headed this way, then I'm sure he'll bring Micah home to us."

"Joshua has forty thousand very disciplined and experienced young warriors." Pepi's voice was urgent as he tried desperately to convince his family of the danger. "I don't care how many kings sign your treaty. If they fight Joshua, they will lose."

"Lose?" Nimshi echoed incredulously.

"The Israelites are invincible," Pepi said. "Nothing but their own folly can defeat them, and nothing can hold them at bay except iron weapons."

Nimshi suddenly smiled. "You mean weapons like those of the Philistine League?"

III

"Philistine League?" Pepi exchanged puzzled glances with Tirzah. "I haven't heard of any Philistine League."

"They are the Sea Peoples who now live along the southern coast of Canaan," Baufra explained. "They settled five cities and so far seem to have no further territorial ambitions." He turned to Tirzah. "They're northerners like your family, but apparently from a different part. They're quite advanced and seem to be a peaceful lot."

"Just try attacking them!" Nimshi said. "A pirate band tried to raid Ashkelon a month or two ago, and they got more than they bargained for. The Philistines can fight, all right, if they have to."

"This is fascinating," Pepi said. "They have the secret of iron?"

"Oh, yes," Baufra replied. "Iron's all over the Great Sea these days."

"Tell me, Baufra, have you had a chance to talk with them?"

"Their representatives won't talk to me. I'm just a journeyman, and I'm not of your line." He caught the look in Pepi's eyes. "They'd talk to you, though. Surely they'd talk to a Child of the Lion. And if you were to go over there—"

"Wait," Neftis said, holding up her hands. "One son leaves home, and we don't know if he's among friends or enemies. Then I finally get to see Pepi for the first time in years, and already you're giving him an excuse to leave. Baufra, how can you do that to me?"

Her husband shrugged and gave her a smile. "Sorry, my dear. You do come from a family of armorers, though."

"The servants are signaling for dinner. Come along. Tirzah, you can sit by me. I can see our men are going to monopolize the conversation with talk of war and weapons. Maybe the two of us can think of what to do about Micah and talk about things that are closer to a woman's heart."

But Neftis did not get to talk with her newfound daughter-by-marriage until after dinner, when the men retired to the great central hall of the big house. She took Tirzah into her own suite. "My son looks happy," she said. "You've been very good for him."

"Frankly, Neftis, I'm worried about him. He's having blackouts. It almost got him killed the other day." Tirzah's face darkened. "And it's my fault." With tears in her eyes she told the story of their first meeting. "The doctors in Jericho told me there's little chance he will ever recover completely."

Neftis snorted. "Doctors! What do they know? Let me keep him here with me, and we can cure him with love and good food." She paused. "If *I* could be cured . . ."

"Pepi told me," Tirzah said. "Something has healed you. I wish I knew what it was."

"You'd be surprised what love can do, if you get enough of it," Neftis said. "Thanks to Baufra I've had that

and the peace and security I need. Coming to Jerusalem
was the wisest thing I've ever done. It's been a fine place
to bring up our sons. Think about it. You'll want a child of
your own soon. And Jerusalem hasn't had a major war for
fifty years."

"Neftis, you must take Pepi's warning seriously.
You haven't seen Joshua's army in action. We have.
Besides, they're getting supernatural help. You should
have seen the way the walls of Jericho crumbled and
broke into thousands of pieces."

"But dear, everyone says that was an earthquake."

"Yes, but an earthquake Joshua predicted almost to
the moment! And what about the way they crossed the
Jordan? They lined their men up at the river's edge and
waited for the river to dry up—something that had never
happened before in the memory of the oldest man in
Canaan."

Neftis's beautiful face fell. All of a sudden she looked
older. Tirzah realized that underneath her calm exterior,
old terrors were still lurking. Anything could plunge her
back into the pit of madness.

Hastily she changed the subject and resolved not to
worry the woman about Micah's safety. "Let's let the men
worry about such things. Tell me about life in Jerusalem."

"Adonizedek may think that this treaty he's signed
will protect him," Pepi told Baufra. "He may think that he
and his friends can put together an army that will stand up
to Joshua. But I know what Joshua is capable of. He will
destroy Jerusalem and kill everyone in it. Then he'll burn
it to the ground."

For the first time Baufra began to show concern.
"Then you must speak to the king. I don't guarantee,
however, that he will pay attention." Baufra paused. "Pepi,
what can we do? I can't leave Jerusalem. It would kill
Neftis to leave. And I hate to think how she would react to
Micah's being in danger. She's not as stable as she looks."

"If you think she'd be upset at having to leave, imagine how terrified she'd be to find enemy soldiers roaming the streets and killing everyone they see."

For several minutes they sat in shocked silence. Finally Nimshi spoke. "Pepi, what if Jerusalem had weapons of iron? What if Adonizedek could strike a deal for iron weapons from Ashdod and the Philistine League?"

Baufra shook his head. "Not a chance. They've always refused to sell weapons. They're not about to give up that advantage."

"But what if Pepi went to see them? What if a fellow member of the craft—a fellow master—appealed to them?"

A thoughtful look came into Baufra's eyes. "Pepi, what do you think? Is there a chance?"

Pepi raised his brows. "I'll do anything I can to save your city."

IV

After the bloody fall of Ai, Joshua's young army swept into Bethel and dealt that city a fatal blow. And among the ranks were two new soldiers, who, if Joshua or Caleb had noticed them, would have been thrashed within an inch of their lives. But because the boys had smeared their faces with ash and since their helmets were a bit too large and sat low, their identity was safe.

"That was incredible!" Micah hooted as he and Joshua's older son, Chaninai, scooted around the corner of a building.

"I have never had so much fun in my life," his friend agreed. "I'm glad you talked me into it. Next time I'd like to get into the fighting a little, though, instead of hanging back the whole time."

"Do you think Shemida would teach us how to use a sword?" Micah asked.

"Probably. Or Caleb, if he has time."

"Well, if he doesn't, we can teach ourselves. You can

learn a lot just by watching, you know," Micah said confidently.

"We'd better put our gear back with the supplies before anyone catches us," Chaninai suggested. "If anyone sees us here, we won't live long enough to learn to be real soldiers."

"Hey!" Micah said, shoving his friend playfully. "We've seen action today. We already are real soldiers."

Joshua assembled the tribes for a solemn ceremony on Mount Ebal. He read to them the teachings of Moses, paying particular attention to the references to the army of Israel. Moses promised that if they followed the Law without question, "The Lord will put to rout before you the enemies who attack you; they will march out against you by the single road but flee from you by many roads." But if the army disobeyed Yahweh's commands, "You shall become a horror to all the kingdoms of the earth. Your carcasses will become food for all the birds of the sky and all the beasts of the earth, with none to frighten them off."

As his final words echoed through the mountains, the great throng broke up, and each person was caught up in a darkly pensive silence.

Shemida, joining Joshua, noted the drawn look on the great leader's face. His eyes were sunk in his head, and there were lines in his gaunt cheeks. The flesh seemed to have fallen off his body. In action he was the same raging whirlwind he had always been, but when his blood was not up, he was a far cry from the Joshua of old.

Shemida took his concerns to Eleazar that night. "I ask after his health regularly," he explained. "But he always tells me he's fine and to stop asking stupid questions. But they're not stupid, are they, sir?"

"No, my young friend. And you do well to keep an eye on him. This constant warfare is a drain on him."

"Is he ill, sir?" Shemida asked.

"No, not in the way you think. You see, Shemida,

most of us are a mixture of good and bad, of strong and weak, of gentle and violent. This is as it should be. God does not make us perfect; He makes us a mixture of elements. This is so that He may have pleasure in seeing us yearn toward His light and strain to attain goodness. So we are allowed to be weak now and strong later, to wander off the path and find our way back to it."

"But what has this to do with Joshua?"

"Patience, young man," the old priest counseled. "While most of us are allowed to be hard today and soft tomorrow, Joshua is allowed only one side of his personality. He has only the one lifetime to conquer Canaan. It is the duty that has been laid upon him by God. Thus, Joshua must always be brave, even when part of him yearns to be soft. He has the capacity for compassion and forgiveness, and great love for his family."

"I know, sir. He is very kind to me."

"But before the assembled tribes he must always seem severe and undeviating. Poor man, he has denied himself more than any of us throughout these years. And it wears on him. He was a kind and loving father to his children but has seen wife and sons so seldom that soon he may not recognize them. He will allow nothing to distract him from completing God's work, so he cannot draw comfort from them as another man might."

"I think I understand, sir. I'll see what I can do to lighten his load."

"You will be doing the work of the Lord if you do," Eleazar said.

When Shemida returned to the command tent, he found Joshua slumped over, fast asleep, on the maps spread across the table. For the first time in days on his face was a peaceful look. But there were signs of fatigue. As Shemida watched, Joshua's lips moved, and tension knit his brow.

Shemida called in three soldiers to help him get Joshua to bed. As they carried him to the pile of furs in the corner of the tent, the commander did not awaken.

But when at last he lay stretched out on his bed, the troubled look remained on his face.

Shemida walked out beyond the camp, beyond the pickets, and into the hills. What the priest had told him weighed on his mind. His master had a heavy burden to carry and that put a heavy burden on Shemida as well. He had to compensate for much that was missing in Joshua's life. He had to shore Joshua up when his master was down and give him strength when his own was gone.

He wasn't sure he had it in him to do what was needed—not while he was lacking those same consolations himself.

As he walked, his eyes roamed over the landscape and lighted on a lone traveler. The figure drew nearer, and Shemida saw it was a woman, small and delicately built. Shiny brown hair peeked out under her hood. When she looked up and saw him, she was startled.

He held his hands up to show that he was unarmed. "Please, don't be afraid."

"You're with the Israelites," she said nervously, backing away.

"But I'm not one of the fighting soldiers. I serve . . . one of the officers. It's not safe to walk alone in these hills. You were right to be alarmed. I don't even trust my own army anymore. How far do you have to go?"

"A league down the road."

"Would you object to my walking with you? I can't walk very fast, but you'll be safe with me." Seeing her puzzled expression, he explained, "I'm nobody, but my—my superior is very important."

The corners of her mouth turned up a trifle in a shy smile.

"Then it's agreed? You'll let me walk you home?" Shemida asked.

"I don't know why not," she said. Her voice was soft and melodious. "I don't need to walk very fast." She paused. "I'm Tamar, daughter of Jochanan."

"I'm Shemida," he said. "Personal assistant to Joshua, son of Nun."

Now her eyes widened even more. "Personal assistant?" she asked. "To a mighty man like that? You must be very important to him." Shemida could think of nothing to say, but Tamar took the initiative. "Then, Shemida, shall we go?"

Stories of the fall of Jericho, Ai, and Bethel spread throughout Canaan, and the invaders were feared.

Some people urged immediate attack against the Israelites. Others advised caution. Many called for the joining of forces to create an army powerful enough to take on the forty thousand fierce young warriors of Israel. These included the Amorite alliance to which King Adonizedek of Jerusalem belonged. The members of that alliance anxiously awaited Joshua's next move and vacillated about what to do.

In Gibeon, the city councillors advocated peace at any price, and after a long debate, they voted to send a delegation to Joshua to sue for peace.

But innate deviousness led them to send the delegates looking not like the prosperous landowners they were but indigents too poor to afford decent clothes. Even the waterskins they carried on the half-starved asses they rode were old and cracked.

Caleb's subordinates mistook them for messengers from one of the northern kings.

"What kind of nonsense is this?" Joshua demanded when the representatives were brought into his tent. "What country sends beggars to represent it?"

The delegates looked to their spokesman. "Pardon me, sir," he said. "We've come a long way. See how worn our clothing is? It was new when we took to the road. We heard of the fame of your God and of how He dealt with the kings who opposed Him. Our leaders sent us to you to sue for peace and to ensure such things never happen to our people."

Joshua's voice was emphatic. "There can be no peace between Israel and its neighbors in the land of Canaan. If you truly are from a distant land, perhaps we bear you no ill will." He turned to Caleb. "What do you say?"

"Cut off their heads, stuff them into their saddlebags, and send their mounts back to their elders."

"My lieutenant is a hot-tempered man," Joshua explained, trying not to laugh at the terror rippling across the delegates' faces. "Give me some reason why I should listen to you and not to him."

The men from Gibeon looked at one another. "Sir," their spokesman said, "we come from far away. You will have no need to invade our lands. Why should there not be peace between us?"

Caleb snorted. "They're a lot of shifty-eyed swindlers, up to no good."

Joshua sighed, again reminded of how differently Caleb and Pepi always reacted to situations. Missing his old friend, a tired look came over Joshua's face. "Why can't we make peace just this once?" he said expansively, then turned to the ragged strangers. "I see that your robes have a distinctive red trim." They looked puzzled but nodded. "Once we've made peace, mark off your lands with banners of the same cloth; then when we approach your land, we'll see the banners and stop. Is that fair?"

"More than fair, my lord," the spokesman said, color returning to his face. "We have your word then? Sworn on the name of your mighty and omniscient God?"

"You have my word," Joshua agreed. "Where we find your banners we will spare the inhabitants. Now go in peace."

Caleb spat on the ground behind the departing emissaries. "If it were any other man but you, Joshua, I'd swear he had gone soft in the head."

"It is true that perhaps I should have made no peace without consulting God in the matter," Joshua said. "But it is good to show mercy occasionally, particularly where there is little reason to be harsh and unforgiving."

"Don't you know that this will be interpreted as a sign of weakness?" Caleb asked. "They'll say, 'Joshua's becoming soft. He's losing the will to fight.'"

Joshua studied his hot-eyed commander. "And sometimes in the middle of the night they'd find me agreeing with them. Then the spirits of all the men and women and children we've slain cry out to me. Caleb, part of me longs to show mercy."

"Joshua, you're tired. Isn't it time that you left the fighting to the younger men?" Caleb chuckled. "Chaninai asked me for swordplay yesterday. If that doesn't make you feel old . . . Nobody can say you haven't given enough to the cause. But perhaps it's time to rest and stop driving yourself."

Joshua put a hand on Caleb's arm. "I plan to die in harness, like an old cart ox. To do otherwise would be to defy God. He put this burden on my shoulders. He alone can take it off. But I don't want my son to die with some Canaanite dagger in his heart. If he asks for weapons instruction again, tell him he's too young or that you're too busy."

"But—"

"It is true," Joshua continued, "that sometimes I act hastily, and I may have done so today. I should listen to your good advice more often, and I will try to do so in the future. But indulge me this once. How can it harm us to show mercy to these ragged strangers?"

A day later Caleb was proven right. Outside Gibeon, advance scouts began running into banners with the distinctive red trim. When the scouts rode around the perimeters of the area marked off by the flags, they realized it guarded the entire northern approach to Jerusalem.

Joshua was fuming when he heard the news. "We've been tricked."

"What now?" Caleb asked. "Do we show them what

happens when they try to fool us? Do we flatten their villages and give them a taste of what we did to Bethel and Ai?"

"No," Joshua said, "I gave my word."

"So we should sit back and let the bastards laugh at us?"

Joshua turned to him. There was anger in his eyes. "What would you have us do that does not dishonor my word?"

"Make slaves of them," Caleb suggested, grinning. "We need laborers to haul water, cut wood, and carry our equipment. What better use of every man and boy than as beasts of burden?"

Joshua's face twisted in disgust, but he said, "You have my authority. Do it."

V

The news that Gibeon had capitulated without a fight set off a panic in Jerusalem—Gibeon had been counted upon to provide a buffer against the advancing Israelites. In Jerusalem's public squares, men made speeches advocating one course or another, but the speakers for peace were hissed off the platform while the fire-breathing advocates of war drew large and enthusiastic crowds.

One day King Adonizedek, disguised as an ordinary man but accompanied by an aide and three stout bodyguards, went out into the streets of Jerusalem and watched as his people were whipped into a frenzy by a spellbinding orator who wanted the people of Jerusalem to rise and crush the arrogant foreigners who had invaded Canaan. The king carried the memory home with him.

He called in Yakim, his chief adviser, and Ulam, the general of his army, and told them what he had seen. "How can I help my subjects maintain that fervor?" he asked.

"Why don't you appear at the window of the palace telling the people what outrages are being committed by these foreign swine and what they can do about it?" Ulam suggested.

"Sire," Yakim said, "we have here in Jerusalem a man who was until recently a trusted adviser to this Joshua and who knows much about him. He has been asking to speak to you. He might have some valuable information that we can use against the Israelites."

"Who is this fellow?" the king asked.

"Sire," Yakim said, "he's of Egyptian blood, born in Nubia, but he was for many years assistant to Iri of Thebes as head armorer to Joshua. He's even rumored to be a Child of the Lion."

"This is interesting! Why did he leave the Israelites?"

"A dispute seems to have arisen between Joshua and him."

"What is he doing in Jerusalem?"

"His stepfather is Baufra, our own chief armorer. He's been telling Baufra much about Joshua's army. He could inform us as to their strengths and weaknesses."

"Strengths!" Ulam snorted. "A band of desert fighters who happened to have a string of lucky victories!"

Yakim smiled grimly. "Are Jericho and its sister cities to be reckoned easy game? Twelve thousand people were killed at Ai and Bethel. Were they all weaklings and cowards? I think not. Sire, I think you ought to talk to this man."

"Ulam," Adonizedek said, "start making those rabble-rousing speeches." He turned to Yakim. "Bring me this foreigner, and I'll hear him out."

"Yes, Sire," Yakim said. "As you know, you have to make a decision by tomorrow, when you meet with your four royal allies."

Baufra brought the king's summons from the palace. "He may not listen to you," he warned Pepi. "Ulam, the head of the army, wants him to go charging out and challenge Joshua immediately."

"Baufra, you must get Mother and Nimshi out of the city before Adonizedek closes it."

Baufra shook his head. "Too late. The order went out this morning. You need a permit to leave. I suppose I could get a dispensation and send them away with the servants, but I don't know how many of our possessions I could smuggle out."

"Forget your belongings. There's a fortune on deposit in Mother's name at Home. Leave everything behind. Just get her to a seaport and look up Demetrios's representative." Pepi put a hand on his stepfather's shoulder. "The alternative is certain death. Gibeon was the only bulwark between you and Bethel, and now it's gone. Jerusalem will be the next to fall."

It was clear from Baufra's face that he had yet to be convinced.

As Pepi was preparing to leave for his audience with the king, a runner entered Jerusalem with good news: Joshua had called for a week of fasting and prayer. There would be no fighting for seven days.

The runner shouted his news to the guards on the city gate; the guards told the incoming shift and then carried the news back to barracks and into the taverns. By the time Pepi arrived at the palace, the news was all over town.

"I suspect you've heard about Joshua?" Adonizedek asked.

"It's only a week's respite," Pepi cautioned. "When the praying is over, they'll fall on you like hawks."

"My officers have been telling me they're just desert rabble," Adonizedek said. "Are they superior fighters, as some people would have me believe?"

"Better," Pepi said flatly. "And they're getting help your other enemies never had. I understand that there used to be believers in El-Shaddai here in Jerusalem?"

"Why, yes. Several of my predecessors were priest-kings of this deity. But the priests of Baal drove them out many years ago. I doubt if there are five believers in that old religion left in the city."

Pepi shook his head. "If Joshua knows this, it will be even harder for you. El-Shaddai has a new name, Yahweh. And it appears that believers can draw upon His power, which has not diminished since the days of Abraham."

"Do you really believe in this supernatural business? You, a man not of their blood or faith?"

"I only know that I thought I was secure in Jericho, behind walls thicker by half than the walls of Jerusalem. And how is one to explain the crossing of the Jordan?"

Adonizedek frowned. "What would you advise me to do?" he asked. "Suing for peace is impossible. And so—if I am to believe your accounts of Joshua's invulnerability—is fighting."

"There is a possibility, sir," Pepi said. "I'm an armorer by trade—a Child of the Lion—and I'm trained in the working of iron."

The king's face rose and then abruptly fell. "But we have no time to work iron. Even if we had a good source of ore."

"No, sir, but what if I could go to Ashdod in your behalf and bargain for Philistine iron?"

"Philistine iron? But they've always refused to sell to us."

"Because you had no fellow master of the craft to deal with them. They may talk to me. I realize it's unlikely they'll cooperate but . . ."

Adonizedek exchanged glances with his adviser. "What do you think?"

"The worst that could happen would be that they'd say no. It's a chance, even if a slim one."

The king turned back to Pepi. "Tell me what clearances and authorizations you need. I've a strong line of credit in Ashdod. You'll have to work through my ambassadors, of course—"

"There's no time for that, sir. We've only got a week."

Adonizedek hesitated. "You would help us to obtain iron with which to slaughter your old friend?"

"No, Sire. I would help you only if you would use the superior weapons to turn the Israelites away, so neither they nor the inhabitants of Jerusalem would fall victim to war. They raised me, Sire, and I have a half brother traveling with them."

The king's jaw firmed, and a look of resolution came into his eyes. "You have my authority to deal with the Philistines, but hurry. Please hurry."

Baufra and Nimshi were waiting for him. So was Tirzah, and her eyes never left his face. "What happened?" she asked. "What did he say?"

"I'm going to Ashdod," he said. "Nimshi, will you go with me?"

The boy turned to his father, who nodded permission. Nimshi's face lit up with excitement.

"Ashdod?" Tirzah said. "But—?"

"I'll only be gone a few days. If my mission fails, we'll all leave the city for the coast. The king will owe me a favor, and I intend to collect it."

CHAPTER SIX

In Aegean Waters

I

After his rage about his wife's behavior had subsided, Menelaus began to consider the political implications of Paris's rash deed and his own political future. Life had taken a turn for the better; Cousin Aegisthus had betrayed his own father by taking him out of Mycenae's impenetrable fortress and, for a tidy sum, handing the old man to Agamemnon and Menelaus. Aegisthus's bribe, although enormous, was gauged by the brothers to be less than the cost of continuing the siege. Now that Mycenae belonged to Agamemnon, the king was interested in increasing his newfound power.

According to the treaty signed at the time of his betrothal to Helen, he could call upon the allegiance of the other Greek kings to gain his revenge on Paris. He sat down and totted up the list. It was an impressive count, and none could refuse his request for aid without losing honor.

Included on the list were the two warriors without whom no expedition would ever prosper: Odysseus of Ithaca and Achilles the Invincible.

119

But Odysseus had sent his regrets and seemed to be trying to back out, while Achilles was nowhere to be found!

Then the cuckolded king had learned that Achilles said he would not fight for any army commanded by Menelaus, although he would consider going to war under Agamemnon.

"You lead, then," Menelaus told his brother. "It makes no difference to me, as long as we split the spoils when the time comes."

"Slow down," Agamemnon advised. "There is a protocol to be followed. Priam has to be offered the opportunity to give Paris over to us for punishment and to restore Helen and your treasure to you."

Menelaus frowned. "But if Priam gives up Paris and Helen and restores my property, I'll have to call off the war."

His brother smiled. "Then you'll look like a peaceable man who's been wronged and who is justified in anything you choose to do in return."

Menelaus grinned, satisfied. "Very well. I'll go myself to Priam and demand restitution."

"No!" Agamemnon said. "You'll lose your temper and destroy the image."

Menelaus pursed his lips. "If only I could get someone else to speak up for me . . . Nestor, perhaps?"

"Nestor used to be all right, but he's not a direct enough speaker anymore. You want someone who won't get lost in his oratory—someone like Odysseus, for instance."

"Yes!" Menelaus said. "If anyone can present the case dispassionately, he's the man. But where is he?"

"Don't worry; we'll find him. He wrote the pact in the first place. He won't wiggle out of his responsibility."

Menelaus clasped Agamemnon's hand. "This might work out very well in the end," he said. "Imagine being the masters of Troy! Imagine controlling access to the Black Sea!"

*   *   *

Iri set up his forge in the harbor at Asine and began to accept work repairing broken swords and spears and bucklers. It was, he told Phorbus, time that the lad started learning a bit of tinkering.

The first thing he learned to do was pump the bellows. It was hot, exhausting work. It seemed to Phorbus the dullest job in the world. But eventually he began to sense the fascination.

"It's almost as if you're playing a game with the metal!" he finally exclaimed to Iri. "You had to fool it, sneak up on it, and get it to go your way despite its own natural inclinations."

One afternoon they walked through the open-air market near the wharf, looking for bronze to melt down. Stalls of every description sold food, clothing, textiles, and services of all kinds. They asked everyone they met about Keturah, but no one had seen anyone matching her description.

Iri purchased a wineskin and a jar and mixed the raw red wine with well water. Phorbus and he sat down with their backs against the well, drinking and watching the passing parade.

Iri's eyes scanned the market, then turned to his friend. "Here, hold the jar. I'm going down to have a look at something."

He rose easily and ran like a man half his age down the stairs, coming to a stop before a burly, black-bearded sailor.

"Sir," said Iri, "that sword at your belt . . ."

The sailor pulled it out and held it up proudly. "It's iron. You don't see this often down here, but it's common up north."

"I'm a fancier of weapons," Iri said. "I also make them. I've never seen anything like this. Could I have a look, please?"

The sailor handed his weapon over, butt first. By this time, Phorbus had joined them.

"Look at this, my friend," Iri said to his apprentice. "The metal's as good as anything the Chalybians can make, but it's definitely not Chalybian. It's not Hittite, either."

"It's Dorian," the sailor said. "They're tribesmen from way up north, beyond Thessaly. Everyone there has them. I traded a fine slave girl for it in Kavalla. It's hard to handle—twice as heavy as a good bronze blade. It has saved my life many times."

"It's all right if you've got a stout wrist," Iri said. In Iri's hands the blade flashed, almost too fast for the eyes to see. "It takes some getting used to. I've a mind to own one of these. What would you take for this?"

"But I wouldn't think of selling it," the sailor replied.

Iri named a sum that represented a sailor's year's earnings, however, and pulled a fat purse from his tunic. The sailor's eyes widened, and he gave in.

II

Paris had chosen Cranae as a refuge until the crisis caused by Helen's and his behavior cooled down. Helen had family holdings on this island, including a fine villa with a splendid ocean view. The staff showed no surprise at seeing the queen of Sparta on the arm of a handsome prince of Troy or the full fleet of ships in the harbor.

Cassandra held her tongue most of the time. During the short voyage to Cranae from Sparta, she had come to expect little in the way of attention, common sense, or civility from either of her traveling companions, who passed most of their time behind closed doors, alone. This was frustrating to Cassandra only because she wanted to ask Helen about the blind slave girl but never had the opportunity.

Bored, Cassandra left the villa to explore the island. She roamed the hills, climbed and strolled the paths, idled under the few trees, and napped in grassy patches and dreamed of Troy.

On the third day she found an untended olive grove and in it, an ancient shrine to Apollo, the god of healing, music, and archery. She pulled with quickening delight at the weeds that covered the worn stones; but even after she had cleaned off the sacred stones and cleared the deadwood from the lone laurel that marked the god's sanctuary, she could not feel his presence. The god often left a site when people no longer came to do him homage, but that did not mean he had abandoned the little grove forever. Perhaps if she prayed he would come to her, and his sacred and powerful presence would bring new life to this blighted shrine.

She knelt before the broken and weatherworn stones, closed her eyes, and abandoned herself to him. "Come to me, bright Apollo," she prayed in her harsh voice, which not even her devout fervor could soften. "Come."

She intoned the god's many attributes, pleading with him to take over her body and fill her mind with his brilliance and wisdom. Sometime during the long recitation, she drifted off into sleep.

When she awoke the morning had slipped away, and the sun was halfway down in the western sky. She sat up feeling refreshed and clean. Apollo had come to her in her dream. She could feel the lingering afterglow of his sacred presence and remember the promise he made her.

A fight had broken out in the port between two of Paris's soldiers. Tisias had insulted Pyrron, and Pyrron had broken Tisias's nose. Tisias, seething with anger and pain, had pulled his sword. Pyrron's friends had come to his rescue, and Tisias, bleeding and outnumbered, had called out to the men of his own squad. Soon the fight spread through the whole market and was overflowing into the main street.

Arkas, commander of the fleet, responding to the emergency, had come stomping into the market with his adjutant, Lykortas. He stood, muscular arms crossed, staring malevolently at the bloody chaos before him.

"What is going on here?" he bellowed in a deafening bass.

One by one the fighters turned to face him.

"What in the name of all the gods do you cretinous, pox-ridden dog molesters think you're doing? Getting in a fight in *my* command? Defying *my* orders? Breaking *my* damned discipline? Do you have any idea what it means to incur *my* displeasure?"

So loud was he bellowing that the men in the front row winced with every brutal word.

Arkas continued. "I would advise everyone here to watch his behavior. If I have to come out again, I'm going to have a couple of dozen men at a time out there in the sewage-filled waters of this charming piss pot of a lagoon, inspecting the barnacles on the keel of every boat in the fleet. Do you understand me, you mongrels?"

There was a stunned murmur of assent as the crowd broke up.

Arkas, his face still livid with rage, turned on one heel and stalked away, leaving his adjutant to catch up with him.

"Sons of bitches!" he seethed. "Of course, it's not their bloody damned fault. It's the fault of the stupid bastard that Priam's saddled me with to lead this misbegotten, botched, career-ruining mission!"

"Sir," Lykortas said, "do you think it's wise to refer to the lord Paris that way when—"

"What does it matter?" the commander groaned. "The by-blow has ruined us, called down the wrath of the world with this latest escapade. Then what does he do? He dawdles in Cranae with his pale-skinned little whore."

"Sir! Please! Your voice can be heard all over."

"Damn it, I *want* him to hear! Somebody has to get it through that thick skull of his that he's done something insane and reprehensible. I've about had enough of running around after him and cleaning up the mess he makes wherever he goes."

"Sir," Lykortas said a little desperately, "lower your voice. Here comes Princess Cassandra."

The commander turned and saw Priam's daughter moving down the path from the hills. He appreciated Cassandra for her sharp tongue and her boldness.

"Good afternoon, Your Highness," Arkas said, saluting.

"Good afternoon, Commander," the girl replied. "I hope my half brother heard you as clearly as I could. It might bring him to his senses." Arkas felt his face color, but she continued, "But in case he did not, I will speak with him again."

"Yes, ma'am," Arkas said with relief. "I'm worried about keeping my men out of action. Boredom usually leads to trouble. I just had to break up a fight within my ranks."

"I'm going up to the brothel—I mean villa—now," Cassandra said. "I'll see what I can do. Since I've had little success with Paris, I'll try to prevail upon Helen."

Arkas watched her nod imperiously, a silent twinkle in her eyes, and pass on. Looking at Lykortas, Arkas spoke softly. "Priam picked the wrong commander, didn't he? *There* goes the right one. . . ."

III

Cassandra sat alone at a long table set for three. The princess had sent messengers to the lovers several times, but still they did not appear. Finally she scowled and called for her meal. But when it came she picked at her food and then shoved the plate away.

She drummed her thin fingers on the table as she argued with herself. Then, after drinking one more glass of wine than was wise, she sent a message for Helen to come alone, so the two women might talk. Apparently this invitation intrigued Helen—or perhaps she merely needed a rest from the lovemaking—because soft footsteps sounded across the dining hall's marble floors.

Helen slid wordlessly into the chair beside Cassandra's and folded her hands on the table, waiting.

Cassandra studied the woman's face in the candle's glow and found herself sadly lacking.

"You are incredibly beautiful," she blurted.

"And you are very otherworldly looking, with those silver eyes of yours." Helen laughed and seemed to relax. "I thought you were going to scream at me and call me names. I am very relieved that you are not. I would like to call a truce between us, Cassandra."

The princess shook her head sadly. "I'm not sure that's possible. You see, I know what is going to happen to my father's kingdom because of your . . . love for my half brother. I also know that you won't believe me; no one ever does. But I must try to make you understand. You have more influence on Paris than I do, surely."

"Agreed."

"First, we must leave here soon for Troy. The sailors are getting restless, and we have left my father's kingdom with a half-strength army. Our original mission, you see, was military in nature, so Priam sent us well armed. Should your, uh, husband mount an expedition to avenge Paris's insult, my father will not be able to defend his lands. There is also the possibility that Menelaus might find out we are here at Cranae and will send troops after us."

Helen nodded her understanding. "That has crossed my mind. Go on."

Cassandra took heart. "Although you and Paris may have taken enough jewels and riches from Sparta to support yourselves, I'm guessing that there isn't enough coin to pay the troops. These men won't want to be paid with silks or furs. If the men don't get what is due them in a day or two, you will have a full-scale military revolt on your hands. It's only fair to warn you that if the officers decide to seize control of this expedition, they will do it with my approval."

"What do you want me to do?"

"You know Menelaus. How do you suppose he'll react?" Cassandra asked.

"This is a humiliating situation for him. He'll want me back. He's a pig of a man, but his pride is strong. He'll start by sending a diplomatic mission to King Priam with a list of grievances, some of which will be valid, some ridiculous." She laughed humorlessly. "As much as Menelaus will want me returned to his bed, he'll want Troy even more—he and his brother."

"So Paris has given them an excellent excuse for attacking Troy," the princess said.

"As have I," Helen added. She thought for a moment, and her eyes filled with tears. "I'm sorry, Cassandra, but I've just been so miserable with Menelaus, and Paris was so . . . willing. I have never had to worry about the consequences of my behavior. Even as a child I always did as I wished. But I see now how selfishly we've acted, and I'll try to make it up to you. I'll talk to Paris right away."

Cassandra eyed the woman and tried to determine, unsuccessfully, whether the tears and the repentance were genuine. "I'd appreciate your help," she said at last.

"Is there anything else you would have me do?" Helen asked, rising.

"As a matter of fact, there is," Cassandra said impulsively. "I was silly enough to leave Troy without a maidservant. I was wondering if you'd give me yours, the blind girl. . .?"

The slave wore a simple white shift, which contrasted with her olive skin. She had a soft, round face, full lips, and dark eyes. She was lovely. She was also the girl of Cassandra's vision. In her arms she carried a baby.

The princess of Troy stepped forward and gently put a hand on the girl's tanned arm. The slave recoiled and turned to shield her child.

"I'm not going to hurt you," the princess said quietly. "Do you speak my language? What is your name?"

"I am Keturah, my lady. And this is my son, Talus.

Please do not separate us. He is no bother—I promise I can take care of him myself without shirking my duties to you." Her speech bore the accent of some faraway country, but her words were clear, spoken in a soft and melodious tone full of sadness and desperation.

"I would never take a child from his mother," Cassandra promised. "In fact, I'll see that you get help with him. I need a companion as well as a servant, and I think you can fill both roles very well—that is, if you don't mind leaving your present mistress."

A small smile tugged at Keturah's lips. "No, my lady. I haven't been with her for very long, and if you take me, I'm sure the queen of Sparta will consider it a favor."

"Tell me about yourself, Keturah. Come, I'll help you to a stool." Cassandra took the girl's elbow and led her to a seat, where she sat down with little Talus.

Keturah shrugged. "There is not much to tell about the happy times of my life and not much I'd like to say regarding my sadnesses. I am a Bedouin, from the land of Canaan. My husband, an armorer, was taking me to the island home of his brother when I was kidnapped by slavers. I have belonged to many people within a short time. Some have treated me well. Others . . . well, I am thankful my baby and I are still together, and I pray that someday we will be reunited with my husband. I know he is looking for us."

Cassandra's heart went out to the girl. "Would he have any idea where to look?"

Keturah sighed. "He's looking everywhere, I'm sure. But it's a big world, and much time has gone by since I was carried off."

"I will make a deal with you, Keturah: Serve me well, and I will help you find your husband."

The girl smiled radiantly and hugged her son, planting a kiss on the top of his head. "Did you hear that, Talus? You will meet your father!" She looked up, and the luminescence of her face shook Cassandra to the core.

"Oh, thank you, my lady! Thank you! I shall be a very good slave and companion, you will see!"

IV

It was the first time in days that Paris had worn the uniform of his office as commander of the expedition. He studied himself in Helen's bronze mirror. Was that fat developing around his middle? Were his jowls drooping?

Scowling, he turned to the big bed where Helen was still asleep. She had kicked off the covers, and her naked body was enticing. Awake or asleep, the woman was extraordinary. He felt heat spreading in his loins.

He hoped he could get away without waking her. Otherwise, he would fall victim to his desire for her. Just now there was a lot more to life than sex; there was power. And power was what he was in danger of losing.

He crept toward the door, carrying his sandals. As Helen had told him last night, it was time to reassert himself. If there was really as much discontent among the men as she had said, it was worth trying to eliminate the problem. What he did not need now was a revolt. He needed to curry the support of Arkas and the other officers, even though he was confident of being able to explain his actions to Priam when the time came. Troy was cash poor at the moment, and the treasure he had stolen from Menelaus would come in handy.

Briefly, a coal black cloud came floating across his horizon. What if Priam were to disapprove of his actions, *really* disapprove? What if Priam were to disavow him? What if Priam apologized to the sons of Atreus, returned Helen, and handed him, Paris, over to those bloodthirsty ruffians?

The thoughts made him stop dead in his tracks. He made the sign against evil. But then he shook the worries off, as he was so good at doing. Squaring his shoulders, he began to whistle as he marched down the hill toward the encampment in the town below.

Cassandra watched her new slave unpack. She had never been around a blind person before. The only ones she saw were beggars, filthy scum who were an assault to the eye. But Keturah was clean and moved as gracefully as if she were sighted. She could even be of good blood, despite her swarthiness.

Cassandra studied the baby sleeping on the mattress they had placed beside Keturah's bed. Babies were also new to her. This little fellow was fascinating, especially since Cassandra knew she would never have a child of her own.

"Is Talus your husband's name?" Cassandra asked.

"No, my lady. His name is Iri. One of the slaves who helped me deliver my baby had been the personal maidservant to a family from Samothrace. She said that Talus was the name of a famous man who invented the compass and the saw. I thought it was an appropriate name for my little boy."

The infant stirred and made cooing sounds. Keturah's gentle hand reached out with uncanny accuracy, touched him, and pulled the coverlet up around his chubby little body. He slipped back into sleep with a small sigh.

"He has a birthmark on his back," Cassandra said.

"I know, my lady. The mark runs in his father's family."

"Is the father's family of gentle birth?"

"They were famous men, my lady. Men about whom songs were sung. My child bears the blood of a noble line of metalworkers. Well, not just metalworkers, I suppose, but artists with metal. Some of them were the famous makers of arms to the courts of the world. One of my husband's kinsmen was even king of Babylon a generation ago." She sighed. "And now his son's a slave, born in captivity."

"But the fates reward as well as punish, Keturah,

don't they? Who knows what the gods will steer into Talus's path someday? Perhaps some kind king will find a use for him and let him apprentice to the craft of his ancestors. Or, well before then, we might find your Iri."

When Keturah did not answer, Cassandra thought about the dream Apollo had sent her as she napped on the hillside: In Keturah she would find a woman friend, a companion who would help her overcome her loneliness and depression. And to be sure, there was a serenity about the girl that was appealing and soothing.

"Yes," Cassandra continued, "one's fortunes can be reversed. Prince Paris spent his first years as an unacknowledged bastard. He was abandoned on a hillside by his mother and raised by poor shepherds. And now look at him, a prince of Troy, leading a great fleet of ships."

It was impossible to keep all the irony out of her voice, but there was truth in her words, and if they comforted the girl, all the better. She watched Keturah put away the last of her robes.

"If you're done," Cassandra said, "I want a bath and would like you to do my hair."

Keturah smiled into thin air. Her voice was low and untroubled. "Whatever my lady wishes."

As she spoke, peace flowed into Cassandra's unquiet heart.

CHAPTER SEVEN

Canaan

I

Pepi's kiss was lingering and loving, but it said goodbye. Even after he mounted his horse, Tirzah clung to him. "If only I could go with you," she said. "I had a terrible dream last night—you suffered one of your attacks in an Ashdod street, and you just lay there. People didn't care; they just stepped over you."

Pepi reached down and squeezed her hand. He was smiling, excited about meeting Philistine ironworkers, learning from them. Since leaving the Israelite camp, he had had no one to talk shop with. But more important, if his mission was successful, it could save thousands of lives, including those of his family.

"Don't worry," he told her. "Nimshi will be with me. And I'll be in contact with you by messenger when I send the king his report."

Beside him, Nimshi swung into the saddle. "Don't worry, Tirzah. We'll be fine. And we won't be long. We *can't* be long. We've only six days before Joshua starts preparing to attack Jerusalem."

"I know," she said, looking from Nimshi to Pepi. "And I know you'll be less than a day's ride away."

Pepi held her hand to his lips. "Take care of Mother. Don't let her worry." He released her hand. "I'll miss you every moment."

Her smile faded as the men urged their horses forward. Pepi was leaving her. And given his sickness, there was no way of guaranteeing that she would ever see him again.

Wending her way through the city streets Tirzah studied the faces she passed, to keep from thinking of Pepi. Since the edict limiting movement in and out of the city, a nervousness had settled over Jerusalem. People did not smile as they once had. In the markets the usual bargaining had turned to ill-tempered bickering. Many people were stocking up on essentials, so others suffered shortages. No one trusted anyone else. All dealings had to be done in coin. Credit was a luxury of the past.

Adonizedek's gruff soldiers inside the city walls aggravated the situation. In addition to the city guard, tough brawling mercenaries with no patience for civilians swarmed over the city. Nightly fights spilled out of the inns into the streets. From midnight to dawn someone was knifed every hour. Bad blood flowed between the guardians and the guarded, and nobody seemed to be doing anything to end the hostility.

As she passed through the large marketplace inside the Yaffa Gate, Tirzah heard a speaker haranguing the crowd. Every day a soldier stood on the platform holding forth, whipping up the citizens' desire for war and hatred for the invaders.

Tirzah stopped to listen.

"At this very moment our king is in conference with his allied rulers. They have pledged their entire armies to our defense. The kings have decided that the only response to the threat of invasion by this foreign rabble is to destroy them before they can destroy us. Joshua leaves us no choice. He kills all Canaanites in his path."

A voice called up from the crowd: "What about the Gibeonites? They're still alive!"

"The Gibeonites took the coward's way out," the soldier responded, "and they've paid for it with their freedom—they're slaves of the Israelites now. Their property was stolen by the invaders, who turned the Gibeonites out of their own homes. The strength of the Israelites overwhelmed the cowards in Gibeon, even though no blood was shed. Is that how you want it, people? Do you want to be slaves? Do you want your children to be slaves?"

"No!" the crowd replied as one.

"Then Joshua and the Israelites must die!"

II

While Tirzah stood in the marketplace listening to the speaker, Jerusalem's king was sitting in council with his allies. Facing him were the rulers of Hebron and the foothill towns of Lachish, Eglon, and Jarmuth. When their forces were joined with Jerusalem's, an army to be feared would be created. But Adonizedek was aware that Joshua held the advantages of momentum and, more importantly, the ability to make unilateral decisions. Kings, Adonizedek knew, did not like to take advice or orders from other rulers.

"I have spoken with a man who until quite recently was in the Israelites' camp, and he tells me—"

"The traitor," hissed Japhia of Lachish.

"And he tells me," Adonizedek continued, after an annoyed glance at Japhia, "that the only possible way to deal with Joshua is to fight him to the death. The Israelite commander is pledged to the total destruction of every city in his path and to the obliteration of our entire civilization."

"Is he mad?" asked Hoham of Hebron.

"No, he's on a 'sacred' mission." Adonizedek smirked. "I have sent the, uh, traitor to Ashdod, in the hope he may be able to procure iron weapons for us."

"What makes you think the Philistines will cooperate?" asked Japhia.

"My man is a Child of the Lion. You have heard of them, of course: Belsenu, Ahuni, Hadad of Haran . . ."

Hoham whistled low. "How could the Israelites have afforded to pay him?" He looked at Adonizedek sharply. "And what is his help costing us?"

Adonizedek smiled. "Not a shekel. His stepfather is my chief armorer, and his mother lives in Jerusalem. By helping us, he will save them."

The king of Jarmuth folded his hands across his belly and leaned back in his chair. "And if the Philistines won't sell weapons even to a Child of the Lion?"

"I have authorized my man to try to buy iron ore. He's an armorer; we'll make our own swords."

The kings digested this strategy for a few moments. Then Japhia spoke up. "And for arranging all this, what will you want in return?"

"I want to direct the strategy of our combined troops, beginning with an attack on Gibeon," Adonizedek replied.

"*Gibeon?*" Debir of Eglon sputtered. "What possible purpose could that serve? The entire Israelite army has evacuated Gibeon. There's no one there but civilians. I doubt if we'll find anyone there worth fighting."

"Precisely." The king of Jerusalem smiled slowly. "Joshua's army is gathered to the east, fasting and praying for six more days in preparation for the attack on my city. This gives us a brief period in which we can safely attack Gibeon."

Jarmuth's ruler nodded thoughtfully. "What you want to do is keep Joshua away from our cities while your Child of the Lion tries to get weapons for us."

"And," Japhia added, "an attack on Gibeon will give our armies a bit of practice without the risk of casualties.

Many of our soldiers are young. They can bloody their swords against the Gibeon civilians."

"Children of the Lion are reputed to bring good luck to armies," Debir remarked.

"I also want to teach the elders of Gibeon a lesson," Adonizedek said. "By tricking the Israelites, the elders saved their own necks but undermined the security of all of southern Canaan." He looked around the table. "Are we in agreement?"

"Agreed," the kings responded.

"Then we're off to Gibeon," Adonizedek said, slapping his palm against the tabletop. "Gather the army before the gates of Jerusalem tomorrow."

He had them now. They would do as he wished.

It was late in the day when Baufra came home from the army's forges. When Neftis was out of earshot he took Tirzah aside. "I have to talk to you." They climbed the stairs to the roof garden. "The kings have come to an agreement," he said. "We're going to attack Gibeon."

She told him about the impact of the soldier's speech in the marketplace. "There must have been three dozen men who stepped forward to sign up for military service afterward."

He nodded. "Neftis is worried enough about Micah, Nimshi, and Pepi. I don't want to add this to her concerns."

"But Baufra, she'll have to know sometime. And she has to be taken away to safety before Joshua attacks."

"She won't leave until she knows that her sons aren't caught up in the middle of this." Baufra had a tortured look. "Gods! If only we knew how Micah is!"

"Don't worry, Baufra," she said kindly. "I'm sure the boy is all right."

"After the picture Pepi painted of the Israelites? It doesn't seem to me that my son is in good hands at all."

"The Israelites will be headed this way. That means that Micah will be brought closer to home. If Adonizedek does attack Gibeon unexpectedly, perhaps in the confusion that will result in Joshua's camp, the boy can leave undetected and come home."

Baufra considered. "Maybe." He smiled. "He's not the timid sort. Never has been."

"And you're going to have to get Neftis out."

He sighed. "I suppose I'm being foolish, trying to put it off as long as I can. I have to stay here with the army, and I hate the idea of being separated from Neftis. She's so dependent on me."

"She'll be happy at Home. From the way Pepi talks about it, she'll be secure there. A whole fleet protects the island. Then, when this mess is over, you and Micah and Nimshi can join her there. The whole family can be together."

His sigh was long and deep. "But if it's the right thing to do, why has Pepi gone to Ashdod rather than taking you with him to Home?"

She had all the answers at the tip of her tongue: Pepi was doing the king a favor; he was protecting the citizens of Jerusalem; he was responding to Joshua's brutal treatment of conquered people. But why had Pepi left her behind? She felt a despairing tug at her heart as she stood looking at Baufra, unable to answer.

III

Shemida watched over Joshua like a mother hen. More and more, he was aware that he was serving a doomed man—a man who would live long enough to achieve what he had set out to do, then expire from sheer exhaustion and pressure. He lived for war and wilted between battles.

At one time Joshua had been the first officer awake in the morning. Now Shemida had trouble rousing him. Approaching him in the first light, Shemida would stare down at the face of his master—a face that should be peaceful and rested after a night's sleep. Instead the adjutant would see the contorted features of a man who had wrestled with unknown demons all night long. Often Shemida found him drenched with sweat from his night terrors.

It seemed unfair to Shemida that Joshua must bear his burdens alone, but when he tried to get Joshua to share his problems, the aide was brusquely rebuffed.

What should he do? Shemida had puzzled over this and had come up with no solution. He asked Caleb for advice, but Joshua's second-in-command was a compassionless man, and he had no guidance to offer. Shemida considered making an appeal to Joshua's wife, but that relationship had disintegrated completely, and Shemida was actually frightened to ignite the woman's emotions.

Finally Shemida tried slipping the poppy-based *shepenn* into his food. Joshua detected the drug immediately and stomped around his tent in one of the worst outbursts of temper Shemida had ever seen.

The adjutant ultimately decided that even though he could not alleviate his master's problems and sorrows, he would not permit others to add to them—not while he could prevent it. So when young Micah and Chaninai came to see the commander and show off their growing prowess with swords, Shemida turned them away. And when Caleb came calling very early one morning demanding to see Joshua, Shemida stood his ground.

"I'm sorry, sir, he's still asleep, and I can't have him awakened now."

"You can't *what*?" Caleb erupted in astonishment, "Who are you to tell me what I can and can't do? Get out of my way. If I'm not talking to Joshua in a moment, you'll suffer for it!"

Shemida looked at Caleb squarely. "No disrespect intended, sir, but I can't awaken my master while fulfilling my present job."

"No—no disrespect," Caleb said, spluttering. "You were raised from the ranks, for some reason Joshua has never shared with me, and you can be cast down again for disobeying orders. Now, for the last time, get out of my way."

Shemida braced himself against Caleb's fury. After Joshua, Caleb was the most skillful and quickest swordsman in the army. And as far as temper, he stood second to none. Shemida's every instinct told him to back down, but he did not. "Whether I'm demoted or kicked out, my status can be altered only by Joshua himself."

"Curse your insolence!"

"Cursed I may be, sir. That's a matter for Yahweh Himself to attend to."

Caleb's eyes flashed, and blood pulsed at his temples as he clutched the sword at his side. It seemed he would strike. Unarmed, Shemida stood trembling, realizing that Caleb could carve him into pieces in a moment.

At last Caleb's hand relaxed, and he stepped back. He looked at Shemida, and the sword in his hand swept up in a crisp salute. "You win," he said, surrendering. "In your place I'd have been equally loyal. But make sure that you keep others away from him the way you've kept me, and when he wakens, tell him I need to see him as quickly as possible."

"It'll be the first thing he hears," Shemida said, returning the salute.

Caleb turned on his heel and stalked away. Only when he was out of earshot did Shemida dare take a breath.

Caleb was fuming by the time Joshua finally called for him. But when he saw Joshua's drawn face, he held his tongue. "Sir, we have a reliable report that a large military force is gathering in the plain between here and Jerusalem."

Joshua looked puzzled for a moment. "Any estimates of size? And does anyone know who's in charge?"

"All the informant said was 'large.' He was a trader coming up from Egypt. He recognized the banners of troops from five cities—Jerusalem, Jarmuth, Hebron, Eglon, and Lachish. The Jerusalem contingent seemed to be taking the lead."

"Odd . . ." Joshua closed his eyes. For a moment Caleb could see how old the commander looked. Violent emotions surged through his heart: a fear and sadness that the great leader might be failing. What would become of Israel without him? Who would lead the army of Israel? He, Caleb, would, of course. Excitement swept through him now. When the legends were repeated and the songs written and the scrolls unrolled for the solemn reading at festivals, the names of the conquerors of Canaan would be listed as Moses, Joshua, and Caleb.

He tried to banish the shameful thought. But still it lingered in the back of his mind. Caleb the conqueror! Caleb the hero! Caleb the successor of the patriarchs! He bit his lip and forced himself to concentrate on the conversation. "Adonizedek, Jerusalem's ruler, has no name as a soldier. But his general Ulam is a most able man. And King Debir of Eglon is no fool."

Joshua's eyes snapped open. "Ulam! I hope for his own sake he assembles a big army. He'll need it if he's going to rattle his sword at us."

Caleb waited. "Could he be planning a sneak attack, sir? Word might have reached him that we've declared a religious holiday and can't fight."

Joshua looked at him. His lips fell into a wry smile, and there was a hint of the old fire in his eyes. "Who says we can't fight?" he asked.

"But, sir, I naturally thought—"

"We can't fight on days of prayer and fasting called by Yahweh, my friend. But I called this week of prayer, and I can interrupt it anytime I wish." Joshua's smile became deadly, and strength seemed to flow through him. "If Ulam is counting on the advantage of surprise, we'll let him think that we're caught off guard. Where do you think he proposes to strike?"

"Our informant says Gibeon."

"They're going to attack a defenseless city?"

"Once they've bloodied their swords on the Gibeonites, they believe they'll be ready to take us on."

"Then Ulam is a fool."

"Mind you, sir, the combined armies are said to be large."

"Let them come. Even if their forces were ten times the size of ours, they would not prevail. Yahweh will strike the cowards down. He will crush them, level their cities, and leave their bodies for the crows."

Caleb looked at him with openmouthed astonishment. When the warlike mood was upon him, the years fell away, and the old Joshua was back!

But for how long?

After Caleb had gone into Joshua's tent, Shemida tried to relax. He wondered if a cup of wine would help, then decided against it. He needed full control of his wits these days. Besides, the entire army was supposed to be observing a fast, so he would have to imbibe behind the commander's back.

Most likely, Shemida decided, he merely needed to take some time off to unwind. He had not enjoyed any respite from his duties since his appointment to adjutant. But what would he do with his free time? He had given himself over so completely to Joshua's service that he had no idea what to do when he was not working.

Suddenly a vivid vision flashed across his mind, of large, melting brown eyes above a beguiling, pert little nose and the reddest lips in Canaan.

Tamar . . . Thinking of the girl he had met and escorted home made him smile. She had been so friendly to him and so grateful for the safe passage he had promised her. Tamar's appreciation of his decency and honor was disarming.

Then Shemida frowned. The girl was a Canaanite, a nonbeliever. He should not become involved with her. Visions of her lovely, delicate hands and feet, and proud and upright stance undermined his resolve. Perhaps Tamar would like to know more about the One God. Perhaps there was time to wash up and walk over to her father's farm before Joshua needed him. Shemida smiled. His tension was already lifting. He would go courting before his courage waned.

IV

Upon leaving Jerusalem with letters from King Adonizedek for the Philistine ruler at Ashdod, Pepi and his half brother Nimshi rode their mounts west at a good clip, out of the hill country and toward the Great Sea. Ashdod was an inland city, but it was not far from the coast.

The pressure on the brothers never relented. On their shoulders rested Jerusalem's only hope against destruction and its inhabitants' sole chance for survival. But Pepi and Nimshi had only six days at most before the Israelites mounted their offensive. And in that short period of time, they had to travel to Ashdod, make contact with the Philistine authorities, present their plea successfully, and have the iron weapons transported back to Jerusalem.

Added to that already awesome burden was the everpresent possibility that Pepi would suffer a seizure or that their horses, ridden hard, might get injured or collapse.

It was thus with great relief that they rode through the Ashdod city gates after relentless travel, their faces streaked with dirt and sweat and their mouths excruciatingly dry.

Isolated from the Canaanite interior, Ashdod's Philistine culture was much in evidence as the brothers rode through a marketplace.

"Where are the armorers?" Pepi, looking around, asked Nimshi.

"Metalworkers are honored here and wouldn't condescend to rub elbows with common merchants in stalls,"

Nimshi answered. "Imagine having clients make appointments with your servants to purchase a dagger and having them bow to you in the streets."

"I like that idea," Pepi admitted, "but right now, it doesn't serve our purpose. The less accessible the metalworkers are, and the more elevated in public esteem, the less easily they'll be convinced to accommodate our needs."

"No one is going to pay heed to anything we say until we get cleaned up," Nimshi said. "Let's find an inn, get someone to take care of the horses, and have a good meal. If we can find a place in the best quarter of the city, we might be able to make some worthwhile connections and save time."

"Splendid idea. I'll follow you."

Nimshi led the way down a narrow, winding street, where Pepi kept his eyes and ears open. Then he relaxed as the houses became progressively more lavish. Finally, in a small but immaculately neat commercial district, Nimshi stopped at an inn.

"Can you understand the language?" Pepi asked as they dismounted.

"They'll probably make fun of my accent, but I can make myself understood," Nimshi replied. "Since Ashdod is inland, I suppose Demetrios won't have a representative here."

Pepi shook his head.

"Too bad," Nimshi said. "That could have proved helpful. Well, let's hope King Adonizedek's credit is good."

They handed their horses to an old servant and removed their travel packs to bring inside, where they were greeted by a friendly and garrulous innkeeper named Binnui. He brought the brothers to an immaculate room upstairs, then excused himself to see to their dinner.

After Pepi and Nimshi had cleaned up and changed their clothes, they came downstairs for a meal. A table had already been prepared for them, and the innkeeper joined them for a bowl of wine. He explained that he had a natural capacity for languages and found it easy to make friends with Ashdod's convivial new inhabitants, the Philistines. He boasted that he had opened an inn, which had prospered, and now owned a comparable establishment in each of the four quarters of the city.

Pepi, taken with the owner's easygoing manner, shared a few facts about his own background.

Binnui's response was one of surprise and respect. "Two Children of the Lion at my table!" he said. "What an honor!"

Nimshi beamed. Pepi smiled and bowed his head. "I'm glad to find a friend here," he said. "Can you tell me about the Philistines? Much depends upon my ability to deal with them."

Binnui shrugged. "I wish I could help you, my friend, but no one seems to know where they came from. When they arrived, though, they had some skills no one else had, including the secret of the smelting of iron."

Pepi confided the purpose of his mission and the fast-approaching deadline. "Can you do anything to help me, Binnui?"

The innkeeper thought for a moment. "I think I can. One of my patrons is Hagab of Ashdod, the master armorer for the king. Tomorrow I'll talk to him and try to arrange an introduction. Will that help?"

Pepi's face split in a grin. "Yes, Binnui. That most certainly will help!"

V

Thus it was that once Adonizedek had mustered his forces, the armies of the five kings moved against Gibeon with the ferocity of an ally betrayed. After all, Gibeon had been an ally for as long as the oldest among the Canaanites could remember.

Gibeon was an open city now. No armed guards stood at the city gate, for there were no weapons left in the city. All had been turned over to the Israelite over-lords.

When the five armies struck under Adonizedek's and Ulam's command, soldiers swarmed through the open gates. Many of the callow young soldiers of Jerusalem's army had never struck a blow before and had to be forced by their superiors to attack the unarmed civilians. Others, how-ever, found the work to their liking, and when the order came down that women and children were not to be spared, rousing cheers erupted from the ranks. Women were seized and raped. Babies were tossed into the air and caught on the points of swords.

Watching these orgies of barbarism, some of the men with humane sensibilities vomited into the street. One of Debir's squads rebelled, refusing to participate in the barbarity, and were themselves put to the sword.

By day's end Ulam commanded a city of killers and death. Bodies were piled in the public squares and burned, and their stench was a pall over the area.

As the night campfires blazed high, Joshua's spy in-side Ulam's army detached himself from the celebration and slipped off into the darkness, heading for the Israelite encampment to make his report.

Baufra stumbled out through the Gibeon city walls, gasping for air. The sights within that devastated town sickened and nearly maddened him. Never had he wit-nessed such crazed savagery, such mindless slaughter. The sweet, thick stench of blood was everywhere. The smell of smoke from fires feeding on human flesh and hair sent him reeling through the streets.

Outside, he leaned weakly against a wall, breathing hard. After a few minutes, he was able to give words to his decision: He would leave the army. He would walk back to Jerusalem, if he had to, gather up Neftis and Tirzah, and take them to Home. He would leave word and money with their friends and neighbors so Micah, Nimshi, and Pepi could join them later.

Feeling better, he took a deep breath and checked the stars for his bearings. Then he turned and began to walk.

"Halt! Who goes there?"

Baufra hesitated, then kept on walking.

"Halt!"

Baufra heard running feet behind him, but now that he had taken the first steps toward Jerusalem, he would not be deterred.

The guards caught up with him, grabbed his arm, and swung him around. "Taking a stroll?" one asked nastily.

Baufra, standing tall, lifted his arm away from the guardsman's grasp. "I want no more of this abomination. I am going home."

"You bet you are. You're a deserter. You're going to prison."

When news of the massacre reached the Israelite camp, Caleb fretted, pacing before his tent and wondering why the army remained inactive. After all, Joshua himself had decreed that the rules for days of prayer did not apply. Caleb tried to reach Joshua but was again stopped by Shemida. The commander, the aide said, was praying with Eleazar and wished to be left alone.

After a night of drunken rioting and looting in Gibeon, morning came, and Adonizedek and the other four kings rode out to inspect the scene of their victory. What should have been a triumphal procession through the streets of the newly conquered city became a sobering experience. Half-burned bodies lay in great ghastly piles. Corpses of women, children, and the elderly lay where they had fallen, in the doorways of their homes or in alleyways as they had tried desperately to escape the crazed soldiers. Flocks of crows feasted on their flesh.

Finally Debir spurred his horse forward and caught up with Adonizedek. "Is this what you had in mind?" he asked in a strangled voice. "We have soiled our own good names. We have—"

"Nonsense," said Adonizedek. "These people betrayed us. They got what they deserved."

Angrily, Debir turned on him. "Are you mad? The children? The aged? What did they do? What kind of revenge is this? We have excoriated the foreigner for his savagery, yet we committed even worse atrocities. At least Joshua defeated his enemies in a fair fight. But whom have we fought? Our men merely marched in the front gate and killed at will." He looked from face to face; none but Adonizedek and General Ulam would meet his gaze. "We have disgraced ourselves, and we will pay. The gods will punish us."

"Don't give us that superstitious nonsense about the gods meting out punishment," Adonizedek said with a sneer. "That drivel is only for the common people."

Suddenly, hundreds of rams' horns blew from outside the walls.

As the sound blared forth, the disorganized conquerors struggled awake, looking for the weapons they had carelessly thrown down during the night. Captains and underofficers alike bellowed desperately to their men, trying to assemble them in some sort of coherent formations so they could mount a defense.

The kings climbed Gibeon's wall and looked out across the plain. They could see the Israelite army come over the crest of the hill and move down toward them, toward the destroyed city of Gibeon.

All that saved the five armies from rapid and utter destruction were the Eglon troops. Debir's soldiers had not been allowed to dissolve in drunken rioting the night before, and now they stood between Joshua's advancing army and the rest of the command.

Watching from the walls of Gibeon, Adonizedek saw that when Joshua's men reached the plain, Debir's troops were waiting for them. A volley of arrows met the Israelites.

Some men fell; the rest pressed forward, holding their bucklers high over their heads.

Eglon's soldiers dropped right and left, but the unharmed continued to fight, giving ground reluctantly before the oncoming wave. Adonizedek realized that they could not stop the Israelites, but they fought and retreated, fought and retreated, trying to delay them, losing a new unit with each onslaught of fresh troops.

Gradually the other armies got organized, and the army of Hebron managed to attack Joshua. Ulam's Jerusalem command, coming to their relief, engaged Joshua's left flank. The king of Jerusalem nearly danced with joy.

While the vicious fighting continued, dark clouds began to drift in from the west. The air became very cold. A freak storm was brewing.

As the five armies gave more and more ground, the sky grew darker. Adonizedek wondered for the first time whether he should gather the other kings and escape before it was too late.

As Joshua's soldiers pushed forward across the plain toward Gibeon, a pair of teenaged boys stood among the wagons and supply carts that were lined up at the rear. Reaching into the back of an open cart, the taller youth whispered, "Don't worry, Chaninai—we won't be recognized wearing these." He lifted out a leather helmet and handed it to his companion.

"I don't know, Micah," his friend replied, brushing back a stray lock of his curly black hair as he took hold of the helmet. "Your parents are in Jerusalem. But mine are here." His dark eyes narrowed as he stared intently toward the Israelite troops advancing on the walled city. "If my father finds out . . ."

"Don't be a baby. You're fifteen. Next year you'll be old enough to join the army, and not even Joshua will be able to stop you. Besides, you said your father hardly has time for you anymore. What better way to get him to notice you than to spill some of the enemy's blood?"

"Aren't you afraid?" Chaninai asked as he donned the helmet and removed a sword and shield from the cart.

"What's to fear?" Micah replied. He waved a sword toward the fighting. "See? Eglon's troops are already falling back behind the city walls. Soon the battle will be won. Don't you want to be in on the action?"

"I'm not so sure," Chaninai replied hesitantly.

"Then why have we been practicing with those swords we made?"

Chaninai hefted the weapon in his hand. "But these aren't wood," he said solemnly.

"Then you're the one who's afraid," the taller boy teased.

"Father says that proper respect for fear makes a fearless soldier."

"Your father is a great man—and a brave leader such as he would have nothing but pride for a son who strapped on a sword and fought at his side."

Chaninai looked at him uncertainly, wavering. Micah snatched up one of the shields and fitted the leather straps on his left forearm. "Come on. We'll have to hurry if we don't want to miss out on everything."

Chaninai glanced behind him toward where his father's army had been camping. Somewhere back there, with the camp followers, his mother was probably wondering where he and his new friend had run off to. She would be mortified to think that her son—her "little" Chaninai—was heading into battle. *But I am no longer a boy,* he told himself as he grasped a shield and held it in front of him. *I am a man!* And today was the day he would prove that to himself—and to his mother and father.

With a ferocious shout Chaninai raised his sword and went running across the barren plain in pursuit of the advancing Israelite troops, not bothering to strap on the shield but clutching it tightly by the straps. Micah had to sprint to catch up to him, and then the boys were charging side by side toward what appeared to be the remaining pocket of resistance on the left flank.

As they raced across the plain, they zigzagged among the bodies that littered the battlefield. Most had fallen victim to Eglon bowmen, who had vainly tried to halt the Israelite onslaught. A few survivors too desperately wounded to go on fighting were struggling toward the back lines. One of Joshua's generals, with one arrow in his side and another piercing his thigh, was being helped to his feet by a foot soldier. Chaninai averted his eyes and continued onward.

Minutes later the boys found themselves in the thick of the battle. It came upon them quickly. One moment they were making their way through ranks of the Israelite infantry; the next moment they were caught in a pincer movement by fresh reinforcements from within Eglon's walls.

Chaninai reacted instinctively when a burly Canaanite suddenly loomed over him, sword raised high. The youth managed to duck under the arc of the big man's blade, then responded with a quick thrust of his own weapon. To his surprise, the blade sank deep in the man's belly, splattering Chaninai with blood. The boy yanked the sword free and leaped to the side to avoid the man's falling body.

Chaninai felt his knees buckling as he stared at the lifeless form below him. Bile rose in his throat. He glanced over to see Micah standing over another corpse, his own sword bloodied. Micah shook the weapon in victory and grinned, then turned back toward the enemy.

Chaninai firmed his stance and looked around just in time to see another Eglonite fighting his way through the ranks. As the man advanced on Chaninai, the Israelite youth realized that this man would not be taken down easily, for he wielded his sword with great finesse.

Chaninai tried to remember all he had learned from watching his father and Caleb. When the advancing soldier moved to his right and drew back his weapon, the youth shifted in the opposite direction, maintaining his distance and using his sword point to keep the man at bay.

Suddenly the soldier lunged forward, swinging his

weapon around in a broad sweep. Chaninai darted back, raising his shield just in time. But the force of the blade was so powerful that when it caught the edge of the shield, it tore it from the boy's hand. Chaninai had nothing to protect himself but his sword.

The soldier, seeming to delight in the youth's predicament, gave a broad, evil grin and moved forward, his shield and sword raised.

Chaninai looked around wildly, hoping that Micah or another Israelite would come to his aid. But in the hand-to-hand combat, the troops had fanned out, each occupied with his individual battle. There was nothing to do but face the man alone. Drawing a calming breath, Chaninai widened his stance and grasped his weapon with both hands.

His opponent's grin widened as he came in for the kill. With a flourish, he slashed the air while nodding as if to urge the Israelite youth closer.

"Help me, Lord," Chaninai whispered, his tone more fearful than reverent. "Help me this once, and I swear I'll never disobey Father again!"

Suddenly the soldier thrust, and Chaninai somehow parried the stroke, knocking the man off balance. The youth's agility surprised the big man, who backed off slightly. Without warning the Eglonite gave a thunderous shout and came at Chaninai, swinging his sword wildly.

The boy, acting entirely on instinct, met the man blow for blow. The crashing of blade against blade jarred Chaninai's entire body, yet he did not ease up—he could not ease up.

The soldier seemed infuriated at the youth's unexpected tenacity. Issuing a silent challenge, the Eglonite dropped his own shield, grasped his sword in both hands, and raised the blade high over his head. With a maddened howl, he came charging.

Chaninai was terrified by his adversary's size and strength but managed to parry the sweeping downstroke and bring his sword back around, thrusting forward and catching the man in the side.

The wound stunned the soldier, who lowered his weapon and staggered backward. At first the injury appeared to be minor, but then the life seemed to go out of the man's arms and legs, and he fell to his knees, his sword slipping from his grasp.

As the man reached toward his weapon, Chaninai stood over him, his own sword raised and ready for the kill. Yet he did not move; he was unable to finish the act.

There was a sudden rush of air, and Chaninai jumped with a start as a sword blade went sweeping past him, decapitating the wounded soldier. As the lifeless body crumpled to the ground, Chaninai shuddered and gagged. He turned, expecting to see Micah but instead stared into the dark eyes of his father's second-in-command. Quickly glancing around, the boy realized that the remaining resistance had been crushed and that the Israelites were surging through the nearby city gates.

"Never leave an opponent wounded!" Caleb shouted, grabbing the youth's shoulder and squeezing it with a fierce, angry grip. "You could get yourself or one of your comrades killed!" The general paused, and his eyes narrowed. "What's your name, soldier?" he demanded. "With what unit do you serve?"

"I . . . I am . . ." Chaninai removed his helmet, lowered his gaze, and fell silent.

Slowly Caleb's eyes widened with recognition. "What are you doing here, boy? Your father—"

"He doesn't know!" Chaninai blurted.

"You came out here on your own?" Caleb nodded toward the body of the dead soldier. "You did this yourself?"

"And that one over there." Micah's grin could be seen, although his helmet was pulled low and his face covered with ash. As he joined them, he pointed his bloody sword toward the body of the first man Chaninai had killed. "You should have seen him in action! Joshua would be proud!"

"That remains to be seen, soldier," Caleb said, glaring at Micah.

"You're not going to tell my father, are you?" Chaninai begged, his face whitening.

Caleb glowered at Chaninai for a long time. His scowl softened. "I'd say you have seen your share of action for one day. If you're so eager to serve in the field, you can see to the injured." He waved his hand toward where the wounded were being helped from the field.

"He will," Micah replied, tugging at Chaninai's arm. "I'll make certain this boy doesn't get into any more trouble today, sir."

"One other thing, Chaninai," Caleb called as Micah started to lead Chaninai back across the field.

"Yes?" Chaninai asked hesitantly.

Caleb allowed himself a slight smile. "Next time, make sure you finish off your enemy."

"Yes, sir!" Chaninai answered.

Pepi was accustomed to towering over most men. But when Binnui took Nimshi and him to meet the master armorer Hagab of Ashdod, the Child of the Lion was astonished to find the Philistine half a head taller. His gigantic hand swallowed Pepi's, and his grip was painful.

"So you're Pepi of Kerma," Hagab rambled in the Canaanite tongue. "My friend Binnui spoke well of you yesterday. He says that you work metal the way I do."

"Well," Pepi said humbly, "I have worked at the trade for some years. But I've only recently seen Philistine work. I'm impressed."

"Is that one of your own swords at your belt?" Hagab asked with a ready smile. "Let me have a look, will you?"

Pepi hesitated, then turned it over. "I'm embarrassed to have a master of the craft look at it. I made this some years ago."

The giant brandished the sword, showing that he was a powerful and quick-wristed swordsman. "This weapon has real merit, even though it's made of bronze. You have a knack for the work, my friend. The balance is good."

"Thank you."

The big man continued, "Of course, it could be much improved. It's too heavy in the blade by a hair." He reached down and picked up a piece of scrap metal and bound it to the handle. "The handle needs to be heavier by this much."

Pepi hefted the sword. "Why . . . why, that's wonderful!" The more he spoke, the more excited he became. "Nimshi, feel this, will you? Now we have met a real master of metalwork."

Nimshi held the sword and grinned like a child. He inclined his head toward Hagab. "Sir, I bow to a master. Would it be possible to see any of your own work?"

Hagab looked up at the dark clouds in the sky. "I don't know why not. It looks as though I'm not going to get any more work done today." He gave instructions to his apprentices, squatting over the forges, then said, "Come over here, will you?"

In the large, impressive shop that adjoined the forge area, his work was arrayed on a tabletop: swords, daggers, battle-axes, spear points, even a metal-and-leather shield of a curious design Pepi had never seen before. Hagab picked up a bronze sword and handed it to Pepi. "This is what we do in the brown metal. Bronze is still good for ornamental swords, but of course they're useless in a fight."

Pepi recognized his opening. "I am in need of weapons that would render bronze swords obsolete."

"Yes," Hagab responded. "Binnui explained your situation to me. As master armorer here, I carry no little influence at court."

Pepi was growing more and more excited. "Then you believe such a purchase can be arranged?"

"I have applied for an audience with the king," Hagab said. "Never have I been denied a meeting—or anything else—at court. I think your request will get serious attention." Then he saw the strange look on Pepi's face. "Is something wrong?"

As he spoke, Pepi's face contorted with pain. Holding his hands to his temples, he began weaving precariously. His eyes rolled back up into his head. His knees gave way, and only Nimshi's quick action prevented him from falling to the tile floor.

"What's wrong?" Hagab asked. "He isn't dead, is he?"

Nimshi knelt over the stricken man. "No," he said, feeling his pulse, "he's alive. He has had these before. I shouldn't have let him get excited. It's all my fault." The boy suddenly looked much younger, and fear glittered in his eyes.

"Poor fellow," Hagab sympathized. "But I don't see how you had anything to do with this attack. Here, I'll help get him up. We'll send for my magus. Perhaps he can set things to right."

"No!" Nimshi said. "I've got to get him back to Jerusalem."

"Jerusalem?" the giant said, picking up Pepi as if he had been a child and laying him on a table. "No, my dear fellow. What he needs now is rest and a physician's attention. In the meantime, you and I can go to see the king and discuss arrangements."

"I—I can't," Nimshi said, his voice rising. "I don't know anything about it. Pepi was the one authorized by King Adonizedek. I can't! I can't!"

"Now, calm down, dear boy. Everything will be all right."

VI

Again and again the armies of the five kings rallied, and again and again Joshua's troops broke through their line. Ulam, desperately improvising, assigned first one unit, then another to hold back the advancing Israelites and allow his remaining forces to retreat and deploy.

Finally the skies opened and disgorged chilling showers, then a bone-freezing downpour. Ulam's men staggered backward in the slippery mud, cursing and falling, but their pursuers fought as if the rain were a help rather than a hindrance.

As the armies of the five kings retreated over the hill toward Beth-horon, the rain turned to hail. Enormous hailstones, such as no one had ever seen before, fell on the retreating men, bruising and numbing them.

Worst of all, the day seemed to last forever. Ulam, desperate for any respite from the relentless assault from the weather and Joshua's army, looked up at the leaden skies, hoping for relief. A rumor began to spread that Joshua's witchcraft had stopped the sun in its course. When Ulam heard one of his soldiers repeating the rumor, he ran the man through with his own sword; but still the rumor persisted.

Darkness finally came as the retreat turned toward Gezer. The Israelites did not pursue them. Ulam spat on the ground and stalked back to his tent.

"Where is Adonizedek?" he demanded of his servant.

"Sir, I have a message from the five kings. They've retreated to Makkedah."

"Makkedah?" the general exploded. "What are they doing in Makkedah when they should be here with their armies?"

Adonizedek huddled, wet, cold, and miserable, in a cave some distance from the town of Makkedah, where he and the other kings had been denied refuge. The townspeople had already heard of Joshua and did not want to harbor the Israelites' enemies.

Across the pitiful fire, hatred reflected redly in the eyes of the kings of Hebron, Lachish, Eglon, and Jarmuth.

"We could have ridden to Gezer and asked for entrance there," accused Debir of Eglon. "They would have been bound by their treaty with Lachish."

The other kings muttered agreement.

"If we had ridden toward Gezer, we would have come too close to the fighting," Adonizedek replied with elaborate patience.

Hoham of Hebron kicked moodily at the stones surrounding the fire pit. "I can't forgive myself for abandoning my troops."

"What purpose would it have served if you had been killed with them?" Adonizedek asked for what seemed to be the fiftieth time. "The armies have their commanders for guidance. As kings, we have the duty to stay alive for our subjects. Look to the future! The survivors of the battle must be assembled at Jerusalem for the final confrontation. We'll destroy the Israelites there, I promise you."

Outside, the horses were blowing and stomping. The men turned and looked toward the cave's entrance for a breath-held moment. Had they been followed? Adonizedek forced himself to chuckle boldly. No one was out there, he assured himself. Who could blame the horses for being restless? No one had taken the time to wipe them down after the hard ride—that was all.

Hagab's Philistine magus was named Sakar, and he was short and pudgy. Quite obviously he was a man who liked his pleasures, and just as obviously these included a well-filled larder. He examined Pepi and then turned to the master armorer and the boy. "Who is closest to him?"

"I'm his half brother," Nimshi said.

"Does he have kin who can take care of him?" asked the doctor.

"Well, yes. But we're from Jerusalem, and I understand that Jerusalem may soon be under siege."

"This Joshua has better sense than to attack our land," Hagab said. "And if he doesn't, well, the more fool him."

"But what about Jerusalem?" Nimshi pressed. "What

should I do about my family there? Would it be better to tell them to come here?"

Hagab and Sakar exchanged worried glances. "Yes. If you have loved ones in Jerusalem, you'd do best to get them here, to the coastal region, where it's safe. And as far as this fellow's returning inland, my friend, even without the war it would be totally out of the question. The journey would be the death of him."

Nimshi bit his lip and looked down at his brother, who was tossing and turning weakly, unaware of what was going on around him. "I don't know what to do," he whined. "I've never been away from home before, and now this happens."

Hagab put a huge hand on Nimshi's shoulder. "I know a boy named Ramoth. He's a good, reliable messenger. You can hire him to send a message to your family. But Ramoth will need a horse."

"He can use mine," Nimshi offered, feeling his panic recede. "I can't tell you how grateful I am for your help."

"Think nothing of it," Hagab said gently. "A mere courtesy to a fellow tradesman. Since your brother can't be moved, I'll instruct my servant to make up a bed for him. In the morning I'll send someone to fetch Ramoth."

On the table Pepi stirred fretfully but did not awaken. Outside the rain poured steadily, with no indication that it would ever end.

Joshua looked up from his table, where a papyrus map lay, held down at each corner by stones. Although his face was drawn, his expression was alert.

"Sir, your two spies are here, Pelet and Gedor."

"Send them in."

Shemida beckoned, and the two young men entered. They started to speak together. Then Pelet said, "You tell it, Gedor."

"Sir, as ordered, we went to survey the enemy's escape route. We stumbled on something rather remarkable."

"It's the five kings," Pelet said. "They have run on their own armies."

"They've *what?*" Joshua said, staring incredulously at Pelet.

"They saw their armies losing and bolted. We spotted them on the road and followed them. They're hiding out in a cave outside Makkedah. We left three men to watch them, with orders not to allow the kings to leave."

Joshua's eyes were bright as he threw back his head and laughed. "Good work. You've earned a reward. How would you like to command the unit that captures them?"

"Sir!" both men said.

"Take fifty men and leave at dawn—earlier, if the weather breaks. If they're in the cave, cover the entrances so they can't escape. I want to find them unharmed when I arrive."

VII

Pepi awoke in a strange room, in a strange bed, to see an unfamiliar face hovering over him. "W-where am I?" he asked, trying to sit up, but strong hands forced him back. He blinked and looked up into the concerned eyes of the Philistine giant he had met the day before. "I know you. But I can't remember your name."

"I'm Hagab," the armorer said. "You're in a room off my shop. We didn't think it made any sense to move you, particularly after the magus recommended that you stay quiet."

Pepi found the air of calm about the big man very soothing. "But where's my brother and why—"

"He's gone to send a runner off to Jerusalem. We thought it best to bring your family here, particularly in view of what's happening in Jerusalem."

Again Pepi tried to sit up, and again the huge hand gently but persistently forced him back. "But our appointment with the king! I'm supposed to bring back iron to save my—"

"I don't want to alarm you, but it's too late. Adonizedek and the four kings have apparently taken the initiative and the offensive. War has begun."

"But that's insane! They were supposed to wait! Joshua is supposed to be fasting and praying." He shook his head. "How long have I been out this time?"

Hagab waved a large, reassuring hand. "Just one night. Sakar, the magus, says this condition could be very serious unless you begin to lead a less strenuous life."

Pepi let out a long breath. "I've heard it all before, but who wants to live like an invalid, afraid to take a step? I know you mean well, and I thank you." He paused for breath. "And I'm very grateful for your hospitality. Is Nimshi all right?"

"Yes, poor boy. He came quite undone when you became ill."

"I hope this isn't too much of an imposition. When my family arrives, they will arrange for me to stay with them, of course, and reimburse you for any expense."

"Do not worry, Pepi. You and your family are welcome in my home."

Pepi recognized the look in his eyes. "What did the doctor tell you?"

Hagab's voice was low and calm. "Things that are beyond our control."

"I know that there's no cure," Pepi said.

Hagab looked him in the eyes. "I think you will feel better when your family arrives."

Pepi sighed. "I'm sure you're right. Meanwhile, will you teach me everything you know about our craft? I want to learn as much as I can."

Hagab nodded. "I will ask Sakar when we can start. For now, rest."

Pepi suddenly felt at peace. "Stay with me," he implored. "Let me ask you questions. I can learn from you even before Sakar lets me near a forge."

* * *

Ramoth, the young messenger, could not resist testing the speed of Nimshi's horse. A good horseman, he had spent his early youth grooming horses for a rich man of Ashdod, only to be let go when his master died. And he had never had a horse of his own.

Along the highroad inland he put the animal through its paces until at last the horse was running at a full gallop. Delighted, Ramoth bent low over the horse's neck and crooned encouragement. "Go! Let's see how fast you are."

The road turned north, then cut sharply eastward. He sneaked a peek over his left shoulder and saw ragged soldiers spilling over the top of a hill, in full retreat. An officer stood at the crest exhorting them to hurry.

Suddenly it occurred to Ramoth that he might be in danger. When Hagab had made him buckle on both sword and dagger he thought the precautions unnecessary, but now he was glad he had them. All along the ridge, men were running, escaping from something. Ramoth slowed his mount. If there were only some way to avoid this road, which would land him in the middle of the retreating army!

But on the left was the defeated army. On his right was rough terrain, which could cause his horse to pull up lame. He would have to dismount and lead the animal, and that would make him slow and vulnerable.

Ramoth had no choice but to run the gauntlet through the line of retreating troops. He knew that it would be dangerous. The men would be angry and frustrated. They would probably want his horse, and he would have to fight to keep it.

The young messenger bent low on the mount's powerful back and kicked it hard. "Come on! Give it everything you've got!" he cried as he directed the horse down the middle of the highroad.

Ulam's horse had taken a spear in its side and fallen, trapping one of the general's legs. The horse had had to be killed, and Ulam had been limping around, cursing angrily, ever since. The men could not hear his orders over the din of their own chaotic retreat. No matter how loudly he screamed, they could not be forced back into line.

He wheeled, favoring his bad leg, and looked around, trying to find a high point on which to stand. Shading his eyes with one hand, he scanned the horizon and saw a horse galloping along the highroad toward Jerusalem.

He grabbed the arm of an archer beside him. "You! Get me that horse!"

"But sir, it's moving at a gallop!"

Ulam swore at him and yanked the bow out of his hand. "Give me that. And your damned quiver." He nocked an arrow and wondered, for a moment, if he still had his old accuracy. His eye followed the form of the rider crouched low over the animal's neck. He pulled the arrow back all the way and let it go.

After a moment he cursed himself for having missed, but then the rider's body straightened suddenly, as if someone had slipped a noose around his neck and pulled him up short.

The rider fell from the saddle, the horse broke stride, and the archer lumbered after the frightened animal, Ulam's curses following him every step of the way.

VIII

The kings' faltering armies regrouped and stood their ground before the walls of Jarmuth, managing to beat back two Israelite attacks. The two forces settled in, and the winded Israelites had a chance to catch their breath for the first time in the two days of pursuing the enemy.

Joshua called for Caleb. "I'm putting you in charge. Pelet and Gedor trapped the five kings in the caves at Makkedah. I'm going after them. While you bleed Ulam white, I'll be cutting the monsters' heads off."

For a moment a look of understanding passed between the two men. Joshua, who had been remote throughout the whole Gibeon campaign, gave Caleb a tight smile. "You've been doing a wonderful job. You're the best soldier I have ever had, maybe the best soldier this country's ever seen."

Caleb was totally taken aback. "Sir, I . . ."

"You don't have to make a speech. Just keep doing what you've been doing." He cuffed Caleb's shoulder in a gesture of rough masculine affection, then turned away, leaving Caleb standing openmouthed, trying to still the frantic beating of his heart.

After Joshua's departure, help came for the Canaanite armies from an unexpected quarter. Joshua's troops were savagely and abruptly struck from the rear by the army of Gezer.

Caleb cursed his own overconfidence. He knew he should have posted pickets. Now he ordered an elite unit of shock troops sent against the interlopers.

He joined them, fighting with the fury of two men. With one blow of his sword he hacked one Gezerite soldier's arm to the bone, and then caught another man in the face with the backswing.

"Come on!" he bellowed in the voice of a raging lion. "Drive them back to the walls of Gezer!"

Adonizedek jumped up and found his way to the cave's entrance in the pitch dark. He pressed his ear to the boulder that blocked the cave's opening.

"Someone's out there!" he said, and nearly began to cry. "We're saved!"

The other kings struggled to their feet and joined him.

"Thank the gods!" Debir croaked. "I was sure we were going to die here, with no one knowing."

"Our luck has changed," Adonizedek predicted.

The rain had stopped and the kings were preparing to

leave their hiding place when the boulder had suddenly crashed down and blocked their exit. At first the men had congratulated one another that no one had been crushed by the freak occurrence, but then they found that they could not budge the rock, even when working together. They had sat down in dismal silence, watching the fire die and waiting for the slow death they all knew they had earned.

Now, however, an erratic sheet of light began to fill the cave as unidentified saviors rocked the boulder. At last it was moved, and as the sunlight poured inside, the kings clutched their hands to their eyes.

"Come out, all of you," a voice ordered.

Adonizedek was the first man to emerge into the sunlight. "Who is your leader?" he asked. "Take me to whoever is in charge, please."

Gradually he began to see again.

Hard-eyed soldiers surrounded him. Their clothing was stained with blood; at their waists they carried swords and daggers. They wore no body armor. Their faces were cold, their expressions severe. To the rear stood Joshua.

It could be no other. His stance was powerful and ruthless, but what struck Adonizedek most vividly were his eyes. They held no pity.

"Are you Adonizedek of Jerusalem?" Joshua asked in a deep and resonant voice.

"Yes, I am," the king said. "And you must be—"

Joshua interrupted. "Your city was once dedicated to El-Shaddai, the One God. Yet His believers were driven out of the city, so that in all Jerusalem there remains no follower of His name."

"That was in my grandfather's time," Adonizedek protested. "Surely, you can't—"

"You have massacred the citizens of Gibeon for their capitulation to the Israelites," Joshua continued. He came forward, raised his hands, and gripped Adonizedek's shoulders, forcing the king to his knees, and then pressing his face into the dust. Before he could try to escape, Adonizedek felt the commander's sandal grinding into his neck. He tried to speak but could not. He tried to wriggle away in panic, but he could not move.

"So perish all who make war with Israel," Joshua commanded. "Impale them. All of them."

Harsh hands grabbed Adonizedek again and hauled him to his feet as Joshua turned and strode away.

Baufra sat on a bench in the city dungeon, lamenting his poor judgment. He should have taken Neftis and Tirzah and quietly gone to Ashdod. It would have been possible before the attack on Gibeon. His status was such that he could have passed through the gate without question. But he had feared losing the position and perquisites as chief armorer to the army of Jerusalem. And he worried about losing his money and property. How unimportant they seemed now!

But Baufra had been born poor and had never been able to believe that he would have next month's rent or, for that matter, the price of a meal two days ahead of time. So when he and Neftis had moved to Jerusalem, he had spent twenty years building up for himself and his family the security he needed so desperately. And it had been difficult—no, impossible—for him to give it all up.

And now his stubbornness had landed him in jail. How long he would be in here, there was no way of knowing. And he knew better than to throw himself on the mercy of Adonizedek.

As if in answer to his despair, he found he had a visitor. When he came blinking into the sunlit room with its barred windows he saw Tirzah standing tall and dignified in the dress of a wealthy matron of Jerusalem.

"Thank you for coming," Baufra said, clutching her hands. "I'd given up hope of being able to get a message to you."

She led him to a bench against the wall, and they sat facing each other. "I paid the guard handsomely for telling me what happened to you. And I've managed to keep the situation from Neftis."

"How is she?"

"Truth?" Tirzah asked.

"Yes, of course."

"She's unraveling. She misses you and her sons terribly, and the worry is getting to be more than she can bear."

"Maybe I can come home soon," Baufra said. "How much trouble am I in? Nobody will talk to me."

"I consulted our bankers," Tirzah replied in a businesslike tone. "Whatever bribe is necessary, I'm sure we can pay it."

"Have you heard from Pepi yet?"

"No," Tirzah answered, "but messengers may not be able to get through. I understand the five armies lost again at Beth-shemesh."

"We're going to lose this war. Pepi was right. I should have listened."

She laid a comforting hand on his. "Don't waste time and energy blaming yourself. The important thing is to get you out of here. Don't worry about Neftis. I'll take care of her."

"If the bribes don't work, you'll have to get me out of here some other way," Baufra said. "Have you hired any men?"

"Yes, bodyguards. Now, don't you worry. You're not trapped here forever."

CHAPTER EIGHT

In the Aegean

I

Khalkeus paced across the large assembly room, nervously pulling at his scruffy black beard. His dark eyes flashed with anger, and for a moment he possessed the old fire and forcefulness of the notorious Minotaur, the fearsome pirate who ravaged shipping in the Great Sea. But the moment passed, and the spark left him. Those days of adventure seemed ages ago; the wildness in him had long since been conquered, first by Demetrios's soldiers and then by his kindness. Now the Minotaur, once Demetrios's sworn enemy, was the heir to his power and the ruler of an empire greater than he had ever dreamed possible.

Khalkeus's anger was replaced with a heaviness that showed itself in his furrowed brow and stooped shoulders. He turned to Akis and Enyo, who had served as Demetrios's chief in-house administrators. When he spoke, there was no trace of bitterness in his voice—only disappointment.

"Are you certain all three ships were taken?" he asked, his tone almost pathetic. "Isn't it possible that—?"

"Our information is accurate," Enyo replied. "All three ships were seized, sir, along with their crews."

Khalkeus shook his head and dropped his big-boned frame into the ornately carved chair that dominated one end of the room. "How could they have been so careless?" he muttered to no one in particular. "If they had followed my simple instructions, none of this would have taken place."

"The captain *was* following your orders, sir," Akis noted boldly.

Khalkeus's eyes narrowed with annoyance, and he seemed ready to berate the man for his insolence. But then his shoulders sagged again.

"It was Demetrios's policy to stay clear of those waters. They have long been a haven for thieves and *pirates*." Akis emphasized the word as if accusing Khalkeus of complicity in the attack upon their vessels.

"Any pirate vessels in that region are acting independently," Khalkeus blurted, pounding his fist on the arm of the chair. "There's no excuse for three of our ships to have been caught off guard."

"What's done is done," Akis replied impatiently. "Now we'll have to accept the brigands' conditions and pay the ransom if we're to have our ships and crewmen back."

"Never!" Khalkeus raged, again pounding on the chair. "I won't pay ransom to thieves!"

Enyo ventured forward and cautiously raised his right palm. "There is no dishonor in negotiation, sir. Demetrios did not hesitate to deal with an enemy if that was the surest and least expensive path. It's said that half the profits of the Minotaur himself"—he was careful to refer to Khalkeus's former incarnation in the third person—"were accumulated at the negotiating table rather than on the high seas."

When Khalkeus frowned but did not disagree, Akis seized the opportunity to press the issue. "The important thing is to minimize our losses. And now that Theon's ship has been sighted in the harbor, you can send him as your representative—"

"Theon," Khalkeus grunted. "He's also to blame for what's happened."

"But sir, he counseled against sending our ships through those waters," Enyo objected.

"I know all about his righteous protests," Khalkeus grated. "He should have made them in private rather than sow discontent among our sailors."

Akis's color rose. "But Theon has always been most discreet. Surely you don't accuse him of—"

"It's no secret that he disagreed with me in this matter. Word of his opposition spread through the fleet before those ships set sail."

"Theon would never undermine your authority," Enyo put in. "Anyone could have spoken out of turn. Why, there were upward of a dozen advisers at that meeting when he voiced his doubts."

"Hello, Father, gentlemen," a soft voice said, and all eyes turned to see Nuhara enter the room. The two administrators bowed respectfully, their distrust of Khalkeus's daughter barely concealed.

"You honor us with your presence," Khalkeus proclaimed. Smiling, he stood and approached his daughter. "We were just discussing some business matters." He took her hand.

"You were talking about my husband's objections to that shipping route you mapped out," she said bluntly, withdrawing her hand and walking over to her father's empty chair. She turned to face the administrators. "It was wrong of Theon to oppose my father at the meeting."

"It is unfortunate that our disagreement became a public matter," Khalkeus commented as he returned to the chair and sat down. "It bred a lack of confidence in my new administration."

"And now I fear he has returned with news that can only disrupt things even more," Nuhara said, frowning.

"News? What news?"

"A messenger has just informed me that my husband will join us shortly. He brings word of a war brewing in the Aegean."

"War?" Akis said. "Among the Greeks, perhaps?"

Nuhara shrugged. "I know only that it involves the entire region—Troy, as well."

"Troy?" Enyo gasped. "Why, such a war could disrupt all our shipping lanes."

Khalkeus clenched and unclenched his fist. "There's no point worrying needlessly. I'm sure it's nothing."

"About that other matter," Enyo said, cautiously raising a paper scroll. "We must respond to these demands if we're not to lose those ships and crewmen for good."

Khalkeus glared at him. "I'm not negotiating with pirates! Are you deaf, man?"

Akis looked outraged. "This stance abandons our crews to the deadly whims of the pirates, sir. Surely you won't—"

"Would you rather wait for Theon—?" Enyo suggested.

"This doesn't concern him!" Khalkeus exploded. "Just do as I say—and don't mention this matter again."

The administrators exchanged incredulous glances, then bowed and left the room.

"You look worried," Nuhara said as soon as they were alone. She walked behind her father's chair and kneaded his shoulders. "Is this matter serious?"

"It's nothing," Khalkeus lied. "If I had been out there with those ships, nothing would have happened." He looked around the enormous, elegantly furnished room. "It's like a prison here. I just can't get used to commanding a fleet from behind a desk. I never should have—"

"You're doing fine," Nuhara said soothingly.

"None of them approve of me." He nodded in the direction that the two administrators had departed. "They all wish that Theon had been appointed Demetrios's successor."

"My husband is still a child," she replied. "He is certainly no Minotaur."

"There *is* no Minotaur," her father said brusquely.

"You're right." She moved around to face him. "But there is a Khalkeus of Gournia. And what Khalkeus needs right now are men who owe their allegiance to him and not to Demetrios."

"And where do you suggest I get these men?"

"You'll find them," she assured him. "I have complete faith in you."

"I can't run this empire alone," Khalkeus declared. "I must find my supporters among the very people I once fought against on the high seas."

"My husband among them."

"Yes. If Theon were more supportive, the rest would fall into line. But if he continues to disagree with me, there's no telling what will happen when we find ourselves confronting a major crisis."

"Such as war in the Aegean," she commented.

He nodded grimly. "If Theon weren't your husband, I'd send him away on a mission that would last a long, long time."

"I'll speak to him," she promised. "I'll convince him that he must present a united front with you."

"And if he doesn't?" Khalkeus looked up at her searchingly.

"He will."

"But if he doesn't?"

"Then I'll give you permission to send him on that extended trip," she vowed. "I will not have my husband undermining my father."

"If it came down to Theon or Khalkeus," he said, "where would you stand?"

Nuhara fell silent as she looked into her father's dark, piercing eyes. A faint smile touched her lips, and she reached out and caressed his cheek. "A husband is easily replaced," she whispered. "But a girl can have only one father." Bending over, she kissed him on the forehead.

Nuhara swung around to glare at her husband. Her lovely face was contorted with anger. "Why don't you try to help him, then?" she demanded.

Theon fought to keep his voice even. "My dear, your father knows I am available whenever he wants my advice or opinions. Apparently they are not wanted. If Demetrios had wanted me to make the decisions, he would not have chosen your father as chief administrator."

"Ha! So you've finally admitted it." Nuhara looked triumphant. "You're upset that you were passed over."

Theon walked across the room to put a conciliatory hand on his wife's shoulder, but she twisted away from his touch. "No, Nuhara, I do not envy Khalkeus his position. Had I wanted to succeed Demetrios, I had but to ask while my kinsman was still alive."

"You don't think my father is capable of managing the fleet."

"I do, truly . . . under normal circumstances." Theon knew he was on dangerous ground, but he did not care. "These are complicated times, and Demetrios could not have foreseen the possibility of war in the Aegean. Extraordinary measures must be taken immediately, to ensure that no disruptions occur in our schedule. As a newcomer to this business, Khalkeus is at a disadvantage. It's not just because he's your father, Nuhara. Any man in his position would be having a hard time of it."

"You want him to fail," she hissed. "Then you can take over the operations and throw us to the sharks."

Theon stared at his wife, openmouthed, as the last shreds of self-control blew away. "Your perception of my character is appalling. Just because your piratical father practiced murder on a daily basis doesn't mean that I—"

A knock sounded on the door.

Theon flashed one last, furious look at Nuhara, then took a breath to calm himself. "Come," he called.

Rhodope, Demetrios's widow, came in, holding a small parchment scroll. "I hope I haven't interrupted anything," she said uncomfortably, after a glance at Theon and Nuhara.

"No, of course not, my dear," Theon assured her.

Nuhara went out to the balcony without a word. "What can I do for you?"

"We have a houseguest." Rhodope handed him the scroll and nodded for him to read it.

My dear Demetrios: Greetings.

Forgive my rudeness in not asking prior permission, but you had at one time assured me that you could be counted upon as a friend in need.

I am sending my dearest daughter Iphigenia to you for what will, I hope, prove to be a short visit. My husband and his brother seem determined to go to war with Troy, and I fear for Iphigenia's safety in these uncertain times. I know, my friend, that you will care for her as if she were your own.

Your humble servant,
Clytemnestra, Queen of
Mycenae

Theon looked up. "Where is the girl?"

"In my apartments," Rhodope answered. "She is a lovely young thing, a few years younger than Nuhara. I had hoped that the two of them might . . ."

Theon nodded. "I'll send her to you. We will, of course, do our best to honor the queen's request."

II

The day was sunny and warm, and the air was fresh and balmy. Beyond the ships' dock along the municipal wharf of Aulis lay the blue strait, and beyond that, the rounded hills. Humming a tune, Phorbus squatted on the quay before his little forge fire and repaired a bent buckle on Agamemnon's war belt. He was holding the buckle up to the light when he became aware of someone standing behind him.

"You, boy, repair this," a voice said, and someone threw a sword and scabbard at his feet, narrowly missing his toes.

Phorbus turned and looked up to see two men. "I beg your pardon?" Phorbus said, offended by their rudeness. He looked from face to face as he got up slowly.

The bigger man was broad shouldered and powerful, with huge, bulging forearms and a flat belly. He was everything that an athlete should be, except . . . something about his face was too pretty. His eyes, however, were harder than any Phorbus had ever seen.

"I'm sorry," Phorbus said. "But I'm not for hire. I'm hardly more than a tinker." He looked at the sword lying at his feet. "The man you should see is my comrade Iri."

"I've heard of him," the big man said. "He's the one with the red splotch all over his face, isn't he? Well, I don't care what he looks like if he can fix my sword. Tell him to come here."

Tell him yourself, you strutting peacock, Phorbus thought. But he forced his voice to sound calm, if not polite. "He's not here just now. My lord Menelaus took him to Troy, with Odysseus and Palamedes. They're demanding the release of Helen and the restitution of the treasure Paris stole."

The big man's lip curled with disgust. "That's a dispute I'll want no part of," he said.

The smaller man stooped to retrieve the sword by Phorbus's feet. "Come, Achilles," he said. "We'll get your weapon repaired elsewhere."

Shaking his head, Phorbus watched them recede along the wharf. One of the rope vendors on the quay came over and chuckled. "So now you've met the great Achilles and his toady Patroclus," he said. "What do you think, country boy?"

Phorbus spat into the water. "Is that the great hero?"

"That's the one," the vendor confirmed. "Achilles can

fight. I'd be surprised if he couldn't beat Hector, despite the Trojan's reputation."

"Who's Hector?" Phorbus asked.

"Paris's half brother. Priam's eldest son. He's the most noble, I think, of that generation, although his sister Cassandra has the reputation of being a good girl, if somewhat odd."

The two men stood in silence, watching Achilles and Patroclus disappear from sight.

Then the vendor said, "Achilles likes three things in life: women, war, and wine. Of those, war is his favorite. If we go to battle, he's the man you'd want on your side."

Agamemnon walked through upper Aulis with King Nestor of Pylos. He missed his brother Menelaus, without whose advice he had always had a difficult time making up his mind. He therefore welcomed the company of an older, wiser head in Nestor.

They looked down at the growing fleet of ships in the harbor. "I am pleased," Agamemnon said, "at the way my fellow kings have turned out to aid my brother and me. But I wish I knew how the peace parley was doing in Troy. I don't trust my brother not to get angry and lose his temper. I hope he leaves the talking to Odysseus."

"Strange," Nestor mused, "the council's choosing Odysseus and Palamedes to go to Troy with Menelaus. Odysseus and Palamedes hate each other. It's as if the council didn't want the meeting to succeed."

Agamemnon tried to hide his grin. "I hope Odysseus talks to King Priam. He is the most diplomatic."

Nestor looked at him skeptically. "You still think a war can be avoided?"

"I doubt it. The Trojans would have to return not only Helen but the gold and other valuables stolen from Sparta; otherwise, Menelaus would lose face. And you know what a proud man he is."

"You are right: It'll be almost impossible to avoid

bloodshed." Nestor allowed himself a very small smile. "We will take Troy."

"You think we can?"

"Have you any doubts? We will outnumber them, and with Achilles among us, I can't see how they can possibly prevail." He smiled. "And then, my friend, comes the matter of what we stand to gain from capturing Troy."

Agamemnon shot him a sharp glance. "It is true that the mouth of the Hellespont is admirably situated to be a Greek colony."

"But you wonder if this can be accomplished?"

"There have been ominous portents, discouraging messages from the gods." Agamemnon sighed, moistened a finger, and held it up. "Not a trace of wind for a week. If the war were to begin this moment, we couldn't sail out of Aulis."

"And you blame the lack of wind on the gods." Nestor stroked his beard. "Well, who knows the minds of the gods or what sacrifice would bring us victory? Young man, I think you need the aid of a seer. Send runners to Thebes and see if old Calchas can be prevailed upon to come to Aulis."

"Calchas! Excellent idea! Yes, that's just what I'm going to do," Agamemnon said, clutching Nestor's hand gratefully.

III

On the first night of their voyage to Troy, Odysseus, king of Ithaca, had sought Iri out, having needed a metal-worker to repair a loose handle on his favorite sword. Iri repaired the handle, then sharpened and polished the blade, while giving Odysseus a probable history of the weapon.

Odysseus had been intrigued by Iri's story-spinning, and every night thereafter, when the ships beached,

Odysseus, who captained the third of the three ships, sought Iri out, and the two would talk. The two men shared a worldly and detached attitude toward the follies of other men, and although both were hardheaded and practical, they spoke sentimentally to each other of home and family. Odysseus had neither seen nor heard of anyone around Ithaca matching Keturah's description.

As the expedition neared Troy, Odysseus pointed out the geographical landmarks they passed.

"You've been here before?" Iri asked.

"No, but I have the sailor's habit of pumping everyone I ever speak to for information. I have a map of the known world in my head, and I'm always adding to it." He chuckled. "I even think I could find that secret island of your brother Demetrios's from what you've let slip in idle conversation."

"I'm getting loose mouthed in my old age."

Odysseus kicked off his sandals. "Don't worry. I won't tell anyone. I wish nobody knew about Ithaca."

"Especially since you've got a baby son there. Your Penelope sounds like a wonderful woman."

"She is. And smart, too. She'll have to be," he said angrily, "taking care of everything while I'm gone."

"You don't want to go on this expedition?"

"Does anyone, other than that silly fool Menelaus?"

"Without Keturah, I don't care if I live or die," Iri admitted, "and one place is as good as another for dying, I suppose. I want to keep traveling, in the hope of finding her and our child. I understand that Troy is quite a city."

"I've no interest in Troy; all I want to do is get back to Ithaca. But fools like Menelaus would never understand that, not with the woman he has to come home to." He paused and looked around, to see if anyone was within earshot before continuing. "Helen's a flighty, stupid floozy."

"What about Agamemnon's wife?" Iri asked.

"A harpy if ever I saw one. They have a beautiful daughter, though. Agamemnon and Clytemnestra dote on

Iphigenia. But there are rumors about Clytemnestra and Aegisthus."

"Aegisthus? Agamemnon's cousin? The one who betrayed his own father so Agamemnon could win Mycenae?"

"That's the one. Admirable man, wouldn't you say? But Agamemnon is not home often, and when he is, I suspect he's no better as a lover than he is at anything else. A woman who's well bedded usually doesn't have a roving eye."

"Then we're working for idiots?" Iri asked. "Do you think Menelaus should let Helen go and forget the whole thing?"

"I'd have paid Paris to take her. These two idiot brothers are going to do their damnedest to get us killed."

"I hope you're wrong and our mission is successful," Iri said, "and that we make peace with Priam and then go home. Even though I came here as a mercenary, you deserve better than this."

"I thank you for the sentiment," Odysseus said. "But it isn't in the stars, I'm afraid. Neither Menelaus nor that fool Palamedes can deal with Priam. War might have been avoided if old Nestor and I had been chosen as emissaries. But watch, I won't even be allowed to speak. Menelaus wants a war, and he'll get one. Many good men will die, but Paris and Menelaus will die happily in their beds— happy as only the stupid can be."

IV

Fishing boats working the coast had spotted the three unfamiliar vessels, and their crews had brought the news to the mainland. Runners carried the warning from the coastal fishing villages across the plain and up the hill to Troy.

By nightfall Priam of Troy knew that Greek warships were in his waters. He summoned his son Hector, and as

blood. My lord, you have no choice but to sacrifice your daughter Iphigenia."

Agamemnon stood as if turned to stone. When at last he faced Calchas, his face was drained of color. His eyes were wide but unseeing. His voice was weak. "Why Iphigenia, the darling of my heart? You must know how I love the child."

"The message to me was clear, my lord. Does the high king of Mycenae want a solution that involves no effort, no sacrifice, and no personal commitment? The gods will have the last word in this matter. Do as I say or the expedition is doomed."

"All right," he said in a choked voice. "I'll write to my wife and tell her to bring Iphigenia here."

In the morning the crews of the three ships stood on the soft sands of the beach not far from the palace of Troy, hauling lustily away on stout ropes and dragging the vessels to a point where the tide would float the boats out onto the blue waters of the bay. Iri looked around for Odysseus but could not find him. Then he was pressed into service to repair a broken chest on Palamedes' ship, and this led to other repairs, and by the time the tide had started to come in, he looked down on the shore to see Odysseus gesturing at him from the beach.

"Here," he said to one of Palamedes' sailors. "You finish this. Just do what I was doing: Scrape away on the oar handle with this knife, and there won't be any more splinters. I have to get back to my own boat."

He went down the rope into the shallow water and waded to shore. Because of the warm air and hard work Iri had stripped to his loincloth, and now the full size of his broad shoulders and huge chest could be seen.

Odysseus slapped him on the back. "By the gods, man, you look like a short version of Heracles."

"Heracles?" Iri said. "Oh, the strong man." He laughed and flexed his arms for effect. "There's an old Egyptian proverb they used to quote back when I was a kid in

Thebes, cautioning against risking the rent money on a test of strength with an armorer. And I'm strong even as armorers go." He smiled a little bitterly. "I had to be, looking the way I do. I had to be able to lick any man half again my size. I can, too—particularly since I spent a few months on a galley oar." He clapped Odysseus on the arm. "I thought you were supposed to meet with Menelaus and Palamedes today, to discuss the strategy of the parley with Priam."

Odysseus snorted. "I just came back. I had hoped you'd spare me having to tell about it."

"It went as you had feared?"

"Worse. The great king Menelaus has decided that he and Palamedes will do all the talking to Priam. They are afraid that I might be able to negotiate a settlement and keep the peace." He grunted. "Priam of Troy might not be the wisest man in the world—otherwise he would not have sent Paris off on a mission to Greece in the first place—but he is, at least, a man of valor and dignity. And that's just how he should be treated."

Iri looked at his friend. Odysseus was of average height, wiry rather than physically prepossessing. He had confessed already to being an average fighter, but Iri had the impression that Odysseus's battles would be won through sagacity and guile rather than brute strength. There was also an air of authority about him, a controlled forcefulness.

Yes, Iri thought, *you'd do much better than either Menelaus or Palamedes in a stretch of negotiation.* But was successful negotiation something Menelaus wanted? Wasn't it more likely that he wanted war? "Does that mean I'll have the pleasure of your company down at the harbor while the two great debaters are up in Troy talking us into trouble?" he asked.

"No," Odysseus said. "I've too much curiosity to stay behind. And I can't let those two idiots blather my life away. Besides, I want to peek at Hector and the others. If

I'm going to be fighting them sooner or later, I want to take their measure. I understand Hector's quite a fellow."

"The match of Achilles, do you suppose? He is all anyone wants to talk about. I've begun to wonder if he—or anyone else—could possibly live up to the expectations raised by his reputation."

Odysseus made a rude noise in his throat. "Achilles! They say he's invulnerable. They say no sword can pierce his body. Well, I wouldn't give him a second thought if I were you. I know damned good and well *you* wouldn't be afraid of him."

To Iri's ears there was a thoroughly satisfying air of appreciation in Odysseus's tone when he said this. "Thanks for the compliment," Iri said, "but I'm not afraid of anybody."

"Look, I'll be bored going up to Troy with just Menelaus and Palamedes. Would you like to come along and keep me company?"

Iri grinned. "I was hoping you'd ask."

Hector came storming down the stairs.

"Husband!" Andromache called. "What's the matter?" He charged past her, then stopped, heaved a sigh, and turned back.

"I'm sorry." His broad shoulders slumped in defeat, but he held out his arms to her. She slipped into them. "Forgive me," he said. "I've had another row with Father."

"It's all right," she said, stepping back and standing on tiptoe to kiss him. "Sit down and tell me what happened." She gestured to a servant to bring wine. "Poor Hector. Was it about Paris again?"

As he nodded she could feel his muscles tense. "I just know the idiot has done something stupid. The damned Greeks are here. Three warships are just off the coast. We've put our own patrol boats on alert, and the city guard is turned out in full force. Four emissaries, under a flag of peace, are on their way up here now." His eyes flashed. "We're not even at war! If Paris has put our lives at risk, so help me I'll—"

"Don't think about that. Let me massage your neck. Relax."

With one huge and powerful hand, he touched her face. For a heartbeat he forgot his worries, then he let out a disgusted sigh. "I can't," he said, his voice filled with bitterness.

As the thought struck him, shock showed on his face. "But what if . . .?"

"Say it," Andromache urged.

"What if Paris got into a fight with the Greeks and lost? What if he squandered our army and fleet on some ill-advised inanity?"

VI

In haste Priam assembled a council of advisers to stand beside him when the Greek emissaries came to court. Hector stood at his father's side. The four strangers were admitted to the hall, and Priam looked them over.

"Welcome to Troy. Is this my old friend Odysseus, king of Ithaca? Greetings!"

Odysseus bowed low, barely managing to hide a grin. He knew that Menelaus would not take to not being the first recognized.

"And is this the king of Sparta, Menelaus? Welcome, Menelaus, and please give my respects to the fair Helen."

Menelaus erupted in a rage.

Palamedes put a restraining hand on his arm and said, "It is indeed Menelaus of Sparta, but the king of Troy uses him ill when making insolent comments about Queen Helen!"

Priam sat up, startled. "Why should I not inquire after the health of the wife of a brother king? Who dares to accuse me of insolence?"

Palamedes raised his voice. "It is I, Palamedes, who speaks. I come with Menelaus to demand the return of his wife, Helen, stolen by your son Paris of Troy, and the restitution of the treasures Paris took when he looted the palace of Sparta in the king's absence, thereby brazenly disregarding all rules of civilized behavior!"

Angry buzzing filled the room. After a quick glance at Hector, Priam leaned forward. "Pray continue," he said in a faint voice. "What has happened?"

Palamedes was insensitive to the uncertainty in the air. "The king of Troy insults us by pretending to know nothing of his offshoot Paris's disgraceful behavior."

An audible gasp burst from the crowd. Palamedes had accused Paris of being a bastard in front of the king.

Priam's eyes were flinty, but his words were calculated to leave room for Palamedes to backtrack. "Tell me how my son and I have displeased you, Palamedes, and offended you, Menelaus."

Palamedes was in no mood for conciliation. Ignoring the angry stir around him, he pressed on. "Surely you cannot be unaware of the gravity of these charges or of the extreme danger in which you place your entire kingdom by harboring a thief and rapist under your walls."

A staccato of astonishment arose from the crowd.

Iri could not believe his ears. He shot a quick glance at Odysseus, who rolled his eyes heavenward.

But Palamedes continued: "Agamemnon, brother of the offended man and high king of mighty Mycenae, chief monarch of the Argolis and foremost among the princes of Hellas, bids me to warn you: 'Return to us the queen of Sparta, whom you have stolen from us, or all of you shall perish.'"

Angry voices were raised. Men's hands flew to their swords. Priam's guards snapped to attention, ready for action. Iri loosened his sword in the scabbard.

But Priam stood, held up both hands, and called for silence. He waited until all the voices had been quieted before speaking. His voice was deep, his impatience and anger held in check.

"I have no knowledge of the offenses my son Paris is said to have committed. We have not seen him or heard from him since the day he sailed from Troy on quite a different errand than that of which you accuse him."

Palamedes started to interrupt, but Odysseus reached over, and his fingers bit painfully into Palamedes' arm.

"The errand on which my son Paris embarked was the precise opposite of that which you accuse him. In fact, we of Troy have suffered a similar insult at the hands of the Greeks. A generation ago Heracles came to Troy and carried off my virgin sister Hesione."

Murmurs of indignation at the affront came from all corners of the room. Iri, looking at Odysseus, saw an appreciation for the king's handling of a difficult situation.

"She was given to Telamon, as a slave," Priam continued. "We are indebted to the goodwill and decency of Telamon, who instead of raping my sister or keeping her as his concubine, chose to make her his honorable wife and treat her with the dignity befitting the daughter of a king.

"But there remains the dishonesty of Heracles and the dishonor done our nation. And mind you, Menelaus of Sparta, we have sent envoy after envoy to you, demanding the return of my sister. And one by one they have returned empty-handed, bearing neither my sister nor apologies."

Menelaus bristled at his words, but Odysseus restrained him, too.

Priam continued, "I sent Paris to you to demand the return of my sister, so that I could enjoy her company in my advancing age. What he has done in the way of carrying out my command—or of disobeying it, as the case may be—I cannot say. But one thing I am certain of: I have not seen him since I sent him off."

Now, little by little, his voice began to rise. "If my son has wronged you and brought with him a married woman he has abducted, she will be restored to you. And so shall any other chattels that belong to you. But there is a condition that must be met." His voice became as hard as stone. "Unless you, who have insulted me, my city, and my people with your boorish behavior, restore to me my sister, you shall have nothing. Nothing but the contempt and ill will of King Priam of Troy!"

Everyone recognized this as a challenge to war. Iri could not help but think that if Odysseus had been allowed to speak, the angry words would have been smoothed over.

Instead, Menelaus nudged Palamedes, who spoke in a voice even more arrogant. "We are not responsible for what Heracles did in the days of our fathers, so we can make no such bargain. Your son is your responsibility. Whatever his original mission was is now irrelevant, as is your maudlin story about your sister, who, when last I saw her, was a happily married matron with children of her own. She is very unlikely to have an interest in returning to Troy, whatever your own selfish wishes in the matter."

Priam's eyes flashed, but he remained silent as Palamedes went on. "Helen, however, was carried off by your own son against her wishes. If you do not restore her once Paris has delivered her into your hands, you will find the entire world of the Great Sea against you, including your sister's own son, Prince Ajax, who has sworn to join us in crushing you."

At the mention of Ajax, Priam paled, but Palamedes plowed on, even more aggressive and arrogant. "Give thanks to the gods, O King, for their having delayed the return of the thieving Paris. It gives you time to make the proper decision. But make no mistake—the proper decision is the only decision: to restore Helen and the treasures of Sparta. Any other response will mean your death and the death of every man in this room, as well as the destruction of Troy."

VII

His words caused a furor among the Trojans. The guards moved to bar the doors, and the nobles on the dais hurried to surround Priam. Several men drew their swords, a reinforcement of guards rushed in, and the four Greek visitors found themselves staring at two rows of bowmen and bronze-tipped arrows pointing directly at their hearts.

Iri reached for his own weapon but then caught a glimpse of Odysseus, standing with his brawny arms crossed over his chest, and dropped his hand.

In the unmistakable voice of command Priam spoke. "Order! Order in my house!"

The commotion ceased immediately, the bowmen relaxed, and everyone turned to face King Priam.

The ruler held up his hands. "We have heard demands of the visitors from Greece. They have trespassed against the very rules of hospitality that they accuse my son Paris of breaking. Now they have threatened our peace and our lives."

Angry shouts of assent exploded from the back of the room.

Again Priam held up his hands. "Nevertheless, it is my policy to answer harsh words with soft ones. Until I have heard Paris's side of this controversy, I will render no judgment."

Scattered groans of disappointment arose.

Priam waved for silence. "It ill behooves a man," he continued, "to answer the boorish behavior of an ill-mannered child with childish behavior. Better that the child be given a lesson in adult manners." He looked pointedly not at Palamedes, but at Menelaus. "Therefore, I ask everyone to pledge that they will honor the laws regarding hospitality while these strangers are on our soil and will let them go in peace."

The nobleman Antenor stepped forward. "My king, I

honor your request and beg leave of you to shelter these men at my own home until the proper tide runs tomorrow and they can again set sail for their homelands."

Priam smiled his approval of his cool-headed courtier. "They shall be in your care. Woe to the man who raises a hand against them so long as they keep the peace of Troy during their brief stay.

"Let no man mistake my response for cowardice," Priam said. "If I find Paris's actions justified, I will answer these insults and threats with words that will sting and with actions that will cut deeply. Let all know that the king of Troy, having once made his decision, will not waver until the last drop of blood has been shed. Let any who bring war to our shores beware! The man who greets us in peace shall be greeted in peace, but the man who comes to us bearing arms will fertilize the fields on which he falls. He will not survive the day he raises a sword against us, and his women and children shall weep for him in poverty and ashes."

He looked around, daring anyone to object; then, his head high, he withdrew.

Menelaus accepted Antenor's offer of an armed escort, but chose to stay aboard his ship. They marched out of the palace of Troy in sullen silence and under heavy guard. No one spoke all the way to the beach, where the escort took leave of them.

"Are you satisfied?" Odysseus asked Menelaus as soon as the guards were out of earshot. "You've killed us all, you damned fool, by letting this ass Palamedes bray unrestrained."

Palamedes started to retort, but seeing the dangerous look on Odysseus's face, he held his tongue.

"Palamedes did exactly what I wanted him to do," Menelaus said happily. "Only a war with Troy can wipe out my dishonor. Besides, we're going to take Troy and dominate shipping throughout the whole eastern Aegean."

Odysseus looked at him with loathing. "You're mad, Menelaus."

The king of Sparta had an amused look, as if he thought Odysseus hopelessly naive.

This made Odysseus more angry. "You and your territorial ambitions! You and Agamemnon can barely subdue your wives, much less keep the peace in the wretched little towns that pay you tribute. Yet you dream of empires."

Menelaus's patronizing smile broadened. "Empty words, my friend. You're bound by oath to do as I say. You're bound by your word of honor to accompany me in my war. You can't get out of it—not without risking the esteem in which others hold you and the esteem in which you hold yourself." He slung an arm around Iri's shoulders. "As your friend Iri here has reported—and Priam has confirmed—the fleet Paris brought to the isles was a large one."

Odysseus's eyes narrowed with suspicion. "I have this uncomfortable feeling I know where this is leading."

"No doubt you do. Our fleet is nearby at Aulis, ready to sail. Priam is obviously telling the truth when he says that he has no idea where Paris is. It's obvious that Paris is hiding out as long as he can, fearful of facing his father's wrath.

"If we can mobilize our whole fleet and get back here before Paris returns, we can strike Troy a blow from which she'll never recover."

In Priam's private apartments Hector was pacing, pounding one fist against the other. "I don't know what I'm angrier about," he fumed. "Hearing him speak to you that way, or knowing that he's right and that Paris has done exactly what they're accusing him of." His fists squeezed the life out of an imaginary neck. "I could kill both of them."

"You may get your chance to kill Palamedes," Priam said. "There's going to be a war right here on the plain

before our city. And while I can understand your anger at
Paris, there's no undoing the deed, if indeed it was done."

"I'll kill him, so help me, if he brings that foreign slut
back here. Menelaus is probably assembling an army already, and preparing a fleet for a rapid return."

"You won't touch Paris," his father said calmly, "because we'll need every fighter we can lay our hands on.
Menelaus and Agamemnon were behind every word
Palamedes spoke. They wouldn't have put him up to such
accusations—virtually a declaration of war!—if they hadn't
already set in motion their military machinery."

"Curse Paris—"

"Calm down," his father advised. "What will happen
will happen. Prophets for generations have foretold this;
it's not merely Cassandra and her unintelligible prognosti-
cations."

Hector glared at him. "But what if Paris isn't—"

"Of our line? Of course he is. If anything, this proves
it." He shook his head. "How I wish Paris would return.
Not only does he have our army and our fleet, but he has
Cassandra. I should never have sent her with him. I need
her. Her own predictions cut deeper than any other,
though she can't always make clear sense of them. I miss
her. I want her home."

Hector studied his father. If only he would be angry!
If only his eyes would blaze! If only the old Priam were
back standing in front of him, proud, powerful, and de-
fiant!

VIII

The servant came back to Aulis from Troy empty-
handed and alone. A league outside the town, his horse
had pulled up lame, and the man had had to walk the rest
of the way. When he hobbled up the plank to Agamemnon's
ship, he was tired and footsore.

Agamemnon saw defeat in his face. "You couldn't intercept my messenger?"

"No, sir," the servant replied. "I was counting on catching him along the long road that spans the Isthmus of Corinth, but he took a ship at Eleusis instead. As I pulled up at the city docks I could see it heading out to sea, halfway to Salamis."

Agamemnon's balled fist smashed into the rail before him. "Curse the luck! He's going to deliver my letter to Clytemnestra tomorrow, and there's not a thing we can do about it."

"Sir, the fault is mine. If I'd anticipated his taking a ship—"

"How could you have known? Ordinarily a man who goes by land continues by land. It's not your fault, it's mine. I have done a foolish and wicked thing, and the gods are punishing me."

"Sir, if there's anything I can do—"

"What could you do? No more than I can do, which is to wish the letter had never been written. This is going to end my relationship with my wife and with Iphigenia, even if I don't go through with it." He closed his eyes and shook his head. "How could I even have considered such a thing?"

Nestor found him there, sitting morosely by the rail. "Agamemnon, are you asleep?" He looked at the Mycenean's face. "Why such a dark look? Everything is going well. Another six boats full of strapping young soldiers joined our ranks today."

Agamemnon stood up, threw his shoulders back, and tried to look like a man shaking off his woes. "Nestor, I've been a wretched fool."

"And so have we all," the old man consoled. "But somehow the gods forgive us. What have you done, my friend?"

Agamemnon took a long, deep breath. "I did as you suggested and called in Calchas."

"But that was a wise decision, not a stupid one."

"He said that the goddess can only be propitiated by the sacrifice of a virgin girl, of my own blood—my daughter Iphigenia."

The peaceful look on Nestor's old face gave way to horror. "Of course you haven't agreed to such a brutal action. Who could kill a lovely child like Iphigenia?"

"I agonized for a night and a day. And in the end, not having slept for a couple of days, I wrote a letter to Clytemnestra, asking her to bring the child here from Demetrios's island," Agamemnon said in a voice that throbbed with pain.

"You didn't!"

"I must have been mad. I . . . I concocted an idiotic story about betrothing the girl to Achilles."

"Achilles? What does he have to say about all this?"

"He hasn't heard about it yet. I must have been mad. I sent a runner with the letter, telling him to take it to Mycenae to my wife."

"And what is going to happen when she arrives here?"

"I'm going to tell her the betrothal is off. I'll claim I misunderstood Achilles, then I'll send her home." He winced. "We'll have a terrible fight over it, of course, but . . ."

"What happens then? The army is ready to sail for Troy, and no propitiatory gesture has been made to the gods to ensure our success. That means that we sail under a cloud of displeasure and that every man stands an excellent chance of being killed."

Agamemnon shook his head as if trying to rid it of the truth. "I know. Either I murder my dearest child, or I risk killing every man on our enterprise, myself included."

"A terrible choice. Is there no other?"

Agamemnon stared at him. "Name one, and you will make a friend for life."

Nestor pondered, then brightened. "It is very simple. Call the herald and have him announce that Agamemnon of Mycenae resigns his command over the Greek troops."

He smiled smugly. "It is but a short step from there to the dismissal of all these good people. Then they can all go back to their homes in happiness, having fulfilled the vow they made to come to the aid of Helen's husband."

Agamemnon had listened with growing interest, but now his face dropped. "But how can I speak for Menelaus? Only he can release the men from their vow."

Nestor raised a brow. "That's true. But if you resign as commander of the expedition and do not accompany the Greeks to Troy—"

"But I, too, made the vow, and only Menelaus can release me from it."

"But you can still resign as commander."

Agamemnon thought for a moment. "I could, and I can still send a fast ship to Mycenae with a message to Clytemnestra, telling her to stay home and leave Iphigenia where she is—that I made a mistake. But I'll delay my resignation until Menelaus returns. Perhaps I can talk him out of continuing with the expedition. When he hears it's doomed, he's sure to agree. Then we can dismiss the troops and all go home. Yes! Yes, I'll do it."

After much deliberation and many false starts, Agamemnon finally finished the letter. "Astrophel!" he called out to his servant. "Astrophel, come here!"

"Yes, sir?"

"Here. Find a reliable runner and tell him to take a fast boat to Mycenae. There's a gold piece or two in it if he can get this letter to my wife by tomorrow night."

"Yes, sir," said the boy. "I'll get to it instantly."

Astrophel hurried down the plank, not toward where the messengers gathered on the dock but in the direction of the tent of Diomedes of Argos. He glanced around to make certain no one was watching, then slipped inside the tent.

Diomedes greeted him enthusiastically. "Good lad. What have you got for me this time?"

Astrophel handed over the letter. "He seemed desperate to get it into his wife's hands as soon as possible. He offered two gold pieces to the runner who could get it to her by tomorrow night."

Diomedes read the letter. "I don't wonder. You've done well, boy. This makes up for your letting the first letter get out without my reading it." He smiled triumphantly. "There'll be a bonus in this for both of us when Menelaus returns."

"Thank you, sir. But, sir, don't you want me to find a runner and send this?"

"No, I'll keep it for Menelaus to see. This is exactly what he warned me about. He wants to make sure nothing happens that will jeopardize his expedition. And that's precisely what would have happened if we had let this letter get through." He clapped the boy on the shoulder. "Return to Agamemnon and tell him that the matter has been attended to. That way you're not lying to him. If he ever finds out, tell him I accosted you and took the letter. Then his brother will take the blame."

Finally Cassandra had goaded Paris into returning to Troy. Now she stood with Keturah at the railing of Paris's flagship, holding the girl by the arm as the sail filled and the vessel slowly began to move out to sea.

"Oh, Keturah!" Cassandra said. "You're going to love Troy."

The blind girl tried to smile. Everyone said war was going to come to Troy. Had Cassandra forgotten her own predictions already? But perhaps her new mistress couldn't face the truth.

"I'm Priam's favorite," Cassandra continued, "after Hector, that is. But Father spoils me, and he never spoils Hector. In fact, he's rather harsh on Hector, considering how much Hector loves him. He'll be pleased that I've bought myself a companion. We're going to have such a wonderful time together."

How could anything ever be wonderful again without Iri? Keturah wondered. "Yes, my lady. It's going to be wonderful. When we're in Troy, will you help me find my husband?"

"Oh, Keturah, you can't guess how lonely I shall be without you. But a promise is a promise. You remind me, and I'll help you . . . although I can't imagine that he'd have come all the way to Troy from Canaan."

"But that's what has happened to me," Keturah ventured, hoping she was not being rude. Cassandra had been good to her and little Talus, but Keturah would not let her renege on her promise. "A man with a birthmark across his face. You will ask?"

"Yes, Keturah. I will. I promised, didn't I?"

Cassandra sounded testy.

CHAPTER NINE

Canaan

I

Tirzah walked quietly into the room and watched Pepi's mother. Neftis sat on a bench within a circle of sunlight pouring in from the window. The light was so intense, it seemed to bleach the woman into a single, colorless brightness.

"Here, now, Mother," Tirzah said with forced cheer, setting a tray of food on the table. "Aren't you awfully warm?"

"No, dear, it feels good." Neftis lifted her face toward the window.

"I've brought you breakfast."

"Thank you, dear. Have Micah and Nimshi eaten?"

Tirzah was brought up short. "I . . . I'm sure they have."

"And Pepi and Baufra? Have they had breakfast?"

"Yes, Mother. Of course." She gently took Neftis's elbow and guided her toward the table.

"Good. I am so grateful you have come here to stay with me. As one gets older, it becomes tiring to take care

197

of a large family. And men can be such big eaters, you know."

"Yes, I know. You eat now."

Tirzah studied Neftis's face as the woman tore a piece of flatbread in half and stuck a piece in her mouth. An impenetrable calm had descended upon Pepi's mother a few days before. One moment, she was fine; the next, without warning, she wore an expression of beatific calm and had no idea what was going on in her life.

Tirzah was left in a turmoil. She did not know whether she should try to break through to the woman by assaulting her with the facts about her family and the inevitability of Joshua's invasion, or leave her in peaceful madness. She finally decided to allow Neftis her fantasies; the woman had obviously needed to wrap herself in them. When Baufra was released from prison, he could deal with his wife in his own way.

The young woman thought of her own husband. *Why haven't I heard from Pepi?* she agonized. Glancing at Neftis, who was happily devouring breakfast, Tirzah was surprised to find herself envying the woman's oblivion.

II

After the execution of the five kings outside Makkedah, Joshua's army marched southeast to Libnah, taking the city after a brief but bloody battle. To the south, Lachish should have fallen without a fight, but another attack by King Horam of Gezer delayed the army's advance by a day. Even conquering Lachish did not slake the army's thirst for battle, so the Israelites pressed southward, destroying the undefended Eglon on the same afternoon. Joshua's goal, gaining control of the hill country south of Jerusalem and the strategic defiles from the lowlands into the hills, was nearly within his grasp.

Now the commander proposed to march eastward

toward Hebron. But Shemida was worried. "He looks like a half-starved lion, sir," he told Caleb. "There's still strength in Joshua, but it's strength of the mind. His body is . . ."

"I know," Caleb said. "We have to face the truth about the old man." He snorted. " 'The old man!' He's not really that old, you know. But I look in his face now, and . . ." He ran his hand through his own thinning hair. "If I'd had the full responsibility on my back, would I look as Joshua looks now? I thank Yahweh that I've been spared. There's a good twenty years in me yet, with any luck. But Joshua? I just don't know."

"Is there any way we can talk him into taking it easy?" Shemida asked. "The back of the southern defense has been broken. His subordinates could easily handle everything that remains to be done."

Caleb looked Shemida in the eyes. "Meaning that minor work could well be left to the likes of me, eh?"

"Come now, sir," Shemida said, carefully avoiding the trap. "You know I had no such meaning in mind. The taking of Hebron—whose army we've already destroyed in battle—and such outposts as Kadesh . . . your captains or even your lieutenants could handle this. Battles remain— big ones, if Canaan is to be retaken. You and my master are going to have your hands full taking the north country around Chinnereth, and both of you need a rest now."

Mollified, Caleb studied him. "I was thinking of suggesting that half the army remain here, in training, or occupy itself with the taking of Jerusalem. The other half could easily subdue Hebron and Kadesh, as well as mopping up the tribes on the edge of the Negev. I could use some time to whip the army back into shape. They think that if they fight well, that's all that's required. They're lax and sloppy looking. I'd be ashamed to march them in triumph through the gates of Jerusalem right now."

Shemida nodded. "And if I might dare make an observation, sir, there may be more to the problem. I believe there's a scandal brewing, if you'll pardon my saying so."

Caleb's eyes flashed. "Out with it."

"Very well, sir. You know what Joshua thinks about graven images, heathen representations of their deities."

"Indeed I do."

"Sir, if you were to hold a surprise inspection, not just of the men but of their gear—"

"Do you mean to tell me the men are back to collecting idols, after I've lectured them?"

"Just hold an inspection, sir, with no warning. But do it when Joshua's otherwise occupied."

Caleb's sharp eyes narrowed. "You're a loyal soldier, Shemida. You're not going to allow anything to upset your master, are you?"

"I hope not, sir. That's why I took the liberty of talking to Eleazar, the high priest, and suggesting that he ride out with my master today to look over the Shephelah and seek the will of Yahweh."

"While you and I inspect the troops?"

Shemida bowed slightly. "I am at your disposal, sir. Anything to save my master anguish and ensure that things continue as they are."

"I'm waiting," Joshua said to Eleazar. "Why, all of a sudden, do you want to go for a ride in the hills?"

Eleazar's face was guileless. "I merely suggested a ride because there is something I wanted you to think about."

The ostlers helped them mount their chargers. Eleazar needed more help than Joshua did, but he couldn't help notice the premature stiffness in Joshua's joints, which slowed his movement. As they rode out of the encampment, a handpicked guard followed at a discreet distance.

"Now," Joshua said, "what is this secret matter you wish me to consider?"

"The beauty of the land," Eleazar replied. "I know your mind is on conquest—as it should be, my friend— but is there a divine commandment that forbids you to enjoy the beauty of the land that you are here to conquer?"

Joshua chuckled. "Would it surprise you to know that I often think what it will be like when the twelve tribes are settled across the land, enjoying their heritage in peace?"

Their path led them up a long slope, and from the top they could look down into a green valley. Eleazar pointed at a distant hill. "Across that hill there is a valley where the Oaks of Mamre still stand. That's where Abraham struck a bargain with the Canaanites to band together to fight the foreign invaders."

"The Oaks of Mamre?" Joshua said, surprised. "I'd always thought they'd have been gone by now, that someone would have cut them down."

"No. They're as sacred to the locals as they are to us."

"I'd like to see them." Joshua studied Eleazar for a moment. "Come out with it, old friend. What is it that you're trying to tell me?"

Eleazar sighed. "I can have no secrets from you. I was thinking of Hebron and of Jerusalem."

Joshua's face darkened. "Jerusalem . . . The thought of destroying it preys on my own mind as well. As for Hebron, I will sack it without a twinge of conscience. The Lord has commanded me to raze it and to vanquish its people. I will obey His word."

"But Jerusalem . . . ?"

The two men rode in silence as their horses slowly walked along the ridge of the hills. At last Joshua reined in his mount. " 'Jerusalem the Golden,' " he said. "The first city we have ever been able to find that was dedicated to the worship of Yahweh."

Eleazar nodded. "It seems to me that if God has not specifically commanded the destruction of Jerusalem, it might be spared, for all the apostasy of its present inhabitants."

Joshua looked down into the valley at an oasis, at the bottom of the slope. "That would be Mamre's Oaks, I suppose." For a long while he was silent. Finally he said,

"I have not been told to spare Jerusalem. So I have been avoiding it, waiting for a sign."

"God has not told you to spare it," Eleazar said. "But has He told you to destroy it? Does not His very silence on the matter say something?"

"It does," Joshua said. "But what? Help me, Eleazar. Help me pray for guidance."

The days of rest gave Shemida the chance he wanted. With his usual difficulty he mounted up and, disdaining bodyguards, rode out into the hills.

After an hour's ride he came to the village, far from the war and on the fringe of the Philistines' domain, where Tamar was staying with her grandmother's people. She had told her parents she wanted to visit her grandmother because the old woman was ill, but neither she nor Shemida had had any doubt of the real reason for her visit.

Shemida was not sure what was happening to him. He had loved girls before—and left them. He had had liaisons with women both of his own people and of the Canaanite tribes. But never before had one woman moved his heart as Tamar did.

Why was she the one? She seemed genuinely interested in learning the Law and hearing about Yahweh. She had great physical beauty, but so had the girl in Bashan and the girl near Jericho and the girl who . . .

But it was more than that. She had total trust in him, and her trust put him on his honor. His conscience told him that he had two choices: Either he could walk away and have nothing more to do with her, or he could do as his heart prompted. He would reward her trust by being faithful and worthy, loving her and making her his forever.

The idea filled him with apprehension. He had never allied himself totally to anyone before he had given his loyalty to Joshua. And now he had to divide that loyalty between his master and Tamar. Could he do that without cheating everyone?

He worried about Joshua. He worried about whether Joshua would make it through this war that was draining him dry. He worried about whether Joshua's strength would desert him in the middle of a battle, leaving him at the mercy of a maddened enemy.

But he also worried about Tamar. So far the war had left her unhurt, but that could not last forever. There was danger from enemy soldiers moving into the area and taking what they needed or wanted—housing, food, animals, women—and his own people would become a menace the moment Joshua died and Caleb took over. Caleb had no trace of Joshua's compassion, and he seemed to have no idea how dangerous it would be to invade Philistine protectorates.

The only solution was to put her under his own protection, as an officer of the army of Israel. And the only way to do this definitively was to . . .

All at once he came over the top of the hill and could look down into the little valley where she lived. He fancied he could even see her grandmother's house, nestled among the olive trees.

Yes! There it was, and there she was, coming back from the well with a jug of water balanced on her slim shoulder. His heart immediately started beating furiously, and he almost turned around, afraid.

But the impulse that drew him toward her was stronger. And he found himself grinning like an idiot as he spurred his horse forward. The animal's hooves kicked up dirt beyond him, and it picked up speed. Down in the valley he could see her look up and wave. Now he knew what he was going to do. No petty fears could stop him. It was the one thing in the world that he was absolutely sure he wanted. He was going to give her his heart forever.

III

Pepi and his brother had taken a room in Binnui's inn in Ashdod. Pepi was applying himself to his lessons in Philistine methods of metalworking as if he were a nine-year-old trying to outdistance the other children. His eyes sparkled with excitement, and he couldn't wait to get to work. Hagab took him on as an apprentice, and Pepi was doing the donkeywork of the forge, as if he were an absolute beginner—pumping the bellows, handing Hagab tools—and he was all too obviously radiantly happy to do so. The work of making iron the way the Philistines did was fascinating. He had not suffered an attack since Hagab began teaching him the secrets of ironworking, and he was eagerly awaiting the arrival of his mother and wife in Ashdod.

Nimshi was also working at the forges, but his interest in the Philistine techniques was overshadowed by his anxiety over his family's safety.

One night when Pepi, exhausted by the hard work of the day, had slipped off to sleep just after dinner, a messenger came for Nimshi from the household of the master armorer. Nimshi followed the man to Hagab's beautiful villa, where Binnui, who had introduced the brothers to the armorer, was also in attendance.

Hagab, huge, gentle, and patient, broke the news to him: "They've found the body of little Ramoth. He never got to Jerusalem with the message for your family to join you and Pepi here."

"I talked to a merchant from Jerusalem," Binnui said. "He bribed someone to let him out. He escaped the city at night with only what he and his family could carry. He said he was frightened to death that they might run into one of Joshua's patrols on the road."

"What did he tell you of the situation in Jerusalem?" Nimshi asked, the color drained from his face.

"Only that King Adonizedek is dead and the army destroyed. The trader thought there might be a revolt very soon. Some vestige of government still exists, and the city guards won't let anyone leave. The citizens are very close to panic." He paused. "It might have already happened."

"What I can't understand," Hagab said, "is Joshua's delay in attacking the city. How has Jerusalem escaped the fate of the other cities in the region? Does he plan to let it stand? If so, it's the closest thing we've seen to compassion in the man."

"All I can say is that he must have gotten a sign from his God," Nimshi said. "That's all that ever alters his iron determination. Pepi told me that Jerusalem was once sacred to the same God the Israelites worship. There may be some shrines in Jerusalem that Joshua doesn't want to disturb."

Binnui frowned. "I wouldn't count on that saving your family for long. We've got to do something about getting them out."

Nimshi looked at him in surprise. "You don't have to get involved. It isn't your fight."

Binnui smiled. "I'm your friend, remember?"

Tirzah hurried through the narrow, moonlit streets of Jerusalem. Her heart was pounding, and she could smell the acrid scent of her own tension. Her hand repeatedly went to the purse of gold coins concealed under her cape. No matter how many times she checked for the pouch and found it, she could not feel at ease.

At last she reached the prison where Baufra was held. She scurried across the courtyard to a great wooden side door to the prison and hid within the shadows, then knocked low. Her only answer was the increased rhythm of her heartbeat. Tirzah drew a breath and knocked again, not so tentatively this time.

The door swung open, and a tall, gangly man with greasy skin and hair slid outside. He raised his eyebrows

206 THE PROMISED LAND

expectantly. Tirzah reached inside her cloak, and his hand snaked out to grab her wrist. He found the pouch, and before he withdrew it, he rubbed the back of his hand against her breast and smiled nastily.

She cringed, then stiffened, afraid to object. Then the man disappeared inside, and the prison door closed. She waited. Long minutes passed, and Tirzah began to wonder if she had been played for a fool. She was too frightened to rap on the door but too desperate to leave.

Suddenly the door reopened, and Baufra was thrust outside, nearly knocking her over. Off balance, they staggered into the moonlight, then righted themselves and walked quickly, wordlessly, toward home.

Tirzah and Baufra did not talk until they were in the beautiful garden of his house. First he had gone to check on Neftis, who was sleeping soundly, and then he had washed and changed his clothes.

"Thank you for arranging my release, my dear," Baufra said when he joined her.

She shrugged away his thanks.

"Is there any chance we'll be able to get away?"

Tirzah's beautiful face was somber in the moonlight. "Not legally, no. But I expect a riot to erupt at the city gate any day. There was a confrontation between some merchants and the city guard this afternoon, and the guardsmen had a hard time quelling the disturbance. Why they won't open the gates, I don't know. Do they think the king is going to come back?"

Baufra snorted.

"This morning I talked with travelers who've seen Adonizedek's head on a pole by the side of the road," she told him.

Baufra looked crestfallen. "Then it's true. The army is destroyed. We're without defenses." He paused. "We're dead."

"Unless we can figure out a way to get out of here."

"What happened to Pepi?"

"I don't know," Tirzah answered. "We should have heard from him by now."

Seeing the look of fear on her face, he took her hand and held it between his own two hands. "Most probably he sent us a message that did not get through. Such things happen these days."

"Yes," she said, forcing her voice to sound calm. "I may just be worrying over nothing. He could be waiting for us with Nimshi in Ashdod."

"In which case it's up to us to pick up and go. I *think* I can bribe our way through the gate. It'll take all the cash I can lay my hands on, but it will be worth it." He looked around him at the great spreading house, the tall trees, and the reflecting pool. He sighed. "Ah, Tirzah, you have no idea how hard it will be to leave this place. I spent so much of my life poor."

"I do understand. It doesn't matter how many times Pepi tells me he's rich, I can never make myself believe it."

"When I think of leaving things behind, possessions I'll never see again, belongings that I know Joshua will put to the torch . . ."

"And yet," she said, "if we stay, we'll all die, and Joshua will still destroy the city."

He shook his head. "The waste. The terrible waste. Why does he do it? Is he such a bloodthirsty man that he can't leave us in peace? Why does his conquest of our land have to mean that he kills everyone?"

"Pepi says that Joshua has sacrificed everything in his own life, too." Her voice was sad. "I suppose we can't change it. We can only try to escape it."

IV

Stripped and given thirty lashes, the soldiers were staked out in the sun and left to the ants and scorpions. At the end of the day, they were brought before Caleb.

His eyes were full of contempt and loathing as he glared at them. "What have you scum to say for yourselves?" he demanded.

None of the twenty offenders would meet his eyes. "Speak up. Anyone who doesn't will find himself repeating the day's experience. Speak up, curse you."

One of the men in the front row cleared his throat and spoke. "Sir . . . my name is Sheshan. I meant no harm, sir, by picking up the golden idol when we took Lachish—nothing in the way of sacrilege. But it was gold, and I thought it would make a nice gift for my wife and daughters."

Caleb's eyes settled on an unfamiliar face, a young face. He took a few steps forward to look more closely. This was clearly a boy not old enough to be in the army, and yet here he was, having suffered the punishment with soldiers twice his age.

"Who are you?" Caleb demanded.

"Micah of Jerusalem, sir," the boy responded.

"Jerusalem?" Caleb exploded. "What are you doing here?"

"I . . . er, am not a follower of your faith and had in my belongings a statue of my own religion."

"No, curse you! What are you doing *here*, in camp?"

"I came here to find my brother—well, my half brother, sir. But he wasn't here, and Joshua let me stay. I had been staying with his family, but then Chaninai and I decided we were old enough to be in the tents with the other soldiers, so we moved out, and then—"

Caleb shook his head in disgust. "What am I running, an army for snot-nosed babies? Get out of here. I don't want to see your face again."

The boy did not wait to be told once more.

"Jerusalem!" Caleb muttered in disbelief, then turned to the next man. "Aren't you Ozni, the fellow Joshua caught beating up Shemida?"

The big man hung his head. "Sir," he said, "you'd

think someone would have forgotten about that after all this time."

"One might if he were ever given the chance. But here you are, back in trouble again. What have you got to say for yourself?"

The ordeal in the hot sun had not yet broken Ozni's spirit. "Sir," he said in a surly voice, "I can't see what's wrong with wanting to make a little money out of all this conquering and burning. If I could send money back to my family in Gilgal, maybe they wouldn't be having such a hard time of it."

"Is that all?" Caleb demanded. "Then let me explain something. When we're done with all the fighting, when we've finished dividing the land among the tribes, there'll be no poverty. Every man will have a fair living. No one will suffer deprivation as we've suffered since the days of Jacob."

Ozni frowned. "But sir, while we're waiting for that glorious day, why should our wives and children go around in rags because a little hunk of gold represents one of these heathen gods?"

"Damn your eyes! Have you forgotten what happened to Achan?"

He looked from face to face and saw that his words had struck home. "As punishment for looting, Achan and his entire family were stoned to death. What if, during the next battle we fight, God chooses to punish your actions by making us lose? How am I to answer to Joshua then? How am I to answer to God?"

When there was no answer, Caleb studied the men in front of him with contempt. "Go now. But carry this thought with you: The next one who disobeys the rule against looting or has anything whatsoever to do with the idols of the heathen will take a long, long time dying."

The men took no time in disappearing, but Caleb lingered before his tent pondering the problem. The problem wasn't looting. The real offense was a more serious one: The Israelites were beginning to drift away from the faith.

Of us all, Moses has been the only one who has ever been able to rule them—and neither Joshua nor I is any Moses, he thought.

Moses had ruled them by love, and they had followed him out of deep respect for the divine authority he represented. But even in Moses' day they had drifted and wandered and had had to be disciplined.

All around Caleb saw signs of laxness, a gradual relaxation of the vigilance against apostasy that Moses had insisted upon. He found himself not just wondering what would happen when Joshua died and the leadership of the Israelites finally passed into his own hands, but *knowing* what would happen.

They would start intermixing. There was already an infidel living among them, and with Joshua's permission! They would start intermarrying. Even Shemida was said to be involved with a Canaanite girl. They would let their children grow up without instruction in the faith. They would stop obeying the Law. They would even stop studying it. The Covenant that had kept them a people chosen, a people apart, would be forgotten. And there would not be a thing he could do about it.

To whom could he turn? Eleazar was little comfort and less help. The high priest was a fountain of goodness and a well of wisdom, but the people did not listen to him as they had to Moses and Aaron. Besides, Eleazar was not a young man. He would be dead early on in Caleb's tenure.

So what could he do? He could pray. But God did not seem to hear his prayers, as He heard those of Joshua and the others. Had he offended God? If so, how could he expiate his sin?

Pepi slipped off into a deep sleep of dreams: He stood on the deck of a beautiful ship with Tirzah, sailing on the azure waters of the Great Sea. The sun shone brightly, the sea air was fresh, and in the cloudless sky, birds swirled and doves filled the air with their cries.

He could hear the joyful playing of the *trieraules* and the steady stroke of the oars. Before them towering volcanic peaks rose jewellike out of the sea. The broken arms of a caldera spread wide as if welcoming them into the harbor.

Pepi knew where they were going. They were going to Home. He watched as the ship entered the harbor. On the dock people were waiting. Pepi strained to see their faces. All of them were waiting for him. His uncles Demetrios and Iri eagerly waved to him. They looked so young!

And there was his mother, younger, too, the terror gone from her eyes. He saw Seth and Mai, who raised him. Incongruously, Moses was there, old and wise and loving, smiling that crinkly-eyed smile that never changed as the years went by.

Waiting impatiently for the crew to dock, he turned to Tirzah to tell her they had arrived at their final destination, where at last they could rest and settle down and fear no one. This was the place where they could raise their children, far from worries.

But even as he looked at her, Tirzah began to fade. He reached out his hand to touch her. She was not there. He looked around. The island had vanished. His ship was moored in the middle of a desolate sea. He was alone. . . .

He awoke, drenched with sweat, crying Tirzah's name. His heart pounded erratically, and his head split with pain. He sat up, holding his temples, crying, "Where did it all go? Where have they taken it? Tirzah! Tirzah, where are you?"

V

"Your back is nearly raw from the lashings," Chaninai said admiringly.

"Yeah, I really got a taste of army discipline," Micah replied, trying not to wince as his friend spread grease on the flayed flesh. "Ow!"

"Sorry. I can't see a way not to hurt you with this."

"That's all right." Micah's voice took on a boastful tone. "It's not as bad as baking in the sun while a hundred ants feast on you."

"If my father had known, he wouldn't have let you be punished. You're a guest here."

"Not anymore." Micah turned around and grinned at his pal. "I'm a full-fledged soldier now. The way I figure it, this was my initiation. I took my punishment just the same as the others. I even told Caleb that you and I had moved into the soldiers' tents, and he didn't say anything against it."

Chaninai's eyes sparkled with excitement. "You mentioned me? By name? And Caleb didn't object?"

"Not a word. That means you're a real soldier, too. There's a formation tomorrow, first thing. I think we should go. We can stand in the back, though, out of respect to the others, who've been fighting longer."

"A real soldier . . ." Chaninai said. "My father will be so proud."

At dawn Shemida supervised the morning formation, cursing and badgering the men until he had troops that looked almost soldierly by the time Joshua arrived.

Shemida faced him and saluted. "They're all yours, sir."

The commander's face was haggard, but when he returned Shemida's salute and stepped forward, the voice that spoke was powerful and stirring.

"Men!" he cried. "Today we march on Hebron. We'll retake the city just as Abraham our forefather did in the days of old. After Hebron we will take Kadesh and all the towns between. We will destroy the last of the old Egyptian settlements. When we are done, the Israelites will control all of Canaan south of Bethel except for the coastal territories."

Shemida rejoiced in his heart that the five cities of the Sea Peoples were to be spared. Everyone knew the Philistines had iron weapons, and they would cleave bronze swords in half. Now that Tamar had agreed to marry him, Shemida wanted to see old age.

Joshua's voice rang with increasing fervor. "Then we move north. And before we have finished executing the commands of Yahweh, we will attack and destroy every army that comes against us south of Mount Hermon."

Shemida breathed a sigh of relief. For some time he had wondered if God had designs on Lebanon or the coastal cities of Sidon, Tyre, and Arvad. But the new Israel would encompass only the old land. Their mission was one of reconquest.

"Then we will have all the land we need to make a good life for ourselves and our descendants for many centuries to come. And that land we will divide equitably among the tribes. We can then live in peace."

Peace? Shemida thought. *Do you really think we can live in peace after what we have done? Do you really think we can disband the armies and settle down to farming and shepherding? No! There'll never be another day here for us without the threat of war. Not if we're here for a thousand years.*

When Nimshi and Hagab came to wake Pepi, they found him dressed and packing for a journey.

"What are you doing?" Nimshi asked.

"I'm going back to Jerusalem," Pepi replied. He turned to face them. "Where's the messenger you sent to Mother and Tirzah? Why hasn't he brought them here?"

"Pepi," Nimshi said, "try not to get upset. It isn't safe for you to get so excited."

"I see, it's better for me not to know my wife and mother are in grave danger. It's better for them to remain in danger, perhaps get killed, while I sit here nice and safe, thinking everything is fine. Is that it?"

Hagab spoke in a soothing voice. "Now, Pepi, no one could have watched over you with more concern than your brother. The messenger we sent has been killed. Now save your accusations, and let's discuss calmly what's to be done. As far as we know, Jerusalem is safe for the time being."

For a moment it looked as if Pepi were going to fly into a rage, but he took in a deep breath and said, "I'm sorry. But I can't sit idly by while our loved ones are in danger, Nimshi."

"Of course you can't," Hagab said.

"I'm going to Jerusalem," Pepi said, "with you or without you."

"Hagab," Nimshi said, "please send for Sakar."

To his surprise Hagab shook his head. "Pepi's right. We'll all go together, but in the center of an armed guard of Philistines. Joshua's people will not be so foolish as to attack us then, knowing it would mean war with the Philistine League."

Pepi grinned. "When do we leave?" he asked.

Baufra had left the packing in Tirzah's hands and at first light hurried to the city gate. Secreted on his person was a purse containing half the gold coins he was able to raise.

He approached the gate with trepidation, then cursed silently when he realized the captain on guard was not one he knew. He swallowed hard; this one would have to be dealt with cold. Slowly he walked toward the locked gate.

Suddenly the smaller gate was opened, and a man rushed in. The guards quickly bolted the door behind him.

"Excuse me," Baufra said. "I wanted to see—"

He was shoved aside. No one would listen to him.

Their attention was on the man who was trying to catch his breath. Finally the fellow was able to speak.

"They're attacking Hebron! Joshua and his army are riding against Hebron!"

The captain of the guard seemed frozen with shock. Finally he said, "Hebron! But that means—"

"Yes!" the newcomer said, his voice still breathless.

"It means we're next," the captain of the guard said. His face was white. "We've got to get the news to the commander of the city guard as fast as possible. Do you know where he lives?"

One of the soldiers spoke up. "I'll take the news to him."

Baufra saw his chance. "Excuse me, Captain. You may know me. I'm Baufra, chief armorer to the—"

"Oh, yes. What do you want?"

"Captain, if Joshua's advancing on Jerusalem and our army has been destroyed, isn't it time to open the gates? Because if he comes here and there's no army to defend us—"

"Just because someone arrives claiming to carry bad news, we can't abandon our laws and discipline. Return to your quarter, if you will. I'll send one of my men with you."

"But we've got to get out of here! We've got to evacuate the city! You know what Joshua does when he takes a city!"

"Go quietly, sir, please. Let us take care of everything."

Baufra stared at the captain. *He must be mad.*

As the messenger ran through the streets he spread the news. "Joshua's coming!" he called out. "The Israelites are coming! Run for your lives! Escape! We're doomed! Doomed!"

Before he reached his destination, concern turned to panic, and panic led to an uprising. Within minutes the streets were full of people fighting, shouting, and looting.

In the confusion a fire broke out, and with no one to fight it, it quickly spread. Flames swept through one building, then another, and soon a block of homes in the poor quarter was ablaze. People stormed the gates, but the guards shot arrows into the mob and dispersed the rioters. Jerusalem seemed doomed, even without Joshua's intervention.

VI

Tirzah looked down on the chaos in the streets from Neftis's second-floor bedroom window. Two men were grappling with a well-dressed man, intent upon robbing him. Farther down the street, a young woman was being assaulted by a heavily built drover who was pulling at her clothes. Running by them were the bodyguards Tirzah had hired, obviously having abandoned their responsibility.

In the distance she could see flames spreading at an alarming rate and coming closer. Unfortunately, the fire lay between Baufra's house and the city gate. And there would certainly be panic-stricken citizens storming the gate. She did not want to get in the midst of an angry mob when Baufra got back from completing the necessary bribes for their escape from Jerusalem.

The sound of atonal humming caused Tirzah to turn around. Neftis was in bed, oblivious to the pandemonium outside, working on a project that involved tying knots in patterns.

She smiled and held it up. "Do you like this? It's going to be a belt. I've made one for each of my boys, and I can make one for you, too, if you wish."

Forcing a smile, Tirzah nodded. "That's lovely, Mother. I'd like one very much."

"Where's Baufra, my dear?"

Tirzah stole another look out the window. A gang of vicious-looking men were striding down the street, kicking in doors and knocking down window boxes with flowers. "He's arranging for us to take a trip. Would you like that?"

"No, I don't think so," Neftis answered mildly. "Will he be home soon?"

"Yes, Mother."

Suddenly there was a crash downstairs, and shouting. Rough men's voices rang out, and screams came from the servants. It sounded as if the house was being destroyed. Tirzah hurried to the bed and whipped back Neftis's blanket.

"We're going to play a game now, Mother," she said urgently, trying to keep the panic from her voice. "I'll hide in the clothes chest, and you'll hide under the bed. We'll both be very quiet if people come upstairs. They'll be trying to find us, but we won't let them. All right?"

"Well, dear, if you wish . . ."

It seemed like an eternity to Tirzah before Neftis was hidden and she was bringing the chest lid down to envelop herself in darkness, but only minutes had passed. Footsteps pounded up the stairs and into the bedroom.

"Hello . . . I'm here under the bed, but you can't find me," Tirzah heard Neftis taunting.

Gods, Tirzah thought, about to weep. *Please spare us.*

But her prayers were not to be answered. Tirzah heard Neftis squeal as the woman was hauled from under the bed.

"Tirzah's in the clothes chest, Tirzah's in the clothes chest!" Neftis chanted.

The lid flew open, and Tirzah looked up to see a horrible visage that leered as it took in her blond hair and golden skin. He gripped her upper arm and half lifted her from her place of concealment. Then he shoved her toward the stairs.

Bleeding, his clothing torn and dirty, Baufra staggered up to his house. His eyes were wide in horror when he saw the door open and hanging from one hinge.

Cautiously he peered inside. He saw no one. Where were the bodyguards? "Neftis? Neftis, are you there?" No answer. He tried again. "Tirzah! Tirzah, where are you? Is anyone home?"

He entered. The house was torn apart. Chairs had been dashed against the walls. Wall hangings had been pulled down and trampled.

He ran through the great central hall and upstairs into Neftis's bedroom. It was empty, but the bed had been slashed, the coverlets ripped. Decorations had been torn off the walls and pried out of moldings and inlaid furnishings. He rushed downstairs. The looters had stolen all the dinnerware and cooking utensils from the kitchen. The larder had been stripped clean.

Perhaps everyone got away . . . he said to himself as he prowled the empty house. Then he tripped over something and looked down.

One of the woman servants lay facedown on the floor. She was naked, and the bracelets his family had given her had been taken from her wrists and ankles. Bruises covered her body.

He knelt and turned her over. Blood covered her thighs. She had been a virgin, and he had promised to free her and give her the money to find a husband. And now she was dead.

Fear tore at his heart. What about Tirzah and Neftis? With an anguished cry he ran out into the garden, searching and praying that he would not find them.

Another slave lay facedown in the reflecting pool. It was a boy, the son of one of the kitchen women. He, too, was naked and had been violated.

Above the wall of the garden he could see black smoke rising from the warehouses at the end of the block. Baufra staggered sideways a few steps from the horror of it, then sat down on the cool tiles, put his hands to his temples, and gave voice to his anguish.

Hagab, sitting tall on the lead horse, was the first to

spot the curling plume of dark smoke. "Nimshi," he said softly. "Isn't that coming from the direction of Jerusalem?"

Nimshi looked at the smoke rising over the hill for a moment, then turned to where Pepi was riding slowly at the rear of the column, chatting with one of the underofficers, as though he had not a care in the world. "It's got to be Jerusalem," he said in a low voice. "But—how? We had reliable information that Joshua had decided to spare the city until he'd pacified the southern area."

Suddenly Pepi noticed the smoke and nudged his mount to the front of the column. "What's that?" he demanded. "I thought Jerusalem was safe! You told me—"

"We don't know what it is," Hagab responded. "I could gallop on ahead and find out."

"I'll find out for myself!" Pepi said, urging his horse forward, first into a trot, then into a canter, then into a gallop.

"We'd better stop him," Hagab said to Nimshi. "He shouldn't be riding that hard and fast. Particularly when we don't have any idea what lies on the other side of that hill." He flicked the reins, and his horse jerked forward. Nimshi followed, but Pepi had a head start and reached the top of the hill long before the others. As he pulled his horse up it reared, and it was all he could do to keep from falling off.

The horse bucked nervously as Pepi stared in horror at the flames shooting over the walls. "It's burning!" he screamed. "Jerusalem's burning down!"

Baufra, not thinking clearly, had come out armed only with a small dagger to protect himself and the money he carried. But he managed to scare off potential robbers as he prowled the streets looking for someone—anyone— who could give him news of his wife and Tirzah.

Fighting his way through the panicky crowd that clogged the area around the city gate, he stopped one person after another, asking after the two women. Although Tirzah was easy to describe and no one else in the city looked like her, he could find no one who remembered seeing her.

His worst fear was that the women had been killed and thrown into one of the burning buildings. Then he would never know.

Suddenly he was aware of a disturbance at the gate. He looked up and saw the crowd fall back as a score of burly men in the uniforms of Philistine guardsmen pushed their way through the small gate.

Philistines? What were Philistines doing here?

Then to his amazement he saw Pepi and Nimshi. "Pepi! Nimshi!" he cried out, waving his arms above his head, relieved to share his burden and thrilled that the brothers were safe. "They're gone! I can't find them!"

Pepi stopped dead and just stared at him, as if he were going to have one of his attacks. Then he regained control and rushed forward, grabbing Baufra's arms and shaking him. "Gone? What do you mean, gone? They can't be gone! Curse you! Where are they?"

CHAPTER TEN

In the Great Sea

I

So beautiful were the young women strolling along the sandy shoreline, that each person coming toward them stopped and watched their approach in appreciation. When Nuhara and Iphigenia found their favorite spot, a large boulder overlooking the sea, they climbed up as they had done every morning since Iphigenia's arrival.

"You are so lucky to live here all the time," Agamemnon's daughter said, capturing her long, thick hair from the wind and securing it in a gold barrette. "It's so peaceful."

"Peaceful? More like lonely. Boring." Nuhara sighed. "Or at least it was before you arrived. Oh, I shall miss you terribly! I never had any girlfriends while I was growing up."

Iphigenia grasped Nuhara's hand and held it. "I hate to leave you, too. I can't remember when I've had so much fun."

The girls sat in morose silence for a few minutes.

"I wish we had had more warning. It's such a shock, your leaving," Nuhara complained at last.

"At least the captain agreed to wait till tomorrow before taking me back to Greece." Iphigenia sat, thinking. "I still can't believe I'm to be married."

"And I can't believe you are marrying someone you've never met," Nuhara said.

"It won't be so bad. I've seen Achilles. He's very brave and handsome. Your knowing Theon before you were betrothed was most unusual."

Nuhara slid down from the boulder, then turned to face her friend. "I'm beginning to realize that everything about my past is odd," she said moodily. "I was raised on a pirate ship in the midst of men, overly protected, of course, by my father. He was everything to me."

"He still is," Iphigenia murmured.

Nuhara's eyes welled with tears. "I want to be a good wife," she snuffled, "but I can't."

"Then what is stopping you?" Iphigenia asked pointedly. "Frankly, Nuhara, you don't have to give up being your father's daughter to be a good wife for Theon."

"I know. . . . I just feel like such a failure." Red blotches of embarrassment colored her throat and cheeks. "Theon wants a baby, and I—I can't seem to manage it. And my father, who was such a—a *god* to me suddenly seems so stupid to everyone. He can't do anything right. He really needs me now."

Nuhara began to sob in earnest, and Iphigenia slid off the boulder and brought Nuhara into her embrace. "That's all right. You have nothing to feel ashamed of."

"Theon would be a better administrator," Nuhara continued after a few minutes. "Everybody knows it. And just being his wife makes me feel as if I am disloyal to Father."

"You could be a great help to them," Iphigenia suggested, standing back from Nuhara to find a handkerchief.

"How?"

"You could be their intermediary," Iphigenia answered, handing Nuhara the square of fine linen. "Get them talking. Then back away and let them continue on their own."

"Do you think I can?"

"I think you have no choice . . . unless you want to end up a very lonely young woman."

Nuhara chuckled humorlessly. "And I married for love, can you believe it?"

Iphigenia hugged her friend tightly. "Yes, I can, you goose. After all, I've met Theon!"

II

All the people of Troy could talk about was the visit of the emissaries from Greece. If they had heard about the despicable behavior of Priam's unpopular son Paris before that, they might well have forced the king to condemn the prince's behavior and order the return of the errant Helen. But Palamedes' rude and insulting performance toward their beloved King Priam had solidified their feelings against Greece.

Thus, when at last Paris sailed into home waters, the mood was almost one of welcome. And when Princess Cassandra appeared on the deck of the flagship, a great cheer arose from the waiting crowd, for Cassandra's fiery and independent spirit was much admired by her people. When she came down the gangplank leading a pretty slave who was obviously blind, and carrying the woman's baby in her own royal arms, the hearts of the people went out to her as they gathered around her chariot and sang songs of homecoming.

Then Paris appeared at the top of the gangplank. The crowd was shocked into silence when they saw the woman at his side. Dressed in regal simplicity, she was the most dazzlingly beautiful woman anyone in Troy had ever seen. But that was not all. Trailing the two lovers were Helen's magnificent handmaidens. Suddenly another cheer went up, as enthusiastic as that which had greeted Cassandra, and all eyes followed the royal procession up the ropewalk to the waiting chariots.

At Paris's command, casket after casket of booty was carried off the ship by armed soldiers. Some of the boxes were open, and as the procession passed through the crowds lining the road, people could glimpse the gold, jewels, and finery that Paris and Helen had stolen from Sparta. The cheers turned to sighs of awe.

Paris had carefully planned the entire performance. Not only would the common people be thrilled to see the treasure, but seeing it carried by soldiers, they would assume it had been won fairly by force of arms.

To make certain, Paris had assigned a number of soldiers to linger behind and explain what had happened—at least Paris's version of it. They were also to announce that Helen's lovely handmaidens were to be offered as brides to the sons of the great men of the city.

When Paris's procession reached the palace, it was met by the palace guard, ordering Paris and his captains to attend the king and the council in Priam's chambers.

So that he could dress properly for a royal audience, Paris asked for a short delay, which was granted. He gathered his men, along with Helen and her handmaidens, to prepare them for what might transpire and how they should respond.

Cassandra, ever curious, peeked out the door of her own apartment and watched them file into Paris's wing. "Paris is planning something sneaky," she called back to Keturah. "I wish I knew what it was."

Keturah, keeping one hand on Talus's cradle and rocking it gently, said, "Surely my lady can satisfy her curiosity."

"I've heard some gossip, but I'd like to know exactly what happened when Menelaus came here. Apparently he made my father so angry that he refused to condemn Paris. I wish I could witness that meeting between Paris, my father, and the council, so that when Paris starts telling his infernal lies, I can make sure my father knows what really happened."

"My lady," Keturah began timidly, "I . . . I don't know much about your customs here in Troy, but doesn't a high priestess of Apollo have some special rights?"

"What are you suggesting?"

"If my lady wanted to witness the meeting, they might be able to stop the king's daughter from attending, and perhaps they could even stop the priestess. But could they stop someone who's both?"

Cassandra considered. "No, they couldn't."

"My lady won't get in any trouble for speaking against Paris?"

"No. Father loves me very much. He doesn't always listen to me, but he wouldn't hurt me. Maybe some of the councillors will heed what I say and can sway him."

"Yes, my lady. And perhaps while you're there you can find some sympathetic person who will tell you exactly what happened the day Menelaus came here."

Cassandra laughed. "Oh, Keturah! How did I get along before I found you?"

"And how will you get along after I leave?" Keturah said under her breath.

The assembled court had taken in good grace the delay Paris had requested, but when at last the herald entered and announced "Prince Paris!" there was an audible murmur of relief.

Paris entered with great dignity, looking his princely best. Although virtually every man in the hall under a certain age was a son of Priam's by one woman or another, none of them, not even those whose lineage was excellent and undisputed, could fool themselves into believing that they could cut such an impressive figure. Paris strode in to the center of the great hall and bowed low to his father and then, in a gracious gesture of respect, bowed to the assembled nobles.

Turning, without a word, he clapped his hands three times. The great doors opened, and his military leaders entered in a slow and solemn procession accompanied by slaves carrying open caskets full to the brim and sparkling with rubies, emeralds, amethysts, and gold.

"My father," Paris said, "my brothers, my kinsmen, and nobles of the court of Troy, may I present to you . . . the treasure of Sparta!"

Cassandra had brazened it out to get into the great hall to watch the procession. Now, looking on from an unobtrusive spot, it seemed to her that it would never end. The slaves laid down their burdens at Paris's feet, then they filed to the rear of the great room to stand at rigid attention behind the military officers, who were all armed to protect Paris if any of the assembled nobles became angry. Grudgingly, she acknowledged a streak of common sense in him that she hadn't seen before.

The protection was not necessary; not one courtier could escape heaving a sigh of astonishment at the rich hoard. A low murmur of appreciation rippled around the great room. Once more Paris bowed to his father and to the court and turned back to the doorway.

"And now, Sparta's greatest treasure," he said, bowing low and dramatically.

In came Helen of Sparta.

The astonishment Cassandra had heard a moment before was nothing compared to this. Somehow Helen had contrived to arrange her magnificent hair in an even more attractive fashion. She wore no jewelry and was draped in a costume of truly stunning simplicity—a white gown that hung in graceful folds all the way to her white, sandaled feet, showing off her long, lovely neck and graceful arms. But nothing drew attention from her flawless face, framed in golden curls. She stood on the threshold with goddesslike dignity, projecting an aura of invulnerability.

Paris seemed to glide to her side and took her hand—as much, Cassandra thought, to show off her graceful arm and elegant hand as anything—and led her forward. To Priam she curtsied, as if to a god, her eyes downcast modestly. And then, like Paris, she bowed, although perhaps not so deeply, to those on her right and left.

"And now, my lords and brothers," Paris said, "brides for my unmarried brothers: the ladies of the household of Helen of Sparta!"

Only a beauty like Helen, absolutely secure of her own preeminence, would have dared to parade a string of long-limbed beauties like this. They came forward wearing the white, sleeveless Doric-styled chiton slave girls wore in the courts of Greece. Their little feet were bare, their arms slender and white, their faces smiling as they looked right and left at the young men of the court.

The eyes of the young men were on the white-clad maidens. The old could not look away from the staggering hoard of riches Paris had stolen from the insulting and despised Menelaus.

But Priam's attention was focused on Helen. And as Cassandra watched, Helen looked up—right into the king's eyes, and held them. Priam could not look away.

By all the gods! Cassandra thought, astonished. *He's pulled it off! Paris has pulled it off!*

III

As the awestruck nobles filed out of the hall, Priam called Paris to his side. Putting his hand on Paris's shoulder, the king said, "You have done well. I think you have won the court over. But there remains the question of, uh, Queen Helen."

"Father," Paris said, "when you get to know her—"

Priam shook his head. "There is no time. The Greeks

are assembling a great fleet at Aulis. They will be here any day. I have much to do."

"But—"

"Patience," Priam said. "Have Helen go to my wife. Have her dress modestly for Hecuba, as she did here. No, make it a trifle more drab—I'm sure Helen will understand how to go about it."

"I will," Paris said, unable to believe his good fortune. "And, Father . . . thank you. I knew I could count on your wisdom."

As soon as Paris left, Hector was at Priam's side. "I can't believe you're going to let him get away with this!"

Priam raised one brow. "Is this the way my son speaks to me? As if I were some drunken tradesman who has passed out in public and disgraced his household?"

Hector's mouth was set, his eyes were ice. "I apologize," he said in a measured voice, "if I give a wrong impression of disrespect. But to condone what Paris has done?"

"My son," Priam said, "Menelaus wants a war, and nothing, I think, will dissuade him from having one. Otherwise he would not have let that fool Palamedes insult me so in front of my own council."

"All this is quite likely true, but—"

"And once Paris had made up his mind to bring Helen here, he was wise to bring along as much treasure as he could possibly carry. This will be an expensive war. Why not make Menelaus pay the cost?"

"Father—"

"The deed is done, Hector. Since there is no way of escaping the situation, we must brazen out the consequences. But I must know whether Helen was raped, as Menelaus claims. It would burden my own conscience unduly if I knew that Paris brought her here against her will."

Hector snorted. "It certainly didn't look like it. Are you going to ask her?"

"No. I'll leave that to your mother. Women are better at getting the truth out than we are, my boy."

"That's right, Father," Cassandra said, stepping forward. "I saw what was going on from the very first."

"It's rude of you to interrupt us when we're trying to have a private conversation, child. Run along."

"I'm no child, Father! I'm a grown woman! I keep my eyes and ears open, and I make mature judgments."

"Now, now, dear. Run on. I'll see you at supper. You may bring that pretty little blind girl. She'll make a decorative addition to the dining hall."

"What an insulting thing to say! She's no decoration! I'm not leaving until you—"

It was Hector who put a hand on her arm. "Cassandra, could I talk with you? I'd be glad to hear anything you have to say as soon as I'm done with Father. Meet me atop the wall, where you used to stand and watch while I did my swordsmanship exercises. Do you remember?"

"All right," she surrendered, and turned to go. It had been a long time since Hector had taken her seriously. But at worst she could get from him an accurate account of Menelaus's visit.

The apartments of the king and queen of Troy were spacious and beautifully furnished. From the terrace one looked out upon the floodplain of the Scamander River as it twisted its way to the dark sea beyond.

Priam's queen, Hecuba, never tired of the view. It was here that she came when she wanted silence and solitude, when her heart was weary and her burdens heavy. She had borne her children here, and nursed them, and worried about them, and she finally returned here to weep when they grew up and left to start their own households.

It was here that she summoned the foreign queen Helen.

Hecuba watched as the woman approached her and curtsied. She studied Helen, taking great pleasure in how well she carried herself, how splendid her manners were, and how carefully and modestly she had dressed. Apparently the Greeks turned out women of royal rank very well. This one certainly displayed the proper deferential manner due a reigning queen, while maintaining her own dignity.

"My lady, I am Helen of Sparta. I come before you at the request of your lord husband the king of Troy."

Hecuba decided to be generous and welcoming. "Greetings," she said, coming forward to take the young woman's hands and look at her more closely. "How lovely you are! One meets few Greek women here and never a woman of rank, breeding, and beauty. Let me welcome you to Troy, my dear."

"My lady is too kind," Helen said with a gracious smile. "My father and his kinsmen told me of the gracious qualities of the Trojans, but I see that their tongues failed them." Noting Hecuba's smile, she continued. "But, my lady, I am not such a stranger to Troy by blood as one might think, and such qualities as my lady is so generous as to find in me may well come from my Trojan forebears." She let her words sink in. "My people and the royal family of Troy are distant relatives."

"It would be pleasant to think so," Hecuba said.

Helen had rehearsed this conversation for an hour and smoothly related the story of her family's derivation from the ancestors of the Trojan royal family. "So, my lady, you may in fact describe me not as a stranger coming to a strange land, but as a long-lost wanderer at last returning home." She gave Hecuba another dazzling smile. "Returning, I might add, in a spirit of joy and deep contentment, as if my whole life had pointed to this moment."

"Indeed?" Hecuba asked. "Then it is not true what Menelaus and Palamedes would have us believe, that you were carried away by force from a happy home?"

Helen had rehearsed *this* moment carefully, too. She brought forth a silvery flood of tears, permitting the hint of a sob to creep into her voice. "My lady, if I had to live another year with the wretched man my father gave me to—if I knew, this moment, that I could never again see the wonderful man who saved my life by bringing me here and giving me his love and protection—I think I would end this poor life of mine."

Hecuba looked hard into the teary eyes, which did not grow red from weeping, and marveled at the performance. *It's a fake*, she thought. *But what a wonderful fake it is. Perhaps, even at my age, there is something for me to learn from her.*

She put out a hand and touched Helen's. "There, there, dear. Tell me all about it. You're home now—home among friends and your new family."

Cassandra, in a turmoil of emotions, had come back from her meeting with Hector. Now, in her own apartment, she poured it all out to Keturah in one great flood: the amazing scene of Paris's conquest of Priam and the entire court, and the long conversation she had had afterward with Hector, alone, on the top of the wall.

Hector had confided to her his total distrust of Paris. And when she had told her own version of the events as they had transpired, she watched the anger grow in Hector's eyes. She had gone on at length, hoping to put Hector in her debt. In return he had given her a very full account of the scene when Menelaus and Palamedes had insulted Priam.

As Keturah listened, her face glowed with interest. She waited patiently while Cassandra began to recount the long, rambling tirade Palamedes had made and Priam's wise and just reply.

"Did your brother describe the men who came to court?"

"There were King Menelaus and Palamedes and King Odysseus of Ithaca. . . ."

"Didn't you say there was a fourth man, my lady?"

"Yes, Keturah. Iri, his name was." Cassandra gasped. "Do you suppose—? Hector did say the man had a birthmark that covered his face!"

"Iri," Keturah whispered in a quavering voice. "My husband. Iri, the father of my little Talus. He's alive, my lady, he's alive!"

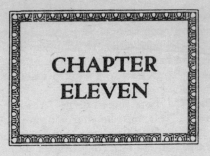

CHAPTER
ELEVEN

Greece

I

As Iri's friend Phorbus watched the three emissaries'
boats returning from Troy, he could hardly contain his
excitement. He dropped the tinker work in his hand and,
stopping only to wipe the soot off his face and wrap a
swath of fabric around his bare loins, abandoned his forge
and set out for the waterfront.

Now, at water's edge, he forced his way forward to
get a better look. At last he saw Iri, standing on the deck
of Odysseus's ship and waving, his ugly face split by a
wide grin.

When the ship docked, Iri, not waiting for the plank,
climbed the rail and jumped the gap over the water,
landing close enough to Phorbus that the two friends were
thrown into each other's arms. Phorbus found himself
hugged so close to Iri's broad chest, it nearly took the
breath out of him.

"Phorbus!" Iri said with delight. "How good it is to
see you again! You're covered with soot! Have you been
working?"

"I have to practice what you taught me," Phorbus replied, "so I've been taking cheap tinkering work."

"Don't make light of it," Iri advised. "Repair work is useful, and a lot can be learned from it."

"Come," Phorbus said. "I'll get dressed and buy you a meal."

Just then Odysseus joined them. "Ah, Iri!" he said in a hearty voice. "This must be your apprentice."

"Yes, this is Phorbus. Here, my friend, meet King Odysseus of Ithaca, the best companion a man ever had on a dull and futile voyage."

"Dull? Futile?" Odysseus echoed wryly. "How could it be dull with a fellow like Iri to talk with? How could it be futile when it guaranteed that we'll all be dead within a year, our bones rotting below Priam's walls?"

Seeing the worried expression on Phorbus's face, Iri said, "Don't mind him. He has a way of overstating things— it's part of his charm. I've got to attend to an errand. Odysseus, take care of Phorbus. I'll meet the two of you at . . . where, Phorbus?"

"I was going to suggest the Golden Lion."

"I'll see you two there in a little while."

On board Menelaus's ship, the king of Sparta remained sequestered in his cabin with Diomedes, who held Agamemnon's second letter to Clytemnestra.

"You're sure Agamemnon doesn't know this never reached his wife?" Menelaus asked. His face was ruddy with anger.

"Not as far as I know," Diomedes answered. "I paid his servant Astrophel handsomely to deliver it to me. When I saw that Agamemnon was retracting his request to bring Iphigenia here, I naturally didn't allow the servant to take it on to a messenger."

"If Agamemnon thinks he can just call the whole thing off—"

"Nestor says that your brother's intention was to re-

sign as leader of the expedition, disband, and send everyone home."

"Idiot! I wonder why he didn't go through with it."

"I suspect he was afraid of what you'd do when you
came home and found out. Or perhaps he was worried
that the men wouldn't leave. They're getting bloodthirsty."

"I would have killed him without blinking an eye.
I've assembled this fleet! We're ready to attack Troy!"

"Can you replace him?" Diomedes asked. "Can you,
as king of Sparta, command the expedition when there are
rulers here of cities of greater size and importance than
Sparta? And you have enemies, Menelaus. One of them is
certain to suggest that Nestor, for instance, would make a
good leader."

Menelaus snorted. "That old fool! In his hands the
expedition would founder in a day. Then he'd give away
three quarters of all the gains in a truce. No! Not Nestor!"

"What about Odysseus?"

"Odysseus would send them all home in the first hour."

"But he has a reputation with the sword."

"He does, curse him. But he only fights when his
back is to the wall—or when he's forced into it. No, it has
to be Agamemnon. Only the reigning king of Mycenae has
the prestige and power. I'll have to whip him into shape."

For the first time a hint of doubt appeared on
Diomedes' face. "Sir, is it worth all this? A lot of lives are
going to be lost."

Menelaus turned on him savagely. "Are you turning
coward on me, too? Either you're with me, or you're
against me! Speak up, curse you!"

Diomedes looked down at the huge fists balled at
Menelaus's sides and tried to answer. It took him three
hoarse, croaking tries to get the words out. "W-with, of
course."

Odysseus and Phorbus took a table on the terrace of
the inn. Odysseus ordered wine, and the men sat back to
watch the harbor below.

"Who would have imagined that so many men and ships, from so many nations and cities, would gather for such a foolish and destructive errand?" Odysseus asked. "Look at them, fools all: Boeotians, Minyans, Phocisians, Locrians, Abantes, Athenians, Salamisians, Achaeans, Laconians, and Messenians; Arcadians and Epeians and men of the western isles; Aetolians, Cretans, Rhodians and Symians and Asian islanders; Myrmidons and Thessalians and Magnesians . . . all here and ready to die ignominiously on foreign soil, with none to bear their bodies back home. And for what reason?"

Phorbus looked at the other man. He understood that this was no rhetorical question, but the way in which he was being tested. "Why . . . for their honor," he responded. "At least, I suppose so."

"And you? I understand from Iri that you and he have come here to work as mercenaries while looking for his wife. Do the two of you fight for money only?"

"I've never fought before for any reason. I was raised to be a farmer, not a soldier. I—I'm here because Iri's here. I follow Iri."

"And what do you expect to learn from him? How to die in battle?"

"I hope not! Perhaps how *not* to die in battle."

"A good answer. But you are not bound by the oath that binds idiots like me and the rest to Menelaus. Is there not a better way of not dying? I wish I were at home, growing green things and minding my own business."

"Iri wants to be here, and as I say, I follow Iri."

"Indeed?" Odysseus said, his sharp eyes on Phorbus, a taunting smile on his lips. "And why would a boy like you follow a man as ugly as an ape? What is there to be gained?"

Phorbus flushed; his words were jumbled and angry. "If you're going to insult my friend, I . . . I can find better ways to spend my time. I don't care where you're the king of."

He made a move to leave, but Odysseus's hand fell

on his arm. "I meant no insult to Iri. If I were young and had no responsibilities, I could do worse than follow such a man. But Iri doesn't avoid death. Why would a boy match steps with a man, however good, however admirable, who has no fear of dying?"

"In the hope of changing his mind, I suppose. My instincts tell me that Iri is a good man." He paused. "I wish he were my father. He's a far better man than my father was. Iri hasn't looked ugly to me for a long time."

Odysseus's smile broadened. It was warm and accepting. "Nor to me. Yes, lad, there's something very special about him. I'd wish for him to have a loving son to look out for him and keep him from feeling lonely. I despair of his ever finding his wife and child. It would please me, as a friend, to know that he has found a son to replace the child he lost." He smiled and raised his cup in salute. "And for you, I would wish the continued good fortune of Iri's favor and friendship. There is much to be learned about life from this man."

Phorbus flushed and looked embarrassed. "I ask for nothing more than to follow him until he is gone. If he has a burden to carry when he dies, I will pick it up and carry it. As far as I'm concerned, he *is* my father."

"Then, your health, my friend," Odysseus said. "May we both get our wish."

II

Iri lugged the sword he had repaired halfway across Aulis before catching up with its owner. The fellow was so grateful, he insisted upon buying Iri a drink, and custom demanded that Iri accept. But then the sword's owner bragged about Iri's strength, and a hulking ox from Samothrace challenged his word, and nothing would do but an arm-wrestling contest.

Bets were made, a space cleared, and Iri put up his

bulging forearm and linked hands with the islander. As the bets rose and the odds climbed, he grunted and strained. Then, when his own bets had all been covered, Iri put the man's arm down with insulting ease. This produced the usual disputes, and only the threat of a riot made the losers pay up.

Iri begged off more drinks, pleading the meeting with Odysseus and Phorbus, but as he got ready to leave, one of the bettors grabbed him by the arm. "Sir, I thought this a good time to talk to you, when you've a fat purse. I'm told you'll pay well for information about a blind slave woman."

Iri stopped dead and looked the man hard in the eyes. "Friend," he said, "I have to warn you: If you raise my hopes only to dash them with some untruth . . ." He grabbed a bronze cup and flattened it with his fist. "So consider your words carefully."

The man raised his hands in protest. "All I know is that someone mentioned your name in a tavern the other day. You're well-known around here, and people got to talking, as can be expected. Somebody said that you'd lost your wife and child, and—"

"Yes?" Iri said, his eyes full of fire and menace.

"W-well, sir, this fellow up and says, 'Damn me if I didn't see someone answering that description not ten days ago, and she had a baby the right age as well.' Anyway, I thought of you, sir, and as soon as I saw you—"

Iri grabbed him roughly by the arm. "Take me to him."

Agamemnon was sleeping when Menelaus burst in the door, threw the coverlet off him, and screamed, "Wake up, you cowardly son of a bitch!"

Agamemnon emerged from his dream frightened and confused, his hands in front of his face as if to fend off a blow. "W-what?" he asked, sitting up. Finally he realized who it was. "M-menelaus! You're back! What are you screaming about?"

"I'm screaming about your attempt to ruin our whole

plan." He spat on the floor. "How could you even contemplate it? Has that wife of yours cut off your manhood?"

Agamemnon rubbed his eyes and stood up. "What are you talking about?" But then, seeing his brother's livid face, he realized. "How did you find out?"

"Never mind that! Did you really believe I'd let you get away with abandoning the entire expedition because it demanded some self-sacrifice?"

"Who says I abandoned it?" Agamemnon asked.

"Nestor, that's who! Did you think the old fool could keep a secret? Not only did you jeopardize the enterprise, but you did it while I was at Troy, ensuring that nothing would get in the way of our war of conquest. But there you were, sniveling shamelessly to old Nestor and trying to weasel out of the leadership of our fleet."

"But Menelaus, the seer said that to ensure the success of our mission, I'd have to sacrifice Iphigenia! She's an innocent, beautiful child who's done no one any harm! How could I agree to that?"

So black was Menelaus's rage that he almost struck his brother. "But you *did* agree to it, and then you turned cowardly. You changed your mind, like the spineless worm that you are. What kind of leader is it who wavers with every breeze?"

"Just wait a minute," Agamemnon said, his voice rising in anger. "Who got us into this mess? Who couldn't manage his wife and keep her content at home? Who was it that—"

"Fool! Did you think that Helen was the real reason why I held everyone to his vows? If Paris hadn't snatched her, I'd have found another reason for invading Troy. Don't you want to get rich? Don't you want to be the most powerful man in the world?"

Agamemnon's face twisted in agony. "You don't understand. Calchas was absolutely certain that if we went to Troy without killing my daughter, we'd die and the expedition would fail."

"So do the right thing for once in your worthless life.

Pay the debt you owe all the men in those ships out there." He jerked a thumb toward the harbor. "And let's get on with it! Now's the time to strike! If we could hit Troy while Paris still has the fleet—"

"Paris already sailed for home; we had a report."

Menelaus waved Agamemnon's objections away. "Then the most important thing is to set sail as quickly as we can. And the only way we can do that is for you to honor your obligations immediately."

Agamemnon paced, afraid to meet his brother's eyes. "I know that. That's why I wrote the letter to my wife to bring the girl here. And then . . . then, I thought of my Iphigenia. How could I betray her trust? Could you with a child of your own, Menelaus? So then I wrote again to Clytemnestra, telling her not to come. How unfair of the gods to ask us to make a sacrifice like this!"

"I know all about that second letter!" Menelaus said, pulling it out of his robe. "One of my men intercepted it. And so now there's nothing standing between you and your duty."

"Give me that!" Agamemnon demanded, snatching it out of Menelaus's hands.

"Clytemnestra is probably already on the way here with your daughter. After all, what mother could pass up the opportunity to match her daughter with Prince Achilles?"

Agamemnon opened his mouth, but the words wouldn't come out. As he stood silently opening and closing his mouth, his servant Astrophel appeared at the door. "My lord, King Nestor told me that I should inform you: There's a ship in the harbor—"

Menelaus gave an angry snarl. "There are a thousand ships in the harbor, you fool! Does Nestor expect you to come inform us every time some fishing boat comes limping into harbor with a hold full of squid?"

"Sir, the lord Agamemnon's own pennant flies from the top of this mast. King Nestor was sure my master would want to know."

Agamemnon's eyes widened with horror. "Clytemne-stra," he whispered in a hollow voice. "She's here! What can I do? What will I say?"

Menelaus ignored him. "How long has the ship been here?" he asked the servant. "Has it docked yet?"

"It docked an hour ago, sir."

Menelaus let out a string of curses. "Damn the luck! Someone should have caught it earlier! Come along, Brother, and may the gods help you if you try to weasel out this time."

III

Menelaus's angry reprimands had carried through the windows and to the ears of anyone below who couldn't resist pausing to listen to his tirade. His words alarmed the men who had forsaken their own wives and families to come to Aulis to prepare for war. And now, according to what they heard, Agamemnon intended to call off the whole expedition rather than comply with Calchas's prescription for success. They realized their valuable time had been wasted by two irresponsible brothers who threatened to abandon their plans, leaving high and dry the men who had believed in and followed them.

The heterogeneous army had already been waiting around in Aulis for far too long. The unexplained delay had occasioned unrest, which vented itself in tavern brawls and fistfights and at least a dozen stabbings. Now, as a version of Menelaus's harangue began to circulate through the port, the men of the expedition, whether of high rank or low, focused their complaints on a single issue: If Agamemnon was going to ask them to risk their lives and fortunes to bring back Helen of Sparta and the treasure she and her lover had stolen, the least he could do was to demand of himself a comparable sacrifice to avoid the displeasure of the gods.

*   *   *

Odysseus and Phorbus had almost given up on Iri, who was long overdue. They had ordered food and were now feasting on ripe, salty olives and on marinated vine leaves stuffed with roasted lamb, washing it all down with wine of Chios. Odysseus had just called for more wine when he spotted a friend. "Zeno!" he called. "Over here!"

The man caught Odysseus's eye and strode toward them, saluting. "My lord, I'm glad I caught you. The most amazing thing is happening. If you—"

"Sit down," Odysseus invited. "Have some wine. Let's not stand on ceremony. No saluting, and none of this 'my lord' nonsense. We're all damned fools here together in Aulis. Meet my friend Phorbus."

Zeno sat beside them and briefly acknowledged Phorbus with a nod. "There's a revolt brewing among the soldiers. I thought you should know, because if anyone can head it off, it's you."

"I'd thought there was more noise than usual down in the street," Odysseus said, "but I was so intent on enjoying my first unhurried meal in days that I paid no attention." He picked up his cup. "I gather you've got all the latest gossip. Out with it, Zeno." He held up his hand and motioned to the server. "Another cup for my friend."

As luck would have it, the first man of princely rank that Clytemnestra met in Aulis was Achilles. He recognized her immediately. "Greetings to the queen of Mycenae," he said. "To what divine intervention do we owe this visit from so great a lady?"

Clytemnestra stared at him as if he had suddenly grown antlers in the middle of his forehead. "Surely Prince Achilles has not forgotten the promise that he made, which brings me and my daughter here."

Achilles, who prided himself on never being at a loss for words, found himself stumbling. "My lady . . . my lady, I hope you will pardon me if I admit that I do not understand. Please explain the nature of my promise, so that I may avoid breaking it."

He paused, waiting, but Clytemnestra merely stood before him, her mouth a thin white line, her eyes full of confusion. Finally she said angrily, "Pardon me. It was my understanding that you had spoken with my husband about a betrothal to my daughter Iphigenia. He wrote me, telling me to bring the girl to Aulis as quickly as possible so that the betrothal could take place before the fleet sails for Troy."

Now it was Achilles' turn for confusion. "I beg my lady to understand that I have not the faintest idea where Agamemnon can have gotten such an idea. I have not, so far as I know, laid eyes on your daughter since she was a small child. I have never solicited her favor, nor have I been encouraged to do so by your husband."

"B-but . . ."

"Don't be upset," Achilles soothed. "Someone has played a cruel trick on you, but I swear before all the gods that I was not a part of it. Perhaps we can inquire into the matter and find out who—"

"Wait!" Clytemnestra said. "There's my husband's slave Astrophel. He'll know what's going on. Could I ask you to catch him and bring him here?"

She watched as the big man fell into an effortless lope down the quay after the servant. To her surprise, when he caught up with Astrophel, the servant tried to wriggle away, but Achilles' strong grip held him. Even stranger was the animated conversation between the two men. At one point Achilles picked the servant up and shook him until he cried out for mercy. At last, he let Astrophel go and came hurrying back to her, his face dark and angry.

As Achilles approached she called out to him, "What's wrong? What did he say?"

Achilles's face was stern. "My lady, go back to your boat and guard your child. Allow no one aboard—not even Agamemnon. Do you understand? I would offer you my protection, but I'm afraid it will take time to muster enough of my personal army. I won't be able to spare many of them if I'm to avert a full-scale riot."

"Riot?" she asked. Suddenly she became aware of a commotion at the other end of the quay. A large crowd was gathered around a man who was standing on an overturned boat, speaking to them. He was too far away for Clytemnestra to hear his words, but occasional angry shouts erupted from the mob. "What's going on? Am I in danger? And what about my daughter? Does someone mean her harm?"

Achilles took a deep breath. "It's your husband, my lady. Some soothsayer has told Agamemnon that our enterprise will prosper only if Iphigenia is sacrificed to Artemis."

"Sacrificed? You mean—"

"He intends to kill her." He told her everything he had forced out of Astrophel, but as he talked he steered her back toward her boat at so brisk a pace she could barely catch her breath.

Finally, she stopped and faced him. Her eyes were dilated with fear. "I hardly know whether or not to believe this. I know I could never dream up anything so horrible." She paused. "I . . . I put myself in your hands. I came here without armed guards, thinking I was protected by Agamemnon's name. It's very difficult for me, a proud woman, to throw myself on the mercy of anyone—even an honorable man like you—but in the name of your own mother, of all the women you hold dear, I beg you to help me save my daughter."

A hot anger flared in Achilles. "I'm bound by my honor to follow Agamemnon and Menelaus on a lawful quest," he said carefully, "but what Agamemnon intends goes against the laws of humanity, and I'll have no part of it. I'll assemble a guard as fast as I can, but word about this has gotten around. Someone has stirred up the men, and they'll turn on us very quickly if Agamemnon comes to his senses and spares your daughter."

"You mean . . . the riot would be in *support* of this—

this unspeakable action? The mob would force Agamemnon
to sacrifice my daughter?"

Achilles nodded grimly. "Please, just get back to your
boat and I'll—"

But it was too late. Agamemnon and Menelaus were
approaching.

Odysseus and Phorbus saw them, too, and Odysseus's
sharp vision picked out Prince Achilles and Queen Clytemnestra on the quay. "Come on, Phorbus!" he said. "I smell
trouble!"

They set off at a jogging pace toward the water.
Phorbus saw Agamemnon approach his wife, and to
Phorbus's surprise Achilles quite deliberately stepped forward between husband and wife. As they got closer he
could hear their words.

"Get out of my way!" Agamemnon demanded. "I
want to talk to my wife!"

"If you'd come on an honorable errand," Achilles
said, "I'd be the first to step out of the way. But I know
what brings you here, and if you think I'm going to stand
by and watch you commit so monstrous a sacrilege, you're
mistaken."

Agamemnon was about to answer when a high-pitched
voice interrupted them. "Father!"

All heads turned toward the boat behind them. At the
rail stood Iphigenia.

Phorbus gazed at her. She was slender and fair, with
a delicate beauty that resembled neither Agamemnon nor
Clytemnestra. At fourteen she stood on the verge of adult-
hood; her hips were still narrow and her bosom still small.
Her features were soft and gently formed, with that unfin-
ished quality of youth. She looked from parent to parent, a
confused smile on her face. "Father!" she called. "Aren't
you glad to see me?"

"You're quite sure?" Iri said. His heart was pounding
hard.

"I watched," the sailor assured him. "The trader didn't even trot her out at first, thinking, I suppose, that nobody was going to want a blind slave."

He caught the offended look in Iri's eyes and shrank back. "Well, I mean, sir . . . I certainly didn't mean anything by it."

"Go on," Iri said. "It sounds genuine."

"I swear," the sailor said, "I wouldn't be telling you this if I didn't believe she was the one you've been looking for. Anyhow, the buyer said, 'Is this all you have?' and then he trotted her out, with the baby in her arms. And the buyer said, 'I'll take her!' Just like that. Took the baby, too."

Against his better judgment, Iri found hope burning bright in his heart. "Who was the buyer?" he asked.

The sailor sighed. "That's the bad part, sir."

"Who, curse you?"

The sailor held up his hands, as if to say the fault was not his. "Queen Helen of Sparta, sir. They left with Prince Paris's fleet a few days later."

Shock and hope mingled on Iri's stunned face. Keturah and the baby were alive in Troy.

IV

The public wharf was no place for an argument, particularly with nearby rabble-rousers stirring the mob to violence, so Menelaus steered them all into one of the warehouses that lined the wharf. Iphigenia, holding tightly to her mother's hand, her eyes wide with fear and confusion, went with them.

Odysseus was ready to bar the door when Achilles said, "Wait. Let me out."

Odysseus stepped back and looked him up and down. "Here I was, thinking you'd shown some guts and decency at last, defending Clytemnestra and the girl. But now I find you making for the door."

"Don't be a fool," Achilles hissed. "That crowd is about to get out of hand. If I can assemble my men and blockade the entrance, perhaps I can hold them all off until this situation is resolved."

Odysseus stepped back. "I've wronged you. My apologies. Please hurry."

"The common men rising against their commanders!" Odysseus grated to Phorbus after Achilles had left. "I smell Menelaus's slimy hand in this."

But Phorbus wasn't listening. He was staring at Iphigenia and shaking his head. "Imagine sacrificing a lovely young girl like her."

Odysseus followed the direction of his gaze. "She is a pretty little thing, isn't she? But if Menelaus insists upon the sacrifice, he'll have that whole mob out there supporting him. I don't think Agamemnon stands a chance; the girl will have to be sacrificed. I don't like it either, but I don't want to be attacked by that angry mob. They would have no hesitation about killing us if we try to get in their way."

"I'm not bound by that oath of yours," Phorbus said. "And I can't see going to Troy for a cause that's been tainted by an act as horrible as this."

"Not even if Iri goes?"

"Iri won't want to go," Phorbus predicted. "I know he won't."

Odysseus looked out the small window by the big door. "It may be a dishonorable thing to do, but—may the gods help me—I'm honor bound to go along." He spat on the floor. "Damn them all. They're going to kill half of Greece and destroy a civilization superior to their own. And for what?"

"Then don't go!" Phorbus implored. "You don't believe in all this! You don't even believe in the gods."

"Although I don't think it proper to go around trumpeting the fact to the four winds," Odysseus said, "it's bad for a society when religion is slighted. It's all I can do to maintain order in my kingdom, and religion helps me do that, even if I don't believe a bloody word of it myself."

As he spoke he kept glancing back and forth from the churning mob outside to the scene inside, where Menelaus and Clytemnestra were shouting almost as loudly as the horde surrounding the warehouse. He watched as Menelaus fixed his gaze on Clytemnestra while he talked to his brother.

"Don't listen to her! You have an obligation to the whole fleet." He grabbed Agamemnon by the upper arm and shook him. "This is the greatest gathering that has ever taken place here, and for the loftiest purpose: to win the keys to the Hellespont and all the treasures of the East! And it was gathered at your behest."

"No!" Clytemnestra protested. "It was at yours, you cuckold! It is happening because you couldn't control my sister. And because you lied to all those people out there." Suddenly the crowd surged against the door. It rattled on its hinges but held. "You told them that Paris had carried Helen away against her will when you knew better."

Odysseus was leaning against the door, bracing it against blows from the mob. "Achilles had better bring his men soon," he told Phorbus. "They've got a battering ram out there."

From the other side of the door came the sound of a bass voice. "Agamemnon! Come out here, you bastard! You coward! Either keep your bargain with the gods, or come out and submit to our justice!"

"Did you hear that?" Menelaus asked, thrusting his face close to his brother's and bellowing into his ear. "They demand justice! They demand that you, their leader, do what must be done. And if you don't, they're going to break down that door and kill every last one of us!" His voice was shrill, and madness gleamed in his eyes. "Is that what you want? What do you suppose the soldiers out there will do to Clytemnestra and Iphigenia? They'll die, too, after being raped by every last one of the wild beasts out there!"

A thin wail came from the girl, who was crouching in a corner, her slender white arms wrapped around her body.

"*That's* your choice, Agamemnon!" Menelaus pressed. "Not a choice between sparing the girl and going home unscathed, or offering her up to Artemis and going off to conquer Troy. The choice is between doing your damned duty to them and me or dying *with* the girl, like an animal!"

Agamemnon looked from face to face in the little circle around him. "Odysseus," he finally moaned. "What can I do? Help me!"

Odysseus started to answer, but he was interrupted by another assault on the oak door. "Make up your own mind—but whatever you decide, do it fast! I don't think that door's going to hold a third time." He cursed as the oak splintered. "Achilles! Where is Achilles?"

"He isn't going to arrive in time to save you from the sacred duty of making up your mind, Brother!" Menelaus shouted. "You have to do it now! Go on, coward! Make up your mind!"

"I—I can't," said Agamemnon, weeping.

"*Wait!*" A clear young voice rang out on the far side of the room.

They turned. Before them stood Iphigenia, her young body frail and reedlike in her simple white *peplos*. She held a bronze dagger to her bosom. Her young face was drawn with sadness. Her blue eyes glittered with tears.

Agamemnon reached out his hand. "No, darling! Give us the knife."

"Don't come any closer," she warned. Her voice quavered with strain. "I don't want to die, but someone has to be sacrificed, and it must be me."

"No, darling! Please!" Clytemnestra called out.

Outside the crowd had grown larger and louder. The walls shook as the mob surged against them. Voices bellowed for blood. The oak door shook a third time under the force of the battering ram.

"It's the only way I can save any of you," the girl sobbed. "My uncle spoke rightly: If I'm spared now, I won't be alive when the mob is finished with me, and all of you will be dead, too."

"Please, Daughter!" Agamemnon started toward her. When her fingers tightened on the knife, he drew back.

"Father, I forgive you. I forgive everyone. As I hope you'll forgive me."

"No!" Agamemnon cried.

The blade was very sharp. Driven by the full strength of the girl's hands, it buried itself in her young body just below her ribs. Blood spurted out, and she crumpled to the floor.

Outside the crowd noises grew even louder, but not loud enough to cover the animal cry of pain from Agamemnon, or Clytemnestra's screech as they rushed to the girl's side. Again the battering ram slammed into the door.

V

Halfway down the quay, Iri noticed the commotion. As he hurried in that direction he could see several hundred men surrounding a warehouse, throwing rocks and shouting curses. As he watched, ten men drew back, then rushed forward, directing a thick battering pole against the door of the building.

Suddenly, from the other direction, came Achilles, at the head of thirty soldiers of his personal army. Without a word they set upon the men surrounding the building, beating them back with the flats of their swords, cursing them, and shoving them away.

Achilles stood, a massive obstacle before the oak door, and faced the men who wielded the battering ram. "Run that thing into *me*, why don't you? See if you can batter down the son of Peleus." His bronze sword was poised in his huge hand.

Iri watched in admiration. This was the hero all the men of the Greek force knew and respected, the man whom even proud Hector of Troy was said to fear. Iri grinned. Drawing his own sword, he elbowed his way into position next to Achilles.

"If you advance beyond this spot," he shouted at the mob, "you'll have to answer to both of us. And I think most of you know by now how I handle this sword. Come on! We're ready for you!"

"Just give us Agamemnon," one of the braver men demanded. "He's going to get us all killed because he won't make the proper sacrifice to Artemis. Because of him we're all going to go into battle with the weight of Olympus against us."

"You bastard," Achilles growled. "You'd take the life of an innocent child in order to protect your own dirty carcass? Get out of my sight, you scum, before I decide to cut your tripes out and feed them to the crows." He spat on the ground. "I'd cut your heart out and your balls off as well, but I wouldn't know where to look for either."

The mob's spokesman looked furious, but he made no move to come closer, and the sword in his hand did not leave his side. "We don't want any trouble with you. Our quarrel is with Agamemnon, and—"

He stopped.

Behind Achilles the great oak door opened.

Menelaus stepped out and held up both hands.

"Men!" he shouted. "The sacrifice has been made. Success is ours!"

Achilles faced him. "Menelaus, what have you—"

Out of the darkness came Agamemnon, his face a death's-head mask. He carried the body of Princess Iphigenia, blood staining her white robe. Beside him, in frozen dignity, walked Queen Clytemnestra.

"Agamemnon," Achilles said through clenched teeth, "you disgust me. How could you—?"

The procession stopped. "The gods have claimed the life of my daughter, Princess Iphigenia," Clytemnestra said emotionlessly. "The honor of the Greeks remains intact. The expedition against Troy can now proceed. Now

I would ask you to leave me and my husband alone to deal with our grief."

Without a murmur, the mob dispersed. Achilles turned to Clytemnestra and asked in a choked voice, "Why, my lady? We came to save her."

She spoke not to Achilles but to her husband. "I will not display my own sorrow in public." The expression in her eyes was unreadable. "There will come a time, Husband, when you and I will have occasion to remember this moment. As you have not kept the faith with me, so shall I fail to keep the faith with you. As you have spoken lies to me, so shall I speak falsehoods to you. And as you have dealt with the delicate matters of life and death for me, so shall I deal with them for you."

When Phorbus saw the sadness in Odysseus's face, the young man went to him immediately. "I'm as sickened by this as you are, but wasn't she a brave little thing?"

Odysseus's face was somber. "What she is, my young friend, is dead. If you'd be so kind, I could use some solitude. I need to think."

Phorbus looked into Odysseus's eyes and saw despair. "Please," he said, "couldn't we talk about it?"

Odysseus's sigh was long and deep. "That magnificent, altruistic act you just saw was the finest you will see before you have gray hair on your head. We will go to eternally damned Troy, and we will waste the remainder of our lives fighting a useless war, when we should be tending to the vines on our hillsides and watching our children grow. And we will all pretend it makes sense for us to be there. We will all pretend that our actions are gallant and admirable. We will pretend that war is as good and honest an endeavor as peace. But it won't make a bit of difference. Our bodies will fall on some Trojan plain, the birds will pick the flesh clean, and our bones will grow white until the dogs and the children scatter them. And then we'll all be forgotten."

"But, Odysseus—"

"Oh, to be sure, some bard will sing some drivel about us, and we'll be lucky if he gets all the names right. But what good will it do my little son, who needs a father?"

"Look, I know how you feel about this, but—"

"You think that girl's suicide made it right back there, don't you? But all it means is that you have to go to Troy, and you have to follow your good-hearted, ugly friend to his death, and you have to watch him gasp out his last in some meaningless patch of pasture in some godforsaken foreign land, and you have to pick up the burdens he lays down, as you promised you would."

Before Phorbus could answer, Odysseus fixed him with a stricken stare and stalked away.

"Phorbus!" Iri called from behind him. "I'm sorry for not meeting you and Odysseus, but I've just heard the greatest news!"

Phorbus turned.

The look on his friend's colorless face startled Iri. "What's the matter? What happened back there?"

"I . . . I'm sorry. I've been talking to Odysseus. Some of the things he said . . . were disturbing. Ideas are whirling around in my head, and I feel drained. I can't think straight. This Troy business seems so futile now. Going all that way to fight people we don't know, to conquer territory that won't belong to us when the war is over anyway."

Iri's face was as happy and animated as a child's. "But that's just it! Now I have a reason to go to Troy! All that wretched melancholy of mine—the drinking and fighting and bad temper—you'll never see it again, boy. I'm a new man."

Phorbus stared at him in confusion. "Agamemnon has ruined our good name and our honor. If we go to Troy, anything we do will be dishonorable."

"You don't understand," Iri said, beaming. "It's Keturah. She's alive. And so is my child. I've talked to a man who's seen them. And best of all, Phorbus—they're in Troy!"

For the first time Phorbus felt the hand of doom that Odysseus had been trying to tell him about. And suddenly he understood Odysseus's warning.

With favorable winds behind them, the great Greek fleet moved slowly out of the harbor. Sailors rowed the black ships into the current, then they raised the sails and let the wind fill the canvas. As each ship set out, a resounding cheer rose from the crowds gathered on the quays to watch the fleet leave on its quest.

Iri stood at the rail of Odysseus's ship and looked happily in the direction of Troy. Odysseus, who had left the navigation to a trusted assistant, joined Phorbus at the head of the rowers' pit. He did not look back at Aulis, nor out to sea. Instead he stood looking at Iri.

"He looks young again, Phorbus. The sap is running strong in him. A week ago he was stumbling around like an old man, as if the burden of the ages lay on his back. Now look at him: his backbone is straight, and his eyes are clear. Everything about him radiates strength. If I didn't know he was well over fifty, I'd say he was twenty-five. If I didn't know he was so ugly, I'd say he was handsome."

For a long time Phorbus was silent. When he finally spoke, his voice sounded hollow. "Odysseus, I . . . I did something stupid yesterday. I went to see Calchas."

"You wanted a look at the future? Men aren't supposed to see into the future! We're supposed to go through life with blinders on. The gods give us the strength we need to deal with problems as they happen, not the ones that *might* happen."

"I couldn't restrain myself," Phorbus said. "I have a terrible feeling that this expedition is going to turn out tragically. I have bad dreams. I wake up in the middle of the night in a cold sweat."

"What kind of dreams?" Odysseus asked, guiding Phorbus toward a far railing and privacy.

"Dark, foreboding ones. I'm in a building. It's on fire, and I'm trying to lead a woman to safety, but all the doorways are full of flames. There's no way out." He shuddered. "Even now, in the bright daylight, it scares me." He closed his eyes and let his shoulders slump. "I have this awful feeling about Iri, that he's—"

"We're all going to die," Odysseus interrupted. "But now it seems Iri's going to be granted some happiness."

Phorbus shook his head. "My dreams make it clear. He's not going to survive."

"Phorbus, it's just a dr—"

"You don't understand. Calchas has been experiencing the same dreams. He says the expedition is doomed, even though Agamemnon—"

"That poor child's death is what doomed us!" Odysseus said angrily.

"Calchas was specific about what was going to happen," Phorbus continued. "He told me who was going to die, and how. He told me what's going to happen to the women and children while we're away. Clytemnestra, for instance, will—"

Odysseus put a hand over Phorbus's mouth. "I don't want to hear any more. Most particularly, I don't want to hear a word about myself. And how can I look another man squarely in the eyes if I know how and where he's going to die? Leave me some surprises in this life, Phorbus. Even if they are unpleasant ones!"

VI

The many vassals and allies and neighbors of mighty Troy had gathered on the floodplain of the Scamander River, ready for the great war they all knew was to come.

Hector led the Trojan contingent—the army's largest and best. Surrounding him were the tents of the Dardanians, Zeleans, and the wild horsemen of the Hellespont; the Pelasgians, Thracians, and Paeonians, great archers all;

plus the Alizonians, the Mysians, the Phrygians, and all the lesser tribes from farther down the coast.

From atop the walls of her father's city, Cassandra looked out over the great gathering on the plain. "Who would imagine, Keturah," she said, "that my father could call in so many men to do his bidding and to defend our city? How could the Greeks possibly think themselves capable of conquering Troy?"

Keturah kept her peace. She remembered Cassandra's visions: dreams in which great Troy was in flames . . . enemy soldiers roamed the halls of the palace raping and killing . . . and Priam and Prince Hector were dead. In the morning Cassandra never remembered her dreams. All she knew was that she awoke drenched with sweat and aching with fatigue.

Every night Keturah was awakened by Cassandra's horrible screams, and every night she sat by the princess's side, stroking her forehead and listening to her tales of horror until her fear subsided and she slipped off into sleep.

Keturah sighed. She would serve the princess Cassandra well and for as long as she needed her. But how much easier her task now that she knew that her Iri was with the Greek army and that he would soon be here to carry her and little Talus to safety before the city was destroyed.

CHAPTER TWELVE

Canaan

I

Pepi had paid the Philistine soldiers personally to search every nearby city and town for a sign of his wife and mother. And when the soldiers were ordered to return to Ashdod, Pepi, accompanied by Nimshi, Baufra, and Hagab, continued the frantic search on his own.

Finally Nimshi decided it was time to call off the quest. Although his grief was as great as Pepi's, he realized they had to face up to the unpleasant truth that they might never see Neftis and Tirzah again.

"I know what Pepi's going to say," Nimshi told Hagab as they rode back toward their wilderness encampment at the end of a long day. "He'll say that if we desert him, he'll continue looking by himself." He shook his head. "And he certainly isn't well enough to go off on his own." He looked up at Pepi, who rode alone at the head of the group. Something in the distance caught his eye.

Hagab shaded his eyes. "Soldiers! There's only one army likely to be moving up from the south—the Israelites!"

"But what can we—" Nimshi began. Suddenly Pepi

kicked his horse into a gallop toward the advancing horsemen. "Pepi! Come back!" Nimshi called, then kicked his own horse into pursuit. Hagab and Baufra followed.

As they rode, they watched the scene unfolding in the distance. One of the Israelites put a ram's horn to his lips and blew two echoing blasts. At that signal a group of horsemen detached themselves from the larger unit in the rear and moved forward.

Pepi pulled up and dismounted to face them. One of the soldiers dismounted to confront him.

"Come on, Hagab!" Nimshi shouted over his shoulder. "Pepi's in trouble!"

The man facing Pepi was Caleb. Sword in hand, he was circling slowly to Pepi's left. "Remember what I swore I'd do if I ever saw you again?" Caleb challenged. "Come on and fight, you traitor!"

Pepi drew his sword and cursed himself, for in the haste of leaving Ashdod, he had not taken the iron weapon Hagab offered him. "I haven't wanted to fight you, Caleb, because we were once friends and I lived among your people for most of my life. But I'm going to kill you, you bastard, because you finally stepped over the line."

"Indeed?" Caleb said, feinting a thrust and then drawing back, looking for a better opening. "And what have I done?"

"My wife's disappeared, lost in that riot in Jerusalem that the fear of the Israelite invasion precipitated. If she's dead, the blame will fall on your head. It's your fault. You could have left Jerusalem alone."

"And you could have gotten your family out," Caleb said, feinting high and stabbing low. "You knew our plans."

"Yes," Pepi said, parrying a well-aimed cut, "and at one time I sympathized with them. You had every right to claim a homeland because you've been without one for so long. But that was before it became obvious that you wanted the entire region and would conquer it with such savage violence. You don't need all that land, Caleb. You're greedy and have an insatiable thirst for blood."

"It's our land," Caleb said, beating back a sudden flurry of strokes. "We won it by force of arms in the days of Abraham of Ur. We were fools to leave. When we get it back, we'll never leave again. We're going to settle the whole land, have children, and populate it from the sea all the way to the Moabite wilderness."

Pepi's companions pulled their horses up sharply and watched. The Israelite patrol stopped at an equal distance opposite.

Pepi executed a complex maneuver that confused Caleb and nearly caught him between the ribs. "But Joshua isn't testing the Philistines' mettle! No, he's giving them a wide berth!" His voice held a note of contempt. "He knows that he'll lose to any army that carries iron weapons!"

"He doesn't need iron!" Caleb said, hacking and stabbing furiously. "We have God on our side!" His attack forced Pepi, blocking the stabs just before they touched his body, to give ground again and again. Caleb pressed his relentless assault.

"You'll need Yahweh on your side now, and half the Canaanite pantheon as well, because I'm going to join the fight against you!" Suddenly Pepi almost disarmed his opponent.

Caleb disengaged and drew back. "At last you admit your treason!"

In reply Pepi again nearly battered the sword out of Caleb's hand with his powerful attack. He caught the Israelite on the arm with his backswing, drawing blood. "I was never guilty of treason," he said evenly, "although you've treated me as if I were. You have mounted a one-man campaign against me, undermining me, since we left the desert and you discovered you could worm your way into Joshua's confidence by denouncing me. Me, his oldest friend!"

"You couldn't be trusted!" Caleb snarled, attacking

with all his remaining strength, only to have his efforts beaten back.

"I was trustworthy then," Pepi said, "before your devious campaign turned Joshua against me. And now, you—and he—have finally made your accusations come true. I began as your friend, but you insulted me and destroyed my reputation. Even that wasn't enough for you; you had to destroy my family! From now on you're all my enemies. I can no longer find any trace of Moses' spirit among you."

Caleb moved back. He was drenched with sweat, and his hands were trembling.

Pepi stopped, allowing Caleb to catch his breath for a moment, an action even more insulting than the ease with which he had beaten down Caleb's defenses. "But your people were falling by the wayside before Moses died. The judges he appointed had already gone bad. The crook who stole my wife's property in Bashan was paying bribes while Moses was still alive."

"Shut up and fight!" Caleb yelled, the anger boiling up giving him strength.

"They're slipping away from you, aren't they?" Pepi pressed. "While you and your men are out in the field, the civilians you're fighting for aren't keeping the Law. They don't keep your Sabbath or the complex laws that govern the way your people are supposed to treat each other."

Caleb came at Pepi with a powerful, quick-handed attack. But Pepi anticipated every one of his moves and deflected them. With powerful wrist action, Pepi bore in and disarmed Caleb. His sword flew into the air, and in the blink of an eye Pepi's razor-sharp blade was at Caleb's throat.

Caleb blinked through the sweat rolling down his forehead. "Go ahead," he said in a strangled voice. "Kill me!"

For the first time Pepi looked around. Half a dozen Israelite bowmen stood with nocked arrows pointing at his breast. Next to them, sitting astride a bay horse, was Joshua. Pepi noted, with shock, his ravaged and drawn face.

"And so if I kill Caleb, you'll order them to kill me. And justice is served, eh, Joshua? Or is it? You've heard what I said, and you know that I'm telling the truth. You know you've conquered Canaan for a people who can't wait for you to die—you and Eleazar—so they can get back to the very sins that Moses tried to break them of."

Joshua said nothing.

"Kill me, Joshua," Pepi said. "You might even be able to do it before I've finished Caleb here."

No one moved. No one seemed to breathe. Then Pepi's sword drew lightly across Caleb's throat, leaving a fine line of blood, just breaking the skin. As the red droplets rolled down Caleb's neck, the archers pulled their bowstrings taut.

"No!" A young horseman from the rear of Caleb's patrol suddenly kicked his mount forward. "Don't kill him!"

"Micah!" Baufra cried out.

Pepi swung his head around.

"Pepi, that's our brother!" Nimshi called.

"Please don't kill Caleb!" Micah begged the half brother he had never seen. "These people took me in and have been good to me, even though I was your brother." His young eyes sparked with anger. "And you're a fine one to talk about savagery and violence. Look at you! Are you any better than they are, with your sword at a man's throat, playing with his life, torturing him?"

Joshua leaned to grasp the reins of Micah's horse as the boy began to cry tears of rage and frustration.

"Well, Pepi, what say you?" Joshua asked. "I'll give you back your brother, but I want Caleb, whole, in exchange."

"No!" Micah cried out. "Please, sir, I want to stay with the army and Chaninai and Shemida! Don't make me go."

Pepi saw the pain in Baufra's and Nimshi's expression. He flung Caleb away in revulsion. The Israelite staggered toward his commander, who tossed Micah's horse's reins away.

"Get out of here," Joshua said to Micah. "That's an order."

Nimshi urged his horse forward to reunite with his brother. Baufra was not far behind.

Pepi replaced his sword in its scabbard. "I let Caleb go, but you'd still better kill me—because if you don't, I'm going over to your enemies and teaching them how to make iron swords to use against you."

Without hesitation he turned on the bowmen and stalked back to his horse. No one moved or spoke. Finally, Joshua broke the silence. He barked out an order in a hoarse voice, and the archers lowered their bows.

Pepi mounted and, with Nimshi, Baufra, Hagab, and Micah at his side, galloped away in a cloud of dust.

II

Not until they were well out of the range of Israelite bows did Nimshi dare speak up. "I . . . I wasn't sure we were going to get out of there."

"Pepi knew exactly what he was doing," Hagab said. "The points he was making were hitting home; Joshua is winning every battle against the Canaanites, but he's losing a war with his own people."

Pepi slowed his mount and fell back to ride with them, leaving Baufra to tell Micah the sad news about his mother. "Unfortunately," he said, "that isn't going to help the people up north, where his army is headed next. And my talk about arming his enemies is just talk. I can't get anything started in time to help the people who are fighting him now."

"Joshua isn't long for this world," Hagab said. "He's either very ill with some wasting disease, or—"

"He's exhausted," Pepi cut in. "He can't last another six months. And then Caleb will succeed him, and Caleb isn't the threat Joshua is."

Hagab chuckled. "You surely got the best of poor Caleb. He looked surprised by your prowess. I thought you two had known each other a long time."

"Almost all our lives," Pepi said grimly. "But we've never had a fight before in which I was seriously intent upon hurting him. I've always held something back, not wanting to wound or humiliate him." He snorted. "The only reason I spared him now was that if I killed him, Joshua would kill you three and maybe Micah." For a long time they rode in silence. Then Pepi said, "Baufra! Will you join me and make iron for the enemies of Israel?"

The expression on the older man's face was pensive. "I'm not sure, Pepi. What if Neftis and Tirzah are slaves of the Israelites? And what if, in retaliation, the Israelites decide to take revenge on them?"

The idea had not occurred to Pepi. "They wouldn't dare," he said quickly, but there was no conviction behind his words.

"Or," Baufra continued, "if they're not with the Israelites, where could they be? I have to keep looking."

While Baufra's attention was diverted, Micah suddenly pulled hard on his horse's reins and glared at his family and Hagab as if they were monsters.

"I'm not staying with you anymore," he told them. "I want to be with Joshua and Chaninai. I'm going back to them."

The color drained from Baufra's face.

"Don't you think we've been through enough, with Mother's disappearing?" Nimshi asked angrily. "What's the matter with you, Micah?"

"Nothing," he retorted. "The Israelites didn't take Mother. We were in the Negev when Jerusalem burned. We had nothing to do with it. I believe in them, and I'm going back. I want to be a soldier, and there's nothing you can do to stop me."

"Micah!" Baufra cried.

But the boy had kicked his horse into a gallop back in the direction from which they had come.

"What can we do?" Nimshi asked.

"Let him go," Pepi said flatly.

"*What?*" Baufra and Nimshi erupted at the same time.

"You can't stop him. He'll just run away again." Pepi turned to Baufra. "They've treated him well enough to gain his loyalty and love. They were good to us once, remember, Baufra?" He thought for a moment. "You know, it's funny: The Children of the Lion and the Children of Abraham have always been connected in their histories. When Iri and I left Joshua, there was no one of our clan with them for the first time in generations. Does Micah by any chance bear the birthmark through Mother?"

Baufra, wide-eyed, nodded. "He does."

"Then perhaps, my friend, Micah's leaving us is meant to be."

As the long columns rode northward, Joshua looked over occasionally at Caleb's dark, brooding face. Caleb had undergone a terrible humiliation in full view of his own army, and nothing Joshua could say or do would lessen it. The hurt would fester within him, to make his fighting, when at last his army squared off against Hazor, all the more ferocious.

On the eve of a great and taxing battle, Joshua did not want to think about Pepi's accusations. The charges that the Israelites were rapidly falling away from the Law were obviously true: The look on Caleb's face had confirmed his own growing suspicions. He was sure Caleb and Shemida had been keeping something from him.

No blow Pepi could have struck with sword or ax could hurt Joshua more than Pepi's outburst and Caleb's silent confirmation had. All of a sudden he felt tired. He had never allowed himself to acknowledge his exhaustion, but at this moment he could not deny it.

It's all over for me, he thought. *Perhaps, with God's aid, I can get through this one last campaign and secure the northern lands; but when I'm done with that . . . no, that is defeatist talk. I must think about the coming battle. That's all that counts now.*

Nothing else mattered—least of all the question of what would happen to him if he survived it.

Joshua's top spies, Pelet and Gedor, had been in the north studying the army being assembled by Jabin, king of Hazor. They made their report before a council of Joshua's generals.

Spreading out a papyrus map, Pelet pointed out the site where Jabin's armies had convened. It was the hill country west of Lake Chinnereth, a narrow valley below Mount Merom, where all the major axes of communication in Upper Galilee met.

"The Waters of Merom," Joshua mused. "That's interesting. Now tell us the enemy battle order."

"Bad news, sir," Gedor replied. "Not only is the army a big one—"

"Yes. I've heard the rumors: 'Like the grains of sand on the seashore.'"

"It's all true, sir. Worst of all, they've got cavalry—not just horse cavalry, but chariots. They can move up to a thousand men wherever they want, as quickly as they want. They are *iron* chariots, sir."

"So the Philistines are relaxing their rules against selling to the inland peoples," Joshua remarked with surprising calm.

"Maybe you don't understand," Pelet said anxiously. "Our front line won't stand a chance against a chariot charge."

Joshua smiled. "There won't be any chariot charge. Once again God has delivered them into our hands. I know because they've elected to gather at the Waters of Merom."

"I don't understand, sir," Gedor said. "When we get there at week's end, they'll be waiting for us."

"Perfect," Joshua said enthusiastically. "We couldn't ask for anything better. But what makes you think we're going to be getting there at the end of the week?"

"Joshua, you aren't thinking of delaying again," Caleb protested. "This time it would be too costly!"

"Who said we are going to delay?" Joshua asked. "We're going to hit them at dawn the day after tomorrow."

"Day after tomorrow?" Caleb sputtered. "But—"

"But that means we're going to march all night to-night and all day tomorrow. We'll come north along the road by the sea in three separate columns. And we're going to attack through these three feeder canyons, right here, here, and here," Joshua said, stabbing at the map.

Caleb leaned over the map and studied it. Then he sat back and relaxed. "Great idea. I—I'd never have thought of that."

"Nor I," Joshua admitted. "But once more God has spoken to me. He told me that there is one thing that chariots are no good for, and that's defense."

On all sides there was silence—respectful silence.

The next day Pepi was back at the forge in Ashdod, working the bellows for his friend Hagab, cleaning up, doing an apprentice's work with a vengeance—all in prep-aration for the day he would be skillful enough to travel north and make iron weapons for the Israelites' future enemies. He had hired a group of trustworthy Jerusalem guardsmen to continue the search for Tirzah and Neftis, under Baufra's and Nimshi's supervision. All day long he assailed Hagab with questions, and then listened carefully to the answers.

When they broke for the midday meal, Hagab took him aside. "Are you all right? You're very pale. I hope you aren't going to have another attack. Yesterday, fighting with Caleb, you looked so strong and healthy."

Pepi shrugged. "If I give in to anger, I'm sunk. And if I get too excited . . . So I've decided to stay calm and plan my revenge slowly and carefully." Suddenly the sadness disappeared, and his tone became brisk. "Tell me, Hagab, is it possible to standardize the methods of making iron weapons so that they can be made faster, on a larger scale? That's what my ancestor Shobai did with bronze weapons back in the days of the Shepherd Kings."

"I suppose it's possible," Hagab ventured. "Although there'd be no way to maintain the high quality I demand in my own work."

"I don't care about high quality. I want lots of iron weapons to put into the hands of Joshua's enemies. I don't care how pretty they are, so long as they'll cut through bronze weapons and drive the Israelites out of Canaan into the desert where they came from."

Hagab raised an eyebrow. "That could take years. And who would command the troops you would send against them?"

"I haven't found the man yet. But there has to be someone out there with the courage and strength to win. And when I find him, I'll train him and arm him myself." He paused, obviously trying to calm himself. "I have a lot to answer for. I helped bring these people into Canaan. And it's up to me to drive them out again."

III

Joshua pushed his men harder than they had ever been pushed before. By nightfall they were within striking distance of the Hazorite camp. But they waited until the hours before dawn to move down into the canyons.

Pickets atop a rise on the southern side of the creek spotted them. The lookouts were the fifteen-year-old Jabin, called Bini by his friends, eldest son of Jabin, the king of Hazor, and his two assistants. One of the boys was sent running down the hillside to notify the army; the other boy, Sisera, a commoner, watched from the heights with young Jabin.

"What are those crazy foreigners doing?" Bini asked. "They're not going to launch a frontal assault against my father's chariots, are they? They'll be slaughtered, every last one of them."

Sisera said nothing, but the look on his face got on Bini's nerves. "You think I said something stupid. What do you know about it, anyway? You've had no training."

"Even so, I can tell a smart move from a stupid one." Sisera rested his chin on the large stone in front of him. "And the foreigner isn't doing something dumb; this is a smart strategy. He'll do a lot of damage."

"Infantry can't stand against cavalry," Bini said.

"Not in an open field. But in this narrow little valley, cavalry's no use—the horses can't charge in an enclosed space. And the ground is uneven. The chariots will destroy their axles, and the horses' legs will break, too. Committing a thousand men to chariots in a space like this is foolishness."

Bini glared at him. "Where did you get these idiotic ideas?"

"Some of my ideas are mine," Sisera said. "Some are my father's. He's a captain in the army of Shimron."

Bini snorted. "Huh! A mere captain!"

"The only reason he'll never make general is because he can't hold his tongue around 'superior' officers who say stupid things. My father won't tell them how smart they are to come up with ideas any donkey would have better sense than to—"

"You've got an insolent tongue yourself," Bini cut in. "Well, you'll soon see how wrong you are. The foreigners are massing for their attack. It won't be long. They're outnumbered four to one."

"The fight will last all day," the commoner predicted.

"It'll take them that long to wipe us out. By then we'll be scattered all the way from here to the sea, and the Israelites will be in full pursuit." He looked young Bini in the eyes. "Your father's head will be decorating a pike by then. My father, if he has the good sense I think he has, will have deserted and lit out for Damascus, or somewhere else where they pay a soldier what he's worth. And, most likely, I'll be scrambling after him."

"Gods!" Bini said. "Don't you believe in anything?"

"Sure," Sisera replied. "I believe in saving my own neck when the odds are against me. I believe in thinking things out in detail, as the foreigner down there in the canyons apparently has." His dark eyes narrowed. "And I believe in revenge. If my father falls in this war he's been hired to fight in, I'm going to make some wretched Israelites pay for it."

"But there'll be no need for revenge," Bini said. "We're going to win."

"No, Prince, they're going to drive us into the sea. This Joshua knows what he's doing."

The sun had barely risen before Joshua struck the enemy. Two Israelite columns hit them broadside; the third column attacked Hazor's right flank.

Prince Bini's runner had carried the reconnaissance information down the hill only shortly before the attack began, so no use could be made of it. The vaunted cavalry was caught like sitting ducks as Joshua's advance units swarmed over them. His second wave of troops hamstrung the horses and incapacitated the chariots.

King Jabin, along with his elite guards, fell back and regrouped with the second-line units. But still the Israelites pressed forward, hacking and stabbing, leaving carnage in their wake.

In the front lines, Caleb, eager to erase the memory of his defeat by Pepi, fought like a madman. Behind him was Joshua. In vain had Eleazar tried to persuade the exhausted commander to leave the active fighting to his subordinates. Joshua, however, insisted upon being in the thick of battle from the first, drawing on his inner reserves of strength.

Joshua, coming up from the rear, took command of a unit of Israelites and broke into Jabin's line. But instead of being encircled by the enemy and being cut off, he managed to widen the hole in Jabin's line. His great sword flashed right and left, hacking through one neck after another, stabbing and battering. His right arm seemed to know no fatigue.

As the engagement against the troops of Hazor got under way, Micah watched Chaninai strap on a helmet and choose a weapon from among the swords stored in a supply cart. Micah could not help but smile when his smaller friend eagerly hefted one of the swords; the last time the two boys had sneaked into battle, Chaninai had been reluctant. Such was not the case today. This did not surprise Micah, for although Joshua had never found out about his son's participation, the great general Caleb had praised him for valor. Now Chaninai had the opportunity to prove to Caleb—and ultimately to his father—that his performance had not been a fluke and that he was competent enough to take his place among the Israelite troops.

Micah picked out his own sword and shield, then the two friends briefly clasped hands before starting into the narrow valley where the Israelite infantrymen were already engaging the chariots of Hazor. Micah shared his friend's enthusiasm.

Each victory, however, brought Joshua's army closer to Jerusalem—closer to disrupting the peace of Micah's family, who resided there. Shaking off his concerns, Micah raised his sword, steadied his shield, and went into battle.

He and Chaninai kept to the edge of the action, joining soldiers who were ordered to intercept any retreating enemy. At first the boys did little more than watch the progress of the main force of infantry. They quickly realized why Joshua's strategy had pinpointed the narrow valley for the assault, because almost as soon as the fighting began, the enemy cavalry found themselves hemmed in, unable to maneuver their large, double-horse chariots. Pandemonium broke out, so the Israelites were able to move in behind each chariot and overcome the occupants, most of whom were armed with long, cumbersome pikes.

As Micah looked around for one of the enemy to engage, he heard a shout from his friend and saw that Chaninai had moved in on a chariot that was attempting to turn and retreat. Micah started to his friend's aid, but Chaninai had already run the driver through with his sword and dragged him from the chariot. The young Israelite yanked the blade free from the man's chest and stood grinning proudly at Micah, who was twenty feet away.

Suddenly Micah spotted a pair of white horses galloping toward Chaninai from behind, pulling one of the Hazor chariots. He shouted and raised his hand in alarm, but Chaninai, not understanding the warning, merely raised his own hand and waved. When the horses galloped past him, Chaninai jumped, startled, but did not have time to leap clear before the driver ran him through with a pike, which broke off in his back as it knocked him to his knees.

Chaninai looked down in horror at the jagged, bloody point protruding from his abdomen. His sword fell from his fingers, and he reached to grasp the pike. He tried to speak, but as he opened his lips, he gagged up blood.

"Chaninai!" Micah shouted again and again, running to his dying friend. He started to kneel beside him, then looked up instinctively and saw that the charioteer had turned his vehicle and was starting back. The man had dropped the broken pike and now wielded a sword.

With a shriek of rage, Micah threw aside his shield and went running directly at the chariot, startling the horses. The left one reared up, and Micah thrust his sword upward into the animal, then quickly yanked the weapon out and made a vicious slash across the horse's legs.

The war-horse whinnied in pain, staggered, and fell

to the ground, causing the chariot to tip to the side. The driver fell out and was scrambling to his feet when Micah came sweeping down on him, swinging his sword in an wide arc and beheading the man.

A moment later, Micah was back at Chaninai's side, cradling the mortally wounded youth in his arms.

"Chaninai," he whispered.

"M-M-Micah," Chaninai muttered, gurgling up blood. There was a curious smile on his face. "I . . . k-k-killed him."

"Yes," Micah replied, and began to cry.

"T-tell . . ." His body shook, and he started to choke.

"I'll tell your father," Micah assured him. "Joshua will be proud of you. All the army will be."

Chaninai's body calmed, and he gave another faint smile. "I . . . I did it, didn't I? I'm a . . ."

"A soldier," Micah said as Chaninai's eyes closed into death. "You're a true soldier of Israel now."

Though the battle raged around him, Micah saw only the peaceful countenance of Chaninai as he held his friend close to his breast and sobbed.

As the two Canaanite boys watched from the ridge, the entire Hazorite line collapsed without warning. The Israelite army rushed forward, and a single officer detached himself from the fleeing troops to stand and face the oncoming horde.

"That's my father!" Sisera screamed out. "He should be escaping with the rest! Father! No!"

Bini crowded close beside and looked down. "Your father is a brave man," he said, admiringly. "Surrounded on all sides and yet fighting on! Look, that's Joshua himself he's taking on. The man's a master swordsman, but your father's his match."

A shrill scream of anguish followed his words as one of Joshua's soldiers came up behind the boy's father and ran him through from the rear. The man crumpled to the ground.

As they watched, Joshua cursed the man who had killed his opponent in so cowardly a fashion.

"I—I'm sorry," Bini faltered.

"I'll make someone pay for this," the young commoner vowed, "if it's the last thing I do!"

"Look!" Bini said. "There's my father! He's trying to get away, trying to fall back to the prepared positions in the rear. But they're cutting him off, the bastards! The damned cowardly foreign scum! Oh, gods! They've encircled him! They've—" His voice broke.

King Jabin fought valiantly but in vain. As he fended off sword strokes, a pikeman came at him and rammed his weapon into the king's throat. The two boys watched in horror as blood gushed out.

"I . . . I'm sorry, too, Prince. Your father died a hero. I swear we'll get revenge for this! Here's my hand on it." The two boys grasped hands. "Now we've got to escape so we can rebuild what your father put together. You're a king's son; I'm the son of a great soldier. If we become partners, someday we can avenge our fathers."

Bini's eyes were full of angry tears. "We'll raise our own army and train the soldiers well, and when the enemy is feeling fat and complacent . . . From this moment, Sisera, you and I are partners."

By nightfall Joshua's army had command of the field. They had only to pursue the stragglers and exterminate them one by one.

Joshua, limping back to his tent, came upon his son's body and suddenly collapsed. Shemida called for guards, who carried him into the tent, and then the adjutant summoned Eleazar and Caleb.

They all gathered around him, and when they saw his pale face and quivering hands, they knew this had been Joshua's last battle.

He knew it too. "Caleb," he said in a weak and disembodied voice, "the army is yours. Go tell the men you're taking over. Tell them to strike in my name, and in the name of Moses and Abraham!"

"I will continue in your footsteps," Caleb vowed in a voice thick with emotion. Then he turned quickly and left.

Eleazar sat down and took his friend's hand. "You knew the day was coming, didn't you?"

Joshua sighed. "There's a time for picking up the sword, and a time for laying it down. Stay with me awhile, will you, old friend? And send for Shemida."

"I'm right here, sir." Shemida's voice came out of the shadows. "I won't leave you."

"Good," Joshua said. "Will you break the news to my wife about Chaninai and take care of burial?"

"It's been done, sir."

"Then I can rest a bit, perhaps."

He slept. And sometime in the night, with Eleazar still holding his hand and Shemida hovering close by, the great hero of Israel slipped away peacefully into another and longer sleep. Eleazar and Shemida looked at each other and sat silently. They both realized an era had passed. The new era might have little use for either of them. What lay in their future, neither had any idea.

Outside, unaware of Joshua's passing or the tragic death of his boy, the army sang songs of victory and thanksgiving.

IV

In the desert, far to the northeast of Jerusalem, a slave caravan stopped for the night. Sometime in the small hours before morning Neftis had slipped away, stolen a knife, and cut her throat. Tirzah found her in the dawn's first light. Looking down at Neftis's body crumpled in the sand, she was not surprised. The rapes and beatings had toughened Tirzah but had pushed Neftis out of the comfort of her madness and into a black, stark reality. Tirzah watched silently through red-rimmed eyes as the Moabite slave masters examined the corpse.

"Toss her by the side of the road," one said. "There wouldn't have been any money in her anyhow. Too old and skinny."

"And crazy. But we won't risk another. Manacle the yellow-haired one. She'll fetch a nice price in the market."

"And if she doesn't bring a good price there, we'll take her all the way to Ebla. Look at her staring at us. *You* put on the manacles. The crazy woman bit my arm to the bone the last time I tried to lay a finger on her."

"Hit her in the head with something and truss her up when she's out. There's no use taking any chances."

Tirzah knew she'd have to change her approach—be nice to them, make them believe she was mellowing. But if they ever let her near a knife, they would quickly realize their mistake.

She held out her hands. "Go ahead. I won't try to stop you. I promise it's safe."

Safe? she thought. *For now. But wait. When you least expect it . . .*

Her people never forgot anything. They never let their enemies forget, either!

V

"It's not much farther," Shemida promised, waving his hand in front of him. "Just over that rise."

"Are you sure your wife won't mind?" The hollow-eyed youth looked tiredly at Shemida. "She doesn't know I'm coming—"

"Tamar will be delighted to have you stay with us, Micah, for as long as you like."

"It will only be for a day or so . . . until I've decided what I should do."

Pausing, Shemida laid a hand on Micah's shoulder.

"Don't rush into these decisions. Take as much time as necessary and stay with us for as long as you like."

Micah looked uncertainly at the Israelite. "Do you think I'm being foolish?"

"In considering the adoption of our religion and the laws of the One God?" He smiled. "Certainly Abraham didn't think it foolish when Yahweh asked him to do the same."

"Then you believe I ought to convert?"

"It is not for me to say." He shrugged. "As I told my wife before she converted, the decision is between you and your God. And if you're convinced that your God and mine is one and the same and that He is calling you to join our flock, then yes, you should follow the dictates of His will." Shemida's eyes narrowed, and he shook his head slightly. "But if this idea of yours stems from some sort of false vanity or pride—perhaps a desire to join Caleb's army and achieve recognition on the battlefield or to avenge the death of your friend—then you should put all of this destruction behind you and go off in search of your family."

"Chaninai," Micah whispered, voicing aloud the name that had been haunting his thoughts ever since he saw his friend get run through with a charioteer's pike.

"You miss your friend terribly," Shemida sympathized. "We all do, just as we miss his father, Joshua."

"Is it wrong to want to avenge his death?"

"Chaninai died in battle, a hero to his people. So did many of the enemy that day. We cannot hate the Hazorites for doing their duty on the battlefield. We should expect nothing less from them—or from ourselves." Shemida drew in a deep breath and let his gaze return to the road. "I smell something cooking nearby. Tamar will be preparing supper, and if you are as hungry as I am . . ." He clapped the boy on the back. "Come. Let's see what she has on the hearth."

"I suppose I could do with someting to eat," Micah admitted, starting back down the road, alongside Shemida.

Shemida and the youth walked up the small hill. As

they topped the rise, they looked into the valley beyond
and saw a small house sheltered by trees. A fire burned on
the hearth, a plume of smoke curled its way homeward
from the chimney—a haven after all the danger, heart-
ache, and loss . . . a place where Tamar would be waiting
for her husband.

Despite his limp, Shemida found his pace quickening
and his heart beating faster. "Come along!" he urged his
friend.

There she was at the window, her little face breaking
into a warm smile. She called to him, threw open the
door, and ran outside. Amid tears and laughter and words
so incoherent that he could make out none of what she
was saying, she threw herself into his arms.

He started to draw a breath, but it turned into a sob.
She understood and hugged him all the closer. Suddenly
she was kissing him, kissing the tears off his face, kissing
his eyes and mouth and cheeks.

"You're safe," she cried. "You're home safe again. I
prayed hard for you. I worried so. They told me . . . they
told me Joshua was dead, and I was afraid that . . ."

He let out a deep breath. "I'm all right," he said.
"I'm safe. I'm home, home to stay. I talked to Caleb and
asked for my pension. The war's over for me. When
Joshua died . . ."

The boy was hanging back, embarrassed by the display of connubial affection. Shemida brought him forward
and made introductions. "Micah will be staying with us for
a while," Shemida told Tamar. "Then, after some soul-
searching, he'll rejoin Caleb or try to find his family."

"Come inside, darlings," Tamar invited. "There's plenty
of food." She turned to Micah and smiled warmly. "Since
our marriage I've always cooked for two, as if Shemida
were here."

They let her lead them through the door into the
cottage and settle them before the fire.

"The fools!" Shemida blurted. "They won't learn.
They'll lose everything within a year or two and have to

fight again. And they'll have to fight their stupid tendency to rebel against their own leaders and against God."

Tamar bent to kiss Shemida's forehead and stroke his neck. "It's over," she said gently. "It's over for you and me, and for you, Micah, if he wishes. Joshua is gone. He lies with Abraham and Moses, and God looks out for him now."

When Shemida looked up at her, his face showed his fatigue. He managed a wan, tired smile. "All I know is war. What am I going to do?"

"You know one other thing," she said with an impish smile. "Which we'll discuss later, after dinner. But there are other things you can learn about—like pruning the trees. Tending the goats. Micah, you are welcome to stay as long as you like and help him. Meanwhile, I'll be taking care of the baby."

Shemida's jaw dropped. "You mean—?"

Tamar blushed and nodded. "Yes, dear. That's exactly what I mean."

CHAPTER THIRTEEN

Troy

I

The man in the chariot was invincible. Three times the Greek had swept across the field below the high walls of Troy, and three times a hail of arrows had rained down upon him from the bows of the Trojans atop the ramparts. Each time the arrows bounced off his gleaming bronze armor. Two horses had been shot from under him, and he had lost one charioteer; but he was untouched.

Around him the bloody battle raged; but from atop the towering walls of the city, the watchers saw only the two champions—Prince Hector, son of King Priam of Troy, bravest and noblest of men, and the valorous Greek. They knew he could be none other than the mightiest of all warriors in the known world, the peerless Achilles.

From the moment he appeared on the field, a spirit of desperation had overcome the Trojans. Their nemesis, Achilles, missing from the Greek ranks for weeks, had suddenly reappeared. Everyone knew that Achilles had been feuding with Agamemnon. It had been a silly quarrel, as most of Agamemnon's many personal quarrels were.

But Achilles, infuriated with the king of Mycenae, had retired to his tent, refusing to fight. And so the Greeks had been forced to carry on the siege without him. For three months they had been fighting the Trojans outside the city walls. For nine of these twelve weeks, they had fought without the aid of Achilles or his personal army.

Suddenly Greek after Greek began to fall before the Trojans; Achilles' absence had given new vigor to the beleaguered defenders of Troy. But while his comrades fell, Achilles sat playing his lyre and composing poems. Every day he stayed away from the fight, the Trojans grew more fierce until they seemed to become a new army.

The Greeks had cursed Achilles under their breath— they knew his terrible temper and obstinacy—and every day they had gone out to meet a fearless Trojan force.

But now it was the Trojans who were falling back on every front as the gleaming armor of Achilles flashed into their dazzled eyes. He drove his chariot back and forth before the walls of Troy, waving his spear at the Trojans as if to say, "Kill me if you can!"

Suddenly, in front of the gates of the city, he was attacked by four soldiers; but to the horror of the watchers, he effortlessly killed every one of them with his lance and sword. The last of them he beheaded, and he held up the head toward the Trojans on the wall before spitting in the dead eyes and tossing it to the ground.

Was Achilles as invincible as legend said?

At the gates of the city, Prince Hector, having retired from battle for fresh horses, paused before stepping into his own chariot. He closed his eyes for a silent prayer.

His uncle Asius mistook his pause for cowardice. "Aren't you going out there after him?" he demanded. "Has he frightened you so badly that you're considering turning tail before him? Gods preserve me, the men of my time wouldn't have hesitated while brave men were dying out on the field!"

Hector opened his eyes, and for a moment he looked

ready to let loose an angry tirade. But then he took a deep breath. "Uncle, you interrupted a prayer to Apollo. May he forgive you!" He paused. "Now watch what a man of my generation does."

Asius moved hastily out of his way.

"Open the gates!" Hector ordered. The guards obeyed, and Hector gave instructions to his charioteer. The fresh horses pranced out onto the field to the accompaniment of great cheering.

Hector made directly for Achilles. His quarry immediately leapt down from his own chariot and picked up a good-sized rock, which he hurled directly at Hector.

Hector ducked, and the missile caught his charioteer in the forehead. The man fell and landed heavily on the ground. Grabbing the reins his attendant had dropped, Hector looked back in horror. The driver lay still.

Hector wheeled his horses around and made for the fallen body, but the armored Greek reached it first. He stood astride one of the charioteer's inert legs. "Look how easily the Trojan dives into the dust!" he called to Hector. "I thought he was a driver. Perhaps he was a diver instead and is used to going headfirst into the sea!"

When Hector heard the insolent taunt, something snapped in his mind. Whipping his horses recklessly, he made for the lone warrior. A squad of Greek soldiers immediately surrounded his prey, however, and Hector had to turn aside. He could not resist calling out a challenge: "You can hide behind them, coward, but I'll find you before the day's over! I swear it!"

Then the battle closed in around him, and Hector had to fight his way out. Those who heard his vow remembered it. Hector was not a man to make idle threats. What kind of man dared to throw words like *coward* at Achilles? Hearing his insult, those on the wall quaked at what the day would bring.

Princess Cassandra stood atop the wall with her blind maid, Keturah.

"Hector's lost his chance," she said in disgust. "He could have killed Achilles, but he hesitated, and the Greeks rushed in to save him. Maybe there's still a chance." She whistled low. "Achilles can fight! He's single-handedly taking on three of our mercenaries and they haven't a prayer! He's changed his style of fighting since he came back. Strange . . . you can usually distinguish one man from another by the way he handles his sword. A man has a certain pattern to his swordwork. If I didn't recognize that armor . . ."

Keturah's face had a faraway look. Her words, when she spoke, seemed to come from a distance, too. "You don't see Iri down there, do you, my lady?"

Cassandra laughed affectionately. "You're a singer with only one note, aren't you, dear? If I'd seen him, you can be sure I would have told you."

"I'm sorry, I just—"

"I understand. Most likely, though, Iri's safely back at the ships working on someone's sword or making new armor. It would be a waste for your husband to fight. Even Achilles couldn't be as much use to the Greeks as a good armorer is." The princess patted her only friend on the arm, then gasped.

"What's the matter?" Keturah asked.

"Hector's got him alone now! Achilles and Hector, they're going to fight!"

It was not Hector who dealt the first blow that day against Achilles. Another Trojan came up from behind and struck Achilles, running a lance through his back. Now it was easy for Hector. He stabbed Achilles so hard in the groin with his spear that the point came through the other side. The figure in the bright armor staggered and fell.

Hector bent over him. "Achilles!" he taunted. "Get up and fight me, brave one! Don't make it so easy for me!"

The figure on the ground stirred, reaching with shaky hands for the helmet that hid his face. "D-dying. Help me take it off."

For a moment Hector hesitated; then he bent down and carefully removed the helmet from the fallen hero's face.

He stepped back in astonishment. "What in the—?" The face was not Achilles'.

II

An uproar sounded from the Greek ranks. From their shouts of disbelief and outrage, it became clear to Cassandra what had happened.

"Keturah!" the princess said, leaning out over the edge of the parapet to see what was happening. In her excitement she grabbed the blind woman's hand and squeezed hard. "It wasn't Achilles! It was that friend of his who was killed—Patroclus! But why would he have been wearing Achilles' armor?"

"What's going on now?" Keturah asked.

"Hector's taking that beautiful armor off Patroclus's body. He looks furious! He thought he'd killed Achilles!" She squeezed Keturah's hand again, and her tone changed. "He's putting on Achilles' armor! Wait until Achilles hears about this!"

Hector, wearing the armor that had fooled everyone, fiercely fought his way back into the fray, slashing right and left with his sword.

Keturah could feel Cassandra's grip loosen. Her hand trembled slightly, and suddenly it went cold as if it were a dead woman's hand. "My lady!" she cried out.

Cassandra's entire body was shaking. Keturah eased her mistress to the ground and cried out for help, but nobody came. She felt for Cassandra's face and tried to get hold of her tongue so that the princess could not swallow it. Hearing footsteps approaching, Keturah called out, "Please help me. The princess is having another one of her attacks."

The man, one of King Priam's slaves, helped Keturah get Cassandra to her room, and when the princess woke, Keturah was sitting beside her, holding her hand.

Keturah felt Cassandra struggling to sit up and gently restrained her. But the seeress pushed the hand away.

"I had another one, didn't I? I remember some of it. Something happened, didn't it? Hector killed Patroclus and ate him. No, that was the dream. He killed him and put on his armor, and now he looks like Achilles." Her tone changed abruptly. "Oh, Keturah! Something dreadful's going to happen! I saw the flames again, and the women were being dragged away."

"Please, my lady, try to rest. It isn't good for you to worry like this."

With a shudder Cassandra pulled Keturah to her bosom and held her. Keturah could feel her heart pounding.

Menelaus, king of Sparta, pulled his spear out of a dead Trojan and looked around through the dust of battle. Coming toward him, nearly dancing with delight, was his brother, Agamemnon.

"What are you so happy about?" Menelaus snarled.

"Patroclus is dead. Isn't that wonderful?"

"Well, if you're so thrilled about it, maybe you'd like to be the one to bring the news to Achilles," Menelaus suggested. "No one else wants to."

"But don't you see?" Agamemnon asked, clutching his brother's arm. "Patroclus's death will bring Achilles back to the fold. His fury at Hector will be much greater than his anger toward me. He'll want revenge and will fight for us again. Perhaps we'll win this war once and for all."

"We'd better find some men to retrieve Patroclus's corpse before Hector's men hack it into pieces and feed it to the dogs," Menelaus said.

"No, don't," Agamemnon protested. "If anything will bring Achilles back into battle, that'll be it. Leave Patroclus where he is. He won't know the difference."

Menelaus gave his brother a long look of disgust. "I wonder why Patroclus impersonated Achilles like that. Didn't he know that wearing Achilles' armor would draw down every Trojan sword on him?"

"That's why I asked him to do it," Agamemnon said lightly. "Of course, I told him that our men would protect him better than they actually did. . . ." He shrugged. "But that's a chance we all have to take in war, isn't it? That we'll die when we're least expecting it. I'll find someone to break the news to Achilles. Nestor's son, perhaps . . ."

Menelaus was left to watch his brother's retreating back.

Iri and his assistant, Phorbus, were repairing a broken chariot axle. "Swab the thing down with grease!" Iri said. "I can't hold it up much longer by myself."

Phorbus seated the axle in the axletree after laying down a heavy glob of jellied animal fat. Only then did Iri set the frame of the chariot down atop it. Phorbus watched him and whistled under his breath. No one else in camp could even have lifted the chariot body by itself, much less held it while waiting for someone to grease the axletree. But the men in camp had begun calling Iri "Hephaestus," the incredibly strong god of fire and metalworking, only half in jest. They said that if you asked Iri to mend the metal fittings on your saddle he would carry the horse away with it, slung over one shoulder, because he was too lazy to take the saddle off the animal.

"Lot of commotion out there," Iri remarked. "I suppose somebody important has gotten himself killed."

Phorbus wiped his grimy brow. "I could send someone to find out."

Iri shook his head. "We'll learn about it soon enough. They'll come home in the evening out of sorts and complain all night about it." He gave a wry smile. "Look at it this way: As long as they're fouling the air with noise, we don't have to listen to Achilles over there singing his verses. I wish he'd get off his butt and back into the battle."

"I wouldn't talk that way where he might hear it."

Iri turned to Phorbus. In the time they had spent together, they had moved from master and apprentice to almost father and son. "You know what I think of the great Achilles dropping out of the war. I want to see my wife, curse it, and Achilles' salving the wounds of his pride is making my wait even longer. The man's a pompous ass. I'll say it louder if you didn't hear it clearly enough. *A pompous ass!*"

Phorbus winced. "It's just that—"

"He's getting the men of our own side killed right and left because of his idiotic temper tantrums. Even Patroclus hasn't been able to prevail upon him."

"Which brings to mind," Phorbus said, pouring water over his dirty hands, "where is Patroclus today? I haven't seen him all morning."

"Someone said they saw him coming away from Achilles' tent with the great man's armor. I suppose he was taking it out to be polished."

"Polished? Achilles always keeps it polished. Why would Patroclus—?" Phorbus stopped and thought for a moment. "Unless . . . no," he said with a frown. "He wouldn't do anything that stupid."

Iri stared at his friend. "You have an idea?"

"You don't suppose that, just for a joke—one of those stupid jokes of his—he decided to dress up in Achilles' armor and impersonate him on the battlefield?"

Antilochus, son of King Nestor, had been ordered by Agamemnon to bring the terrible news to Achilles. Afraid to face Achilles by himself, the young man took Odysseus with him. As they approached Achilles, Odysseus urged Antilochus forward. "He won't kill you for bringing the news—at least I don't think he will. If he tries, I'll be here to defend you."

Odysseus could have imagined any number of reactions to the news. But what Achilles did took Odysseus by surprise. He put his lyre down carefully and placed his hands over his face. He sat with his eyes closed and head bowed for a long time, as if he were communing with a god. To Odysseus's astonishment he did not even appear to be weeping. Then, as if nothing had happened, he opened his eyes.

"The Trojans have his body?" Achilles asked.

Nestor's son nodded.

"And Hector is wearing my armor?"

"Yes, my lord. It is the ultimate act of arrogance and insolence."

"Yes, so it is," Achilles said. "That armor belonged to my father. I cannot go into battle with ordinary armor. I must wait until special armor, fit for the greatest battle of all time, can be made for me. By Hephaestus himself."

Odysseus rolled his eyes heavenward. He was about to tell Achilles that he thought he was insane, when Achilles continued, "Bring me the armorer that men call Hephaestus. Tell him I have a special commission for him. I want him to make me armor to wear when I kill Hector."

This time, although his voice dripped with malice and suppressed rage, it sounded entirely sane.

III

At the dawn of this long and bloody day of fighting, Hector had been the first man to come through the gates of Troy. Now, as the sun lay low in the west and all his men came trudging wearily homeward, he lingered behind. Even after the Greeks had retired to the ships in the harbor, he was still carefully checking every fallen Trojan to make sure that no wounded soldier was left for dead on the plain. At last he slogged slowly up the hill and through the massive gates. He nodded to the guards to close them and throw the bolt.

Suddenly he found himself alone in the street. Two hours before he had been a hero. The citizens had lined the walls of the town and cheered as he had fought for them, hewing at the hard bodies of the Greeks with ax and sword and lance until it seemed his arms were too weary to move. After the exhaustion had set in, he had forced himself onward, plumbing new depths of his strength. He had fought until he could no longer tell whether he was winning or losing. He had fought until there were no Greeks near him to battle and his legs had been too weak to seek out new ones to pursue.

Now he was not certain he could get home again. He almost fell, but he forced his legs to continue. Taking off the once-gleaming helmet of Achilles, he tossed it carelessly into the street. He saw that it was covered with blood and dust. Hector looked down at his chest and forearms. His arms were black with clotted blood, some of it his own. His body armor was splashed with blood. Cursing, he reached down to unbuckle it. The bronze armor no longer gleamed as it had when he had stolen it from the dead man. He let it drop into the street.

Stumbling, he bent and pulled the greaves from his legs and tossed them aside. Even his legs were streaked with blood and filth. Somewhere he had lost a sandal. The sword he was wearing was taken from another man, but whom? He could not remember. One of his legs felt numb. He knew a rib was broken as a sharp pain shot through his side.

But he was alive. And that was a lot, he told himself.

It was the end of the day, but the battle was still not over; the enemy would come at him again the next day, and somehow he had to find the strength to go out to fight again.

He looked down the long street. Was it possible he still had so far to go?

If only he could reach back into the day and change the outcome of his fight with Patroclus, for today he had sealed his fate. Achilles might have remained beside the ships, taunting the Greeks, refusing to join them in the fight, and lowering their morale. Perhaps he might even have eventually called his personal army together and sailed home.

But now there was no chance. Achilles would return to the fight, ignoring his quarrel with Agamemnon. His love for Patroclus would prompt him to forget his anger against everyone but Hector. And Achilles would devote all his vast energy to killing him.

Only Hector's death would satisfy Achilles. He would destroy one detachment of Trojans after another until he had hewed his way through them all to find Hector and fight man to man to the death.

And Hector knew how that fight would end. He had known it from the first day the Greeks had landed.

He looked up. At last, there was the staircase to the palace. He lifted one weary foot and felt his legs turn to water. He almost fell. He reached down and steadied his leg and forced it onto the step. How many steps were there to the top? Seventy-six. He had counted them every day. And now he was not sure he was going to make it.

But of course that was absurd. He would make it home. He would try to get some sleep and rise the next morning and tempt fate by trying to live through another day.

And once more he would conquer the fear he felt of Achilles. He would because there was one thing he feared more than facing the Greek hero: It was the vision Cassandra had told him about . . . Troy in flames . . . the fiery-eyed conquerors rampaging through the streets, their filthy, blood-smeared hands reaching out to grab the women whose men had lost the war.

In the end Achilles put on the show Odysseus had been expecting. Standing on the shore by the Greek ships, he wept and wailed and tore his hair; he snarled and threw things and swore revenge; he roared like a lion and cursed. But he waited until he had a proper audience.

Bored with the performance, Odysseus went looking for Iri.

Iri sat before a roaring fire, drinking wine and eating olives. "Sit down," he invited. "You look like a man who has either been counting the grains of sand on the beach or listening to Achilles. What you need is some of this atrocious wine I won in an arm-wrestling contest."

He tossed the wineskin over to Odysseus, who drank from it thirstily and then spat out the last gulp on the sand. "That *is* atrocious," he said. "You've got to start wrestling a better class of people. You need a manager. Maybe I'll quit fighting Trojans and manage your career."

"No time for wrestling now. I suppose you've heard: I'm making armor for the great Achilles, armor to turn aside everything from sword thrusts to lightning bolts." He grinned. "You are now looking at a miracle worker, a man who can make magic armor. Of course it will look and feel just like ordinary armor. Maybe a little prettier. But he pays well for magic, or so he says."

"He's no swindler," Odysseus said. "He can't afford to be. Appearances are too important to him."

Odysseus frowned and took another long drink. "Your wine is strong enough, that's for sure. And that'll have to do, even if it does taste like piss dipped out of a trench." He wiped his lips. "Despite everything, Achilles really can fight. And there is a decent side to him." He spat into the gathering darkness. "I wouldn't be Achilles for all the money and power in the world. I wouldn't be Achilles even to get back home to Penelope and my boy." Suddenly his tone turned thoughtful. "Yes, I would. I'd do almost anything to be home with my family."

"Odysseus," said Iri, taking the wineskin, "I'm going to sneak inside Troy some night soon, when there's a commotion down here and nobody will notice. Maybe we can bribe a few of the boys to start a fight, one of the ships against another. Anything to draw the attention of the guards on the wall."

Odysseus looked at Iri. "What did you say?"

"I'm going into Troy. It'll take planning, but I'm not going to wait any longer. I've only gotten a glimpse of Keturah once or twice from the field, while she was standing on the wall with Princess Cassandra. That's not enough, Odysseus."

"You damned fool! What sort of nonsense are you spouting now? Give me that wineskin. You're drunk."

"Keep it," Iri said, handing it over. He pulled out another. "Plenty more where that came from." He uncorked the new skin and squirted a long stream into his mouth. "Bah! This is even worse than the last stuff. These heathen bastards must have cut it with pig sweat."

"About sneaking into Troy . . ." Odysseus said. "Both of us know how heavily guarded it is. You'll get your guts cut out before you've gone twenty steps."

"I don't care," Iri said. "Better dead than living separated from Keturah." He took a long drink and stopped only when the wine ran down his cheeks and neck into his tunic. "I'm going to go by myself. Less danger that way."

"No, you're not," said a voice out of the darkness behind them. Iri turned. "Either you take me along or you're not going," Phorbus said.

"Both of you, hold off a bit longer," Odysseus said. "Otherwise you'll get yourselves killed."

"Time to go now," Iri said, his words slurring. "Any night now."

In the morning Iri took fittings for Achilles' armor. He turned out to be the same size as one of his own army's lieutenants for whom Iri had been making a helmet and breastplate, and Iri decided to adapt these. But he did not dare mention this to Achilles.

That afternoon Iri worked on the armor. On the breastplate there was a picture in half-relief of Achilles himself in battle. Iri polished this until it shone like the sun and then added feathers to the helmet. Achilles, he knew, was fond of such useless decorations.

In the field there was a day of rest as the Greeks mourned Patroclus.

"You missed another big show," Odysseus said sourly when he came again to visit. "Achilles outwept us, outbragged us, and outdid us with his threats against the Trojans. I fell asleep."

Iri checked a fitting and tightened a leather strap. "I'll bet he liked that."

"He snorted a bit, I'm told. I didn't stay around to hear all of it. He threw a lot of insults in my direction, but I'm past the point when anything he says can touch me."

Iri held up the armor to catch the afternoon light, then passed it to his friend to admire.

"Gorgeous," Odysseus said moodily, then handed it back. "We have to get this battle between the two heroes out of the way. Then when the personal score has been settled, we'll have to realize that if we don't do something drastic, we're going to be here for years, fighting before the damned walls of Troy. We'll all be palsied old men with weak legs and unable to hold our piss anymore, but we'll still be staggering out every morning to fight the Trojans. Only it'll be their fresh, strong young sons we'll be fighting, while *our* sons will be home in Greece, doing something sensible like making money or bedding women."

"I see the war continues to keep a fine edge on your wit," Iri said. He held the helmet between his knees as he worked on it with a hammer.

"I'm tired of this. I want to do something that will get us home before we're so old our wives won't recognize us." He grunted. "I guess I trust Penelope, but most of these fellows here—if they were to go home right now, they'd find the old woman flat on her back with her heels in the air, doing it with some upstart half her age."

Iri grinned at him. "Rumors are already beginning to circulate. About the august king of Mycenae, for instance."

Odysseus looked at him with amused surprise. "Ah!

Clytemnestra!" His expression darkened. "After what happened to Iphigenia, though, I'm not surprised."

"I was there, too," Iri said, "and I remember the look on Clytemnestra's face. She would be within her rights to want revenge. A terrible waste, terrible. And such a beautiful child." Iri put down the helmet and looked at Odysseus. "I don't even know what my child looks like." His jaw firmed. "I can't wait. I've put it off too long. First chance I get, I'm going inside Troy to find my Keturah."

IV

Hector's wife, Andromache, awoke in the night and found herself alone in the bed. She sensed that Hector had not been beside her for a long time. She arose and threw on a light robe and, barefooted, walked across the moonlit bedroom.

The next room was empty, but beyond, on the terrace, she could see her husband sitting in the moonlight, naked. His whole body seemed to sag.

She paused to pick up a sheet and drape it over her arm. Distraught, he hardly noticed her until she stood beside him, arranging the sheet over his shoulders and sitting close to him.

"I missed you," she said.

He did not speak for such a long time that she thought he was not going to. But at last he said in a flat voice, "I'm frightened. I'm afraid of Achilles. Afraid of dying. Afraid of leaving you alone." He could not look at her. "Don't worry, by tomorrow I'll have figured out how to conquer my fear, and I'll be out there fighting as if Achilles were some weakling upstart who didn't know one end of a sword from another—and not the Greeks' strongest and most resourceful warrior." He took a deep breath that was almost a sob. She shot a glance at him, but his eyes were dry. "But tonight . . . the nights are the hardest."

"Of course they are," she said, putting a soft hand on his arm. "Hector, my dear, now you know what it's like being a wife, waiting at home and not knowing."

Suddenly he looked at her with wide eyes. "I'd never thought of that. Forgive me."

"There's nothing to forgive." She smiled, and her voice was gentle. "Did you suppose I'd think less of you for admitting you're afraid?"

He was silent.

"Who wouldn't be afraid? Only a fool! How much more difficult it is for a man who's frightened, as you are, to go out and face down his fears every day. That's true bravery. Anyone can easily confront death if he isn't afraid of it."

His expression was blank.

"Come to bed," she said. "Bring your fear to me. I'll give you a love poultice for it. I'll rub your back. I'll make love to you. And you'll sleep soundly, and when you arise in the morning, it will be with a clear head. You'll do what you have to do, and everything will be all right."

"But—"

"It will be all right. Even if you lose. This life is short. We'll be together soon enough. Do what you have to do—be Hector, the great man you are."

"Andromache . . ."

"Come to bed now. I love you. I'm not worried about myself. Why should you be?" She took his hand and all his fear flowed into her. She took it upon herself and buried it.

In the morning the Trojan troops, who had gathered inside the gates, looked at one another and felt the same fear Hector had known. "What if Achilles comes back today? What if . . .?"

"Forget everything you've heard about Achilles' being invulnerable," Hector said. "He's just another man. Do you know what we're going to do tonight? We're going to slaughter the lambs and eat like the gods themselves. If we have something to celebrate, it'll be best celebrated with a feast. If we have to mourn, we can mourn better on a full stomach. And if we've lost the war and have only one last night, better that we, rather than the Greeks, should eat all the food we have hoarded. Let's not leave a morsel for them. When we go out to fight them today, my friends, think not about how mighty their fighters may be but how good the food's going to taste when we return from the battle."

"But Hector, Achilles has new armor."

"Good. I'm wearing the armor he loaned to Patroclus. Someone was kind enough to collect it and bring it to me. It seems appropriate that I wear it to fight him, if that's what I'm fated to do today." He grinned, a fierce and fearless warrior's grin. "If I'm not afraid of Achilles and I'm the man he's sworn to kill, why should any of the rest of you be? I feel like a conqueror today. I feel like a man who, at the end of the day, is going to wipe the blood off his sword and stack arms in the corner of his own house, then go to dinner with his wife. Now who's with me?"

Odysseus pulled Iri and Phorbus away from their forge and dragged them down to the beach where Agamemnon's flagship lay. "You don't want to miss this," he said. "Achilles is going to make a speech."

Iri tried to twist away. "I don't want to hear any damned speech. I've got work to do, plans to make."

"I know. Today's the day you're going to do something stupid, isn't it? Phorbus, can't you talk him out of it?"

Phorbus snorted. "I've tried. There's nothing to do but go with him. Don't worry. I'll stick to him like a barnacle, although I'm a fool for doing it."

They found Achilles standing by Agamemnon's ship. Agamemnon appeared in his best armor and stood by his side. A profound quiet spread through the crowd.

Achilles stepped forward to face Agamemnon. "Son of Atreus," he said, "I have been long away from battle—too long. Let me spend the day dirtying my sword with the blood of Trojans, and then, when we have returned at nightfall, let us celebrate our renewed friendship with feasting and merrymaking. But first things first—to battle! Let all the Trojans, and above all let Prince Hector, beware, for today I mean to send him to lie with his ancestors!"

The applause was thunderous. Achilles and Agamemnon embraced and then held their swords high to acknowledge the cheers of the crowd.

"That damned fellow can act with dignity when he so chooses, and he even managed to get dignified behavior out of the clod Agamemnon," Odysseus said. "Aren't you glad you—?"

He turned around and realized he was talking to himself. "Iri?" he asked. "Phorbus? Where did you go?"

"What madness is this?" Phorbus demanded. "In the middle of the day? I thought we'd be going over the wall at night, when the world can't see us."

Iri hurried along the riverbank behind the hill on which Troy stood. "I didn't ask you to come along," he said. "As a matter of fact I forbade you to come along." He let out a snort. "A lot of good it did."

"We were a team as recently as yesterday," Phorbus said, "but all of a sudden you decide to do something crazy without even consulting me, and when I try to get you to talk sense—"

"I don't want to talk sense, Phorbus. I want to see Keturah again. And I want to see my child."

Phorbus, puffing, caught up to him. "I know you want to see them, but in your place I'd—"

"This will probably be a perfect opportunity to find her. Today everyone in Troy will be on that wall looking down on the plain. They'll all be sweating out every moment of the confrontation between Prince Hector and Achilles. What better time to get in over the rear wall?"

Phorbus stumbled, but Iri did not slow down to let him recover. He had to rush to catch up. "I know it sounds like a good plan," Phorbus said, "but there we'll be, right in the middle of Troy, and . . . Do you even know how to find Cassandra's apartments?"

"I know from a former servant at the palace who used to come through here trying to drum up tinker work. He drew me a map, and I memorized it. Her quarters are two floors up in the palace, near Prince Hector's rooms."

"People say Cassandra's crazy. What if she does something weird to ruin your plan? Don't you remember seeing her back in Greece?"

This made Iri break stride. He stared at Phorbus. "I did? When?"

"Back in Pylos, when you had the shouting match with Prince Paris on the waterfront. She was standing at the rail, and she smiled at the scene. I watched her face. It's a hard face, and her eyes looked so strange."

"We'll just have to take our chances. I have to get Keturah out of here." He spat. "I'm going to take things in my own hands at last. Faster! Why can't you keep up?"

V

On the one day when bright sunshine would have been most welcome, a trick of fate sent a thick, low-lying fog down on Troy. It came on quickly, as fog does along a seacoast, and soon the armies pouring forth onto the battlefield could barely tell friend from foe. And the watchers perched on the city walls caught only occasional glimpses of the soldiers as they groped about in the thick mist.

Blindly the two forces stumbled toward each other. A warrior feeling his way through the fog might suddenly find himself face to face with an enemy—or a friend he might mistake for an enemy. Blows were struck, and men fell.

Achilles, raging like an angry lion, confronted Prince Aeneas of Troy in the mist. Achilles cursed that the gods

had not delivered his enemy Hector into his hands and
hissed scornful words at Aeneas. "Get out of my way,
damn you!" he said. "Tell Hector I'm waiting for him!"

"To find him you'll have to cross my dead body,"
Aeneas said. "As for killing me, you talk a good fight. The
Trojans don't boast idly the way you Greeks do. First they
kill you, then they talk about it."

"If that's the way you want it," Achilles said, "I can
oblige you. First I'll practice on you, then I'll kill Hector."

"Kill away," Aeneas challenged, and, without warning, cast his lance. It hit the shield Iri had made for
Achilles and clattered harmlessly to the ground. Achilles
laughed and threw his own spear. It pierced Aeneas's
bronze-and-oxhide buckler and grazed his shoulder before
coming to rest in the ground.

Aeneas, sobered by the near miss, picked up a large
rock and heaved it at Achilles. But as it left his hand a
cloud of even thicker fog surrounded them, and he could
not tell if the stone had hit its mark. He cursed and
pushed forward through the mist.

Achilles, dodging the rock, blundered ahead. The two
men passed so close to each other they could have touched;
but they could see nothing. Achilles continued on, prob-
ing the grayness in front of him with his sword.

Suddenly he stumbled over something. He bent over,
ran his hand along the ground, and found a fallen spear.
He put his sword in its scabbard and, holding his buckler
before him, moved forward, spear at the ready.

Without warning the mist rose slightly, and he found
himself facing a party of Trojan soldiers. With an animallike snarl he lunged at them. His spear caught one man in
the forehead and split his skull; the Trojan fell at Achilles'
feet. When another came at him, the Greek caught him in
the eye and drove the spear deep into his brain.

Achilles realized he was completely surrounded by
Trojans and felt a surge of excitement. There was nothing
he liked more than a fight against overwhelming odds. He

stabbed a third warrior in the kidney and withdrew the lance just in time to see one of Priam's sons rushing toward him. With a roar he rammed the spear into the boy's groin and was rewarded with a piercing howl of pain.

Then, suddenly, coming out of the fog toward him he saw Hector! He was wearing the armor Patroclus had worn on the day of his death!

"There you are, you bastard!" Achilles cried. "You might as well fight me now, because I'll catch you before the day is out!" He looked into his enemy's eyes and saw fear. He felt a great surge of triumph in his heart. "You're afraid of me," he screamed savagely. "You murdering son of a whore, well you should be. Stand and fight!"

The two men stood staring at each other for a moment. The fog settled between them. When it drifted past, Hector was nowhere to be seen.

Losing his prey drove Achilles to a peak of insane rage. "Hector!" he screamed. "Hector, stand and fight, you coward!"

But it was not Hector who bore through the fog at him. Spear-carrying young Trojans confronted him. Achilles snarled and laid into them like an avenging god, killing a Trojan youth with a single blow to the neck and wounding his comrade in the knee with the backswing. He killed two young warriors with his sword and then, ignoring the pleas of one weeping youth who cowered at his feet, stabbed the boy through the liver.

This still did not satisfy his bloodlust. A Trojan came into view, and whirling, Achilles drove his lance into the young man's ear with such force that it went right through his skull. The boy's falling body pulled the spear from Achilles's hand. He let the lance go and drew the sword Iri had given him.

Still they came at him, but his strength did not diminish. It seemed to flow into his arm from the sword. "This Hephaestus fellow makes a good blade!" he roared to himself. "Let's anoint it properly." And he killed an oncoming Trojan with a single blow to the head and wounded another with the backswing before finishing him off with a mighty slash that nearly decapitated him.

"Give me more Trojans to kill!" he screamed. "Here am I, Achilles! Test my strength and skill. Give me Trojans! Give me Hector of Troy!"

The towering walls of Troy rode above the fogbank like a ship on the waves. Peering down into the mist, the watchers could see little of what was happening. But Achilles' last onslaught had been plainly visible, and the sight of the invincible Greek slaughtering Trojans until his forearms were red with blood threw fear into their hearts.

Only Cassandra viewed the battle with a certain detachment. She believed that nothing could save her from the fate the gods had decreed for the city. It was not fear she felt so much as an objective admiration for Achilles' catlike grace as he mowed through her people.

What did awaken feeling in her was the sight of Prince Paris standing atop the walls, his bow and arrows by his side, sitting out the battle in which so many of his people were dying. There was no other man of fighting age on the wall. Except for King Priam every man was either in the field, fighting the Greeks as he should be, or recovering from honorable battle injuries.

The sight of Paris indulging his well-known cowardice began to eat at her, and she found her temper rising. At last Paris picked up his long bow and his quiver. With a malicious smile on his face, he drew the bow and loosed an arrow. Below, on the plain, the arrow pierced the arm of a Greek who fell and did not arise.

Curious, Cassandra approached her brother. "What sort of sorcery is this?" she asked. "That man should have been able to pull the arrow out and go on fighting. Yet he died in his tracks."

Paris grinned and shot another arrow. It sped, swift and accurate, to its destination, striking a Greek in the neck. He dropped, wriggled weakly once or twice, then was still.

Paris turned back to her. "I bought a poison on the islands," he explained. "You thought I was merely dallying with Helen, but I was trying to find something to make up the difference in strength between other fighters and me. Why should a slightly built fellow like I am fight a great ox such as Achilles one on one, as though we were physical equals? No, my dear sister, I have advantages other than strength, and I'm going to use them."

"Don't call me sister," she said in a tone dripping with contempt. "I refuse to share blood with a coward like you! Poisoned arrows! Shooting at braver men than yourself from cover! If there's a more despicable snake on the face of the earth, I don't know who it could be!"

He continued fitting a shaft into his bow. With an insolent grin he said, "Bluster all you want. Hector will fight Achilles, test his muscles, and fall. Hector's a fine fighter, but he's never been a match for that magnificent animal down there, who hasn't any idea what the word *fear* means and who can cut off heads all day and not tire his arm." He took aim. "But me? I'm going to be the one who takes Achilles down. Just watch."

"Haven't you any shame?"

"Shame? For killing Greeks? I'm surprised at you, Cassandra. You act as if I weren't defending my city, as if I didn't deserve praise for repelling the hated enemy. Yet while you've been watching, I've killed two Greeks, who, I might remind you, darling, might have set fire to this house and hauled you off into slavery."

"You're not only shameless, you're as slippery as a serpent," she said. "Don't other people's opinions of you ever bother you?"

"Why should they? Do they bother you? If they did—if you ever gave them any credit, or started believing there was any truth in them—you'd have to hide your head in shame. Surely it can't have escaped your notice that most people consider you crazy? A loudmouthed, petulant termagant who goes around spouting incoherent auguries to anybody and giving herself airs about how holy she is?"

Cassandra stared. "I'm a priestess of Apollo," she said, shocked. "I don't have to give myself airs. The god chose me—"

"So you say. And because of your rank, nobody challenges you. But do you really know what people say about your fits and spasms? They say that you wouldn't be half as crazy if you'd open your legs to some young upstart from the lower classes and learn what it is to be a woman."

"*What?*"

"The gossip is that you and the blind girl are lovers, and she's the reason you don't give yourself to a man. Nobody believes that nonsense about your being consecrated to Apollo."

"Paris, beware, he may strike you dead as you speak! This is the worst blasphemy!"

"That's just what the common people say about your own ridiculous claims. They say, 'Why would a god who can have any woman he wants choose a skinny, flat-chested, loudmouthed bitch who takes her pleasure with women?' And of course you know what the answer is. Nobody believes it."

VI

Palace protocol demanded that one person visiting another request permission. But Princess Andromache, wife of Prince Hector, was not about to ask humbly to be allowed into the rooms of Princess Helen, who was now accepted as the wife of Prince Paris.

Although Helen, as queen of Sparta, had once outranked Andromache, she had voluntarily given up this rank to become the bigamous wife of Paris of Troy while her husband Menelaus of Sparta yet lived. As a result the servants who guarded the door of Helen's chambers made no more than a token effort to stop Andromache when she went visiting with fire in her eyes and a grim and determined look on her face. When Andromache barged into Helen's bedroom, she found Paris's wife involved in her usual activity: primping before the mirror.

Helen wore only a light dressing gown, and the secrets of her pink body were visible through the translucent cloth. As she turned to face Andromache she held a paint pot in her left hand and a brush in her right.

"To what do I owe an invasion of my privacy, Andromache?"

"I think it's time you and I had a talk, Helen. The field outside is full of men facing their death because of you. Their number includes my husband."

"This is true," Helen said lightly.

"Achilles is back, and he's full of anger and desire for revenge—revenge against Hector! And if something happens to Hector today, or any other day, I'll see that you pay dearly for it!"

"Why me?" Helen asked. She turned back to her mirror and continued making up her eyes. "You know as well as I do that this is all a matter of money and power. If my ex-husband and that stupid Agamemnon hadn't found this excuse for attacking Troy, they would have found another. They want the Hellespont. They want to control trade at this end of the Aegean. Even I know that!"

"And you know that any other excuse would not have drawn all those other men over here to battle. It was only the oath to your husband that forced them to fight."

"*I* think it's quite a tribute to me," Helen said, "that they'd take the oath and consider themselves honor bound to keep it."

"Yes," Andromache said, "and it makes you the reason for the war. Achilles intends to kill Hector. Now is the time for you to intervene. You could end the bloodshed. All the other Greeks are waiting for is a good excuse to quit and go home."

Helen cocked her head one way and the other, studying the effect in the mirror. "What do you expect me to do?"

Andromache grabbed Helen's shoulder and spun her around. "Find Priam. Tell him you're willing to go back to Menelaus. Offer to bring along the treasure of Sparta that Paris and you stole. I'm sure Priam would be willing to add some interest. And then the Greeks can go home, and this war will be finished. The war hasn't worked out the way Menelaus and Agamemnon wanted it to, anyhow. They're looking for an excuse to get out. Give it to them, Helen. Now!"

Helen put down the paint pot and brush. She looked at herself in the mirror and then looked up at Andromache's reflection.

"Are you insane?" she asked. Her eyes were hard and unyielding. "Go back to Menelaus? Do you have any idea what that would mean? No, obviously you don't—Hector's not a bad sort. He's gentle with you, gentle and protective, right?"

Andromache nodded.

"He's probably a good lover. He's not bad to look at, and his eye doesn't wander." She smiled a secret smile. "Goodness knows I tried to attract him. Just for practice, you understand. I have to try with every man, just to prove myself. It's the way I am." She paused. "You're probably a good wife to him."

"I try to be."

"Imagine that instead of Hector you had this big lout who came to your bed reeking like a boar who's been wallowing in manure and who didn't care whether you wanted him or not. Imagine that he had absolutely no idea of who you were and didn't care about finding out. Imagine that he wanted you only so that he could brag about having the prettiest wife around. But that he'd never, ever tell you that you looked nice or show you in any way that he approved of you."

"Look, Helen, this is all very—"

"Now imagine his growing more insensitive every day. Coming home at day's end bellowing and complaining and never having a kind word to say about anything.

And then . . ." She gave a disgusted sigh. "I'm very good in bed, Andromache; with a man who appreciates me, I'm even better. I really enjoy making love. But every night I spent with that monster, that ugly, foul-smelling, bad-breathed satyr, was rape. He never bothered to learn the proper way of approaching a woman."

"I'm sorry, Helen," Andromache said coldly, "but in the meantime my husband's out there risking his life."

"I sympathize, but I have to say no to going back to Menelaus. I know other women don't appreciate Paris, and certainly the men don't. But since I've been with him, I've been able to think well of myself again. Whatever deficiencies you may see in me now, I'm twenty times the woman I was when I met him."

Andromache's eyes narrowed. "You're remarkable, Helen," she said. "Although I never thought I'd hear myself saying anything good about you. You're worth a man's taking chances over. But your own man, Helen, not mine. And your actions are putting Hector in danger, and this is something I won't tolerate. I'm going to find a way to make you go back to your husband. I'm sorry, but either you give in, or I'll break you."

"I'm afraid you'll have to break me," Helen said. "I like you this way, Andromache, direct. If things had worked out differently we might have been friends." She frowned. "But then again, perhaps not. I'm not one for making women friends. They all seem to feel threatened by my beauty." She looked up at Andromache's angry and determined face in the mirror. "I'd give almost anything to keep harm from coming to your man. Almost. If you mean to fight me over this, be prepared for a real fight. I fight just like a man, Andromache, a smart, determined man who means to win, so beware."

Under cover of the thick fog Iri and Phorbus found their way to the far wall of Troy without being seen. There Iri stopped.

"So far it's been easy," he said to Phorbus. "But the moment we climb over the top of the wall all the odds will

be against us. We'll attract attention everywhere, particularly with this face of mine, which is why I wanted you to
stay home, my friend. Too many people will notice me."

Phorbus smiled bravely despite his fear. "Why don't
you just accept that you've got someone to look out for
you?"

Iri grinned. "Don't think I don't appreciate it, but I
wanted to remind you how ticklish this business is going
to be. Stick close, and keep your eyes wide open."

In the field the fog had begun to break up and to
blow away. King Priam, looking down from the wall, could
see the terrible carnage Achilles had wrought. More than
a score of young Trojans lay dead, and still Achilles roamed
the field, smeared with the blood of other, better men.
The Greek looked strong and savage and invulnerable;
Paris's poisoned arrows had reached their target but merely
rebounded off the armor. Not one of the swords, spears,
or arrows aimed at Achilles had harmed him.

Now, howling with rage, he led a squad of his personal army in pursuing a Trojan detachment that had
broken and run toward the city walls. The fleeing Trojans
paused before the gates, and Hector called out to the
gatekeepers to let them in.

The gates swung wide. The men dashed inside, but
Hector held back, calling up at the gatekeepers. "Close
the gates!"

"But, my lord, you're alone outside."

Hector's voice boomed out. "Close the gates! I know
what I'm doing!"

Priam knew what his son was planning and cried out
in his weak old man's voice. "No, Hector! Don't!"

No one could hear him.

VII

As the gates were slowly closing, Hector saw that the Trojan soldiers were turning around to return to the field. "Shut the gates!" he repeated. "Don't let them out!"

Obediently the gatekeepers slammed the gates. *I have to get Achilles away from the city. I have to make sure that after killing me, he doesn't vault over my dead body and into the streets of Troy.* Hector looked at Achilles, followed by his personal army, heading toward him with fire in his eyes, and made his decision.

To Achilles's astonishment, Hector set off away from the gates at a jogging clip, circling around toward the far corner of the field. "Catch me if you can, Achilles!" he called.

Achilles stopped abruptly and took off his helmet to wipe the sweat from his brow.

"Should we catch him for you, sir? We could round him up and—" one of his men asked.

"I'll track my deer myself and bring him down," Achilles said impatiently. "Although I'd thought it was a bear I was hunting. Either my eyes aren't what they were, or this is a lesser man impersonating Hector. Whoever it is, I'll catch him and kill him."

He set off after the Trojan, who was now far across the field.

Iri cautiously put his hand up over the top of the stone-block wall. He probed around and got a good purchase. After pulling himself to the edge, he looked furtively for guards. They were all far away at the other end of their patrol along the wall.

"Come on!" he said in a loud whisper.

Phorbus's hand appeared, and Iri grabbed hold of it and pulled him up in one mighty motion.

"Now! Get down!" Iri whispered.

The two men looked around. A chest-high inner wall surrounded a palace garden and courtyard, with a doorway allowing access to the royal apartments. The elevation afforded a commanding view of the area surrounding the palace: In one direction they could see the broad flood-plain, veined with streams, then the hills and groves nearer the river, and finally the river itself, snaking through the countryside. In the distance were the Greek fleet and the Great Sea beyond.

Iri and Phorbus scrambled down the wall they had just climbed, then made their way over the low, inner wall to reach the courtyard of the palace.

"We're in luck!" Iri whispered. "I wasn't sure I could trust the floor plan that fellow gave me, but he was right. Now if we can only get past that guard—"

Phorbus followed his gaze. "Leave him to me. You're the master of the sword, but he's too far away for the sword to be of any use. There's an old shepherd trick I know that ought to work."

He reached inside his clothes and withdrew a leather harness. At first Iri was puzzled, but then Phorbus poked around inside a pouch at his waist to retrieve several rocks. He chose one and put the others away.

Phorbus studied the guard, whose back was to them. Sling in hand, Phorbus crept across the courtyard, using potted trees for cover. Ten paces away from the guard he stopped and fitted the stone to the sling. He began spinning it around rapidly.

The guardsman did not turn, and Phorbus reached inside his garment and withdrew another stone. He tossed the rock with his left hand, and it struck the guardsman lightly in the back. He yelped and turned around.

Quickly Phorbus let his missile go.

The stone caught the guardsman right between the eyes. There was a splash of blood. He crumpled and fell.

Almost before he could hit the ground Phorbus was upon him, cutting his throat with his knife. Then he motioned for Iri.

Iri dashed across the courtyard at full speed.

Hector sprinted along the wagon tracks that bordered the banks of the Scamander River and past the bubbling springs. Only once did he look back to see Achilles gaining on him, slowly but steadily.

What if the stories told about Achilles were true?

What if he was invulnerable? The man was a braggart, but his strength and endurance were more amazing than any of his lies.

The tracks led to a stream, and Hector weaved through a grove of olive trees along its bank. When he emerged, he saw the walls of the city. When the people caught sight of him, a cheer went up. The sound was masculine, deep and strong. That meant that the men of the city had abandoned their foolish idea of coming out to help him.

Good, he thought, *let's give them something to watch.*

He knew what he was going to do. Perhaps he had known it ever since last night. He turned and wound up the hill by the river. At its top he stopped and faced the man who had been chasing him. Without hesitation he took out his sword and formally saluted Achilles.

The big Greek warrior came to a halt ten paces away and looked Hector up and down. He did not even seem to be breathing hard. "Well?" he asked harshly. "Aren't you going to run any farther? Are you out of strength? Did you pull up lame? Surely you're not going to face me as an equal, knowing that you're not half the man I am."

Hector took a deep breath and closed his eyes for a moment to compose himself. "I am done with running," he said strangely. "I will not budge from this spot. I will either vanquish you or die. If I were to live a thousand years, I would never find a better place to make my stand than this hilltop."

"Then let's make an end of it," Achilles said, slashing the air with his sword. "You've worn that stolen armor too long. I mean to take it back today."

"Come and get it," Hector challenged. "But let there

be one covenant between us: If the gods grant me victory, I swear never to abuse you after death. Once I have taken the armor from your body, I will give your body back to your people. Will you then do as much for me if I lose

A look of disbelief contorted Achilles' face, but he said nothing. When he finally spoke, his voice was ugly and rasping. "I make no covenants! Only a coward's law binds both the lion and the lamb! When you die—and die you will—I'll do as I like with your wretched bones. Prepare to die, coward!"

He hurled his lance.

Hector ducked, and the shaft flew over his head. He feinted once, twice, and launched his own.

The lance struck Achilles in the middle of his chest, but the metal tip glanced off the heavy bronze armor and fell to the ground.

As Achilles came at him, Hector braced himself, but his knees shook as he prepared for the assault.

Iri stood in the deserted palace hall, looking in one direction, then the other. "If I remember correctly, Hector's apartments are down to the right, and here, to the left would be Helen's and Paris's, and beyond them . . . Cassandra's."

Phorbus allowed himself one frightened shudder before saying, "Lead on."

Iri, padding down the hall on bare feet—both men had abandoned their sandals—did not know what he expected to find in Cassandra's apartments. Perhaps the princess and Keturah were elsewhere; rumor had it the two women were inseparable. What would he do then? Go hunting through the halls, taking his chances that nobody would see him, or wait in her rooms for someone to come back?

Cautiously he crept forward.

Achilles's attack was the most ferocious Hector had

ever experienced. How foolish he had been to assume that he could tire this unconquerable monster by running him around the field! The man's arm must be made of iron, and he seemed not to breathe at all. He came at Hector right, left, above, and below. Achilles' arm beat down Hector's parries until he could barely hold the Greek off. Achilles' strokes were never more than a handspan away from where he aimed them, and his great sweeping cuts threatened to take off Hector's head if he did not move quickly.

The Trojan prince gave ground again and again, content merely to parry, fend off, and survive. He had no time to think of making an assault of his own. All his energy was concentrated on keeping the flashing blade away from his throat where Patroclus's armor left a dangerous gap.

And Achilles knew it. His every second stroke was aimed at Hector's throat. Everything in between was a feint. His eyes remained on his target as his face twisted into a savage grin.

All at once Hector felt the strength drain out of his body. He stepped back and saluted Achilles once again.

The huge crowd atop the walls of Troy understood and let out a sigh.

Hector smiled. His heart was already halfway into the next world.

Achilles rushed forward, feinted, and lunged.

The blade went through Hector's neck in a spurt of blood!

VIII

Cassandra, standing atop the city wall with Keturah, had expected disaster; but when the blow finally fell she was unprepared. "No!" she cried. "Not Hector!"

But her words were buried in the wails of hundreds

of people gathered on the wall. Keturah turned to her and, in an uncharacteristic gesture of familiarity, put a timid hand on Cassandra's forearm. "Please, tell me what has happened."

Cassandra's voice was a constricted rasp. "My brother, Hector . . ."

"Is he—?"

"Achilles cut his throat, and he's bleeding terribly. Oh, Keturah! It's the beginning of the end! I can't look. Come with me. I refuse to stay here and watch."

Cassandra grabbed Keturah's arm and pulled her away. Keturah, stumbling, let herself be dragged to the stairs.

On the field Achilles straddled Hector's legs and looked down at him. "So this is the great hero of Troy, who was going to kill me with ease." Achilles looked the dying man in the eyes and spat on his chest. "Remember Patroclus, my friend whom you killed! Take his memory to the underworld with you!"

He turned to the guards who surrounded them. "Strip his body and bring my chariot. Then pierce his hamstrings and string his feet up to the chariot. I've waited a long time for this victory, and I'm going to make the most of it."

Iri and Phorbus crept into Cassandra's rooms. Just then came the great groan that could be heard all the way on the far side of the palace. The two men exchanged glances. "If that means what I think it does—" Phorbus said.

Iri nodded grimly.

"Then it's bad news for Troy," Phorbus continued. "But for us it might be enough of a distraction to allow us to slip away." He whipped his head toward the door. "Someone's coming." He drew his sword and stood by the door. "Back against the wall!" he whispered to Iri.

The door opened, and Cassandra stood there with Keturah by her side.

Iri pulled his sword, but he stood transfixed. The face that turned his way was as lovely as he had remembered. If anything she had grown even more beautiful.

Cassandra was the first to recover. "Close the door!" she said. "Quickly, before anyone sees you!"

The sight was enough to turn even the strongest stomach. Achilles drove his chariot back and forth before the walls of Troy, dragging Hector's naked and befouled body and hurling insults up at the Trojans. Soon the other Greeks joined in. They had had little opportunity lately for jubilation. Now Achilles had returned to the field.

Two of the Greeks, however, refused to join in the humiliation of Priam and his people. Nestor and Odysseus walked back to the ships together. For a time neither spoke. Then Nestor looked over at his companion. "I take it that rejoicing isn't something that appeals to you now."

"It's good enough news," Odysseus allowed. "Not that the death of Hector means the easy victory everyone thinks it does. The Trojans still have a lot of fight in them, and they're getting reinforcements soon. We intercepted a messenger bringing news of an army of blacks from Nubia. And some women's army. No, the Trojans will fight on. We won't be going home tomorrow, although half those idiots out there probably think so."

"Is that why you left?"

"No. I think it's dishonorable to insult a fallen foe."

Nestor nodded. "How much longer do you think we'll be here?"

Odysseus shook his head. "I've no idea."

Nestor pursed his lips. "Well, for my part I think the death of Hector will break their spirit. Priam won't hold out forever—not with his favorite son dead. I wouldn't be surprised if he sued for peace just to get the body back."

"No," Odysseus said. "Priam will get Hector's body back only when Achilles has insulted it sufficiently to befoul his own honor forever—and not a moment before."

*   *   *

The hall was full of people who had come in from the wall. Each reacted in his own way—some with grief, some with horror, some in fear of the future—to the death of Troy's great defender. Cassandra and Phorbus hovered by the door, listening for signs that the crowd had dispersed homeward.

Iri sat by the window talking with his wife. He held his sleeping son in his arms. "I can't believe it. To see you at last! And Keturah, you're even more lovely than I remembered you!"

"I'm a little older. I feel much older. I hope that doesn't displease you."

He kissed her hand. "Nothing about you or Talus could displease me. I can't believe I have this beautiful son, and a Child of the Lion, too! I can't wait to get you safely out of here and across the sea. I heard terrible rumors that you were dead, and I thought I would lose my mind."

"Ah, poor Iri. And I was here, safe and sound. The princess has been very good to Talus and me."

"I've heard your voice in my dreams."

"And I've heard yours in mine. The way you sound and feel are all I had of you, that and the memory of how you treated me, how you made me feel." She smiled. "Phorbus, tell me what Iri looks like."

Iri protested in a voice full of tension. "He doesn't have to do something that—"

"He's got large, piercing eyes, Keturah. They look right into you and see what's inside. It's as if there is too much emotion in his eyes."

"Intense," Keturah said. "Iri is very intense. He always was." Her voice rang with warm affection. "Go on, Phorbus, please."

"But once you know him you realize that he's a very kind person. A very warm and loving person, but maybe one who hasn't had too many people love him back."

"That's very true," Keturah said, squeezing Iri's big hand in both of hers. "But that's a thing of the past. You and Talus and I are going to make up for all that. We're going to give him so much love for the rest of his life that he'll forget every hurt he's ever suffered. Tell me more."

"He has the broadest shoulders I've ever seen. I guess he's worked so long with his hands that his arms seem longer than other men's. He's very, very strong."

She smiled, and Iri almost let out a sob of emotion. He was so very happy. "Look at his hands," she said.

"They're very strong. He is fearfully strong, in fact—as strong as a demon. He could easily kill a man by strangling him to death with one hand. I'm sure all the Greeks are afraid of him."

"Achilles isn't afraid of me," Iri said gruffly. "Neither is Odysseus. But everyone else walks a large circle around me."

Keturah turned back toward Phorbus. "But he's also as gentle as a lamb. He used to take care of me as though I were a newborn baby. He would do everything for me, as if I could do nothing for myself. He lived in constant fear that something would happen—that I'd trip and fall or somehow harm myself." She smiled. "Maybe when we're safe at Home we'll make Talus a little brother or sister. You'd like that, wouldn't you, Iri?"

Iri did not speak, and Keturah turned to Phorbus with a puzzled expression. "Phorbus? Tell me what—"

"Keturah," Phorbus said, "he's crying."

Paris fitted another arrow to his bow, but as Achilles' chariot careened past, he relaxed the tension on the bowstring. "It's no use," he said. "He's out of range. A pity someone hasn't invented a bow strong enough."

King Priam stared at him disconsolately. When Achilles had begun dragging Hector's body back and forth across the field, the old man had been unable to watch. He had sunk down, a crumpled wreck, on one of the stone benches. "Hector . . ." Priam said in a dull voice, "Why did Hector have to fall?"

Paris shot a sharp glance at him. "Why him and not

somebody like me, you mean? That's what you're thinking, isn't it?"

"I didn't say that," the old man protested.

"I know you didn't, but you're thinking it, I can tell.
You all are, especially Cassandra and Andromache. Anything to end this war. Well, I'm sorry to disappoint you,
but I have no intention of dying heroically on the battlefield." He let the words hang in the air for a moment,
then added, "Nor unheroically, either, if that's what's
going through your mind."

"Why did he have to die?" Priam repeated. "And at
the hands of that barbarian, that monster, that—"

"We all have to die," Paris said coldly. "And when we
do, it hardly matters what happens to our bones afterward. Do you think Hector's spirit is suffering more now
because that great ox out there is hauling his meat back
and forth and yelling insults at us?"

"Hector . . ." his father moaned. "My son . . ."

Paris scowled and replaced the arrow in his quiver.
Taking the bow in hand, he looked once more at Priam,
then shrugged. "If all you can do is snivel over the dead,
I'm leaving. I have better things to do."

But Priam did not hear his words. Nor was he aware
of Paris's leaving.

Cassandra looked at Iri, Keturah, and Talus in the
corner and then over at Phorbus. A realization struck her.
"You're going to try to get them out of here, aren't you?"
she asked.

"The thought had crossed my mind," Phorbus said.
His tone told her that he did not like her. She did not
care. "Take me with you," she asked.

Phorbus stared at her. "Are you mad? It's going to be
hard enough smuggling a baby and a blind woman out of
the palace, without adding a spoiled princess who wants
her own way."

"Spoiled I may be," she said. "But I can be of more
help than a simpleton like you could imagine. I know

every way of getting out of here. I know every path within fifty leagues. I can hide outside the walls, and Zeus himself couldn't find me. And I can call in favors owed me in the villages around here. People will hide us in case you've no intention of going back to the Greek ships."

"Why wouldn't we return to the fleet?"

"If you take us to the ships, you'll have to share us, as captives, with the Greek kings and princelings. Imagine how your friend will take to the idea of having to give Keturah to Agamemnon, Menelaus, or Achilles."

Phorbus had not thought of that and wondered what they could do.

IX

Helen passed Andromache in the hall. Hector's wife had a taut look on her face, as if she could barely control her emotions. She did not acknowledge Helen as she rushed toward the stairs, a grim-faced servant at her side.

"Andromache!" Helen cried out. "What's the matter? Why are you—?"

There was no answer. Petulantly Helen stamped her foot and vowed never to speak to Andromache again. Then Helen remembered the woman's expression. What if that groan she had heard through her window had signaled a terrible reversal in the fortunes of Troy?

She paused to think as Paris entered the hall, bow in hand, his quiver slung over his back. "Paris, Andromache just came by. She wouldn't speak to me."

"Achilles got Hector," he explained. "They're making a lot of it upstairs. Father acts as if we'd lost the war already." He made a wry face. "As if one man could make that much difference. Hector didn't fight well today. I never could understand what everyone else saw in him. Yet everyone followed him as if he were extraordinary. The truth is, Achilles was always the better man. You don't face a man like Achilles; you cut and run." He shrugged. "Well, now it's too late."

Helen considered his words. "What does this really mean? Is Troy going to lose?"

Paris snorted. "Of course Troy isn't going to lose. You've been listening to Cassandra again, haven't you?"

"I haven't been listening to anyone, Paris. You know I never have anything to do with these stupid Trojan women. They're all jealous. It's just that I have to think of my future. If Troy is going to lose, it means a change in my plans."

Paris glared at her. "A change in your plans? Don't tell me you're considering going back to Menelaus? You always told me you'd die before you'd ever—"

"Now Paris, don't act like that. You know I have to think about myself. If the walls are going to fall down and all those foul-smelling Greek boors are going to come swarming in here raping and killing . . . well, I'm not going to sit and wait for some stupid oaf to throw me on the ground and—"

"Stop it, Helen. Hector is just one man. There are plenty of us left to defend the city. And let me tell you, my darling, the city'll be in more trouble when and if *I* pass away than it is right now." He took a deep breath. "Look, I'm sorry about Hector. I'm sorry for Andromache. But this isn't the great earth-shattering horror everyone seems to be making of it. We knew it was coming. Hector was no match for Achilles. Now that the worst has finally come to pass, we must get on with the war."

Helen looked at him and seemed to soften. "Then I needn't worry about the Greeks invading Troy?"

"No. Go back to our rooms. I'll join you in a few minutes. First, I have to find the armorer and order more arrows. I used up all but these few in that last siege, trying to hit Achilles. When I come back, I may have some other ways of reassuring you."

Her smile was the old one: seductive and inviting. "Don't be long," she said.

* * *

Iri looked Cassandra in the eyes. "Why would you want to go with us? You're the daughter of the king. You're a priestess, revered and respected. Why would you want to become a fugitive?"

Cassandra unflinchingly returned his gaze. "What do I have here? This city is soon going to be pounded into dust. With Hector gone, we're lost. I've had visions of the palace in flames, with soldiers raping and killing the inhabitants. I want to see if I can escape my destiny. Troy will fall, and I don't want to fall with it." The look in her silvery eyes told them how serious she was. "If you're afraid I'll betray you, ask Keturah if I would ever knowingly do anything to bring harm to her."

Iri turned to his wife. His arm went around her shoulders. "Is she telling the truth?"

"I believe so," Keturah said.

Phorbus's eyes locked with Cassandra's for a moment, and he could see that she was silently pleading with him. "Well," he said, "if she'll agree to follow orders . . ."

Cassandra flushed, but then she bowed her head submissively and nodded.

"All right," Iri said. Then he turned to Cassandra. "What's the best way out?"

"There's an old abandoned conduit that was used for draining the latrines," Cassandra said. "When the new system was installed, they walled this one up, but with only one layer of bricks. A couple of strong men ought to be able to break through it. After that it's just a matter of sliding down. It's a fairly steep slope. But if someone goes first and is there to catch the others—".

"How do we get there? We're too large a group to pass unnoticed, and nobody is going to forget my face."

Cassandra's expression was grim. "I know. Paris will recognize you if anyone will. He was furious at you in Pylos."

"Is there a back way that we could take?" Phorbus asked.

"Yes," Cassandra said suddenly. "It's down near Cleomedes' forge. It's the fastest way, and we're less likely to run into anyone."

"Can we trust Cleomedes?" Iri asked.

"I don't know," Cassandra replied. "He is in my father's army."

Phorbus began to move toward the door, then stopped. "Don't you need to take anything along, any belongings?"

Cassandra smiled. "If we're caught, we'll die. We won't need anything in the next world. And if we escape, we'll have to travel light, stealing and begging for whatever we get. Don't look surprised. I know about the world, and I'm not afraid. I'm a woman in a household where only men count—men, and beautiful women like Helen. Anything I get I have to take."

The look Phorbus shot her was full of respect. "Lead the way," he said. "Iri, I'll take the baby, and you bring Keturah."

A sword in one hand and the baby in the other, Phorbus followed Cassandra out into the hall.

"What's wrong?" Paris asked Cleomedes. "You won't look me in the face. You're hiding something."

The old man swallowed nervously and tried to stare his questioner down. "Sir," he said, "I d-don't know what you're talking about. I'm not feeling well today, and that's a fact."

"Rubbish. Why do you keep staring past me at the door? You act as if you had stolen something."

"Sir, I beg you to believe me. I've stolen nothing."

Once more the old man's eyes darted to the door of the armorer's chamber. With a curse Paris decided to investigate. As he threw the door open, he stood facing a group of people standing, startled, in a shaft of light: Cassandra; the blind girl and her baby; a stranger in the dress of a Greek warrior; and a burly man whose face was covered with a red birthmark. A face he had seen somewhere before. A face that—

"*You!*" he said as his hand closed on the sword at his side.

X

Iri recognized Paris immediately. In a terse voice he gave instructions to the others. "Phorbus, take Keturah and Talus to the exit. Princess, stay with me so you can show me the exit after the others have escaped."

Cassandra nodded. "Paris, this is Iri of Thebes. You're up against someone who can kill you easily. He's feared even among the upper hierarchy of the Greek army. Let him and his family go, and everything will be all right."

Paris smiled nastily at Iri and Cassandra, watching as the others disappeared around a corner. Both men were armed. "Well, Cassandra," Paris drawled, "so you've added treason to your other accomplishments. I wonder how Priam will take this news, coming on the same day his favorite son got himself killed."

"Tell him whatever you like," she said. "I'm letting Keturah and her baby go. They were my slaves, and I can do whatever I want with them."

"Get behind me," Iri said to her. "There's more than one way of shutting his mouth, and my way is the best for all concerned." He looked at Paris. "Come here, Princeling. Come here and learn how to die."

"I remember you," Paris said. He was careful to stay out of Iri's reach and backed slowly down the hall as Iri advanced on him. "You were the one who was insolent to me in Pylos."

"Watch out, Iri," Cassandra warned. "He's backing into the main corridor. The coward's going to make a run for it and get help. We'd better go."

"We?" Paris asked with a malicious and deadly smile. "It's even worse than I thought. You're going with them? Wait until Priam hears about this! But perhaps I'll let him think you were raped and carried off by these blackguards. That will hurt him more. He may well resign his crown. You never know what a depressed man is apt to do. But as king of Troy I'd know what to do about these Greek pigs."

"Have at you!" Iri cried, and attacked.

"Have at you yourself!" Paris cried.

The prince was an experienced swordsman, and despite Iri's superior strength and skill, he sidestepped the first lunge and parried, catching Iri a glancing blow with the edge of his sword and opening a thin cut along his arm. Their positions reversed. Now it was Iri who stood with his back to the open corridor.

"Iri!" Cassandra called. "There are people out there. Get out of view. This way!"

Iri obliged, pressing an attack that drove Paris back, back, and brought into play every bit of Paris's skill. Iri's moves were Egyptian ones, different enough to provide Paris with surprises. It was obvious that Iri, although keeping the prince on the defensive, could not touch him. All at once Paris tied Iri up with a parry that nearly disarmed him. Once again Paris began forcing Iri back toward the corridor.

"Princess!" Iri said, defending himself against every lunge. "Is there any way you can look out to see if they've escaped?"

Cassandra hesitated, afraid to take her eyes off the two fighting men. "There's a window in Cleomedes' room," she said. "I'll try to see from there."

"Go!" Iri urged. "Now!"

When Cassandra looked out the window, she could see Phorbus leading Keturah across the plain. Relieved to see they had escaped, she turned to see Cleomedes coming up behind her, dagger in hand.

"So you'd betray our king and our country as easily as that, would you?" he asked. "If I'd known you were going with them instead of just helping your slaves escape, I'd have informed on you, princess or no princess. I refuse to allow you to betray King Priam in his hour of need! People have called you a witch, and I always defended you, but now I see they were right. I'm holding you for the guards, and then I'm going to tell the whole story to Priam myself."

"Get out of my way!" she ordered. "What do you mean, pulling a dagger on—". His hand reached out for her. Without hesitation she grabbed it and bit down. Cleomedes let out a howl. "Iri!" she screamed. "Iri! Help me!"

Cleomedes still held the dagger in his free hand, and he turned the blade and brought the hilt down with great force on her head. She fell to her knees, numb from the shock. As she fought to stay conscious she saw Cleomedes throw the bolt on the chamber door.

Iri heard the scream and reacted with fury, beating back one of Paris's attacks and disarming him with a twist of his powerful wrist. As Paris stood in disbelief, watching his sword spinning down the hall, Iri tried to open Cleomedes' door just as the armorer bolted it shut.

"Damn you! Cleomedes, let her out! Let her out, you worthless bastard!"

Paris retrieved his sword and was coming at Iri again. Realizing he could do nothing about Cassandra now and had to save himself, Iri set out at a dead run down the hall.

Around the corner he found a dead guardsman and realized Phorbus had been here. But the guard had obviously wounded Phorbus, and Iri followed the trail of blood down the second hall and around another corner. He paused for a moment and listened. He could hear nothing. Paris was not following him.

The trail of blood led up the stairs to an old latrine room. In the far corner was a hole where someone had smashed through a mortared-over door. He knelt and peered inside to where a steep ramp led downward. At the bottom he could see daylight.

Replacing his sword in its scabbard, he slipped feet-first into the opening and propelled himself down the long, dark chute.

Outside, Phorbus, having led Keturah and the baby to what looked like safety in a little grove beside the Scamander River, came back looking for Iri and Cassandra. The Greeks had returned to the ships now that Achilles had finished humiliating the dead Hector. From the waterfront came the sounds of funeral games for Patroclus, which had been delayed until Achilles took his revenge.

As Phorbus approached the palace wall, he looked up to the parapets. There was Paris, a bow in hand. *Damn you!* he thought. *If you've killed Iri, so help me I'll—*

Suddenly there was a scraping sound inside the wall, and Iri came slipping down the chute to land with a thump.

"There you are!" Phorbus said with relief. "Let's get out of here!"

Iri stared at him with horror. "You left Keturah and Talus alone?"

"They'll be all right. I had to make sure that you—"

"The only reason we came here was to rescue my wife and child. My life doesn't matter!"

"You matter to me," Phorbus said. "Come along." He looked around. "Where's the princess?"

"Cleomedes locked her up. I had to make a run for it. Paris is a better hand with the sword than I expected."

Paris watched them. He was pleased that he had been a match for Iri; the armorer's superior strength would, however, eventually have worn him down. Iri had a wrist of iron.

But there was more than one way to beat him. He pulled one of his special arrows from the quiver and nocked it to the bowstring. Then he bent the bow and drew a bead on the two men hurrying across the plain below. He pulled the arrow back and let it fly.

*   *   *

"Is that the grove?" Iri asked. "I don't see anybody. Where are they? Phorbus, if you've—"

"Patience," Phorbus said. "This is the grove. I told Keturah to stay hidden exactly where I left her. Don't worry."

Suddenly there was a *whoosh* and then a *thunk*! Iri staggered forward. Phorbus wheeled to see an arrow protruding from Iri's shoulder.

Iri cursed. "Keep moving! We're almost out of range." He tried to reach up and pull the shaft out, but it was so shallowly embedded that the force of running shook it out. It fell in the path behind them as they lurched into the shelter of the grove.

Phorbus maneuvered Iri to safety behind a big oak tree. "Let me have a look at that," he said. "Does it hurt?"

"No, curse it! It doesn't hurt at all! Now go find Keturah and Talus! I'll be all right here. Get them to safety!"

Phorbus studied Iri's face. It was odd that he was choosing to rest instead of looking for his wife with Phorbus. "Sit down here. I'll get Keturah and Talus and bring them back here. They're nearby. I won't be long."

"Go," Iri urged. His voice was phlegmy.

There was no doubt in Iri's mind what had happened. The numbness had begun to spread through his body immediately. When Phorbus and he had reached the grove he could hardly move his legs to sit down. Now he could not feel them at all, and his vision was beginning to blur.

You've failed. You've failed again. The thought rammed its way through Iri's mind. He could not fight it. There was little fight left in him mentally or physically.

Rescuing Keturah had been an impossible dream. He refused to waste his last moments in regrets. Their time together today had been painfully brief. But he would die the man she had loved and cared for: a man worthy of her devotion.

He had found Keturah during the bleak days when

Moses was leading his people on that tortuous course through the desert. Jacob's scouts had found a blind girl. When her husband had died, no one wanted her. Unable to feed herself or contribute to the welfare of a wandering tribe, she had been left by the Bedouins to die in the desert.

Iri had been enchanted first by her gentle beauty, then by her sweetness of spirit. And he had found that, unable to see his ugliness, she could not conceive of it. For the first time he had found someone who could accept him as he was.

And he had found someone to love. She had called forth in him a new Iri, a whole man with strong emotions. Then when he lost her to the kidnappers, he had returned to being the old, distant Iri, a man who needed no one and cared for no one.

It was getting dark. Perhaps it was day's end, or perhaps it was just the end of his days. It did not seem important. If he would never see her again, what would it matter if he lived one day or fifty or a thousand? He had the one splendid memory, and he had seen the fine son he had fathered.

He closed his eyes, and his thoughts turned inward to a place where he did not need physical sight. He was with her again, and he had his arms around her. She was asking him to describe the sunset as they stood atop a rocky ridge in the Negev, and he was struggling for words. She was laughing gently with him at his fumbling attempts. And he was happier than he had ever been in his life. Her small, warm body in his arms was the dearest and most precious thing he had ever known.

Phorbus could see no sign of Keturah and Talus, whom he had left only minutes before. He ran frantically through the grove, then stopped abruptly.

"Oh, no!" he groaned under his breath.

Across the plain a squad of Trojan soldiers had Keturah by the arm and were taking the baby and her back to the palace. The soldiers appeared to be part of a grave patrol, finding slain Trojans and carrying them to the city for proper burial. Phorbus's heart sank. He had failed his friend! All of their dangerous work had been in vain! He squared his jaw.

"I'll get them out again. I promise you that, Iri. If it's the last thing I ever do."

He shuddered and turned and walked slowly back to where he had left his friend.

Iri was sitting with his back braced against the oak. "Iri," Phorbus said, "I know what you're going to say to me, and I deserve every word, but . . ."

He saw no sign of motion.

"Iri? Are you all right?"

He came closer. Iri's eyes were wide open, but they were staring at the sky.

"Iri!" Phorbus cried. He knelt beside his friend. Gently he shook Iri's arm. "It wasn't a bad wound! It was hardly more than a scratch!"

Then he remembered the stories about cowards who wouldn't stand and fight, preferring to hide and kill with arrows dipped in the juice of the black hellebore root—poison that made one's legs grow cold and death creep through the body. He clasped his friend and mentor in his arms. But it was too late. Life had fled.

"Iri," he said with a sob. "I'll get them out, and I'll take care of them. I'll raise the baby as if he were my own. Nothing will ever happen to them again. I promise you, Iri!"

But the dead eyes stared sightlessly. Finally Phorbus reached out with a trembling hand and closed them.

XI

The knock on the door came again, insistent, peremptory. "Who's there?" Cleomedes demanded. He looked over at Cassandra, who was sitting by the window. "Stay there, Princess. I'll deal with this."

Cassandra did not care. She had seen the guards dragging Keturah, who was carrying Talus, into the palace. She had never felt so discouraged. Not only had she failed to escape, but her friend had been captured, also.

It was no consolation that Keturah would be with her again—she was returning to the palace of Troy a prisoner.

When Cleomedes had locked her up, her heart sank, but she had been happy that Keturah had escaped. But now? Keturah and the boy would wind up slaves again, and she was in trouble herself.

Cleomedes was letting Paris in. He stood before her and smirked. "It was all for nothing. I saw them being brought in through the front gate."

"Her husband will rescue them. Just watch."

Paris's laugh was light and mocking. "So that's what you think, eh? You think he'll be back to carry the three of you away. That the fellow with the ugly face will save you. I'd advise you not to hold your breath, my dear."

To her surprise Paris's grin looked triumphant. "What do you mean?" she demanded.

He ignored her question and turned to Cleomedes. "You disgraced yourself by not telling me of her plot to free the others."

"Sir, I didn't—"

"Shut up. But you did redeem yourself by locking this one up. That took guts, more than I'd credited you with, considering what it would mean to have a princess of the blood angry with you. If she were to report you to Priam, it would be your word against hers, and everybody knows Priam dotes on her. He'd have your head cut off."

"Sir, I beg of you—"

"It's all right. I'm going to forget this ever happened. But Cassandra, I have something on you now."

Cassandra was suspicious. "You know something you're not telling me. What happened, Paris? Did the same soldiers capture Iri and Phorbus, too?"

Paris's smile was sly. "The young one got away. It's all right—he doesn't amount to much. The red-faced fellow is another matter. He would have been a man to fear."

"Would have?"

"Yes. I made the shot of my life. A pity no one was watching. Nobody will believe I could shoot him from that distance."

"Paris!"

"And, yes, my dear sister, I poison all my arrows now, on the off chance that Achilles will wander within the range of my bow."

"You bastard," Cassandra said. "You filthy bastard."

"You always called me that. In fact my blood's the same as yours." He shrugged. "Not that I care what you call me. I've got you where I want you. Keep out of my way and I'll keep my mouth shut about today. Otherwise . . ."

As evening came on, a low mist hung over the water's edge. Odysseus, chilled to the bone, busied himself with starting a fire, but it stubbornly refused to warm his bones.

He had declined to attend the victory feast and insulted Achilles by not paying his respects at the opening of the funeral games for Patroclus. The last thing he needed were drunken louts celebrating the brutal death of a man so far superior to them. Nor could he bear to be around Achilles as he reveled in his victory.

Odysseus added more fuel to the fire and sat back on a piece of driftwood to warm his hands and feet and study the dancing flames. His mind was far away when he saw Phorbus coming toward him, bearing a large burden in his arms. He knew instantly what it was and sprang to his feet. "What happened?"

"The worst," Phorbus said, laying Iri's body on the sand. "Iri's dead. Keturah and the baby were taken back to the palace. It's all my fault, Odysseus. If only I'd stayed with them. I wish I were dead, too."

Phorbus sank heavily on the driftwood log and told

the story in a broken voice. "We'd all escaped and, Odysseus, he was happy! I'd never seen him so happy."

Odysseus clapped him on the shoulder in sympathy. For a long time the two men sat silently staring into the fire.

Finally Phorbus spoke. "I want to go back and get them out. Will you come with me?"

Odysseus stared at him, one brow raised quizzically. "Me? No, lad."

"But—"

Suddenly they became aware of a presence beyond the circle of firelight. Achilles, drunk and still wearing his bloodied tunic, stood glaring resentfully down at them. "I missed you at the party in honor of Patroclus." His voice was slurred.

"We have our own dead to bury," Odysseus said. "Iri the armorer died today from one of Paris's damned poisoned arrows."

Achilles blinked slowly, and when he spoke, his words were still slurred, but there was a sober tone of respect in his voice. "I'm sorry," he said. "I came to congratulate him and thank him for the fine suit of armor. 'Hephaestus' —a fitting nickname we gave him. I share your sorrow." He paused. "He was a good man and a skilled worker. I respected him. Let me bear the cost of seeing him into the next world. It's the least I can do."

Without waiting for an answer he turned away, leaving Odysseus and Phorbus to exchange surprised glances. "I don't think I'll bother telling him how rich Iri was," Odysseus said. "Or how rich you are, as his heir."

"Heir?" Phorbus asked.

"Didn't you know? He had you registered as his adopted son. So you and the baby are brothers now. And you, my friend, whether you bear the birthmark or not, are now a Child of the Lion. And as the son of Iri of Thebes, your half of his fortune makes you, I suspect, the richest man in this camp. Well, maybe not richer than old

Nestor, but you could buy and sell Agamemnon on the best day of his life and still have money left over."

Phorbus gaped at him. "If I could only trade all of it to have Iri back here beside us—"

"I know," Odysseus said. "And take comfort in the fact that he knew how you felt about him, too."

XII

Cassandra could not put off confronting Keturah any longer. She found her in the dungeon, sitting on a cot, her lovely face expressionless. "Princess?" Keturah asked, holding Talus to her breast. "That is you, isn't it, my lady?"

"Yes," Cassandra said. "Sit down. It's all right."

"There's something wrong," Keturah said. "I can tell by your voice."

"He's dead," Cassandra whispered. "You suspected, didn't you?"

A tear rolled down Keturah's cheek. "Yes. When he didn't show up . . . I know Iri. The only thing that could have stopped him . . ." She paused and backhanded her tears. "I hope there wasn't any pain, that it went quickly for him."

"There was no pain," Cassandra said. "It was Paris. He nicked Iri with one of his poisoned arrows. He would have felt tired, then he would have . . . gone to sleep."

"I'm glad he didn't suffer," Keturah said. "It was too much to hope, I suppose, that we all could have escaped safely."

"Keturah, I'm so sorry."

The young woman's voice was barely audible. "I can tell you are. It's kind of you to say so." She pressed her lips to the top of Talus's little head.

"No, I mean it. I've never felt like this before. I don't even feel this bad about Hector's death, and he was my brother." Cassandra fell sobbing to her knees on the hard stone floor and hugged her close.

Keturah dashed the tears from her face. "There's a certain comfort in knowing that Iri is beyond pain. He is done with loneliness and people calling him names because he's ugly. He's at rest now, I know it. I can feel him, and the feeling I get is one of peace."

"Keturah, do you really believe it?"

"I can feel his presence. He won't let anything bad happen to me. And one day Talus and I will go to Home, as Iri wanted." She smiled. "He charged Phorbus with the task of taking care of us, and I know he will."

Cassandra looked at her and dried her tears. "You think that Phorbus will try again?"

"Of course."

Cassandra was silent for a long time. "I still want to go with you," she finally said.

Keturah allowed herself the familiarity of stroking Cassandra's long, tangled hair. "Then Phorbus will take you along." She smiled reassuringly. "I'll insist upon it. I'm his mother now. How could he disobey his mother?"

Epilogue

In the distance a wind sighed eerily. The Teller of Tales paused, raising his head and listening to the wind sweeping down from the high desert. His face was barely visible in the light from the guttering coals, but his eyes shone in the darkness.

"Hear," he said. "Hear the demon winds. Now, as always, they bring with them the seeds of conflict and war. Such a wind blew on the day the Children of Israel entered Canaan; such a wind was blowing the day Jericho fell and when Joshua fought his last battle at the Waters of Merom.

"The same winds continued to blow as the Israelites divided and occupied the land Joshua conquered for them. But the winds did not bring wisdom or piety or justice. They did not bring peace.

"What they brought, sweeping down from the empty lands, were confusion, disobedience, and inequities.

"When the Israelites should have been purifying themselves and adhering to the Law Moses had given them, they chose to fall away. As soon as the land was given to them, they became unfit to rule it. At a time when they should have governed with wisdom, they fought wisdom *and abandoned the One God who had given everything to them."*

His voice grew harsh. "And as, little by little, they began to deserve enemies, they began to acquire them. On all sides—along the sea, in the Arabah, in Moab, in the wild lands of the North, and in the desert kingdoms of the Negev—among the people the Israelites had mistreated, the seeds of revolt were sown. The son of Jabin of Hazor, who had sworn revenge when his father fell before Joshua's might, and his friend Sisera apprenticed themselves to strangers in the warlike North, to learn the ways of battle. When they grew to manhood, they looked southward at the lax and lazy Israelites and began to dream of winning back what their fathers had lost.

"Israel had had no prophet since the death of Moses, and there had been no firm hand to guide them through the snares of evil. With no man fit to lead them, they foundered. And as they foundered, their eyes looked to the heights for a leader. They could not see the great and mighty prophet in their midst: a woman sitting under a tree, speaking truth to the humble people who sought her out."

A questioning murmur arose, but the Teller of Tales did not explain. "Thus we seek the large and neglect the small, my children, and in the end we build nothing that will last. Israel was adrift, and so it was with the Sons of the Lion. Chaos and confusion reigned in Canaan, in the Aegean, and on the shores of Troy.

"Tomorrow," he said, drawing them close with a single mighty sweep of his sorcerer's hand, "tomorrow you shall hear how all their great schemes failed—until men learned to look to the small and humble for wisdom.

"Tomorrow," he said. "Tomorrow."

The best-selling saga of the Children of the Lion continues, with a new generation. . . .

Here is an exciting preview of **THE INVADERS** Volume Thirteen of the *Children of the Lion* Series, by Peter Danielson.

On sale in 1991, at bookstores everywhere.

Prologue

All day long the dreaded hamseen *had blown*, bringing the madness that could still be seen on many of the haggard faces around the campfire. When night fell the wind had changed directions and brought fresh air that carried the smell of the sea.

The evening seemed softened by the sea air. Gulls, their huge wings spread, glided in to land on the oasis waters. Far above the western horizon sat the clouds that would bring rain. The travelers looked at them and realized the hardest part of their long journey had ended. The morrow would bring new terrain unlike the parched track they had followed through the desert wilderness.

As the lank figure of the Teller of Tales stepped out of the darkness and into the warm pool of light from the campfire he could see the hope in their faces. He raised his long arms and bade them be silent.

"After the harsh desert, the smell of the sea," he said. "After travail, silence and rest. After sin, repentance. After bitterness, reconciliation and forgiveness. After a sundering, a healing. After the trials of life comes God's benison, although sometimes the wait seems longer than one man can bear and the suffering more than he can endure."

The old man raised his voice, and his conjuror's hands wrought magic in the firelight. "So it was," he said, "for the tribes of Israel in the ten years that followed the conquest of Canaan. So it was when the children of Jacob fell away from the Law given to them by Moses, turned their faces from God, and felt the fury of His displeasure."

The last of the sea wind died, and the flames of the campfire stopped dancing. "There came a time," the Teller of Tales said, "when, as man had deserted God, so God began to desert man. The people began to forget Him and turn toward the wretched baalim of the heathen among whom they lived. Some even courted the favor of the evil demon Ashtaroth. All the strength and power that the men of Israel had wielded suddenly left them, and they became less than men.

"Then it was," he said in a voice that carried a hard edge, "that the nations Joshua had conquered began to rise from the dead, and Israel's enemies, old and new, rose against her. In the south the warriors of Moab swarmed across Jordan to enslave and oppress Israel's southern tribes, men who had lost the will to fight. And from the north there came a new threat, the son of Jabin of Hazor. As a youth he had seen his father killed by the Israelites and his father's army scattered. Now he wanted revenge.

"Ten years after his father's fall, the young Jabin established a new kingdom, enslaving the men of Naphtali and Zebulun, dishonoring their women, and oppressing the old and the poor. Suddenly it was as if Joshua's fiery sword had never flashed through the northern hills, had never carved a new empire for the Israelites."

The Teller of Tales shook his bony fists. "The men of Israel were no longer men! In their weakness they had lost all their friends, even the Children of the Lion, who had been their allies since the days of Abraham. They stood naked before their enemies. Finally the cry rang out from one end of the Promised Land to the other: 'What can we do? Who will rise to lead us? Who will win back the power Moses gave us?' "

The old man's hawk eyes peered out from under white beetling brows to scan the crowd. His thin lips curved in a wry smile. "Well you may ask!" he said. "God's eye traveled up and down the land He had given them, searching for a prophet to speak the bitter truth to His people. And among the weakened men of Israel he found no one through whom His words could rightly be spoken."

He paused. The crowd waited. "So in His infinite wisdom He chose a woman to do the work the men could not do."

He paused again. When he spoke his voice was low and soft; his hands wove their spell. "Hear now," he said, "of the rise of Jabin of Hazor and of his evil general Sisera. Hear of the shame that fell upon Israel and the wickedness that drove Pepi of Kerma to the enemy camp, to arm the Hazorites for war.

"Hear, too," he said, "of the wanderings of the Children of the Lion after their exile from Israel: how Phorbus, Iri of Thebes's adopted son, carried on the struggle for Keturah's freedom, and in Canaan, how invaders brought war and destruction to lands that had known peace. Brother fought brother, and the madness of men made mockery of the mighty words of God!"

He paused and drank in the expectant silence as the crowd waited for the tale to begin. Then, in a strong voice full of emotion, he spoke.

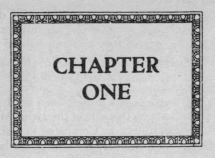

CHAPTER ONE

Canaan

I

Micah pulled his wagon to a halt and motioned to his second-in-command, Zuriel. "Here's where I leave you," he said in a taut voice. "You know what to do, don't you? Just deliver the tribute to the warehouses as if nothing were wrong. As if you haven't any idea what I'm up to. Right?"

Zuriel's eyes anxiously searched his superior's face. "I'll do my part, and I'll try to have our party out of the city before trouble breaks out. But what about you? You're sure you'll be all right?

Micah shook his head, afraid to speak for fear his voice would break. He cleared his throat. "Don't worry about me. I'll just do it and get out of here. When you've left the city, have our men blow the ram's horn through the hill country, then send the most reliable messengers by the fastest horses."

"How will I know that you've been successful?"

Micah gave a nervous snort. "You'll know. I'll do what I have to do, whether I manage to escape or not."

"Micah, this is suicidal."

"I'll get away. Don't worry. And what if I don't? The important thing is that we stop the Moabites at the Jordan. So long as we control the fords, we're all right. They've only a token patrol here, and we can handle them. But if their main army crosses the Jordan . . ." He shook his head sadly. "I'm sure we can prevent it and win the victory we need. Then it will only be a matter of mopping up the force on this side of the river. Moab won't soon forget." Micah stiffened. "Compared to that, it hardly matters whether one person like me comes back alive, does it?"

Zuriel looked at him with admiration. "You're a true hero of Israel, Micah, especially since you were not born among us. I'm proud to . . . know you."

Micah had not missed the painful hesitation in his friend's voice and knew he had started to say "to have known you." But it was true. What did his own life matter if they could drive the Moabite oppressors out of central Canaan? If only the Israelite irregulars now hiding in the forests of the hill country awaiting his signal were successful, too!

Seeing the anguish in Zuriel's eyes, Micah dismissed him with a nod. "Get out of here," he ordered.

"Go with God," Zuriel said as Micah separated himself from the procession of wagons and headed toward the house Eglon of Moab had commandeered as his headquarters in Canaan.

For more than a year Micah had delivered the Israelite tribute, and for most of that time the plot upon which he was now embarked had been hatching. Accordingly, he had gotten to know the Moabite guards well and had spent time with them, gambling for low stakes, drinking with them, joking. By now he knew several men on each of the shifts and had shared many good times with them: He knew who drank too much, who had a shrewish wife, who had a taste for lowlife.

As he approached Eglon's headquarters he spotted Saleh, commander of the day shift, and greeted him with a broad smile. "Saleh!" he said. "I see you haven't got the field commission you sought. What happened? Did you bribe someone with a pig that died before he got it home?"

"Bribe?" Saleh asked with a grin. "Me? Offer a bribe? The gods forbid that I should ever offend the honor of my superiors by offering any of them a bribe!" He winked broadly. "Call it rather an expression of admiration—a love offering." His mouth turned down comically. "In fact, dear fellow, it was a donkey, fat and pregnant. It should have made a splendid gift. But the damned thing had a breech delivery and died, and the foal was deformed and blind in one eye. The son of a dog I'd given it to blamed me for the whole thing. Now I'll be lucky if I can merely remain with the palace guard. The last man who fumbled one of these little love offerings wound up supervising the digging of a sewage trench." He gave an exaggerated shrug. "What brings you here, my friend?"

"The usual," Micah said. "An expression of love, as you put it. A love offering for the excellent Eglon."

Saleh's eyes rolled heavenward. " 'The excellent Eglon,' a curious description for a disgusting boar hog with a fat belly that would have done more than justice to that she-ass of mine before she dropped her foal. Can it be that you do not understand our language as well as I thought you did? 'Excellent?' I would have thought *excessive* a better word."

Micah looked to right and left. "Isn't it dangerous to say things like that so close to Eglon's house? How do you know there's not a spy hiding behind one of those boarded-up windows?"

"I don't, my friend. I'm just making an educated guess. But I've been patrolling the area for the last ten minutes. Of course someone could have been sneaking into the building while we talked. You're right: I should watch my tongue." He clapped Micah on the shoulder. "Look," he said, "when you're done with your errand—"

"Errand!" Micah snorted.

"Whatever you wish to call it. When you're done, come see me. We're on half staff today, and there's nobody worth a damn to talk to. Perhaps we can go have a drink later. There's a tavern I wanted to take you to. They've managed to get their hands on some beer that—"

"Beer? You expect me to match the likes of you drink for drink, after that last time? Don't you know it's against my religion?"

"So is bedding Canaanite whores, but that didn't stop you from trying out half the house down at the Sign of the Red Sails. The girls are still talking about you."

"God forbid," Micah said with genuine regret, and thought, *What one has to do to put these people off their guard!* "But look, perhaps I can see you. You'll be off duty when? An hour or so before sunset?"

"Yes. The tavern I was talking about is the Two Terebinths. It's in the Street of the—"

"I know where it is. You hang out *there*? Why, the last I heard—"

"No, no. There's new management. And the dancing girls are the kind you like. There's a little one with great brown eyes and great big br—"

"I see." Micah shook his head in mock disapproval. "It's not enough getting me in trouble with the tribal priests and elders. Now you want to expose me to sexual diseases."

"Guaranteed clean. My word on it."

Micah sighed, wondering if he was not being too obvious. But when he looked into Saleh's eyes, he could see no suspicion. "All right," he said. "I'll see you then." Saluting the Moabite, he headed once more to Eglon's headquarters.

II

"You don't need my signature? My seal?" Nimshi asked.

"No, sir," Elizai the banker assured him. "The funds will be transferred to your account in Ashdod by the first caravan heading into Philistine territory. You're very wise not to carry gold with you from Jericho. The roads are full of bandits."

Nimshi looked around at the banker's lavishly appointed rooms. In the old days a banker would not have been so ostentatious about his wealth; it would have put his clients off. "Things have indeed changed in only a decade," he said. "In the days of Joshua, the roads were kept clear of robbers and brigands. Now that Moab rules the southern half of Canaan, guard patrols are few and far between."

The banker dismissed this with a wave of his beringed hand. "Surely, sir, you wouldn't wish those days back? Joshua's hand lay very heavy on those of us who did not share his people's religion and ways."

"I'm making no apology for the rapacious ways of the Israelites of that generation," Nimshi said. "My family suffered at their hands, too. My mother and sister-in-law disappeared during the riots that broke out when Israel destroyed the army of Jerusalem. I don't even know if they are dead . . . or worse; my brother Micah joined the Israelite army, and I haven't seen or heard from him since." He paused. "We also lost most of what we owned."

"Well, I'm glad I've been of help, sir," Elizai said. "Not everyone, let me tell you, appreciates what a good banker can do for you in times of difficulties. I'll say this for Eglon of Moab, sir: He appreciates us. He knows he wouldn't have been able to rebuild Jericho without our loans."

Nimshi looked at him and thought: *What about the*

heavy taxes levied on Israelite and Canaanite alike, to repay those usurious loans? But he said nothing about this.

"Well," Nimshi said, "that finishes my work here. It's back to the coast for me. I prefer to be where I can smell the sea."

"The coast, sir?" the banker asked. "I thought you lived in Ashdod."

"No, I've only business there," Nimshi explained. "But I've begun building a second home in Ashkelon, within sight of the sea." He smiled. "There's a wanderer buried somewhere in every Child of the Lion. We all have an itchy foot, whether or not we get to exercise it."

"Ah, I envy you, sir," said Elizai. "But I see I'm keeping you, and you'll want to catch the noon caravan for the coast, I'm sure. May you have a pleasant journey and return to us soon."

"I doubt that," Nimshi said. "This completes the work I contracted for here with Eglon. I've plenty more work lined up back in Ashdod and Ashkelon." He extended his hand. "Good-bye, and thank you for all your help."

The banker looked crestfallen. He had apparently hoped for more business with Nimshi. Doing business with any Child of the Lion was regarded as a necessary step on the road toward doing business with Khalkeus of Gournia, proprietor of the vast family trading fleet.

All the known Children of the Lion shared in the profits of the shipping empire, although not all chose to enjoy them or to live in luxury on the secret island called Home. Some of them had chosen quite different lives.

Nimshi's half brother, Pepi of Kerma, had simply vanished during Joshua's time, after his beloved wife, Tirzah, disappeared during the riots in Jerusalem. Nimshi knew Pepi had quietly gone underground and begun working, under assumed names, for the enemies of Israel. Most of those who remembered Pepi now assumed that he was long dead—victim, perhaps, of the head injury that had plagued him for years.

Pepi's aging uncle, Iri of Thebes, had died in Troy, trying to save his blind wife, Keturah, from slavery and the uncertainties of the war that still raged there.

Nimshi had chosen to do as his father, Baufra, had, maintaining a strict neutrality in the wars of Canaan after the time-honored tradition of the armorer, whose job it was to sell weapons to all who came to him, regardless of the justice or injustice of their causes.

In truth, it was difficult to distinguish one cause from another. Nimshi had not liked the ruthless and brutal way in which Joshua had conquered the land a decade before. Now, Israel, having lost its ascendancy in the wake of the death of Caleb and Joshua, was once more a vassal nation, and Nimshi was angered by the oppressive behavior of Israel's enemies.

Walking through the streets of the new Jericho, a wall-less, unfortified settlement that had sprung up near the gutted ruins of the old city, which had been destroyed by earthquake and Joshua's army, Nimshi could see evidence of that oppression everywhere he looked. Israelites who had been prosperous landowners only a year or two before now worked as common laborers in the warehouses or hired themselves out as beasts of burden. Their children, once kempt and bright-eyed, now begged in the streets. Many of their women had been reduced to worse pursuits. The Israelites had been taxed off the land, and every day brought new homeless victims of the Moabite tax collectors into the city. Joshua's bitter and violent campaign had exhausted the Israelites, and they had lost their sense of purpose. Leaderless, they fell from the ways of their religion and became vulnerable to their enemies.

Looking around him at the Israelite faces, Nimshi saw the hopelessness in their eyes. Were these unfortunates the same people who had swept through Canaan like a mighty wind only a decade before?

He saw, coming down the street, a procession of wretched-looking Israelites driving wagons filled with tribute destined for the Moabite storehouses. A large percentage of their harvest was extorted by the Moabites as condition for the continuation of their poor existence in Canaan.

As he watched the wagons pass and saw the haggard faces of the drovers, he forced himself to remember his own suffering during Joshua's war and harden his heart against them. His eyes followed the pitiful column as it turned into the street of the royal storehouses.

A few blocks farther along he suddenly spotted a familiar face. "Micah!" he cried out. "Micah, is that you, Brother?"

To his surprise the man did not show any sign of having heard him, although they had been no more than ten paces apart.

Nimshi hesitated for a moment, then set out after him. Why should his own brother, whom he hadn't seen for ten years, choose to ignore him?

"Micah!" he cried. "What's the matter? Don't you recognize me?" Micah refused to look at him. "Have you risen so high in the Israelite society that you've no time to bandy words with a mere metalworker?"

The moment he said it, he wished he could call back his jest. He remembered the procession of wagons. It was obvious why Micah was here: He was delivering tribute to the hated Moabite oppressor because his proud, adopted people were hardly better than slaves.

Micah turned his head slightly. "Go away, Nimshi. I can't talk to you now. And you can't afford to be seen talking with me. It's too dangerous."

Never once did he look directly at Nimshi or slow his pace. Nimshi hesitated; then stepped back and let his brother pass.

"What do you suppose. . .?" Nimshi said to himself, his heart breaking.

Then he shrugged and headed toward the livery stable. He had to meet up with a caravan that would be heading to sea.

*　　　*　　　*

Once Micah had gotten past the guards, he made his way to the upper floor of Eglon's headquarters, where he was told that Eglon was resting. He was heartsick about Nimshi, but he had no choice but to reject his brother utterly.

He found the Moabite, huge and bloated, enjoying the cool breezes and looking out over the long rows of palms that lined the streets of the new Jericho. "Ah, there you are," Eglon said. "Did the transfer go all right? You didn't short us on the tribute, did you? Because if you did . . ." He let the threat hang.

Micah studied the misshapen, porcine face, with its bad skin and tiny, red-rimmed eyes, and loathed the man more than ever. But he forced calm into his voice and bowed politely. "I think your overseers will find, my lord, that we have overpaid slightly. I myself gave the order. I thought it better than having the payment disputed. We barely have time to produce the crops without having to spend time arguing with the Moabite auditors."

Eglon scowled. His face, ugly in repose, took on an even more loathsome quality when he was angry. "You're insolent," he said. "But I'll let it go. If your accounts aren't accurate, we'll find out about it." He dismissed the problem with a wave of one fat hand. "What else have you for me? Remember, I asked you to keep your ears open and let me know if any of your people were plotting against me."

Micah's heart was beating fast. He tried to speak but could not. "M-my lord, my throat is dry. Could I perhaps have a drink from the wine bottle I see beyond you?" His throat was so constricted, he could hardly get the words out.

"I suppose so," Eglon said. Micah reached for the goatskin wine bladder, uncapped it, and squirted a generous draught of raw, red Moabite wine down his throat. Then he wiped his lips and recorked the vessel. His heart was still pounding, but his resolve was firm. As he stood with his back to the Moabite leader, he felt with his left hand for the dagger, secure in its scabbard, concealed to the right of his navel.

"Well?" Eglon said. "Your throat can't be dry now. Get on with it. What information have you for me? If any of your thieving countrymen have hatched some plot to defraud me of my tribute, so help me, I'll impale every last man and all his women and children as well. I won't have anyone holding out! Do you hear? Answer me, damn you!"

Micah took a deep breath and slowly turned around. "My lord, I have indeed found evidence of a plot against you. But it isn't among my people. It's among yours. There's a conspiracy among your own guards. They intend to kill you and replace you."

"My guards?" Eglon asked, incredulous. "What are you talking about? No Moabite would ever—"

Micah made a shushing motion. "Quiet, my lord. They might hear you. If I could only whisper in your ear . . ."

The idea of getting that close to Eglon was repugnant, but it had to be done. Eglon stood, facing him, his huge body fat and shapeless in its flowing robe. "Tell me," he said. "But first close the doors. You're right. I want to make sure we're not overheard."

As Micah turned, his hand loosened the dagger in its sheath. He bolted the doors with the heavy crossbar. Then he slowly moved to face the Moabite. "Now, my lord," he said. "Come closer. This is for your ears only."

Eglon approached cautiously. "Tell me. Tell me!"

Micah reached inside his garment and his strong fingers closed on the knife. "All right, my lord," he said. "This—for the honor of Israel!"

The knife came from below with all the force he could put behind it.

Eglon had just enough time to blink with shock before the knife caught him in the belly and ripped upward. Micah could see the fear and horror in the Moabite's eyes. His loose mouth fell open.

The dagger, cutting through Eglon's many layers of fat, found his heart.

III

Micah watched the life leave Eglon's eyes. Then the great lump of flesh collapsed. The knife had split open his guts, and they spilled onto the floor. Micah gagged.

He looked right and left and listened. There had been no one else on the top floor, but now he heard footfalls coming up the stairs. Someone banged at the barred door.

He heard voices: "Didn't you hear that crash? Do you suppose he's fallen and hurt himself? You know how he'll be furious if something's happened to him and we don't come fast enough."

Micah began to panic. Where could he go? He knew there was a secret passage put in by the builder for Eglon's convenience. But how to find it? He looked down at the Moabite's body and felt the bile rise in his throat. Sooner or later they would find some other way into the room. They would find Eglon and him.

The pounding and voices continued: "He's not answering. I don't like that. Go around and climb up to the balcony while I call for help."

Micah studied the long wall that was covered by woven hangings. He peered behind each one and finally found a suspicious-looking panel. But how to get it to move? He ran his fingers up and down the crack, searching. At last he found a handhold. He pulled, and the door started to open slowly.

The banging and the voices grew louder, more frantic.

Micah pulled hard, and the door swung open to reveal a staircase leading downward into darkness. He pulled the door shut behind him and fled down the stairs, feeling his way along the wall and wishing he had retrieved his dagger.

When he reached the ground floor, he pushed the door open and found it led to a kitchen pantry. Around the corner he heard voices and hurriedly picked up a bag of flour and hoisted it over one shoulder. He walked boldly out into the kitchen and through a crowd of servants. Even if someone noticed him, the bag covered half his face.

Once in the great hall he kept his head down and hurried along, trying to look like someone who knew where he was going. At one end of the corridor was an entrance tradesmen used. If only he could reach it.

Suddenly one of the servants recognized him. "Micah!" he cried. "Where are you going? You can't take that bag of flour!"

Micah swallowed and hoped his voice would sound natural. "I was looking for someone to give it to. It fell off a cart outside in the street."

He handed the bag over, smiled, and took off through the door. Outside, blinded by the sunlight, he blinked.

Screams sounded from the roof: "Help! Someone come help! It's the master! Someone's killed the master!"

Micah's urge was to run. *Steady and slow*, he told himself as he walked along, pretending he had somewhere to go to but was in no particular hurry to get there.

When he reached the corner—a narrow alley piled high with garbage—he fell into a jog and moved swiftly into the next cross street.

He could still hear shouting. By now all the guards would know that the last man to see Eglon was Micah the Israelite. He cut through more streets and alleys, making it difficult for anyone to follow him. At least the new Jericho had no walls to trap him.

Yahweh, Joshua and Caleb's God, had commanded that the city of Jericho was never to be rebuilt. In fact, the new town that had sprung up around the ruins of the old had not been constructed until after the Israelites had taken up Canaanite ways and forgotten the Law and Joshua's commands. The people had even called it Jericho—the final insult to Yahweh.

Micah began jogging again, and after a dozen steps the jog turned into a run. He remained in the narrow alley, nearly knocking over the pedestrians who wandered into his path. But then he looked up and saw city guardsmen ahead. He slowed to a walk and then stopped, watching them cautiously. A chariot drawn by a fast horse sped into view.

The chariot stopped, and soldiers surrounded it. Micah flattened himself against the wall, hoping no one would look in his direction. He could not hear their words, but he had no doubt what they were talking about. Finally the guards split into groups and took off in different directions.

To his horror one soldier headed down the alley. Micah sank back into the shadows and dared not to move. The guardsman obviously was not watching where he was going, and he did not see Micah until he was right on top of him.

Micah had only one choice. He lunged out of the shadows and slammed into the guardsman, driving him into the far wall. Both men hit the wall with a crash, but the soldier had the wind knocked out of him. Micah seized the opportunity and grabbed the soldier's dagger. Without a word he ran the guardsman through.

This time he retrieved the weapon. After dragging the body into the shadows and covering it with garbage, he set out again. When he reached the corner, nobody was in sight. He sprinted, dagger in hand, across the street and headed down another alley at a dead run.

At the end of the street he found ordinary people going about their daily business. Trying to pretend he was one of them, he slowed to a walk and hid the dagger inside his robe.

But then his luck failed him. He looked up and saw the sign of two spreading trees—the Two Terebinths. Who, at that moment, should come out of the front door but Saleh.

They saw each other at the same instant. It was obvious from Saleh's broad smile that he had not heard about the assassination. "Micah!" he cried. "Just the man I wanted to see! Come and have a drink with me!"

There was nothing Micah could do but force a smile onto his face and pull Saleh into the alley behind the Two Terebinths. "I have to tell you a secret," he said. "Come closer, now. . . ."

Saleh gave him a strange look but bent toward him as Micah pulled the dagger out from under his robe. Just as he had with Eglon, he brought it up from below. But Saleh was wearing body armor under his uniform, and the blade hit it with a loud clank.

Saleh pulled back, his eyes wide with alarm. "What are you trying to—"

Micah panicked and drew back his stolen dagger and stabbed Saleh in the throat.

Blood gushed forth, staining his robe a bright red. Now he was a marked man. He watched as Saleh fell to his knees, clutching his throat. Then he stabbed him in the temple, watching the sharp point of the dagger break through the thin skull. Saleh cried out softly, a sound Micah would hear for the rest of his life: plaintive, accusatory. Micah let his man fall.

He cursed softly. His whole front was gory with blood. He could never go out into the streets without attracting attention. He tore off his robe, leaving himself naked except for his loincloth and sandals.

He kicked the stolen dagger under his discarded robe and moved back out into the street. The almost silent death of Saleh seemed to have attracted no attention. Micah felt fairly sure he could pass as a body slave or, perhaps, a day laborer. To make certain, he kicked off his leather sandals. Then he stepped into another alley, scooped up a handful of dirt, and smeared it over his naked body.

Feeling safer, he walked at a brisk pace down the street. Suddenly he felt a hand clutch his arm. His blood grew cold.

He was pulled through a doorway; the door was shut behind him. Then he saw the familiar face of Nefeg, one of his confederates inside the city. "We've got to disguise you so you can get out of town!" Nefeg said.

"Why can't I pose as a slave?" Micah asked.

"You're too pale. A real worker would be burnt black by the sun. Don't worry. Nobody was paying attention to you."

He stopped and looked at Micah. "You did it."

"Yes."

"The city is full of soldiers. And our man in Eglon's headquarters sent a signal—black smoke."

"Who is he?"

Nefeg shook his head. "The less that people know about him, the better. Our people in the hills will have seen the signal by now."

"Good," Micah said. "Is a unit at the river to cut off the runners sent to warn the main Moabite force?"

"Relax. Your part is over."

"No, it isn't," Micah said. "I've got to get out of the city. They know I did it."

"For that very reason this is probably the safest place to be right now," Nefeg said. "We've been using this house to hide our people for some time. Someone who stayed here was probably your size, so we can find you some clothes." He grinned. "Tell me about old Eglon."

Micah grimaced. "It was disgusting. I left my knife in him because I couldn't bear to touch him again." The whole horror was coming back. "I killed another man—a man I knew. He wasn't a bad fellow, and . . ."

"Was he a Moabite?"

"Yes, but—"

"Bah! That's all you need to know. Be glad he's dead, whoever he was."

IV

Nimshi's caravan wound slowly through the pass of Beth-horon above Jericho and came to rest on the table-land called the Shephelah. Nimshi fretted during the caravan's slow progress through the hills. Impatient at its slow pace, he decided to take action. He separated himself from the long line of wagons and pack beasts and approached the caravan leader. "I'm leaving the caravan," he said. "I want to go into Ekron."

The drover shook his head. "Are you sure? The hills are full of bandits these days, sir."

"I've been warned about the bandits already," Nimshi assured him as he set off along the southward track.

An hour later he turned his mount toward the dusty road to Ekron. The road led through flourishing olive groves; olive oil was one of the principal sources of Philistine wealth in the region, and every bit of spare ground was given over to the trees. As he rode he thought about Micah. His brother had behaved so strangely. And why the unexpected warning that talking to him was dangerous?

In one flash of insight he suddenly understood. *Why, they're planning something. A revolt against Moab? And Micah was going to see Eglon to deliver the tribute. . . .* It was the only explanation. Could he have been planning to assassinate the Moabite overlord? Nimshi felt fear for his brother, who would risk his life for the Israelites.

The Israelites had seemed so docile when Moab moved in and began demanding tribute, unlikely behavior for the sons of Joshua, the soldiers who had slashed their way through city after Canaanite city. It wasn't like the Israelites to sit peacefully by while Moabite taxes bled them white.

So, he thought, *the worm turns at last, and a good thing, too.* Moabite dominion was bad for his business. Moab would not patrol the roads, and trade was suffering from the constant raids on the caravans.

A revolt! That's why the rams' horns had been blowing in the hills when they had come through Beth-horon.

The entire garrison at Jericho turned out, and runners were sent to summon help from the main Moabite force across the Jordan. But the runners were quickly cut down by Israelite bowmen at the ford. No message got through to the large Moabite force stationed farther down the valley.

When the Jericho guard appeared, Israelite soldiers fell on them. Wave upon wave of young men, directed by the older men who had ridden with Joshua, poured down from the hills. They attacked, hacking and stabbing, and won an easy victory.

In the city one of Eglon's aides hurried to the roof of Eglon's headquarters and sent up a distress signal—three puffs of smoke, followed by a pause, then three puffs again.

The signal was finally picked up by the Moabite army, and they sent out a unit of cavalry to the river. They were met by the Israelite irregulars, and after a brisk and spirited fight the Moabites realized they could make no headway in recapturing the ford. So they sent runners for reinforcements, and they dug in, vowing to give no ground.

In the Israelite camp Micah was welcomed as a great hero. Men, women, and children had come down to the river's edge to see the army that would drive the Moabites out of central Canaan. When they were told that Micah had assassinated the hated Eglon, a rousing cheer went up.

"Long live Micah!" some cried.

"Let Micah come forth to lead the army!" another voice said.

But the young man held up his hand to stop them. "I'm no leader of men, my friends. Right here there are fifty, a hundred men who would be better than I, men who were born among you, of your blood. You have to believe me. I'm not being modest."

Some people would not easily take no for an answer, but Micah held firm, waving aside their suggestions. In the end they let him alone, and he crossed the river to meet with the leaders of the resistance.

These were all older men, men who had fought with Joshua; some of them had even been with the army when they first conquered Sihon and Bashan.

One of those was Shemida, Joshua's former adjutant. After Joshua's death, Shemida had retired, but when the ram's horn had blown, he had ignored his lame leg and had ridden to the ford to offer his services. Not much older than Micah, Shemida had been a special friend to the young convert from Jerusalem, and the two had been happily reunited upon Shemida's return.

"Congratulations," he said to Micah. "You've done great service for the nation today."

The young man shook his head sadly. "I didn't mind killing a disgusting man like Eglon. But I had to kill another man, someone who thought of me as a friend. I'd known him for some time, and he trusted me."

Shemida understood. "Our numbers include many men who actually enjoy killing the enemy—every army does—but when it comes to murdering a man you know and like, who can blame you for feeling guilty about the deed? But you did what was necessary for furthering our cause."

"I keep seeing his face. Just before I stabbed him, he was so glad to see me."

Shemida looked Micah in the eyes. "Did you know that the people Joshua killed rose up to haunt him at night? For the last months of his life he had a hard time sleeping because of his conscience?"

"I can believe it," Micah said. "I'm sure that I'll see my friend's face as soon as I close my eyes." His features twisted with pain. "Shemida, the people acted as though I were a hero, a man to lead the Israelites in battle. I think they expect me to become another Joshua."

"Be glad that you're wise enough to see that you're not. No one would ever want to be the new Joshua if they knew what the old one went through during the conquest." He put a hand on Micah's shoulder. "Besides, a man doesn't elect to become a leader. God chooses him to become one, and the price he pays is terrible."

Shemida limped away and sat down on a broad rock, motioning Micah to join him. "My leg doesn't let me stand for long without pain." He looked at his friend. "I keep wondering if God is going to send us another man like Moses or Joshua, to lead us against our oppressors. But I don't think so. Not now." Shemida let out a long, disgusted sigh. "Look around, my friend. Moses said that if we obeyed the Law, if we kept to the dietary regulations and followed the Commandments, we would prosper. But he warned that the moment we started straying from the path, we would become weak."

"Canaanite superstitions are turning up here and there, aren't they? Everyone feels he has to have one of the little stone *baalim* in his pocket for luck. Astrologers and diviners wander through our villages. There are even cults of Ashtaroth."

Shemida shook his head. "What we need now is not a great warrior to lead us in battle against the enemy. No, the enemy is not the Canaanites but ourselves. We have begun to drift away from the One God. What we need is a spiritual leader, a prophet. We could train or appoint a military leader, perhaps, and he might serve well. But only Yahweh Himself can create a prophet, and He doesn't seem to have given us one."

"FROM THE PRODUCER OF WAGONS WEST COMES YET ANOTHER EXPLOSIVE SAGA OF LEGENDARY COURAGE AND UNFORGETTABLE LOVE"

CHILDREN OF THE LION